The View From Prince Street

MARY ELLEN TAYLOR

A Letter from Patience

NOVEMBER 5, 1751

Dearest Mother,

The witch's voice rode in on a frigid wind, heavy with the promise of snow, and tugged me from a restless sleep. Fresh on the heels of her witchcraft trial, I feared the beautiful widowed sorceress had arrived to curse me. I glanced to Mr. McDonald, only to find rumpled sheets and a fading crease in his pillow.

Moonlight streamed through the unlatched front door and drew me from my bed and across the one-room cottage, past the glowing embers of the hearth. My aching heart momentarily forgotten, I peered into the night and saw the witch standing just outside. Her fiery, unbound red hair and gaunt face were illuminated by the heavens. She spoke in hard, desperate tones to Mr. McDonald, who wore work pants and boots pulled on hurriedly under his nightshirt. When I heard a babe's squawk, I knew she had also brought her infant twin sons, who lay swaddled and tucked in a small cart she must have pulled over the three miles of rutted paths from the Alexandria settlement.

As I leaned against the doorjamb, I watched her drop to her knees in front of my husband and beseech him to give her and the babes shelter. "I will do anything to save them," she said.

They spoke in whispers and for a long moment she did not move before she slowly nodded and rose. When I saw him lean into her and raise his hand as if he wanted to touch her, I shouted, "Witch! The good wives have banished you, Faith, from the settlement!"

Faith did not dare look in my direction, but I saw her fingers curl into fists. My husband avoided my gaze as he continued to whisper. Faith nodded again, never looking up. I realized a deal had been struck, and I was too late. The witch had spun her magic. My husband would allow her and the twins to stay.

That witch has cursed him, us, our lost children. Of that, I swear. God help us for what evil Faith Shire will do now that she lives under our roof.

Yours Faithfully,
Patience McDonald

Chapter One

RAE, MONDAY, OCTOBER 3, 2011

The headline glared on the page. *Dr. Rae McDonald: Matchmaker with a Heart of Stone?*

When the reporter first reached out to me and explained she was doing a profile on successful businesswomen, I assumed her focus would center on my doctorate in psychology and my private family practice. The interview began well enough. I discussed my undergraduate work at Georgetown, graduate studies at the University of Virginia, and my thriving family practice. The reporter scribbled notes and appeared interested. Then she mentioned a friend of a friend who was a client of mine. "Not a family practice client," she said, leaning forward with a grin. "One of your matchmaking clients."

I am not a matchmaker. There are times when I make suggestions to couples, I explained, but I was not a matchmaker. Then, she detailed my high success rate and shared several glowing quotes from couples that had found happiness because of my marital advice. I supplied more statistics about my family practice, and she listened. Took notes. Nodded.

And when she left my home, I assumed the matchmaking was a forgotten diversion.

Rae McDonald: A Matchmaker with a Heart of Stone?

People read the weekly Lifestyle edition of the paper, but also the online version that had the potential to reach far beyond the limits of Old Town Alexandria to every corner of the world that had access to a computer. *Dr. McDonald, whom some would argue has a heart of stone, cuts through her clients' emotional chaos to find love and happiness.*

It felt like a tabloid exposé.

Heart of stone.

It did not set well. I was not the Tin Man looking for a heart, nor a robot. In fact, sadness nearly destroyed me when I was sixteen. My older sister had died, and I subsequently made reckless choices that resulted in a pregnancy. I carried a healthy baby boy to term, gave birth, and when he was a day old, laid him in another mother's arms forever. The loss and pain were crushing. Devastating. And on that day, I realized my very survival depended on suppressing all my feelings.

Heart of stone, my ass. Such are the traits of sociopaths, and my pain had been very real until I exorcised it.

My detachment had served me well. I survived abandonment guilt, and I also thrived academically as well as professionally. My ability to keep feelings at bay is the reason I can navigate my clients' emotional maelstroms. Because I remain detached from all their turmoil, my perspective is unencumbered and clear. I can see the forest for the trees.

As I stare out the window at the square, muddy patch of dirt in my backyard, raindrops roll lazily down hand-blown glass. The panes were original to the home, which was built over two hundred and fifty years ago. I thought about the couple sitting behind me on the couch. They were here because of the article. They wanted a matchmaker to politely analyze and approve their union. They needed no counseling, but rather a rubber stamp on their self-proclaimed rock-solid relationship.

Each had a clipboard, paper, and pencil. Their charge was to perform a simple exercise. *Write your deepest, darkest secret. Fold the paper in half and wait for my instruction.*

These two individuals, like many of my clients, were successful in their own right. They were well on their way to enviable careers and shared high IQs, elite educations, and ambition. But as valuable as all those traits were on the corporate ladder, they did not necessarily translate into thriving marriages.

Today, *He* was Samuel Morris: mid-thirties, a lawyer on track to be a partner in a Washington, D.C., law firm. He had a passion for great food and intended to have at least three children. *She* was Dr. Debra Osborne, a surgical resident at Georgetown Hospital who loved hiking, visiting Paris, and skiing. Though she spoke briefly of children, she neglected to check the box regarding children on my questionnaire.

In the first minutes of our initial interview today, they said that as soon as I gave my blessing on their match, they would formally announce their engagement. But this office was not a drive-up window, and I did not give out gold stars unless they were earned.

Pencils scribbled, stopped, and scribbled again as I continued to stare out the window at the freshly grated square patch of land in my backyard.

This spot had once been the location of the original McDonald homestead hearth, which had long ago fallen into a tumble of moss-covered rubble, entwined with weeds and strawberry vines. It had stood on the property like a sentry since the Native Americans walked this land.

As legend had it, the stones were collected from the rivers and streams of Scotland to serve as ballast on merchant ships bound for the Virginia Colony. They were then loaded into the hull and placed around cargo so that in the event of a storm, the goods would not shift, throwing the vessel off balance and sinking it. These stones arrived with the 1749 voyage of the ship *Discovery*, which also carried two newly married Scots, Patience and Michael McDonald. They had fled Scotland and a cholera epidemic to start afresh and tame the wild Virginia woods into profitable farmland.

According to my mother, *Discovery*'s captain had been ready to dump the stones into the deep harbor at Hunting Creek and fill his hull with tobacco hogsheads for the return voyage when my ancestor, never one to waste, offered to transport the stones ashore. The captain, anxious to anchor and see his wife, agreed. Michael McDonald and his wife offloaded the stones into a cart on shore and built the hearth that would be the centerpiece of their cottage. Those stones warmed two generations of McDonalds before lightning struck the hearth in 1783, sending loose cinders from it onto the cottage's thatched roof. Fire broke out and within minutes devouring the roof before setting upon the cottage's contents.

The blackened stones were forgotten, and there they lay for over two centuries. Someone in each generation suggested that the stones be dismantled and hauled away, but there was always an elder at the ready to prevent their removal. The stones, the old ones said, warded off evil and protected the family. How many times had crops been spared from gale-force winds? When the Union troops marched through Virginia, why was the McDonald house left untouched? The stones protected the house and the land. But perhaps, not its inhabitants.

I did not believe in talismans or curses, but if I did, I would note that the stones' powers were tall tales of those who needed to believe in a higher power than their own. The McDonald farm, which had been reported to cover a thousand acres at one time, had dwindled to a one-acre lot. Generations of McDonalds had died young, including my sister. And my son was gone. Where had their magical power been when it was needed?

After my mother's passing a couple of years ago, the stone sentry grew increasingly unsightly to me. It was an embarrassing reminder of superstition and outdated fears of ancestors.

My contractor had finally dismantled the hearth six weeks ago, but the angry patch of red clay it sat upon still looked startlingly out of place each time I glanced at it. I still expected to see the stones. My gut was beginning to tell me I had made a grave mistake.

The near-monsoon rains prevented any new construction, and with each passing day, the bare soil looked more and more like a sunken grave. Whatever relief or sense of accomplishment I might have anticipated was sorely missing.

Turning from the window, I studied the couple. They each sat rigid, their hands gripping their papers. Body language spoke volumes. "Have you finished?"

Debra tugged her black skirt, sitting a little taller. She was petite, with dark brown hair and eyes that carried an intensity that was difficult to miss. She was the type who studied hard, made good grades, and played by the rules. "I'm not sure of the purpose of this exercise," she quipped.

Samuel raised a soft hand to his mouth and coughed. "Doesn't really make sense. You've heard us talk for an hour today. Surely you must see we're nearly perfect for each other."

"Exchange papers," I said, ignoring his comment.

"What?" Debra asked.

"You tell Samuel your darkest secret, and he'll tell you his. If you truly love each other, then you should be able to know the worst and still find acceptance. Long-term relationships demand that kind of trust."

Neither moved, as a heavy silence settled between them.

They exchanged nervous glances until Samuel asked, "What does the past have to do with now? Today is what matters."

"The past isn't separate. It's part of us," I said.

Debra glanced at Samuel. Her grin was uneasy and neither budged. "I have to agree with Samuel. We accept each other for whom we are now. The past is over and done. Neither one of us wants to dredge up yesterday's missteps."

A grandfather clock in the hallway chimed ten times, indicating our session was over. "When you two can exchange papers, then call me for another session. Otherwise, you're wasting your time and mine."

Samuel shoved his paper in his pocket. "We didn't come here to create a problem where there is none. All we want is confirmation that we're a good couple."

Arching a brow, I studied him, not with anger or frustration, but with mild interest. "If you're looking for a yes or a no, I would have to say given the current conditions, my answer would be no."

"What?" Samuel asked. "That's absurd."

"I would wager you've done more due diligence on prospective corporate mergers than this marriage," I replied.

"*No?*" Debra nearly shouted, glancing at Samuel. "We paid three hundred dollars for a *no*?"

Staring her down, I replied, "You paid for my opinion. I've given it."

Debra rose, straightening to her full five feet five inches. "We get a lousy *no*, because we don't want to open the past. Our future does not earn a *no*!"

"I won't give you a patronizing yes. Past, present, and future are links in a chain. For a chain to hold, all the links must be strong. You can't simply pick and choose." I traced the face of my watch. "There's also the fact that Debra didn't check the box for children on the questionnaire."

She turned a bit red-faced. "I missed it. Give me the form and I'll check it now."

"Not until you exchange pages." I looked at my watch. "Now you must excuse me. I have another appointment."

Samuel stood, wrapping a protective arm around Debra. "This was a waste of time and money."

"I disagree," I said. "I have saved you the cost of an expensive wedding and a more expensive divorce. This session was well worth it to you."

"But we *love* each other," Debra said. "That must count."

"You've been dating three months," I pointed out. "Yes, you have an affection, but what both of you are feeling is sexual attraction. It'll fade in less than a year. And then you'll be left with each other. If the foundation is not solid and the goals are not aligned, the marriage won't survive."

"This is ridiculous," she said.

The front doorbell chimed. "That's my next appointment."

Samuel shook his head. "I'm telling everyone who'll listen that you're a fraud."

Slowly, I turned back toward him. As a family practice psychologist, I was accustomed to dealing with raw nerves, tears, and anger. This couple's determined need for my approval was the first red flag. Debra's worried expression and Samuel's ire were the next. My approval was an excuse for a deeper reason. "Show Debra the paper in your pocket."

His eyes narrowed. He was now opposing counsel, and in his mind's eye, we were facing each other across the negotiating table. "Fine. I will." He dug the crumpled piece of paper out of his pocket and handed it to Debra. "Go ahead, read it."

She lifted a chin. "I don't need to read it. I trust him."

Whereas he took her words as an act of faith, I saw it for what it was: a diversion. The front doorbell rang again.

"Return when you both agree to exchange papers in front of me."

The couple looked at each other, but Debra did not look at his paper or share her secret. Samuel's face lost some of its ire. Instead, he took Debra by the arm and exited through the pocket doors.

As they marched down the center hallway toward the wide front door, I followed.

My house is a two story built in the Federal style and fashioned of red Virginia clay brick. The first floor had four large rooms divided by a wide center hallway that stretched from the front door all the way to the back into a thirty-year-old addition that housed a recently updated kitchen. My office and a dining room occupied the east side, and on the west, there was a parlor and a small room where I sometimes watched television or read. Upstairs were four bedrooms and two bathrooms. I used the smallest bedroom, the one that had been mine as a child, because it caught the morning sunlight. After my mother died, I had her room and bathroom updated but had never gotten around to moving into the larger space.

"You aren't being fair," Debra argued. "Not everyone comes into relationships with such intimate secrets."

"I agree. But for those who do, those secrets, like the tiny seeds of a cancer, grow freely until one day they destroy your life."

"That sounds more like personal experience," Samuel jabbed.

"That's not relevant."

"So, this is about you?" he countered.

"No. It's about you and Debra."

As Samuel reached for the front door he turned, his mouth in a grim line. "I suppose you've written your darkest secret and shared it with your partner?"

"I have no partner," I said.

His lips curled into a snide snarl. "Because you won't practice what you preach?"

I was engaged six years ago and performed this same exercise. My fiancé was happy to discuss what he considered the most guarded of his past. I however, sat for a long moment, pencil gripped in my hand, unable to write the first sentence.

In the end, I could not do it. Recording my past mistake made the boy's existence far too tangible and threatening. The weight of it grew as we sat in the minister's office.

I had carried this secret for so long, but the additional weight of that single sheet of paper was the straw that broke the camel's back. I could not share my past with my fiancé for fear that the sharing would resurrect the pain. Within a couple of months, my fiancé and I broke up.

If there were ever proof of the past's power, that moment was it.

The doorbell rang again. "I must meet my next appointment."

"Heart of stone sums it up," Samuel said.

My well-practiced smile was polite and restrained as I opened the door. "Thank you for visiting today."

With hands clasped tightly, the couple stormed out of the front door over the damp slate walkway toward a late-model black Volvo sedan parked in the driveway.

Without another look in their direction, I shifted my attention to my ten o'clock appointment. Addie Morgan and Margaret McCrae, owners of Shire Architectural Salvage Company, were the contractors who removed my stones six weeks ago. Addie was petite with brown curly hair that graced slim shoulders, and she favored collared short-sleeved shirts and crisp navy shorts that skimmed the top of her knees. Addie's notable trait was not her professional demeanor, but the infant pack strapped to the front of her chest. Tucked inside was her niece, Carrie, now eight weeks old.

Beside her was Margaret McCrae, a vibrant redhead who barreled through life with no trepidation. She wore her hair in a loose topknot, along with a green T-shirt that read *Well-Behaved Women Rarely Make History*, faded jeans, and worn leather sandals.

After Addie and Margaret hauled away the stones, I followed their company's news and learned they were making a name for themselves in the salvage business. From what I had gleaned, Addie was saving her family's business from the brink of ruin.

Margaret now worked full time with the salvage company but still maintained close ties to the archaeology center. From what I gathered, she had a PhD in history and was a qualified expert in local Alexandria history.

Whereas I sensed a calm, steady energy around Addie, the opposite was true of Margaret. Energy sparked when she entered a room. She was oblivious to it.

"Ms. Morgan and Ms. McCrae."

"Please call us Addie and Margaret," Ms. Morgan said. "Safe to say you can tell by looking at us that we're informal."

"Please come inside." Despite Addie's offer to use first names, I rarely did. The formal address maintained a comfortable distance.

"Thanks for seeing us," Margaret said.

Both women wiped their feet on the doormat and entered.

To my great relief, the baby made a small sucking sound but otherwise was content to sleep. The idea of hearing a baby wailing today was not ideal.

"I read about you in the paper," Margaret said. "I knew you were a psychologist but didn't know you were a matchmaker. I didn't think matchmakers, other than on cable television, were real."

"I'm not a matchmaker. I'm a trained clinical psychologist."

"Right. I get it. How did the reporter find you?" she pressed.

"She had a friend of a friend whom I assisted with several sessions."

"The article said this client and several others found love thanks to you."

"Not thanks to me. To themselves."

"That *Heart of Stone* headline was below the belt," Margaret said. "What was the deal with the writer? Did she have an ax to grind?"

Addie cleared her throat. "We didn't come here to talk about the article, Margaret. What was it you wanted to ask Dr. McDonald?"

"Oh, right. Sorry about that, Rae. We have a bigger purpose."

Addie absently patted the baby's back. "Dr. McDonald, Margaret did some research on your house after we dismantled the stone hearth. You remember the bottle we found?"

"Dirty, brown bottle from what I recall."

"A witch bottle," Margaret reiterated.

"Ah, yes, of course. Please come into my office."

Once the women were settled on a Queen Anne sofa, I took a seat on a Chippendale chair across from them. Addie leaned back in her seat, gently rubbing the baby's back while Margaret sat forward, her body a coiled spring. Bracelets rattled as she tucked a stray curl behind an ear festooned with three hoop earrings. "This witch bottle is an incredible find."

Though politeness dictated that I offer them coffee, I was not in the mood to extend the visit. "Again, what exactly is a witch bottle?"

"Protection spells," Margaret said without hesitation. She scooted closer to the edge of her seat as if nerves electrified with excitement would not allow her to relax. "They were created centuries ago by people who feared black magic. They were designed to ward off a witch's spell or an evil curse. They were typically made of wine bottles, filled with all kind of sharp objects."

"Why sharp?"

"To penetrate the magic."

"Of course." How had I found myself here listening to such an inane explanation?

A sly smile tugged at the corner of Margaret's lips. She had read each of my thoughts. "I try not to judge the past by today's standards. I report the facts, Rae."

"Rae. No one has called me Rae in years. Always Dr. McDonald."

"Right," Margaret said. "Basically, the bottles were buried by the home's front door or by the hearth, both considered open portals through which evil could enter. One of the bottles we found belonged to Addie's family. Sarah Shire Goodwin buried that one. Patience McDonald buried the one we found on your property, and Imogen Smyth made the one we found on the Prince Street property. All three women lived in Alexandria around 1750."

Margaret wore her love of history on her like a Girl Scout merit badge. "Judging by the tone of your voice, you consider this a remarkable find," I said.

"You have no idea how amazing it is to find three intact bottles," Margaret said. "Before I found the Alexandria bottles, only one has been found in such remarkable condition. That one is in a museum in Maryland."

"And now you have three."

"Two remain intact." She nodded toward Addie.

Addie absorbed Margaret's excitement and maintained a steady demeanor, regardless of the storms around her. "The Goodwin bottle fell and broke. My bad." She held up a hand. "We've had this discussion a million times. Baby Carrie was weeks old and I wasn't sleeping much. My nerves were frayed. End of story."

"It's a shame the bottle broke," Margaret said. "But it gave me a chance to study the contents. Four nails, a lock of hair, a penny, and what must have been herbs."

The grandfather clock ticked in the hallway. "Why are you here, ladies? I appreciate your passion for these bottles, but what do they have to do with me? I gave my bottle to you."

Margaret looked at her associate and drew in a breath, wrangling her excitement. "You're one of the families who could be considered original settlers of Alexandria. And one of a handful who has continuous ownership of the same land, although a much smaller plot now."

"That's correct," I said. "For good or bad, we've been rooted to this land."

Margaret looked beyond the window to the barren patch of earth. "When we were removing the hearth, you mentioned you have lots of family papers."

"I've a collection of boxes that hold many papers and letters kept over the generations but haven't paid much attention to the family's past other than what my mother told me as a child." My association of pain and its past created a general dislike of it. Unearth one part of it and you get the whole lot.

"I remembered you saying you had letters dating back to the eighteenth century."

"And I believe I shared information from the family Bible that helped you with some puzzle you were deciphering."

"And I do appreciate those," Margaret said," I truly do. It was a huge help." Her foot tapped before she stilled it. "But I would love to have all the papers and build a full picture of the three women who made these bottles. I think any documentation you have may shed a great deal of light on the lives of these women."

"Why do you care about them and their past?"

Margaret's eyes widened, and then blinked. Her mind did not compute such a question. "Why wouldn't I care?"

For Margaret, the past was a curiosity to be studied and admired. From my perspective, it was a billowy, dark place filled with demons lurking in the shadows. To tug at one brick threatened the structural integrity of the entire firewall I had built around my heart. "Why does this matter? These women are long gone."

"History matters, Rae. You've heard the old saying that those who do not study history are doomed to repeat its mistakes."

Though I never looked back, I would also never repeat my mistakes. I would never lay one of my children in another woman's arms again if the price were a life of solitude. "What kind of mistakes are we talking about? These women feared witches and curses. I don't think you or I are in danger of repeating that."

"I have read every document I could find about the Goodwin's, McDonalds, and Smyths, and though I have enough historical facts and figures that give me a general look at their lives, I have no information that tells me who they really were. That's what I'm hoping the papers will reveal."

"Again, why does it matter?"

Margaret looked at Addie, searching for a better way to put forth her argument. "What am I missing here?"

Addie laid her hand on Margaret's arm. "Since I'm now raising Carrie, I'm far more aware of the past and how it affects us both. Our history is intertwined. I know you don't have children, Dr. McDonald, but one day you might, and perhaps then you may find Margaret's research has a great deal of value."

I did have a child—or at least I had for the minutes I held him. Suddenly the wall dividing the past from the present shifted as if the ground beneath it shuddered. I did not care about the past. It could wither in the darkness for all I cared. But the boy could have a very different view of his biological heritage. He might care.

"What would you do with any information you discover? I have no wish to dig up dirt on anyone's family history."

Margaret leaned forward, trying to close the deal. Just a little nudge would do the trick. "I would give you the final approval on what is released to the public."

Tugging at a speck of lint on my skirt, I wondered if the boy ever thought about his biological past. "So, if you find a fascinating bit of information that I do not want publicly discussed, you would honor my request to squelch it?"

"Yes, completely."

That might be acceptable. Thanks to my mother arranging all the documents into protective boxes when I was a child, they were preserved. My aversion aside, it made logical sense to inventory the boxes. Especially for the boy. "All right, Margaret. I'll give you access to the papers, but you'll have to study them here. I'm not comfortable with them off the property."

Margaret clasped her ringed hands together. "That would be amazing. And I won't get in your way. Put me in a corner or the attic, and I'll be happy as a clam."

"I think I can do better than that. I have a large farmhouse table in the kitchen. When would you like to start?"

Margaret nudged Addie. "Now would be awesome. But I'm assuming you might need a day or two."

"I do have appointments today. How does tomorrow look?"

She pumped her fisted hands in the air before quickly folding them in her lap as, no doubt, Addie had counseled restraint. "That would work."

"We have a salvage job in Prince William County in the morning," Addie said.

"Right, the old church. How does afternoon sound?" Margaret asked me.

"That would be acceptable." I imagined all the meticulously stored boxes belonging to generations of McDonalds waiting to be opened. Even if we did not care about the past, we were careful scribes of the present. "Four o'clock?"

"Done," Margaret said.

The doorbell rang and I was relieved to end the conversation. "That's my contractor. We need to go over the plans for the garage."

Addie rose, cradling the baby's bottom with her hand. "You're using Zeb Talbot?"

"Correct."

"I haven't seen him in a couple of weeks," Addie said. "I know he's been busy with his son and work."

From what little Zeb had said, I knew that Addie and Zeb were once related by marriage through Addie's sister, Janet. Janet was Carrie's mother, but also the mother of Zeb's seven-year-old son, Eric. Mental illness prevented Janet from parenting her children, but she was trying to maintain her fragile hold on sanity and be in their lives as best she could.

Zeb put on his best face when he spoke of Janet, and I sensed he and Addie were a united front in their love for the children. In fact, they made sense as a couple.

Margaret stood and I could see she was already counting the minutes until she could examine the documents. Though her enthusiasm could be annoying, I admired her passion. "See you tomorrow. Four o'clock sharp."

We walked to the front door, past an oil landscape that depicted Alexandria after the War of 1812. Margaret paused to study the painting, completely absorbed with it. "This is amazing," she said. "I don't think I've ever seen it before."

"It's been in the family many generations," I said. How

many times had I passed the painting and not even tossed it a glimpse?

For the first time in a very long while, I studied the soft brush strokes of the English painter commissioned by a McDonald to capture the city that this clan now proudly claimed as home.

Gone were the sweeping concrete skylines that trailed along Duke and King Streets, the eight lanes of the Beltway that wrapped around the city, and the roar of planes landing at Reagan National Airport. Instead, the painter had captured tall ships anchored in a harbor transformed by settlers who sheared off the cliffs and created a gentle slope to the waterline and a larger commercial waterfront. At the water's edge, a collection of warehouses and brick townhouses clustered close to the north shore. In the middle ground, sprawling brick and wooden homes were surrounded by wide swaths of land, enclosed by split rail fence. In the distance, Shuter's Hill had not yet become home to the tall stone spires of the Masonic Temple that was built in the 1920s. In the painting, Shuter's Hill sported a single plantation, known today as the Mills/Lee//Dulaney house. This elegant Italian mansion was built in the late eighteenth century and owned by three prominent Alexandria businessmen over a fifty-year span, until fire destroyed it.

"This is incredible," Margaret whispered as Addie pulled her closer to the door.

"You can look at the painting later, Margaret. I need to feed Carrie." Addie looked at me with a rue grin. "Carrie is not a happy camper if she doesn't eat on time."

"We wouldn't want that." The sound of a baby's cry always triggered visions of an awkward teen mother trying to soothe a child who sensed her lack of will to fight for him.

I opened the door to find that the heavy rain had yielded to a fine mist. A very tall man with wide shoulders and closely cropped black hair peppered with strands of white at the temples filled the doorway. My contractor, Zeb Talbot, wore a red T-shirt with *Talbot Construction* printed over the breast pocket, jeans, and well-worn work boots recently brushed clean of dirt. Long, weathered hands wrapped around the rolled-up plans for my new garage.

"Mr. Talbot," I said, feeling an odd sense of relief. "I believe you know Addie Morgan and Margaret McCrae."

He looked past me and nodded to the women behind me. "Addie and Margaret, what brings you out here?"

"Historical riches," Margaret said.

"The McDonald papers," I added. "Ms. McCrae is doing research on the witch bottle she found when the hearth was removed."

"Ah, the witch bottles." He grinned at Addie. "Casting more spells these days?"

Addie's laugh was easy and relaxed. "Every chance I get."

"Do not mock our kinfolk," Margaret said. "These bottles are a time capsule into the lives of women who dared to cross the Atlantic and make the wilderness of the New World their home."

Addie tugged Margaret's arm. "Save the lectures, Professor. We need to prep for tomorrow's demo, and I have to feed the kid before she blows."

"We're dismantling windows in an old church in Prince William," Margaret added. "The church was built in 1922. I can already tell you more about it than you'd ever want to know."

Addie pushed Margaret past Zeb and me. "We can't wait to hear all about it."

Margaret, sensing she was pressing her luck, went to the door. "Another fascinating tale but I'll save that for our ride south tomorrow."

Carrie squawked and I tensed.

"Addie, the baby has been sleeping the whole time, which means she'll blow in less than twenty minutes," Margaret said.

"You two make her sound like a bomb," I said.

Addie rubbed the baby's back with a mother's affection. "She can be vocal when she's hungry, and it's nice not to be stuck in traffic when she wakes up. Dr. McDonald, thank you for your time."

As the two women hurried past Zeb, Addie nudged him affectionately and he tossed her a grin that I could not judge as either romantic or brotherly. I watched as Margaret leaned close to Addie and said in a voice that carried a bit more than she realized, "*Heart of stone* may just fit."

Addie replied with a frown and herded Margaret closer to the privacy of the beat-up Shire Architectural Salvage truck.

Zeb's expression hardened, a clear indication he had heard as well. "Sorry about that. Margaret can be a whirlwind."

I had mastered the art of not hearing from my mother. We McDonald women did an excellent job of ignoring what did not suit our immediate purposes. "I missed it altogether. Please come inside."

Tapping the roll of plans on his leg, he paused at the front door, wiped off his boots, and entered the hallway. "Once the ground dries for a few days we can get started on the garage. It's been one of the wettest seasons on record, and I've shifted all my men to indoor jobs."

The rain had fallen just about every day for the past six weeks. The soil was waterlogged, the river high and fast, and the skies forever dreary and gray. "One of the last clear days I can remember was the day Addie and Margaret removed the stones from the land."

"I wonder if Margaret has made the connection," Zeb said. "She's sure to link it to the bottle."

"It's a stretch but a coincidence, nonetheless. The removal

of the stones certainly could not be associated with the weather."

"You might be interested to know that those stones were sold to a family in Loudoun County. They built an exterior hearth with it."

"Hopefully, they built it a safe distance from their main house." I shared the somewhat irrational inside thought before I realized it.

"Why do you say that?" he asked. My comment had piqued his attention, as if this were his first glimpse into my personal quirks that simmered just below the surface.

"The cinders from the original hearth burned the first McDonald home. Family lore states it was struck by lightning...but on a clear day."

"Fire was a constant threat in those days," Zeb said. "Homes were built of highly combustible material due to cost. To add insult to injury, the fire department would let your house burn down if you didn't show proof of having bought fire insurance."

"That's horrible, but it shouldn't be a surprise."

He cocked his head, sensing that a small door had opened and trying to peer inside. "Are you worried about fires, Dr. McDonald?"

I found holding eye contact with his clear gaze a challenge. "I have a healthy respect for anything that puts off over five hundred degrees of heat while consuming life and property."

"I've noticed you've installed double the usual number of smoke detectors in this house. And the fireplace in your office hasn't been used in years."

"Those are odd details to notice."

"I'm a contractor, Dr. McDonald."

"It's an old home, and it's also my place of business. The extra smoke detectors defray some of the cost of insurance.

And I've no need to use the fireplace. It's inefficient and messy."

He studied me, and I sensed that if we had met as two people in a social setting, he would have pressed the issue. But he was too professional to dig deeper. "Understood."

I held out my hand, indicating a round table nestled under the large window that overlooked the raw patch of yard. Hard now to remember what it looked like dry.

We both sat, and he carefully removed the rubber band from the roll of plans and unfurled them. "I've made the changes you requested and expanded the attic for extra storage space."

Carefully, I traced the lines depicting the layout. "Now that I think about it, I'm not sure I'll have a need for more storage."

"What about an apartment? You mentioned that once."

"Not a bad idea."

He rolled his head slightly to the side, unwinding tension. "If you ever have family that visits, an apartment would be ideal."

"I'm the last of the McDonalds."

The subtle scent of his soap mingled with the smell of rain. "You're the last McDonald?"

Ten generations of McDonalds had lived in Alexandria, and each generation saw the survival of only one or two McDonalds. With my sister's passing seventeen years ago, I became the last in the clan.

The last female.

There was the boy, of course, but I had surrendered all claims to him when he was just hours old. Yes, I was thirty-two and capable of having more children, but I would not. I had squandered my chance at motherhood. I could have fought for him.

"I'm the last McDonald and have no real need for an

apartment. But I'm considering turning the space into an office. It would be nice to have some separation from this house. Too much time is spent here."

He scratched the side of his head. "An office?"

"Correct."

"If you've a mind to do that, then it makes sense to rough-in communication systems as well as several more electrical outlets."

"That's a good idea."

"It will be some added cost."

"I understand. Perhaps you could also draw up a plan that breaks the space into two areas—one designed for reception and the other for my office."

"There will be another delay while I draw up the design."

"What's a few days with more rain moving in our direction?" I reasoned.

"I don't mind making the changes, but this will be your third set. You sure you even want a garage out back?"

He was intuitive. Lately, I was not as certain about the addition nor why I was unsettled about the plans that had been so clear only about a month ago. "Better to make the changes now than later when it will be far more expensive."

The sun-etched lines feathering from the corners of his eyes deepened as he squinted. "Okay. I'll get back to you."

I traced the edge of the plans. "Thank you. I appreciate your good work."

As I walked him out to the front door, he paused, the plans held tightly in his hands. "That was an interesting piece they wrote on you in the paper. Never occurred to me you were a matchmaker. I figured you were some kind of family counselor."

"I'm not a matchmaker." I readied for a joke about my heart of stone. "But I've seen too many couples make tragic mistakes, so I offer sound advice."

He had the ability to look at me with an unwavering and somewhat unsettling intensity. "The article says you've matched up quite a few couples."

"Not really matched."

"How many?" he pressed.

"Two dozen."

"The newspaper article said that you have a ninety percent success rate. What happened to the other two couples?"

"One divorced. They were not entirely truthful during their sessions with me. The other is in counseling."

"Impressive statistic," he said as he opened the front door. "Can't argue with it. I could have used your advice before I married, but then if I hadn't married Janet, I wouldn't have Eric. Sometimes mistakes carry blessings with them, I suppose."

If I could take back my mistakes and wish away the boy, would I?

Would I wish away the boy?

Hell, no.

The answer came loud and clear. "I suppose you're right."

He jabbed his thumb toward his truck. "Which reminds me, I have something for you. It's in the truck."

Zeb jogged to the truck, his long legs crossing the drenched walkway easily, opened the passenger side, and tossed in his plans as he reached across his seat. A quick jog back and he held out a stone to me.

I took the smooth stone from his callused palm. "What's that?"

"It's from your hearth. The mason had a handful of stones that didn't quite work and were tossed aside. I loaded up what he didn't want and thought of you when I saw this one."

The stone was lighter than I expected and had an irregular surface, with a vein of gray running through the center. But it was not the texture that caught my attention as I turned it over, rather its shape. There was no doubt about its shape. A heart.

"Ah." Margaret's earlier parting comment barely registered with me, but this cold rock jabbed sharply in my stomach. "A stone heart."

"I had read the article just a couple of days before I visited the job site in Loudoun County."

I traced a small center crack with my thumb. "And you thought of me."

"You have to admit, for a stone it's an interesting shape."

"What are the chances?"

"You don't like it." He shifted his stance. "I didn't mean it that way. I thought you would find it amusing."

"It *is* amusing." Was he mocking me or giving me a memento of a family relic? I tightened my grip on it. "I'm sure I'll be getting a lot of mementos like this in the future. Perhaps I should incorporate this into my logo."

He studied the stone and then my expression, which I purposefully kept neutral. "They have you all wrong."

"How so?"

"Your heart. It's nowhere close to stone."

"I come from a long line of women like me. We might begin our lives as emotional creatures, but we always end up the same." I held up the memento. "With one of these."

"Why do you believe that?"

How many times had I asked that very question of my mother? "I'm sure there's some genetic anomaly."

"Have you ever tried to break the cycle?"

Carefully, I shook my head. "I can see you're a good man, Zeb. You care about people and you want to fix their lives as easily as you restore an old building or build a new structure. But sometimes a person has to find their own way." He looked as though he would say more. "Thank you." I turned to my house and slowly closed the front door.

Long seconds passed before I heard the engine turn over and the sound of Zeb slowly driving away. Letting my head fall back against the door, I pressed the stone to my chest and allowed the cold weight to seep through my silk blouse and against skin. Back to the last bittersweet moment I felt pure love and pain; the moment I laid the boy in another mother's arms.

Letter from Patience

NOVEMBER 6, 1751

Dearest Mother,

The morning sun peeked above the horizon as I watched Faith swaddle the freshly fed babes in thick wool blankets and lay them carefully on the blankets near the fire. As much as I feared her, I must confess that I was drawn to the babes. My breasts still heavy with milk, I ached to hold my lost children in my arms again. When she caught me staring, she said, "I prayed never to leave the loving embrace of my intended, Mr. Talbot, but fate stole him along with happiness. Here I am again braving not the vast seas, but the thick wilderness." Her barely whispered words gave me the courage to ask why she chose to return to our farm. "It is all I know. And if not for the babes, I would not be here." Mr. McDonald came in the room at that moment. Uneasy, he looked me in the eye and said, "Faith needs us." When I rose off my bed to argue, he said, "You're unwell. You need her. We need her. Like it or not, we are all bound."

Yours Faithfully,
Patience McDonald

Chapter Two

LISA, MONDAY, OCTOBER 3, 2011

Years of living on the open road had dulled my memories of Northern Virginia rush-hour traffic. One look at my watch and I remembered that the rush of cars and drivers clogging the Beltway that encircled Washington, D.C., started as early as two-thirty in the afternoon. With so much humanity crammed into a small space, it was a wonder anyone accomplished much. As I inched along the southern side of the Beltway, I regretted my late start. Rookie mistake.

But the noon AA meeting had lasted longer than expected and I had lingered. I, Lisa Smyth, needed an extra dose of support. I quickly hurried by the Prince Street house and collected my aunt's dog, Charlie, a seven-year-old chocolate Lab. We took a quick walk around the block before I put him in the car, and we made the trip to the nursing home.

The Braddock Road exit directed me away from the traffic snarl and through a collection of stoplights past endless strip malls and housing developments. Finally, I was able to turn off a primary road onto a tree-lined side street that fed into the arched half-circle driveway of the assisted-living home.

I parked Aunt Amelia's 1989 Buick LeSabre. The car had been sitting in the garage for at least six months and I realized that if someone did not start driving it soon, the gas would go bad and ruin the engine. So instead of driving my truck, I was driving Blue Betty, as Amelia called the car.

I leashed Charlie and we both moved toward the plain brick building while I tried to be upbeat for Charlie and Amelia's sake. "Grant me the serenity to accept the things I cannot change." I repeated the AA mantra, realizing right now it was easier said than done.

Accept what you cannot change, I thought, as I moved toward the front entrance. Charlie regarded me with so much trust that I pulled back my shoulders and dug deep for a smile. The daily visits did not last long and though some might argue they were unnecessary, I refused to miss one, given the debt I owed the woman inside.

Through the front doors, antiseptic smells mingled with a sickening sweet minty aroma that never failed to steal my appetite and challenge my resolve. They called it assisted living. This was not a place of life, but of pending death. The people who lived here were too old or ill to live on their own. Some no longer dreamed of a bright future but looked forward to the day it would end.

I paused at the nurses' station and smiled at a middle-aged woman with thinning black hair and large glasses. Her name tag read *Delores,* and I knew from past visits that she liked to bake chocolate chip cookies on Fridays, loved the romantic comedy *Love, Actually*, and had a wicked crush on the grandson of one of the center's patients. She liked to share details of her life and might well have told me far more if I encouraged her. Conversations were meant to be a back-and-forth kind of event, much like a tennis match, but whenever she lobbed a ball of information my way, I rarely returned it. It was all I could do to contribute to the weekly AA meetings, let alone go a second set with this woman.

Tug on one thread of information and then, suddenly, the entire tapestry unraveled.

I signed *L. Smyth* and dug my driver's license out of my wallet. After a cursory check, Dolores smiled up at me. "Ms. Amelia is having a good day today. She's sitting up in bed and more clearheaded than normal."

"Thanks."

"Hey, Charlie," the nurse said, grinning.

The dog's ears perked up. Since I had arrived, we were both trying to get the hang of this new routine.

My Aunt Amelia's more lucid moments were a blessing and a curse. I enjoyed visiting when she remembered me, and we could talk about her younger days living in Alexandria. She was born in 1942 and just an infant in the city during World War II. She enjoyed reminiscing about the city during her teen years, when her parents moved the family to the Prince Street house. After a stint in New York trying to make it as a singer, she moved back to Alexandria and became a music teacher. She was twenty-six when she met Robert Murphy, the man she would marry. Two weeks ago, she talked about her first dance with him, and tears glistened in her pale gray eyes. Her parents never knew how Amelia and Robert met, but they were thrilled they had. Her eyes glistened with mischief as she said, "You know, Robert and I had sex on our second date. We were alive for each other."

"I never knew." I tried to sound a little scandalized.

"We Smyth women are good at keeping secrets, aren't we, Lisa?"

No truer words were spoken. We Smyth women were lip-locked when it came to secrets.

My worn brown cowboy boots, which I had purchased

from a street vendor in Nashville several years ago, clicked against the tiled floor in time with Charlie's steady steps. I wore jeans and a loose-fitting black T-shirt that skimmed the top of my hips. Corded rope hemp bracelets, now a faded blue, wrapped around my wrist, and long silver earrings tangled in my shoulder-length blond hair. As I pushed open the door, a glimpse of my slightly yellowed fingertips had me self-conscious. No matter how much I scrubbed, I could never erase the silver nitrate stains that plagued wet-plate photographers. I had chosen this antiquated, cumbersome, and time-consuming method of capturing photographic images as a teenager when I found a large bellows camera at an estate sale. My mother did not roll her eyes, but she clearly considered this one of my fads. I was drawn in by the camera and soon found a tripod on which to mount it and assembled the collection of chemicals to treat the eight-by-eight inch glass negatives. My first attempts to re-create the black-and-white images made popular during the Civil War by Matthew Brady, produced misty frayed photographs filled with technical flaws. As imperfect as my first efforts were, they offered a different perspective that still fascinates me to this day.

No matter how many times I coated the large glass negatives with the wet collodion mixture, sensitized the plates in silver nitrate, or stood with the large lens cap exposed while the camera slowly trapped the image on the glass, I was always amazed by the images that materialized in the final developing process. The textures, the lines, and the grains created depth.

I tried art school for a couple of semesters after high school, but in the end, I found the routine of college too limiting. At nineteen, feeling I was wasting my life, I hit the road in a beat-up truck with my photographic supplies.

I had made a name for myself in photographic circles by using this particular camera, but artistic success has not garnered many financial rewards. Several grants, sales at several art galleries, and a showing at a museum in Arizona have earned enough to keep me going. But I am still scrambling for the next photographic job to pay the rent.

My gypsy life changed three months ago when I received a call from my aunt's attorney. She had suffered a bad fall and broken her hip. He had her dog but could not keep the animal long term. I drove up from Florida and moved what little I had into her Prince Street house. When the doctors diagnosed her with Alzheimer's disease, I throttled back on plans to drive to Maine and found this facility for her. Though expensive, it was one of the best.

Aunt Amelia's mind may have abandoned her, but her hip healed quickly, and her heart was strong as ever. Her doctors expected she could live another decade. I accepted that her house would need to be sold and the money put in a trust to pay her bills. Like it or not, I was tethered to the area for now.

Of all the places I ever toyed with living for more than a few weeks, Alexandria was not, nor would it ever be, on the list. My dreams always favored the Florida Keys, the desert southwest of the United States, and even Alaska. And yet, here I was.

Charlie and I pushed through the door of her room and found her sitting up in the center of her hospital bed. Her thick white hair was brushed to a silken sheen that draped over thin shoulders. At seventy-eight, she had smooth skin, though months in bed had robbed her of a pink glow, leaving her as pale as buttermilk. The only hint of color came from a soft blue nightgown I had brought from her home last week and fingernails I had painted bright red a few days ago.

"Aunt Amelia," I said. "You're looking well." I no longer burdened her with the job of remembering, which created stress for her and disappointment for me. But Charlie wagged his tail as he pulled me toward the bed.

Each time I greet her, I casually hinted at the basic information to help jog her memory and not upset her should she be having a bad day. That was what dementia had done to both of us. It stole real and insightful conversations we once had and replaced them with staged events. I love my aunt, but we rarely connected any more.

She rubbed the dog's head. "Charlie. How's my big boy?"

The dog licked her hand and wagged his tail, clearly thrilled to see her, as he was every time.

"You remember me, too, Aunt Amelia."

A silver brow arched, annoyed, as she folded her hands over an old scrapbook in her lap. "I may have a bad hip, but I have not lost all my faculties. I know who you are . . . Lisa."

Grateful for this gift of time, I lowered my purse to the floor. I kissed her on the cheek before taking the seat next to her bed. Charlie settled on the floor and I fished a chew stick from my purse and gave it to him. "You know how it goes; some days are better than others. I like to play it safe."

"You've never played it safe in your life."

"Old dogs can learn new tricks," I said.

Amelia patted the spot beside her. "Charlie can get up here."

"The doctor says no. It's too hard on your hip."

"My hip is fine."

"No, it's not."

Before she became sick, Amelia had been a straight shooter and did not appreciate being treated like a fool. In one of her rare lucid moments after she was hospitalized, she made me promise never to treat her like a child, but rather like a grown woman with a lifetime of experiences. I agreed, thinking then that we would have more good times than bad. No sugarcoating for Amelia. Straight talk, hard news and politics that always made for good arguments, were welcomed. But the better days were now rare and in the last couple of weeks had whittled down to hours.

Amelia wagged a manicured finger, the vibrant red

drawing attention to her pale skin. "Ha, you don't know old. What are you, sixteen?"

Tension rippled up my back as I braced for the light in her to vanish. "I'm thirty-four, Amelia."

Hearing the concern spike in my tone, her head cocked. "I'm teasing, Lisa. I was there the day you were born. Your mother, my sister-in-law, Monica, was in labor for twenty hours. After it was all over, she looked like she'd been hit by a beer truck when she laid you in my arms. It was hot that July day. Bright sun." A brow arched. "I'm still here."

"Just checking. You do fade in and out."

Her lips curled into a snarl. "I would rather have cancer than this. At least cancer is up front and in your face. And you have your mind. When your mind is gone, you've lost yourself."

I leaned closer, studied her, and nodded. "You got that right. Let's not waste time worrying about it."

She gave a small shrug. "I want you to know, I'm never so lost that I don't know my favorite niece. Even when you can't see that, I'm there."

Sadness swirled like a maelstrom, but I swerved clear. "I'm your only niece, Amelia. Reaching favorite status isn't a huge feat."

"Simply because you have no competition doesn't mean you get to be favorite. It's a compliment."

I dug a small bag of cookies from my purse. Carefully, I unsealed the Union Street Bakery medallion and opened the top, allowing the soft scents of brown sugar, chocolate, and cinnamon to waft. Charlie looked up from his chew stick, expectant. As pet owners went, I probably did not win gold stars for all the table scraps I gave him. "Do me a favor and do not rat me out to the doctor about the sugar again. Last time when you faded, you went on and on about how good the cookies were. The doc gave me a lecture last week about the evils of sugar."

"Can't say I won't spill the beans again. You know I get a little confused."

I gave her one brown sugar cookie and kept the second one for myself. I broke it and gave half to Charlie. "If I have to be arrested for a crime, it might as well involve sweets."

Amelia bit into the tip of the cookie, closing her eyes as she savored the sweetness. "If chocolate is wrong, then I'll choose never to be right."

"I couldn't say it better." I laughed, glad that the woman I had loved since I was a child was here with me today. Tomorrow, an hour from now, she might be gone again, but for now, we were together. "Daisy and Rachel asked me to say hi. They worry about you."

"I do enjoy those girls. How is that bakery doing?"

"Doing great. Their online business has really taken off."

"I was really worried that the bakery would close when their parents retired. I'm glad they're still there." She studied the cookie. "So much of what I love is vanishing, and I don't want to lose my favorite bakery as well."

"Business is booming."

"Do the sisters have any gossip for you? Those girls always had the pulse of the town."

I bit into the cookie. "You know me, I'm not the gossip type. I never linger long."

"Even if you don't like gossip, do it for me. How is Daisy's baby?" Amelia asked.

"Walter is fat and happy and Rachel's twin girls are entering the second grade soon."

"Now if we can just get Rachel married off."

"She looks pretty happy to me," I said.

"You said her French baker moved back to France."

"You remember? I'm impressed. On your game today."

Satisfaction coaxed a small smile. "What's happening in town is far more interesting than the social calendar of this place. Honestly, Lisa, if I hear one another old lady bitch about a bad hip, I might break her good one."

There were times when I wondered how Amelia and I could have been genetically linked. She was as outgoing as I was introverted. And yet, we always got along and were a good match for each other. "Margaret is working for Shire Architectural Salvage now," I said. "I didn't realize it at the time but she and her business partner, Addie, cleaned out your basement about a month ago."

At the mention of the basement, her head cocked. "You had the basement cleaned out?"

I should not have mentioned the basement. The last time we had this discussion, I explained that her attorney had suggested we sell the Prince Street house. Big mistake. The idea of giving up her home upset her terribly. She still clung to the notion that she would return one day.

But Amelia would never be able to move back to the Prince Street house, and we needed the money to pay for her care.

"I told you." I kept my voice relaxed. "I had it tidied up. It was getting a bit cluttered."

She relaxed a fraction. "It was chock-full to the rafters. There were items in that basement that dated back hundreds of years. I bet Margaret enjoyed finding all that history."

"She loved it. She squealed every time she discovered a new detail. It was like a kid opening gifts on Christmas morning."

"The girl loves history." She plucked a stray thread off her blanket. "I wish she could get as excited about the present."

"She's a free spirit," I said.

"Margaret McCrae flitters from place to place. Frustrates Daisy, who says her sister has never stayed in one job long enough to get settled."

Like me, she was unable to put down roots. "Margaret flitters more than I do?"

Amelia immediately shook her head. "No, you're different. You're a photographer and you travel the world to work on your art. Margaret can't hold on to the present long enough."

My aunt described what I did in such a purposeful, nice way. The truth was, I was a gypsy, unable to stay anywhere for an extended period of time. "Margaret McCrae and Addie Morgan get on well."

"I don't know Addie well. Her aunt Grace is a good woman." She straightened her shoulders, proud of her clarity. "You know the Shires, the Smyths, and the McDonalds go back centuries."

"I know we've been here forever, but I never really gave it much thought." I nearly failed history in high school.

"Colonial times, from what my mother used to say. You know, a Captain Smyth built our house on Prince Street."

I resisted rolling my eyes. I had heard the story about the Scottish captain who built the lovely brick home overlooking the Potomac River for his young bride so many times. I hated hearing about it as much as she loved telling the story. "I bet it's a great story."

She nibbled her cookie. "Don't patronize me, Lisa. You hate the story."

I laughed. "Busted."

"I might be forgetful, but I'm not *that* forgetful, Miss I-got-a-D-minus-in-history."

"Fine."

Her expression grew serious. "I don't know how long all this clarity will last. Each time, I feel I'm back for good. But it isn't true, is it?"

"I'm sorry."

Nodding, she set her cookie on her top sheet. "Look in the nightstand. There's a book."

I handed the last of my cookie to Charlie and after wiping my hands on my jeans, opened the bedside table. Inside was an old scrapbook covered in silk fabric that had once been a pale green but was now faded to a dull gray. The binding along the spine was torn in spots, but enough of the fasteners remained to hold together the dozens of yellowed pages.

She held out her hands. "May I look at it?"

Carefully, I laid it on her lap. She traced a large *M* embossed on the front of the book, and her frown deepened as she searched for the memory that skittered out of reach. "I didn't know this book existed until I was thirty years old. I wasn't who I thought I was." She closed her eyes and nibbled her bottom lip, choking back tears.

"Can I see it?"

She leaned forward and looked at me. "Sure, dear."

Carefully, I slid the silk book away from her fragile hands, which were knotted with arthritis. I brushed off the cookie crumbs and opened the cover. Inside it read, *Baby's First Year*. "It's a baby book. Is it yours?"

"I believe it is," she said, smoothing her hand over the first page. The yellowed page creaked as we turned it to the title page. In a thick bold handwriting, it read: *Amelia Elizabeth McDonald. Born July 1, 1942, 6:24 P.M. Six pounds, six ounces.*

"Amelia, are you sure this is your book? Its family's last name is McDonald, not Smyth."

Slowly, she traced the name McDonald with a bent finger. "I was born a McDonald."

I had never heard this story before and suspected she was recalling someone else's life. The blending of reality and fiction was not uncommon. "I didn't know that."

"I was adopted when I was a year old by your grandparents, Sam and Marjorie Smyth."

"I never heard a word about that. Ever."

"I don't think anyone beyond my parents knew. The Smyths are good at keeping secrets. You should know that by now."

She was right. My mother had battled cancer on her own terms while my father gambled the family money on the stock market. In my seventeenth year, Dad lost everything before having a fatal heart attack. Mom died six months later. If not for Amelia moving back into the Prince Street home with me, I would have been deep in trouble. "You never kept secrets."

"Keeping secrets was a quality I learned from my mother. What came naturally to her was always a struggle for me."

Scooting to the edge of my chair, I was anxious to confirm the truth of her words. If fact and fantasy were blending, I wanted to snatch as many truths as I could before they floated away like a handful of balloons released into the air.

"My mother, Marjorie Jones Smyth, and Fiona Winter were good friends growing up. They were born on the exact same day and met in elementary school. They were like sisters, from what my grandmother Smyth used to say."

"Fiona Winter. She married a McDonald." I was a friend to a McDonald once. Jennifer McDonald. We were like sisters, too. "I never heard any of this."

A slight shrug of Amelia's shoulder did not hide the hurt radiating from her now. "Marjorie and Fiona were in love with the same man. His name was Jeffrey McDonald. Very dignified and handsome."

"A love triangle. Always a good story, but are you sure?"

Amelia stroked the yellowed page, absently tracing the elaborate *M* of her born last name. "My adopted mother never wanted me to know about her love for Jeffrey." A sly smile tweaked the edges of her thin lips. "She was pulling Christmas decorations out of the attic one year and asked me to help. The phone rang and she went to answer it. As I was searching for the decorations, I spotted a trunk. Inside the trunk were dozens of letters bound together with a faded red ribbon."

When I was younger, Amelia had been the energetic older aunt who had always been quick with a fun idea. She loved life. When I was six, she took me for a ride in her new convertible along the George Washington Parkway. When I was ten, she hired a hot-air balloon and we drifted over the waters of the Potomac. And when I was nearly eighteen, in the dark days after my parents' deaths and then the car accident, she allowed me to cry when no one else thought I had a right to my tears. When I was twenty, she dragged me to my first AA meeting and told me not to contact her ever again if I did not start working with the program.

Aunt Amelia never shied from a challenge. A bundle of letters would have been irresistible. "How long before you doubled back and read them?"

Eyes twinkled. "Three days. I had to wait for Mom and Dad to leave the house. I pulled the steps down and crept up the stairs."

"Where was Dad during all this?" My father was ten years younger than Amelia and his older sister's constant shadow until she moved out of the family home for college.

"Your father was about four at the time. I was supposed to be watching him, and of course, when I put him in bed he did not sleep. He was always a terrible sleeper, much like you."

"I can picture it now. You're in the attic and Dad is on the bottom rung of the stairs threatening to tell." I had loved my father, but he could conveniently keep his own secrets but no one else's. It was why I had never been able to really talk to him.

"Your father sensed I was up to no good, and he took great joy in threatening to tell Mom that I was in the attic." She glanced at her polished nails, her grin as devilish as a young schoolgirl. "I told him I'd tell Santa he had been naughty, and

Santa would never again come to our house. His eyes grew as wide as saucers, but he tried to hold his ground and insist I was lying. But I wanted to see the letters so badly that I kept twisting the Santa threat until he burst into tears and ran to his room."

"And you read the letters."

"I snuck them to my room and slowly read each and every one of them." Her eyes glistened. "I discovered my adoptive mother was in love with a man named Jeffrey. The letters were dated several years before my parents met. Which made them all the more delicious."

"What happened?"

She opened her mouth to speak but hesitated and frowned. I recognized the expression. The words and ideas on the tip of her tongue flitted away, out of reach. "She married, so I suppose it did not end well for Mother and Jeffrey. I never really knew what happened to him until I found this book. He married another woman."

She fumbled with the frayed edge of her blanket and I could see her frustration. A woman who had prided herself on her quick wit and memory was now losing both to a disease that mercilessly robbed the mind.

I laid my hand over hers and then kissed the back of her hand. "Let's look at the book and see if it will tell us what happened."

Worried eyes rose to mine, and for a blink, she searched my face, staring for the familiar. Slowly, she nodded. "It all must be in the book, shouldn't it?"

"It must be, otherwise you wouldn't have it."

I turned the first page to a picture of an infant girl dressed in a white christening gown. A round button mouth curled into a wide grin and her little hands were splayed wide open. The photographer had caught her mid-belly laugh. Amelia had been a pretty baby, with wisps of lightly colored hair that I guessed had been red. I had seen pictures of her as a young woman and her hair was a vibrant copper. As she aged and silver threatened to diminish the luster, she turned to the salons to maintain a color that grew increasingly dark, out of step with her pale skin. However, since she had arrived here, there was no one to dye her hair, so time and washings had faded it to a silver that I found far more attractive.

I angled the book so Amelia could better see it. Age had degraded the pages, and I wondered if given a couple more years locked away, they would not have crumbled. "You were a pretty baby."

She traced the infant's wide, expressive eyes, and with a little more confidence said, "Yes, I was. I always wondered where that red hair came from. I never quite looked like a Smyth."

"Did your birth mother have red hair?" I asked.

Her light blue eyes darkened with an intensity that hinted of a truth no one in the family had ever mentioned. "Yes, she did."

Turning the page of the baby book, I stared at a picture of a young couple holding a baby. The inscription at the bottom read: *Fiona and Jeffrey McDonald with their precious daughter, Amelia.* "Amelia Elizabeth McDonald. You really were adopted."

Her chin lifted up in defiance. "I told you I was."

I ran my hand through my hair. "Holy cow."

"I know. Shocker. I was as surprised as you when I found out."

"That was decades ago. You never said a word."

"I was in shock at first. Didn't want to believe it. And then my husband became sick. I tried to talk to my mother once, but she said she didn't know what I was talking about. I pressed her, but the conversation went nowhere, and she told me not to bring it up again. I thought about talking to my dad, but if Mother didn't want a subject discussed, he always obeyed her wishes. I thought I could ask her again one day, but she passed and so did my father. Time slipped through my fingers."

Over the last month Amelia's condition had worsened. Bringing with it all kinds of crazy claims. Once she confused me with her doctor and thanked me for her discharge papers, telling me her niece would arrive soon to take her home. Another time she told me my late mother had come for a visit. We had many conversations, but many were rambling threads of what I thought were delusions.

But now, as I stared at the page, I understood better. "Explains why you and Dad were so different." My father was as closed as Amelia was open.

"We were never really close. I always felt that once he came along, I became nearly invisible. He was the son my parents thought they would never have. Of course, to get everyone's attention, I had to become more and more outrageous. My parents were never amused."

I turned the page of the book and studied a collection of telegrams wishing Fiona and Jeffrey congratulations on the birth of their daughter. Time had weathered the telegrams, making them appear all the more ancient. We all exchanged words easily today. Quick texts, or if time really allowed, an e-mail. Letters and note cards were relics. But when Amelia had been born, to send a note of congratulations took time, effort, and money.

Carefully, I ran my hands over the beautiful cards that still had a silky, delicate quality. On the next few pages were photographs of smiling strangers surrounding the young couple and their baby.

Here were two people full of life and love. It was clear that Amelia had been a much loved and cherished child. "What happened to Fiona and Jeffrey?" I whispered.

"Jeffrey died."

I studied the face of the man who shared the same jawline and glint in his eyes as Amelia. "How?"

"I don't know. It was during World War II and he had been shipped overseas."

"Do you know why Fiona couldn't keep you?"

"No," she sadly whispered. "She left Alexandria after the adoption and then returned several years later married to David Saunders. They had a daughter, Diane, who oddly also married into the McDonald family."

"Diane McDonald. She was Jennifer and Rae's mother."

"Yes."

The faded page creaked as I turned it. The families were intertwined like the thick honeysuckle vines growing on the back fence of the Prince Street house. "And you asked your birth mother about all this?"

She studied the page so closely, recalling distant memories fading fast. "Fiona never admitted to any of it."

"You must have talked to someone. Who told you about the adoption? How did you end up with this book?"

A frown furrowed her brow. "I don't remember. I've been trying all morning to remember the details of how the book came to me all those years ago, but I can't dig up one memory. This damn disease is stealing my life." Tears moistened her eyes. "If I had one wish before I die, it would be to learn what happened to Jeffrey and why Fiona gave me away. Why didn't she ever want me back after she remarried?"

Although a lot of time had passed, the pain on Amelia's face was as raw as if it all happened yesterday. Her wound had never healed.

"How did you get this book here, Amelia? I didn't bring it from the house."

Her eyebrows rose. "I called my attorney. I asked him to bring it to me. It's been with my papers for years."

"Colin West?"

"Yes. I think it was Colin."

I had met Colin to get Charlie and discuss Amelia's finances. In his late thirties, he was polite and reserved. Not classically handsome, but very intense. He always wore a suit, and once I jokingly asked if he had come into this world fully attired. He was not amused. Jokes and Mr. West were strangers. I would have written him off if Charlie had not liked him.

Amelia laid her small hand on mine, her grip tight. "Maybe you can talk to your friend, Jennifer McDonald. I bet she would be able to find out more."

I drew back. Her addled mind was missing critical bits of information and she did not realize it. Still, the words sliced. "Jennifer is dead, remember Aunt Amelia? She died in a car accident when we were in high school."

She clutched her white blanket as though holding onto memories. "Jennifer is gone?"

"You remember the car accident, don't you?" There were so many times that I wished I could forget it. But not a day passed when I did not hear the screech of locked wheels or my screams blending with Jennifer's as the car struck an old tree by the river.

"The accident." Amelia's lost eyes stared back at me. "Jennifer was killed?"

Carefully, I closed the book, sensing the frail woman who had greeted me when I had entered the room minutes ago had been overtaken again by the shadows. Her memory flickered. "It was a long, long time ago, Aunt Amelia. Don't worry about it."

Still holding my hand, she offered to console me. "But it was an accident."

"Yes. A very bad accident."

"Maybe you could ask Jennifer's sister, Rae, about Fiona. Rae was always such a smart girl. Always had the answers."

"I haven't seen Rae since the accident, Amelia. She and I aren't friends like we used to be."

When Jennifer died, Rae's world was turned upside down with grief. She acted out, rebelled against her own mother's stoic acceptance of Jennifer's death. She went looking for love and comfort anywhere she could find it. Rae soon found herself pregnant at sixteen.

I moistened my lips, the constant craving for alcohol elbowing to the front of my mind. I thought about drinking every day since the accident and most days could list all the reasons why I was grateful I no longer drank. But today, the gratitude list was woefully short. All the true and sure reasons for sobriety which usually remained at the ready were not holding water. They had scattered like vapor, leaving me to think about the bittersweet taste of cool white wine trickling down my throat. I imagined releasing my firm grip on sobriety.

Nearly a decade had passed since I had touched a drink. But in a blink, none of that mattered. What mattered now was that I was desperately thirsty for the release of one glass of wine. One small glass. Not a bender. One to soften the edge and soothe the swelling sadness that was consuming me.

But AA did not work that way. One glass, the first glass, was the destroyer.

"Honey, I'm sorry you and Rae and Jennifer don't get along anymore. You were all close."

The window to Amelia's clarity had nearly closed. No sense reminding her of what now skittered out of her reach.

I gently tugged the scrapbook from Amelia's hands and carefully placed it in the drawer of the nightstand. I leaned forward and kissed her on the forehead and tucked her hands under the folds of the white blankets. "I'll be back tomorrow, Aunt Amelia. Sleep well."

Her eyes drifted open for a moment and she stared up at me with cutting clarity. "You were in the car when Jennifer died."

A sigh shuddered over my clenched teeth. "It was a long time ago."

She shook her head. "But not for you. For you, it's right now. I can see it. I can see her."

"See who?"

"Jennifer. She's behind you now."

A tingle shot up my spine, and despite logic, I turned and looked. Jennifer's presence had always lingered close since the accident. There were times I sensed her standing right behind me, pushing me forward to fill my life with experiences for both of us.

Turning, I found only the glow of the overhead light.

I smoothed my hand over her forehead. "No one is here, Amelia."

Sympathy warmed my aunt's confused, sad eyes. "I know you didn't mean to kill her. She knows that, too. We both understood you didn't mean it."

No one knew what had happened in that car before the accident. No one. Except Jennifer and me.

"Get some sleep," I said.

When she drifted off, Charlie and I left the room. The urge to drink now yanked and tugged at me. At moments like this I stood at the cliff's edge, tempted to jump back into the delicious oblivion of alcohol.

To combat the terrible craving, I moved with precision, slowing life to microseconds and analyzing each of my actions, hoping the cravings would pass. I feared that if I lowered my guard, time would jump forward and I would find myself sitting in a bar with my second or third glass of wine in my hand. There were moments when my sobriety felt as fragile as a robin's egg. I needed another meeting, soon.

Smiling at the nurse, I walked toward the elevator, Charlie at my side. What came next was a blur to me. Charlie hopped into the front seat and we drove back to Alexandria fast enough to earn a hefty speeding ticket if caught. I slowed when I exited the Beltway and worked my way into Old Town and the Methodist church where AA held meetings. Out of the car, Charlie and I slowly walked around the block to kill a little bit of time before we went inside the church basement. I took a seat in the empty circle of chairs with Charlie settled on the floor next to me.

"The meeting doesn't start for a half hour," a man's voice said behind me.

I gripped the strap of my purse a little tighter but made no move to stand. "If you don't mind, I'd like to sit here and wait."

"Sure, sure. That's fine. I'll have the coffee and donuts out soon. Unless you need it earlier."

"No, that's okay." I peered into his familiar face with a slight smile, in what I hoped was a friendly gesture. He was of medium build with thinning brown hair wearing a tan sweater, jeans, and white tennis shoes. His name was Grant and he ran our meeting.

"Do you need to talk?" he asked.

"No, I'm good."

"He's cute," the voice whispered softly. I assumed, as I always did, that it was my own thoughts echoing Jennifer. But deep down I knew better.

"You sure?" he asked again.

I hugged my purse a little closer. "If you see me running for the door before the meeting, tackle me. Make me stay."

A grin warmed his face. "Consider yourself stopped."

"Thanks."

Here I felt a little bit safer, knowing Grant was on guard and soon I would be surrounded by kindred souls. Once the meeting started, the room would fill with folks from all walks of life, and then I would listen to their struggles.

If I stayed right here in this chair, forgiveness would not visit me, but I might find a reason not to drink for another hour, maybe another day.

"You'll find a reason. You always do."

Letter from Patience

NOVEMBER 10, 1751

Dearest Mother,

Faith and her babes have been here five days. I awoke to the sound of one crying and the milk in my breasts that I thought dried, stirred. I rose from under my covers and saw the infants lying on a pallet. Faith was nowhere to be seen. Perhaps she went to the barn to fetch milk for breakfast. Pulled by the babe's squawks, I moved to the pallet where the boys lay side by side. Though they were twins, they did not look at all alike. One was as light in skin and hair as the other was dark. Good and evil. Light and darkness—one cannot exist without the other. I picked up the smaller of the two, his hair as pale as mine, and held him in my arms. He rooted, fussed and searched. Unable to resist the powerful stirring in my womb, I unfastened the front of my nightshirt and bared my breast. As soon as I teased his lips with my nipple, he hungrily suckled. For a moment I stood frozen, my body overwhelmed. Though my heart did not beat as it once did, soft whispers of hope stirred.

Yours Faithfully,
Patience McDonald

Chapter Three

RAE, TUESDAY, OCTOBER 4, 2011,
ALEXANDRIA, VIRGINIA

I dreamed about the boy last night.

Because I was young and tall, my pregnancy did not really show until I was six months along. Loose clothes and sweaters bought me another month until finally there was no denying it. By the time I finally confessed my condition to my mother, I was nearly seven months pregnant.

Mom promptly poured a stiff scotch, swallowed it in two gulps, and then poured another shot as tears streamed down both our cheeks. "You are not even seventeen and will not be keeping that baby. You're sixteen and not ready to be a mother."

My trembling hands instinctively slid to my stomach as the baby kicked and stirred.

Mom stared at the amber liquid in the crystal glass, lost. "I cannot do it. I cannot go through this."

The idea of motherhood terrified me. I did not know what to do or how to handle the weight of its responsibility. When my mother told me she would not help, I knew I could not do it alone.

I moved fifty miles west to live with a friend of Mom's in

Winchester. The car ride was a solemn tense affair. Staring out my window, I watched the malls and housing developments give way to rolling hills and pastures. Mom gripped the steering wheel, staring at the road ahead.

Her friend was nice enough and tried to make me feel welcome. But when my mother drove away, and I sat in my room tugging at the loose thread on the bed quilt, I felt alone. My sister was dead, and my mother had abandoned me emotionally. Even the baby in my belly refused to move while the heaviness in my heart grew with my belly.

When the boy was born, I had thirty minutes to hold him. The first minutes brought a rush of love that was so, so sweet. I had never experienced this kind of love from my mother. And when I looked into his face, I saw perfection. When the nurse returned with his adoptive mother, I was required to tell her I would not keep custody of him. When I laid him in the other woman's arms, a switch clicked off somewhere deep inside me to keep me sane. The sadness retreated, but so did most of me.

I picked up the stone heart given to me by Zeb Talbot. Heavy and cold in my palm, it carried far more weight than the original gesture intended. Although an odd-shaped rock to him, it epitomized me. I might have been annoyed by the reporter's words, but perhaps she was right. I had a heart of stone.

The front doorbell rang, shifting my thoughts back to the present. I moved from my study and was a tad irritated to see Margaret McCrae through the small windows that trimmed the side of the door. She was early. I was a rigid scheduler, and as a psychologist, I recognized that my obsession with time stemmed from a need to control a world that was oblivious to my wants. I understood the futility of it but could not stop.

Opening the door, I found Margaret standing on the front porch, her hair damp from what must have been a quick shower after the trip she and Addie had taken to Prince William County today. There was always traffic, so for her to arrive early meant she had wasted no time.

Margaret grinned at me, shifting her weight from foot to foot. She reminded me of a young trick-or-treater at Halloween on the doorstep of the house with the best candy.

"I know I'm early," she explained, "but the job went faster than expected, and I can't wait to get started."

I stood back, watching as she wiped her damp boots on the front mat and entered the foyer. "I was sorting through the boxes of papers, trying to isolate the time period," I said.

"You were sorting through boxes. How many papers do you have?"

"I've never stopped to count, but we McDonalds were always detailed record keepers."

She laid her hand over her heart. "So, you have over two hundred years' worth of documentation?"

"Perhaps a bit more. Some records came over from Scotland with Patience McDonald," I said. "I hope you don't mind, but I went ahead and set up the boxes on the kitchen table. I'll show you the way."

She clapped her hands together. "I swear this is amazing, Rae. I live for days like this."

My heels clicked on the hardwood floor a couple of beats faster than her boots. "I've sorted them by dates. You should be able to zero in on the time period in question."

Margaret entered the kitchen and paused to stare at the long farmhouse table covered in sturdy brown boxes. This part of the house had been an addition when my mother still could summon a bit of emotion. My father was dead, but Jennifer and I were doing well, and our family was the closest that I ever remembered us being. Mom decided the old kitchen needed to go, so she hired an architect to build this large addition. The old was demoed unceremoniously without another thought. Last year, I hired Zeb to renovate the space. Though I kept the structural design, I replaced mauves and grays with an eggshell blue color, stainless steel appliances, and white marble countertops. The large kitchen table was the single holdout from the first kitchen that was built in the late eighteenth century. I still found the kitchen one of the most comfortable and inviting spaces in the house.

"Kitchen looks new. What's prompted all the changes on the property?" Margaret asked as she dumped her satchel purse on the table by a box.

"A house needs to be updated from time to time to maintain its market value."

Her curls glistened with a slight dampness. "Are you thinking about selling?"

The idea had crossed my mind once or twice, but whenever it did, I always opted to stay. This was the McDonald family home, a legacy. But more importantly, the address I gave the boy's parents, and to leave risked him not being able to find me. "It's a big house and it's only me here."

"Part of the house's foundation dated back to the mid-1700's when the McDonalds arrived. That means there's been a McDonald continuously on the property for nearly three hundred years."

"Yes. Though I'm the last of the line."

She ran a callused hand over the top of a box. "Adopt me, Rae. I'll become a McDonald and parade the legacy with pride and glory."

With a slight grin, I replied, "We McDonald women live a long time."

"How old are you?"

"Thirty-two," I replied.

"I'm thirty-six." She beamed. "If you never marry or have kids, can I have the house?"

"Check back with me in sixty years."

"It's a date. Looking forward to it." She glanced out the window toward the raw patch of land. "Why get rid of the hearth? I mean, I'm glad we excavated the site for you, but why?"

Deep inside me, fear whispered: *Because every McDonald before me insisted it stay.* Logic said, "I'd like to have a garage."

She visibly shuddered. "When I think about all the history that has been lost because people need parking."

I'm tired of carrying the weight of the past. "My practice is expanding, and I have more clients coming and going."

"If it were me, I'd make them park at the end of the street and hoof it in before getting rid of the hearth." Margaret held up her hand, realizing her candor was not always her best asset. "But if you had not dismantled the hearth, then we would never have found the witch bottle. Thank you, Rae."

"If you consider finding that old bottle lucky, I'm glad for you."

Margaret moved to the first box. "The question is, why did a McDonald, whom I'm guessing was Patience, feel the need to create a witch bottle?"

"Superstition was common in the days when sickness and death were never far, and families had little control over their fate."

"So, Rae, you don't believe in spells and curses?" Margaret asked as she contemplated the box marked *Eighteenth Century* and then carefully removed the lid.

"Are you saying that you do?" I asked.

Margaret grinned as she reached in her pocket and pulled out a pair of white cloth gloves. "Hell, yes."

"That's not logical, is it?"

"Spoken like a shrink." She tugged on the pristine gloves and removed an old leather-bound ledger from the box. She moved her hand reverently over the worn, cracked surface.

"When I hold pieces of the past like this, I believe there's a lot we could learn if we're open to it."

"It's a journal," I said. "An artifact."

"To me, it's a voice from the past reaching out to me." She eased open the pages, wincing when the spine creaked. "I believe that there's more to this planet, this life, than the physical world."

"Ah, you believe in ghosts, spirits, and goblins and all creatures that go bump in the night."

"Do I detect a bit of disbelief, Rae?"

"I'm more science minded."

"But you're a psychologist. The mind and thoughts are not exactly a tangible science. More art than science," she challenged.

"Behavior can always be traced back to a specific source. We may not be able to identify it, but it's there."

Margaret pulled out a wooden chair and sat, never looking up from the page. A frown furrowed her brow as her fingers moved over the page. "So, my obsession with the past can be traced back to a specific event."

"Or events."

Margaret raised her head, considering what I had said. "I had a pretty normal upbringing, if you consider my indentured servitude in a bakery normal."

"That bad?" Rae smiled.

She tugged a pair of reading glasses from her shirt pocket and perched them on the bridge of her nose. "Not exactly. If you haven't noticed, I tend to exaggerate. But our family was all about keeping the bakery running and making a buck. As Dad always said, the bakery was our past, present, and future. And since the present meant work and the future was always a little daunting, I found myself drawn to the past."

"I understand you're a scholar when it comes to Alexandria," I said.

She reached in another pocket for a cell phone. "That and a few coins will buy you a cup of coffee."

"Yes, I don't suppose history is the profession of the rich and famous."

"Not generally." She slowly turned a page. "Mind if I snap pictures of the documents as I go along? That way I can study them at length when I get home."

"That won't damage the pages?"

"No. I would never, ever damage these documents."

"And you won't share the pictures?" I asked.

"Not without your approval."

"Okay, you may photograph." I had a paper to finish and several follow-up client letters to write, but I found myself fascinated by Margaret's utter absorption in the journal. "I tried to read the notes in that book before you arrived but found the script challenging."

"I've read so much of this that I can decipher the penmanship pretty quickly. Another one of those quirky specialties that doesn't earn me a dime."

"So, what have you discovered?"

A frown furrowed her brow as she stared at the first pages. "It's a household account kept by Patience and Michael McDonald."

"Michael?" I had wanted a strong name for my son and had chosen Michael for the archangel who commanded the angels in heaven. When my mother tried to object, I insisted and she realized I was pure tinder, ready to ignite. All parties agreed to the boy's name.

"Yes. He was the one who started it all in the Virginia Colony. I know from other research that Patience and Michael McDonald came to this country in the mid-1700s," Margaret said.

"They were the first from the old country to own land on these shores." Michael was not an uncommon name, but it was an odd coincidence that the line began and ended with the name. "Interesting."

"What, the name?" Margaret asked.

"The name Michael has always been a favorite of mine."

"Oh, okay." When I did not expound, she did. "As you might know, Patience and Michael hailed from Scotland with the intention of being tobacco farmers. I know that somewhere along that time they purchased the indentured servant contract for Faith Shire."

"Shire? As in the Shires of the architectural company?"

"One and the same. I know from previous research that Faith lived on their farm for about a year before the McDonalds sold her indentured servant contract to Mr. Ben Talbot, the manager of Hugh West's tobacco warehouse. That was located where modern-day Union Street ends and Oronoco Street begins."

"Where Robinson Bus Terminal is now?" I asked.

"Yes." She sat back and tugged off her glasses. "I know that many women in town considered Faith a witch and were afraid of her."

"They created the witch bottles as a protection against spells, but especially hers."

"Exactly." She tapped her finger on the ledger. "This is a household account that Michael McDonald created when he began his farm."

"Is there mention of Faith?"

"Yes. He purchased her contract from the ship's captain for the promise of a hogshead of tobacco. A hogshead was a giant wooden barrel. Currency was a rarity then, so many farmers used tobacco as money."

"Why would a man want an entire barrel of tobacco?"

"He'd have sold it back in England and made a sizable profit." She carefully turned several more pages. "Here I see that Mr. Talbot paid for Faith the following spring. He traded two hogsheads of tobacco for her."

"Her value doubled in a year."

"Very few women in the city at that time," Margaret said. "They were at a premium, and if she survived here a year, that meant she had to be tough."

"What happened to this witch?"

"She later 'married' Talbot and bore him twin sons."

"Why do you say 'married' that way?" I asked.

"I'm not so sure they legally wed."

"Ah."

"The women of Alexandria formally accused her of witchcraft after Mr. Talbot's death, and then she and her sons vanished from the records. I'm hoping that Patience will make some kind of mention of her."

"You've quite the task. There are dozens of letters along with the ledgers."

Margaret raised a white-gloved hand to her heart. "Letters."

"A couple of decades' worth."

"Rae, this is like historical porn." She cleared her throat. "I mean, I'm very happy to study it."

It was hard not to be impressed by her excitement. "Sexual fantasies are not my forte, but I'm glad you have found a distraction that's of interest."

Her laughter rang clear and loud. "Rae, I think you made a joke. There might be hope for you, yet."

"I didn't realize I was hopeless."

"Not hopeless," Margaret said. "But you did get labeled as the lady with the heart of stone. At least no one called you the Ice Queen."

"My clients like my detachment."

"That can't be much fun for you. What gets your motor racing?"

I fingered the pearl bracelet encircling my wrist. "I choose not to engage in high drama. Calm and order are needed to remain objective."

Margaret shook her head as if she pitied me. "Unless I'm dealing with documents like this, order drives me insane."

"To each his own."

I left her hunched over the papers and returned to my computer. Without really thinking, I pulled up my e-mail, hoping for minor tasks to occupy my time. I was scrolling through my inbox when I saw his name: *Michael Holloway.* The boy.

Sitting up in my seat, I stared at the name, stunned. I was not intimidated much but was now scared to read his message.

My index finger anxiously tapped the mouse button before I drew in a breath and clicked it twice. The e-mail opened.

Dear Dr. McDonald . . .

Dr. McDonald. That made sense, of course. Polite. But distant.

> Dear Dr. McDonald,
>
> I read about you in the paper. You might not know it, but you and I are related. I guess you could say I'm your son. I'm not writing to ask for anything, but I was hoping you could answer a few questions for me about the McDonald family tree. My mom was trying to help, but she does not know any names other than yours and your mom's.
>
> Thanks,
>
> Michael

I read the e-mail again slowly as the full spectrum of emotions washed over me. His request required a simple and straightforward answer. And yet, I was clueless as to how to proceed.

Answer the boy. An e-mail took less than five minutes. So little time. But what were the right words? I did not want to ruin our first interaction. What if he wanted to know why I gave him away?

"Holy shit!"

Startled from my thoughts, I found Margaret standing in the doorway. A look at the clock and I realized an hour had passed.

Margaret held a letter in her hand, her eyes dancing with excitement just as they had when she stood on my porch with that old bottle.

Pulling off my glasses, I quickly closed the e-mail and rose. I cleared my throat. "What did you discover?"

"Patience feared Faith."

Grateful for the distraction from the e-mail, I moved from my desk, hoping to distance myself from a new and growing restlessness rubbing against the underside of my skin. "Why?"

"I'll get to that." Margaret looked up at me, eyes dancing. "How much do you know about Patience?"

"Only what's written in the family Bible."

She clasped her hands like a teacher addressing a class. "She and her husband, Michael, had four children. Two of those children survived to adulthood. One was a boy, Patrick, and the other a girl, Hanna."

I remembered the feel of my empty arms after I gave the boy away. The emptiness was so acute my skin burned. God only knows what it felt like to bury a child. Absently, I folded my arms over my chest and rubbed my forearms. "I've counseled women who've lost a child. The pain is devastating."

"Death was a fact of life in those days, but you're right, the loss must have been excruciating. Patience McDonald must have been heartbroken."

"What happened to the children?"

"Despite my colonial script deciphering skills, parts are hard to understand. Time and improper storage had taken its toll."

"Improper?"

She raised a hand. "I won't lecture you on proper storage when you've done a fair job for an amateur. But there are better ways to preserve these papers."

"I've never done any task *fair* before."

"Well, there's always a first." And then, presuming my response didn't matter, she said, "All these papers need to be in a special room, Rae. I've photographed each page before I touched them for fear they'd break apart. Consider yourself lucky none has."

"Noted. What did Patience McDonald say to her mother?"

"I'm still sifting through that, but I do know she lost a son in 1749 and another in 1750. In 1751 she references her third son, Patrick, and later a daughter, Hanna, born a few years later. They both lived."

Margaret scrolled through images on her phone. "After Faith's witch trial, she and her sons came to live with the McDonalds. Odd that Faith would return to this place, but then again, this was the only other home she would have known in Virginia. And she was likely smart enough to know that she could not survive alone with her babies. Also, the McDonalds might have needed help. Faith must have suspected Patience wasn't in good health."

"You figured all that out from two or three letters?"

"That and what I already knew. Survival was always at the forefront of every decision back then."

"What does Patience say about Faith?" The answer did not matter to me beyond the fact that it would keep Margaret talking. When she talked, my focus shifted away from the boy's e-mail.

"Patience actually nursed one of Faith's babies. She says her breast milk still stirred, suggesting a child might have recently died. But that doesn't jibe with the Bible, which records Patrick's death in 1831." Margaret shook her head. "Always missing puzzle pieces. It's maddening and exciting all at once."

"Why would the McDonalds take Faith back if they feared her?"

"Faith was a healer, a midwife, and the early 1750s was a tough time for the McDonalds. She could have helped tend to Patience, or nursemaid her baby if it were still alive. She would have been a valuable asset."

"The loss of the children was good reason to keep Faith out of their house," I argued. "Why invite a witch into your home?"

"To keep the other two children alive."

"What became of Faith's sons?"

"There's mention of one of them in the history books. Marcus Talbot Shire. He became a prominent innkeeper in Alexandria. There was a time when I thought Ben married Faith, but I don't think he ever made it legal."

"What happened to the other son?"

"I don't know," she said softly.

"What about the McDonald boy, Patrick?"

"He became a successful lawyer and farmer," Margaret said. "Lived to be eighty."

"Faith arrives with two infants and there is a reference to an empty cradle," I said. "Only one of Patience's sons survives and Faith's second son . . ."

"Cullen."

"Cullen vanishes. It didn't require a historian to figure out what had happened."

Her head cocked to the side and I imagined her thoughts swirling. "Rae, are you suggesting the McDonalds took one of Faith's children?"

"Conjecture at this point."

Margaret snapped a finger. "What if the McDonald son did die and Faith was invited to stay provided, she gives the McDonalds one of her babies? Maybe Faith had to give up rights to one son to save them both."

"Interesting theory."

She wagged her finger at me, and I sensed theories swirling. She was forever consumed with piecing together the past, at the expense of the present. "I like the way your mind works. Of course, proving this is another issue."

"Adoption is as old as time," I said.

"Do you mind if I make a pot of coffee? I've been on the go since the crack of dawn and I need a second wind."

"I'll make us a pot." My heels clicked on the wooden floor, echoing through the house with a purpose, just like my world.

"Do you always wear high heels?"

The question caught me off guard. "Though I work out of my home, I do consider this my office and want it to be professional."

"Yeah, but high heels? The last time I wore heels was to my senior prom and they hurt like hell. I kicked them off five minutes after Ronnie Stevens and I arrived at the school gym. I lost the heels."

"What did your mother say about that?"

She laughed. "I suggested there were worse things I could have lost."

"Let me guess, she wasn't amused."

"Not at all. Before the prom she gave me a serious lecture about sex. One look at Ronnie's van and she was sure I'd get knocked up. I told her I wasn't throwing away my upcoming summer in Greece by having Ronnie's kid."

I removed two white porcelain cups from the cabinet and carefully set them on the countertop along with the milk from the refrigerator. I recalled the night I had slept with my beau.

His name was Dan Chesterfield and he was a year older than I. Three months after Jennifer died, Dan came by the house and offered to take me out. I was desperate to get away from the grief that engulfed my family, so I agreed. We drove along the George Washington Parkway and parked in a spot offering a stunning view of Georgetown on the opposite side of the Potomac. He had a bottle of whiskey and offered me the first sip. So polite. I drank and immediately coughed as liquid fire burned my throat. I shoved the bottle back in his hands, certain I was finished with it. But as the warmth of the whiskey spread through my body, I realized the pain had numbed a little. I tried another sip. Coughed only a little this time. He laughed. Called me a lightweight. And the pain eased a little more.

There were no high heels to lose that night, but my virginity went by the wayside in an awkward and painful exchange. Nine months later, I gave birth to the boy.

"I wear the heels because they make me feel in control," I said as the coffeemaker dripped out a fresh pot.

Margaret leaned forward, resting her chin on her hands. "You're about the most controlled person I know. I can't imagine you need the heels to keep you on the straight and narrow."

"They're a reminder not to get too well acquainted with my circumstances."

"Control is an illusion, Rae, believe me. It's like El Dorado, the mythical city made of gold. It isn't out there. I stopped looking a long time ago."

"But I'm not searching for great riches." As the coffeemaker gurgled the last drops of coffee, I removed the carafe and poured a cup for each of us. "Peace is more to my liking."

Margaret ladled in two heaping spoonfuls of sugar. "And you find peace in the routine?"

I poured two splashes of milk into my cup. "I find it in routine and predictability. I'm not a fan of surprises." And yet, this day was unlike any I had in a long time.

"Tell me about this matchmaking gig of yours." She splashed milk in her coffee and took a sip. And then another. "Don't suppose you have cookies?"

"Sorry. I don't eat sugar."

"My God, woman, how do you function?"

"Sugar isn't good for you. No nutritional value."

"It's a major food group, along with fats and chocolate." Margaret grinned. "You're a doctor, you should know that!"

"I'm not a medical doctor."

"Rae, we need to work on you detecting sarcasm. In the meantime, explain how you became the matchmaking queen. Is there a degree for that?"

"I'm not a matchmaker. I find people who share similar traits and introduce them from time to time."

"But they come to you and ask you to find someone?"

"Sometimes."

"The paper called you a matchmaker and if it's written in a paper then it's *always* right."

"Hardly."

She winced. "Sarcasm alert, Rae."

"Yep, I caught that one."

"I'll say that 'heart of stone' crack was below the belt. Though, if I have to be completely honest, Rae, and please don't take this the wrong way because anyone who saves history like you have is a goddess in my book, but you're a tad reserved."

"I'm objective, not Victorian," I countered. "I'm able to

see couples, people, situations, and analyze their strengths and weaknesses. I keep sentiments out of the equation. Introduce it and it's a free-for-all with completely random results."

"What about the chemistry, Rae? What about sex? Isn't that what makes the world go around?"

"I'll concede that sexual attraction is a key ingredient. But other factors must come into play, otherwise you just have two hormonal people who soon realize they're ill suited. Eventually, the sex suffers and there is no glue to hold them."

"I've had a couple of relationships like that. Sex was great, the project ends, and we go our separate ways. We promise to call and write, and *yada, yada, yada*. Two months later, it's gone completely. I guess I've never been good at planning the future."

"The past is safe. Its ending is known. Certain."

She leaned back and grinned. "Could be." She picked up her phone and typed in several notes. "Which reminds me, have you wondered why Patience wrote her mother so many letters? Normal to write Mom, but why not post the letters?"

"Perhaps they were returned after her mother's passing."

"Solid theory." She sipped her coffee.

When I had first met Margaret on that hot day in July, she had irritated me. If not for Addie Morgan, I might have closed the door in her face, treating her like a solicitor. But now she was growing on me. And she could build a history of this family that might be of real interest to the boy.

"If you're free, you can come back on Saturday." I could explain to Margaret that tomorrow was Jennifer's birthday, but I didn't want to crack that door yet."

"I was really hoping I could take the letters home. I'm a night owl and do some of my best work in the wee hours of the morning."

"They've likely not left the property in generations."

"If you don't want to lend them out, I get it. But I can tell you I'll move faster if I can work at home. And I'm a trained professional when it comes to this."

I imagined my mother stiffening at the idea of lending out the papers. My mother never, ever would have given Margaret the letters.

"That would be fine," I said. "I know you'll be careful with them." First, the kitchen remodel. Then, the stones. Now, the letters. No need for a PhD to recognize rebellion.

She paused with the cup close to her lips. "Really? You're saying yes."

"I am."

"You aren't practicing sarcasm, are you, Rae?"

"No. I'm sincere. The letters are yours to examine. Though they're for your eyes only. I'd like to know what's in them before any information is shared with the public."

"You bet. I'll keep them safe and show them to no one."

"Then we have a deal," I said.

She gulped the last of her coffee and absently tapped a ringed finger against the side of the cup. "And when I return on Saturday I'll bring you an assortment of cookies and prove that sugar and fat are vital to a healthy life."

I calculated the average calories of a cookie and balanced the number against the calories burned during my Saturday morning run. "We shall see."

"Sounds like a challenge."

"When do you think you'll know more about Patrick McDonald?" I changed the subject. "If there were no formal adoption papers, then there can really be no real way to determine if he was Faith's or Patience's child."

"I would argue that if Old McDonald—excuse the pun—had wanted a son, he'd have seen to it that there'd be no way to prove the boy was not his. He'd want a direct line of uncontested succession. Maybe Patience hinted at the truth in her letters."

"The McDonalds had another child that survived," I said.

"The surviving child was a girl named Hanna," Margaret replied.

"Real, as in biological."

She cringed. "Poor choice of words. My sister Daisy is adopted, and she gets a little tense when I say 'real' in association with a parent."

I had not met Daisy, but she was now an adult. She would understand much of what the boy might feel. "How old was she when she was adopted?"

"Three. Her birth mother abandoned her at the bakery."

"Abandoned?" The word's nasty ring needled up my spine. "That was her plan?"

"No. It was more like 'Here are some cookies, baby girl, Momma's got to jet.'"

"That's horrible."

"Yeah, but Daisy wasn't alone for more than two minutes before my mom swooped in and rescued her."

I culled the interest cropping up among the syllables in my tone. "Did your sister find her birth mother?"

"Yeah." Margaret shook her head. "Whoever said adoption reunions are all happy endings is full of it. They're complicated."

If the boy showed up on my doorstep, would I welcome him? Or would I be so fearful that he might hate me that I would reject him as I had almost all other feelings? "I'm sorry to hear that."

"Daisy keeps trying to connect. She's stubborn, so maybe one day she'll get her reunion." Margaret held up her empty cup to me and automatically, I filled it. She sipped, savoring the taste. "But common law back then stated property was passed to the eldest son with no rights for the daughter. Therefore, Patrick became the sole male owner of this farm."

Margaret rubbed her hands together, her rings clinking

together. "Don't you love digging up old secrets? God, I live for digging them up."

"I imagine you're good at this."

"I can hold my own, if I do say so myself."

Patience and Michael McDonald's secret was so old, there was no one left alive for it to hurt. Time had long washed away the pain, rendering it safe to be exposed.

But other secrets . . .

Well, they were too powerful to ever see the light.

A Letter from Patience

NOVEMBER 16, 1751

Dearest Mother,

The snows have arrived, and the air has turned bitter. We spend most of our time inside the cottage. I still have not recovered from my loss and my head spins with grief each time I stand by the open hearth to cook. Daily tasks are impossible. After I burned the stew last week, Faith, without a word took over the cooking and now prepares all the meals for us. She is a good cook, and though Mr. McDonald has not said a word, he clearly relishes the hot fare waiting for him when he returns from the fields and barn. He enjoys the babes who lie on their pallets, fat and cooing. In the span of days, Faith has given Mr. McDonald everything I cannot.

Several times, I caught Faith staring at the empty cradle. Though she rarely speaks, her expression softens. Maybe even a witch can understand.

Yours Faithfully,
Patience McDonald

Chapter Four

LISA, WEDNESDAY, OCTOBER 5, 2011

With the "*Hello, my name is Lisa*" tag pressed to my shirt and Charlie at my side, I sat at the early-morning AA meeting the next day, fidgeting with the sobriety chips I had collected over the past years. One year. Two year. Five year. Decade. After all this time, the process of staying sober should have been easier. I should have finally vanquished the demons and have this figured out. Was not sobriety like a muscle? The more I use it, the stronger it becomes.

God, if it were that simple.

But as strong as my convictions can be in one moment, they remain susceptible in the next. Each time my guard drops, they appear, singing promises of relief. *Drink and all will be forgiven.*

Last night, after Charlie and I left the meeting, thoughts of Jennifer's death chased me all the way back to Prince Street. I was in her car again, bruised and bleeding, trying to undo my seat belt and then Jennifer's. She was unconscious, but alive, when I pulled her from the wreckage onto the damp grass. We were twenty feet from the car when I saw the first flames rising from under the hood. Terrified, I ran to the road, hoping to flag down a car.

In the shadow of this memory, my sobriety lay before me, brittle as a dry leaf. Closing my eyes, I imagined the cool wine rolling over my parched tongue. Easing tension, unfurling knots, it promised bliss and redemption.

But of course, it lied. I remembered this hard-learned lesson about falling off the wagon the first time I attempted to get sober. On the heels of one glass of wine came several more of its friends and I lost track. And bliss turned to guilt and to more self-loathing.

I did not drink last night, but when I awoke, Jennifer's presence, along with the cravings, was near.

"Are you a wine drinker?"

I opened my eyes to find an attractive blonde holding a cigarette to her lips and reaching for a lighter. "Excuse me?"

"I'm a beer drinker, and on special days I reach for the tequila. Those are the wild and dangerous days." She grinned and held out her hand. "You look like a wine girl. Hi, I'm Janet Morgan."

"I'm Lisa and this is Charlie."

Janet tossed an apprehensive glance at the dog and made no move to pet him. "You're new to the meetings here. You recently move to Alexandria?"

"I'm visiting." I sat a little straighter, trying to relax the tension banding my shoulders. I needed to open up and talk about what haunted me. Instead, I smiled.

Janet took a long pull on her cigarette. "I'm here for the duration. Both my kids are in Alexandria, and I'm sticking around, even if it kills me."

"Is this place so terrible?"

"It's not the place." She stared at the glowing tip of the cigarette as smoke trickled out of her mouth. "It's me. I'm not happy anywhere, as it turns out. I'm always ready to jump to the next lily pad on the pond. Only this time, I've run out of pads. End of the line for me."

"How long have you been working the steps?"

"Five whole weeks. Jesus, it doesn't sound like a lot of time, but it feels like a lifetime. I've never seen the minutes move so slowly."

"Absolutely."

Janet held my gaze for an extra beat, sizing me up. "You come regularly to these meetings or is this kind of an emergency situation?"

Mentally, I released the grip on my words. *Talk about them. Get them in the open and destroy them.* "Today's a bad day. A lot of memories. It's always a tough time for me. I like to visit a meeting on this day no matter where I am."

Today was Jennifer McDonald's birthday. She would have been thirty-four if not for the car crash. Every summer since her death, I made a point to be as far away from Alexandria as possible, but this year I was at ground zero. "I'm going to the cemetery to pay my respects," I said.

The meeting leader began, and we all introduced ourselves. There was a familiarity to the meetings that I'd encountered, no matter if I were in California, Kansas, Florida, or Virginia.

The meeting leader wore her thick gray hair back in a ponytail. Her dress was made of denim and hung loosely around her round body. Clogs, athletic socks. I refused to look at her legs to see if she shaved. TMI as far as I was concerned.

Despite her grandmotherly appearance, her attention was sharp as she moved around the room and listened closely, asking pointed questions. This grandma had a bite.

After introductions, most did not have much to say. Newcomers spoke of struggles that the old-timers knew all too well. There was comfort in knowing I was not alone.

Fortunately, it was promising to be a quick meeting. I felt a little more grounded and was ready to soldier on.

The leader zeroed in on me. "So, Lisa, what brings you here today?"

"Checking in," I said as lightly as I could. Since I was originally from Alexandria, I wondered if someone in the room might recognize me. "New city, new circumstances, and I always expect some new kind of trigger that could catch me off guard."

Grandma folded her arms over her ample bosom. "What kind of triggers catch you off guard, Lisa?"

"A new bar. New people who don't know I'm an alcoholic. There's always a trigger."

"Have you been to Alexandria before?"

Bracing, I did not look away. "I was born and raised here but haven't been back in a long time."

"What brings you back?"

Not what drove me away but what brought me back. "My aunt is in assisted living. Her house is being sold. I need to handle all the arrangements. A bit overwhelming."

"That kind of job comes with a lot of stress."

"It does." Absently, I rubbed Charlie's head.

"And what are you doing to cope?"

She was not so much digging into my life as she was trying to get me to share coping strategies for everyone else. I understood that. "Sitting here, right now."

"What about your aunt's place?" Pale eyes darkened. "Free of booze?"

"I've searched the cabinets and tossed the usual suspects." It had been a cursory search that lasted less than fifteen minutes. Normally, a new place received the entire once over, but not this time. This time I had been sloppy and quick.

She shook her head slowly, picking up the meaning

between the words. "Sounds like you didn't put your heart and soul into it."

"What makes you say that?"

A sly smile twisted the edges of her lips, and for a moment, I did not see an old woman but a young hellion who had mastered every trick in the book. "A half-ass search means we're either complacent or we're thinking there might be a little hooch somewhere. Might be thinking if a rainy day comes it will come in handy."

I sat a little straighter and announced, "I've been sober eight years."

"I was sober twenty-one and a half years. I woke up that morning in a great mood, had the world on a string. Next thing I know, I'm with friends from work and belting back whiskey. It took me another two months and more Jack Daniels than I can remember before I hauled myself back to a meeting. Time away from the sauce is good, but it's a poor guarantee for a drunk."

For a moment I did not speak. Instead of spinning a lie that would set off this lady's BS meter in a blink, I said, "Seventeen years ago my best friend and I were in a car accident. She died. I walked away without a scratch. Today is her birthday and I'm sitting here screwing up the courage to visit her grave and pay my respects. I owe her that much, but I'm being a chickenshit about it."

The woman smiled as if she had finally gotten to the truth. "Paying respects or asking forgiveness?"

"Both."

"What do you think your friend would say to you right now if she were here? Would she still want to be your best friend?"

"That's irrelevant. My friend is dead."

"Don't dodge the question, Lisa. Your friend is standing right here. What does she say to you?"

The weighted stares in the room shifted onto me. If anyone had come into the room with a worry or concern, it would be tabled until I answered.

"She hated self-pity."

The group leader leaned toward me. "So, she might be saying . . ." She left the question open.

Jennifer's laughter suddenly rang in my ears, and for a moment, I could swear she was standing right behind me. "She'd tell me to ditch the pity party and do what needed to be done."

"Then what's holding you back?"

"Nothing," I said. "As soon as this meeting is over, I'm driving straight to St. Mary's Cemetery."

"Good. Would your friend expect you to stand by her grave and beat yourself up with old memories?"

"No."

"Good. But in case you do, we also have another meeting tonight."

Pride demanded I tell her I would be fine. *Don't worry about me. I got this.* Instead, all I said was, "Thanks."

The meeting broke up and Janet came up to me as I moved toward the door. Fumbling for a cigarette in true chain smoker fashion, she lit the tip of another about to burn down to its filter.

"You did a good job. Thanks for speaking up," Janet said. "Nice to know I'm not the only one carrying a barrel of guilt."

"Here's to good days."

"Amen. See you soon."

"I'll be here."

I did not linger, no longer willing to scratch at a wound that had never healed. With Charlie riding shotgun, I slid behind the wheel of the Buick.

Sweat dampened the back of my neck as I drove through the wrought iron gate at the entrance of the cemetery. Shifting in my seat, I tightened my hands on the steering wheel and followed the road to the left, winding past the gray tombstones that dotted the rolling green landscape. Many of the plots were decorated with urns filled with flowers, making me feel guilty that I had forgotten to bring flowers. I should have brought some. "Who comes to pay homage without flowers, Charlie? Jennifer loved sunflowers." The dog rose, sensing we were close.

"Shit," I muttered as I shifted my dark sunglasses to the top of my head to get the hair out of my eyes. Irritation snapped through my body.

Charlie wagged his tail and barked.

"Maybe I should leave and buy flowers. I could be back within a half hour with a bouquet." Charlie barked as his gaze trained ahead.

The flowers offered the perfect escape. I could leave now, find a florist or a grocery store and buy flowers. I could delay this meeting and keep carrying the all-too-familiar weights of remorse and guilt.

"*Wuss.*" The word echoed in my head.

As tempted as I was to turn the car around and leave, I did not. I was the master of delay tactics. I could find perfectly legitimate excuses to put off what needed to be done. Do not do today what you can put off until tomorrow. Or better, next month. Did not matter if it were sobriety, developing the box of neglected glass negatives from last winter, or apologizing to an old friend for my role in her death.

Pushing on the accelerator, I drove deeper into the cemetery until I found the section, I knew belonged to the McDonald family. I parked by a neatly trimmed curb and shut off the car. The silence hummed around me as the clouds overhead grew heavier and darker with rain. Jesus, more rain? What the hell was it with this city lately?

I closed my eyes, savoring the silence, wondering if this is what Alexandria sounded like centuries ago.

"Get it over with already," the voice whispered in my head. "It won't be better tomorrow."

Charlie barked. Nerves crawled up my spine and I shook my head to clear it.

Refusing to delay another second, I leashed Charlie and we pushed out of the car. Charlie walked ahead to the moist green grass surrounding a large granite marker that read *McDonald*. Surrounding the primary stone were a dozen smaller headstones of various family members. Instead of walking to Jennifer's spot, which I knew was in the back on the right, I searched for Jeffrey McDonald. His simple gravestone was in the center, beside his parents. To his left was the marker for Stuart McDonald, two years his junior, and likely his brother.

A thundercloud clapped overhead, drawing my full attention to the task at hand. The clouds had darkened as if on cue. Soon, I would be deluged. Hell, the first time I stood here it was raining. That day, I barely took notice. I was seventeen and still battered and bruised from the accident. Painkillers dulled my throbbing head but had done little to ease my guilt and heartache.

I had not wanted to be at the funeral, but my mother insisted I join the mourners. "You have nothing to hide," she said. "You were her best friend and people should see for themselves that you're grieving for her. And if anyone asks you about the accident, I don't want you to say a word. It's between you, me, and our lawyer."

Large dark sunglasses, unnecessary on that gloomy day, had hidden Mom's eyes. Whatever she had felt was buried deep, as she did with so many other bits of information from her life. Mother wanted—no, needed—the world to believe we lived a perfect life, so she became a master at hiding the unpleasant truths. A smooth veneer. And on that day, she did not want everyone to know her daughter was responsible for her best friend's death. When Mom came to get me at the hospital after the accident, I told her the truth. She closed the door, locked it, and took my tear-streaked face in her hands and told me, "Never tell anyone. This secret is your punishment. It's your burden to bear."

"My punishment," I whispered as I turned from Stuart's grave toward Jennifer's and crossed the neatly trimmed lawn past much older grave markers worn smooth by time.

Jennifer's resting place was at the back of the McDonald section, tucked next to her parents' graves. Bright yellow sunflowers rose out from a brass urn, their blossoms reaching toward the heavens like outstretched arms. Not a leaf or twig marred the neat grass of the three graves.

I knelt. As Charlie stood beside me, I traced her name with my fingertips. Jennifer Patience McDonald. Patience. I was always puzzled by her middle name. Such an odd name for a girl who had so very little of it.

My gaze fixated on the day of Jennifer's birth—August seventeenth. And then to the day of her death—August fifteen. Just shy of eighteen years old. It should be me lying here.

A life of laughter and potential was forever reduced to two sets of dates that spanned way too little time. The pale gray granite stone designed to memorialize her life forever seemed woefully lacking. It did not mention she had auburn hair, her contagious laugh or her mastery of the guitar. No mention of her singing; her love of her cat, Sparky; her crush on Jerry Trice. None of that was memorialized. It pained me to know that whoever visited her would never know those details. The stone ignored all that.

I rose and sat on a small gray bench stationed in front of her marker and tried to tamp down my guilt. Charlie settled at my feet. "It's been a while, Jennifer. I'm sorry for that. But I've kind of been on the run. Not from the law or anything. That might actually be a little romantic and fun. I've been running from you and this moment."

AA had honed my ability to be honest. "I could sit here and tell you that I meant to visit. I could say life kept getting in the way, but that would be crap and you'd know it. You deserve better."

A wind whispered through the trees and reminded me of her faint laughter.

"Frankly, Jennifer, you and Rae are the last on my list of atonements. I've made peace with all the people I hurt in the early years of my drinking. I wasn't able to talk to Mom before she passed, but I'm sure she was glad to avoid it. Even if she'd been alive, the conversation would have been one way. It was always lopsided with Mom."

"I'd like to have seen you talking while your mother tried to change the subject to anything but the ugly truth." Jennifer's laughter rattled in my head as it did when she would toss me a sideways glare and raise a bottle of diet soda to her mouth. *"Truth is Mommy Smyth's kryptonite."*

The corner of my mouth ticked up. "Yeah, I know she was glad she checked out of this world before my honesty atonement tour." An unexpected chuckle bubbled in my throat.

A chill blew between the stones, and as I looked up, I imagined Jennifer. Her thick hair was pulled into a ponytail, and her hands hitched on hips. I rose slowly. Rational thought dictated that I should be scared. Sane people do not see dead people. Amelia said she saw Jennifer, but she was in a nursing home with dementia.

But the sight of Jennifer was oddly welcoming. Charlie barked at nothing as he wagged his tail.

"So, you said sorry to her and everyone else. Why did it take you so long to get to me? I'm your very best friend." Jennifer

lowered her hands from her hips, and she held my gaze. She did that when she was pissed.

"Because they were easy." I leaned forward. "You were always the tough one. Always the one I disappointed most." I tugged off my sunglasses and caught my stricken expression in the lenses.

"There was a time you could tell me anything. Why are you having so much trouble talking to me now? We were as close as sisters."

I lifted my eyes to the grave marker and dropped my voice to a faint whisper. "Because . . . I killed you."

Closing my eyes, I listened for her voice but found only a heavy silence.

The rustle of feet on grass snapped my attention back. Charlie wagged his tail as I turned to see Rae McDonald standing, her arms loaded with a fresh bouquet of yellow sunflowers. She wore a simple white blouse, a black pencil skirt, and very sensible black heels. Her auburn hair was secured back in a round bun at the base of her neck that showcased round pearl earrings dotting her earlobes and the strand of June Cleaver pearls encircling her neck.

I was aware that I had come here not only empty handed but dressed far too casually for such an emotional meeting. Couldn't I have dug out a damn skirt? "Rae?"

Rae stood as still as a statue, her chest barely rising and falling with each breath. "Lisa. It's been a long time." Her expression softened a little as she studied the dog. "Charlie. I heard you had him. He looks good."

Her cool voice transported me back to the days Jennifer and I would sit in the McDonalds' kitchen and her mother talked to us about college and the future.

"Wow," I said. "You look so much like your mother. For a second I thought I was staring at her."

Rae did not smile, nor reach out to welcome me with a hug. Time and life had changed her.

Two years younger, Rae was an impetuous kid sister who had always wanted to tag along. That last time Jennifer and I went out, Rae begged to come along, but Jennifer said no. We left a crying Rae, yelling that she would tell her mom where we had gone. She never told, but I now wished to hell she had.

"I didn't realize you were still in Alexandria," Rae said. "I thought you'd be gone by now. You don't stay anywhere very long."

Her honest directness sounded harsh. "No. I've not been good about establishing roots."

"Has your aunt Amelia taken a bad turn?"

"She's in and out of it," I said. "Some days are better than others. However, she did say your mother came to see her last week. I attributed it to dementia, but that was you, wasn't it?"

"I check in on her from time to time. She often confuses me with Mother."

"That's kind of you to visit."

"She and Mother were friends."

Rae cleared her throat and, shifting the sunflowers in her arms, moved toward the urn. Carefully, she removed the old flowers, holding the stems over the ground until the old water dripped free before gently laying them on the grass. With tender care, she unwrapped the new flowers and meticulously arranged each in the vase.

My emotions burned hot in my chest, like a boiler in an old steam engine. When would I reach critical mass and blow up? I shifted from foot to foot, suddenly cold and restless. However, Rae was steady, taking an extra moment to adjust a blossom before she slowly rose. She looked as cool as a mountain lake in the morning.

Annoyed by her composure, I said, "The old flowers are still good," I said. "Seems a waste to get rid of them."

"I'm not fond of wilted flowers."

"They aren't wilted."

"They will be soon." She gathered up the old blossoms. She touched the browned tips of a petal.

So perfect like her mother. "I read about you in the paper."

"And?"

"And nothing. I keep forgetting that you're Dr. McDonald now. PhD is a huge deal."

She tugged a plastic bag from her purse and prepared to dump in the old flowers.

"Are you throwing them away?" I asked.

"Yes."

I stepped toward her. "If you don't mind, I'll take them. They're still pretty."

Already, I knew I would carry them back to the Prince Street kitchen, arrange them in one of Amelia's pots, and photograph them. Fresh-cut flowers were a symbol of life. And like us, their life spans were so fleeting. A photograph would extend their life for decades, if not forever.

Rae handed the flowers to me in a neat bundle. "They're all yours."

The stems were slick and damp. "Thanks."

She brushed her palms against each other, knocking free what little dirt clung to her pale skin. "I never expected to see you here today."

"I owed Jennifer a visit."

"Have you been here since the accident?"

We both showed up at the grave that day, too surprised and hurting to really speak to each other. "No. I've been traveling."

A neatly plucked arched brow said more than words. "Ah, traveling. How nice."

Polite and controlled words did not hide the underlying

accusation. She was calling me a coward. Which, of course, I was, each time I avoided Jennifer's death or thought about escaping to the land of drunk and numb. But it was far easier to hold tight to long-festering guilt than to actually deal with the pain we shared.

Suddenly annoyed, I wanted to shatter the ice and jab at her heart to see if it really had turned to stone. "Are all the McDonalds buried in this plot?"

"All?" She understood immediately what I was deflecting. "I'm not sure all are here, but there are nearly two dozen McDonalds in this plot."

"I saw a stone for Jeffrey McDonald. Your grandmother's first husband?"

Genuine curiosity darkened Rae's blue eyes. "Yes. Why do you ask about him?"

I turned back toward the stones. "He was married?"

"That's right. He died young. In World War II."

"Whatever happened to his wife?"

"I have no idea. Why are we having this conversation?"

"I saw Amelia yesterday for a little bit. Her mind was clear and sharp."

Rae moistened her lips. "Glad to hear it."

The lack of inflection telegraphed indifference, but I knew where to jab to make her hurt. "She told me a very interesting story about herself. Did you know she was adopted?"

Her eyes widened a fraction. "I did not. But I'm not very familiar with your family."

"Don't do this. She really doesn't need this today."

Ignoring the warnings, I pressed. "She gave me a baby book that her birth mother and father created for her. Her birth mother and father were married, and they raised her for the first year of her life."

Rae remained silent while watching me closely. Spurred on by the sense I'd struck a nerve, I kept pushing. "According to Amelia, her birth father died in World War II and then her birth mother struggled to care for her. After about a year of trying, she signed over full custody to the Smyths."

A shade of pink faded from Rae's cheeks. "Amelia gets very confused. She always calls me by my mother's name."

"True, but she has moments of pure clarity. Yesterday was one of them."

"I can't help you with this."

"No one in your family ever mentioned that Jeffrey had a child?"

"No. Never. Why are you bringing it up?"

"It bothers Amelia that her birth mother remarried, then had another child, and never sent for her first daughter. I've never seen Amelia look so hurt."

Rae's chin raised a small fraction. "I'm sure her birth mother had her reasons."

"Are there any reasons that justify a mother turning her own child away? I mean, I get giving up a child to protect it, but never to acknowledge it in the future? Seems cruel."

Rae fingered the pearls. Swallowed. "I can't help you, Lisa. I came to pay my respects to Jennifer and now I must go. I have a client meeting me at my office in thirty minutes."

She turned to leave. Sadness and guilt collided, sending shards cutting into every corner of my body. "How can you turn off all those emotions?" I asked. "What do you do that makes you so impervious to pain and suffering?"

Rae stopped walking.

Tears welled in my eyes and spilled. "Pain slides off you, Rae."

She did not face me.

I shook my head. "How do you do it? How do you not feel anything?"

She turned, cocking her head slightly as if she considered a complicated problem. "What would that accomplish? It won't bring Jennifer back. It won't undo what Amelia's birth mother, or I did."

I did not need a translator. She referred to the baby she had given up a little over a year after Jennifer's death. Smart Rae with the bright future rebelled after Jennifer died. She drank, snuck out of her mother's house, and found a boy more than happy to oblige her. Few knew about the baby. She had kept her secret well. I found out right here in this very spot when we had both returned on the first anniversary of the accident. She was sitting on the little stone bench, her very full belly pear-shaped, crying, confessing to her older sister about the baby she feared no one would want. When I approached, she fell into my arms and sobbed. She told me she had snuck back into town to visit Jennifer. I asked her about her plans, and she told me her mother chose adoptive parents to raise her baby. She did not want to give up the child, but her mother refused to help. She left me that day, still sobbing. I never heard another word from her until this very moment.

Tears welled in my throat as I remembered that teenage girl, who must still be inside this cold and aloof woman.

"You're such a bitch, Lisa. Why'd you dig into Rae about the baby?"

I wiped a tear away from my cheek. "Rae, I'm sorry. I shouldn't have churned all this up."

A cool breeze blew between us. "Lisa, it's a fair line of questioning and I would do anything for Amelia, but I can't tell you about her birth mother. Amelia never uttered a word to me about this."

"You sound so calm."

"I *am* calm."

Shaking my head, I raked my fingers through my hair. "I wish I could be more like you and simply shut off all emotion and not feel."

Rae was silent for a long moment. "Be careful what you

wish for, Lisa. Be very careful. It's a harder road to travel than what you think."

Rae turned and slowly walked away, her heels clicking on the concrete, leaving me to watch her move to a sleek, black BMW.

"Lisa Smyth . . . super bitch."

"Guilty."

A Letter from Patience

NOVEMBER 19, 1751

Dearest Mother,

Faith and the babes sleep in the corner of our farmhouse, near the fire. The boys are small, but they grow, and their complexion has the color of health. It was a bitter, cold night when I awoke to find little Cullen was awake. I rose up and my bare toes curled when they touched the wooden floor. I quietly crossed to the child, lifted him and carried him to the rocker. I sat, baring my breast so he could nurse. To my surprise and delight my milk flowed as he suckled greedily.

When Faith awoke, she searched for her babes. Seeing the bare spot, she scanned the cottage wild-eyed until she saw the boy in my arms. "Give me my child."

Her harsh whisper woke Mr. McDonald and he quickly understood. He rose up, his nightshirt billowing around his bare legs. "Leave them," he said to Faith.

The warning beneath my husband's words silenced her protest. Outside, the wind howled as snow fell. The witch's eyes burned, but she wisely lowered back to her blanket. However, she did not sleep until the babe was fed and returned to her arms.

Yours Faithfully,

Patience McDonald

Chapter Five

LISA, WEDNESDAY, OCTOBER 5, 2011

After seeing Rae at the gravesite today, self-pity raced out of the shadows and slid right up next to me. I was suddenly very tired of living my life moment to moment while reminding myself that sobriety was the only choice. Charlie looked up at me with a curious gaze. He sensed a change.

"I'm fine," I said. "Right as rain."

I drove out of my way to a grocery store north of the city. I normally did not stop here, but I had heard about it at the meeting. Many in the group avoided it because it was known for its extensive wine selection.

When I parked, I fished the last chew stick out of my purse and gave it to Charlie. "I'll be right back." I left the car running with the AC on and dashed across the parking lot. Inside the store, I grabbed a cart and moved along the perimeter, grabbing a bag of apples, milk, a carton of eggs, more chew sticks, and bread before I made my way to the wine section.

I skimmed my fingertips over the bottles of reds and wanted so desperately not to care. I wanted to be like Rae and find a way to shut off the feelings, set aside the mantle of guilt, and savor the numbness.

"Is there a wine I can help you buy?"

Startled, I discovered a plump woman with very pleasant features standing nearby. She wore a burgundy store apron decorated with a collection of wine bottle pins.

"No, thanks." I rummaged and found a smile not used since I joined AA. It was an overconfident and relaxed smile that messaged that I did not have a care in the world. I chose a red blend, caring neither about the price or the vineyard. "I found exactly what I want."

She didn't remark on the label as she handed me a white invitation. "We're having a tasting in a half hour. If you're still in the store, stop by. We have some lovely blends we'll be highlighting."

I tucked the card in my pocket. "Thank you. I might just do that."

Pushing the cart, I moved toward the cashier, grabbing a bag of chips and a bottle of soda. I wanted everyone to know I was not here simply for the booze. I was grocery shopping for supplies. Maybe I'd have a glass. Maybe two. Maybe I wouldn't have any. I could handle this. My God, I'd had it under control for a long time.

The old but familiar lies turned over and over in my head. I moved through the checkout and carefully loaded the groceries in my car. Charlie looked up from his half-eaten chew sticks.

"What are you looking at?" I asked as I settled behind the wheel. "Don't judge."

The dog continued to stare.

"I bought you more treats."

His attention lingered a beat before it dropped back to the task of demolishing another chew stick.

When I reached Old Town, I took a right onto Washington Street and then a left onto Prince Street. The cobblestones of Prince Street rattled the bottles in the bag, making them clink gently against each other as if dancing. A parking space opened up and I quickly parallel parked in front of Amelia's place. The bags in my hand, Charlie and I hurried inside.

Inside the house, I slowly walked the center hallway to prove I was in no rush, past the collection of pictures I had developed and framed in the last six weeks. I had not taken any new pictures since arriving in Alexandria. They had been taken during a hike through Montana. God, had it really been three months since I pulled the camera out?

In the kitchen, I set the groceries on the counter. Charlie ran to the back door, the stub of a chew stick hanging out of the corner of his mouth. I opened the door and let him outside to the narrow, fenced backyard.

Grateful Charlie was not watching me, I flipped on a light and moved directly toward the utensil drawer, where I found a wine bottle opener.

The afternoon sun streamed into the large room that was outfitted with marble countertops, stainless appliances, and an overhead pot rack that held several copper pots Amelia had collected. She had been a marvelous cook and could transform the most random ingredients into a stunning meal.

The kitchen had been updated three years ago when Amelia had renovated. No one had expressed concern that she was foolishly spending money at her advanced age, but she enjoyed the idea of giving her home a new life and transformation. She had transformed the house into a real showplace without destroying its historical charm. Her sights had been set on the basement remodel just as her hold on reality began slipping in earnest. She had left this part of the house for her final project.

Using my thumbnail, I dug into the gold foil seal of the

bottle. I tossed it aside and jabbed the corkscrew into the cork and twisted the handle. I should have heard the confusion in her voice and come home earlier. I should have. . . .

Refusing to think, I pushed the levers and worked the cork free until it released with a delicate *pop*.

The scent of the red wine teased my senses as I reached in the cabinet for a coffee mug. I ignored the doubting whispers deep in my brain. I filled the mug nearly to the brim and stared into the ruby depths. I raised it to my nose and let it touch my lips.

The pull was stronger than any rip tide.

"Remember how we used to get hammered in high school?"

I was not sure if it were my voice or Jennifer's, but whoever spoke, it was unwelcomed.

"Go away."

"My God, Lisa, we were hellions back in the day." Laughter bubbled. "Remember how much beer we could slam back?"

I touched one of the velvet-soft sunflower petals. "You complained about your mother's coldness, and I could only talk about Jerry Trice and wondered why he didn't like me. All I cared about then was boys."

"And remember the hangovers the next day? We'd order pizza and sit in bed all afternoon? If I had a nickel for all the times, I ended up with a jackhammer pounding in my head." Laughter rose and swirled around my head like storm winds off the Potomac. "Man, those were the good old days. Sure, beats too many years wasted not drinking."

As I raised the stoneware mug to my lips, I spotted my keys, discarded recklessly next to the sack of groceries. Front and center on the key ring were the sobriety chips.

Sobriety was a heartless bitch. It was relentless and uncompromising

Remember that time you got drunk.

Charlie scratched at the back door.

I studied the wine's liquid depths and suddenly my head cleared. The wine had transformed from a craving to a poison. I moved quickly to the sink and turned on the water without a second to lose. I poured out the wine from the mug and bottles. I flipped on the water faucet, hoping to obliterate any trace of it.

"Shit." I rinsed out the bottles and tossed them in the trash. The mug went into the dishwasher. I hurried to the back door and let Charlie inside. His tail wagging, he looked up with such trust I could hardly bear it. I fished another chew stick from the grocery bag and gave it to him.

Jennifer sat on the kitchen counter, crossing her long legs and laughing. "You were so close to a good time.'

"Zip it."

I walked out of the kitchen into the living room and switched on the television to a cable news show. Dropping my head back against the plush couch, I closed my eyes, pinched the bridge of my nose, and considered how close I'd come to embracing the demons' seductive lies.

"So, are you going to lie here all day and mope?" She clucked her tongue against the roof of her mouth, mimicking a ticking clock.

"Go away!"

"I think," she said, close to my ear, "that you should stop worrying about me and focus on Amelia where you can do some real good."

"Amelia is fine. She naps this time of day."

"I'm talking about the baby book, dumbass. Why are you letting it sit in that hospital room, forgotten?"

I shoved a jittery hand through my hair, trying to brush away the buzzing imaginary voice. Over the years, I'd felt Jennifer's presence, but she never actually spoke to me. "I don't need this."

"Well, you sure as shit don't need a drink."

"Shut up."

"Back at you."

A Letter from Patience

JANUARY 2, 1752

Dearest Mother,

I want to banish the witch away. I can find no shred of charity toward her. Her presence is a reminder of all that I am not. This morning, when she found me nursing Cullen again, she did not get angry or demand the boy back. As she cut a strip of salted pork into small pieces for stew, she told me she could create a mixture of herbs designed to strengthen my constitution and fortify my infertile womb for another babe. As much as I cherished holding Cullen, I long to carry one more child. I desperately want to give my husband a son. I stared into her piercing blue eyes, knowing the dangers of striking a bargain with a witch. But desperation makes fools of us all. I agreed. Smiling as she dropped the salt pork into the simmering pot on the hearth, she told me when Dr. Goodwin made his rounds, I should not let him bleed me. Later, she made a tea with herbs. I hesitated, but when she bade me to drink, I did. Perhaps a devil's bargain, but a new babe would resurrect my broken heart.

Yours Faithfully,
Patience McDonald,

Chapter Six

RAE, WEDNESDAY, OCTOBER 5, 2011

After the visit to the cemetery, I returned to work. I toyed with cancelling my afternoon appointments but knew work would keep my mind off seeing Lisa. Now, as I stared at the rain-soaked yard, I wondered what else could happen.

My patients arrived in good order, and by three in the afternoon I was listening to a young man who had outlined all the traits he sought in a perfect wife.

"If it will help, Dr. McDonald, I've prepared a list."

"I'm not a matchmaker, Mr. West. I'm a family psychologist. Don't believe the paper."

"I rarely do." Unconvinced, he held out the neatly typed and organized list. "But I've heard from several people whom you've assisted."

I scanned his wish list for the perfect mate. "This is a tall order."

"I know of several people in my firm who speak highly of you and your mother's talents," he persisted. "I have a client who swears your mother introduced her to her husband. Grabbed him right off the street."

"You're with West & Murphy, correct?"

"Yes."

"Would that client be Amelia Murphy?"

Green eyes sharpened. "Perhaps."

"Her husband was a partner in your firm a long time ago and she was a friend of my mother's. Not such a stretch. I heard a story or two about the day Amelia met her husband."

He nervously brushed his pant leg. "This client was certain your mother had made several successful marriages."

He was careful not to confirm Amelia's identity. That kind of discretion won him points in my book. He might have unrealistic expectations, but he was not a bad guy. "I don't know what to tell you, Mr. West. I can't speak to what my mother did."

"No. But I can see you have an analytical mind. Now that I've met you, I'm more convinced you can find the right match for me."

My mother never admitted to being a matchmaker, but she did have a knack for tossing out a name or making an introduction just at the right time. Often, her suggestions led to successful marriages. When I asked her once about it, she said she simply tossed out the first name that came to mind. "Have you met Amelia's niece, Lisa Smyth?"

The question caught him off guard. "We met once when she came to pick up Charlie. She strikes me as a free spirit. Attractive, but not for me. How's Charlie, by the way?"

"I suspect Lisa is spoiling him with chew sticks and table scraps."

A half grin tugged at the corners of his lips.

Lisa had been on my mind since this morning when I saw signs that she was struggling. Shaky hands. Watery eyes. Depressed. Having someone like Mr. West stop by the Prince Street house might offer enough of a distraction to help her through a rough patch. "I wasn't suggesting she was your type at all. But I know Amelia would appreciate you helping her with the sale of the Prince Street house."

He tugged at his cuff. "She's not reached out to the firm for help."

"As a favor to Amelia, please do so. And I'll see you again as a family practice patient if you're willing to talk further about your high standards for a mate."

He wasn't classically handsome, but his intensity set him apart. "There's nothing wrong with lofty standards."

"No one's perfect, Mr. West."

"I don't believe that."

We debated the subject of perfection for the next fifteen minutes, but clearly, he would not be returning. He wanted a matchmaker, not a therapist.

Another client arrived. More talk about perfect love. I made notes, listened, but my thoughts continued to scatter.

I again read the boy's e-mail, analyzing each word for clues. I could not think of a word to write but knew the delay might be sending the wrong message.

When the phone rang with Margaret's name on the caller ID, I was relieved by the distraction. "Dr. McDonald," I said.

"Rae, I have mucho facts." She sounded breathless and barely able to contain the words. "Can I come by?"

"Sure. I'll be here."

"Great. See you in a few."

"Okay." I rose and moved toward the kitchen, where I set the coffeepot to brew. I had never wanted to be the keeper of the flame of the McDonald family history, or to be responsible for others knowing about our accomplishments. But as I stood at Jennifer's grave today, surrounded by generations of McDonalds, I realized it was no longer about me.

I was not the last McDonald. There was the boy. For his sake, not mine, I would do whatever was best for him, even unearth secrets long held.

The front doorbell rang, and when I opened it, I found Margaret brimming with excitement. Clutching the strap of a large leather satchel, she pushed past me, smelling faintly of boxwoods and cinnamon, scents from recent visits to the bakery and the salvage job in Prince William County.

"Any salvage trips today?"

"Same as yesterday. Old church. We retrieved several amazing stained glass windows. They date back to the 1920s. Not exactly ancient, but they deserve to be saved." She grinned, much as she had when she stood on my front porch over the summer and announced the discovery of the witch bottle.

"I'm guessing you've read some of the letters," I said.

"Just fascinating."

A glance toward the kitchen and widening eyes prompted, "Is that coffee?"

"Help yourself."

Margaret dug in her purse and pulled out a pink Union Street Bakery bag. "Excellent. I have cookies."

"Ah."

Margaret started toward the kitchen but paused in the hallway to study the painting of the Potomac circa 1920. "Three women found their way to Alexandria, Virginia, by 1751. A doctor's wife. A farmer's wife. And a sea captain's wife. I know it sounds a bit like a limerick or a bad joke, but it's a kickass story."

"Kickass. You aren't the shy, deferential type, are you?"

Margaret grinned. "Well-behaved women rarely make history, Rae. You should know that."

"Really? Then I'm doomed to obscurity."

"You, Rae? Never. There's a wild woman in there somewhere."

"Have you looked at me lately?"

Margaret laughed. "I bet, given half the chance, you could kick off those high heels and really shake it up."

Even in my very young days, I had been well behaved and followed the rules. Part of me craved excitement, but I always found an excuse to toe the line. Until I did not.

Ironically, if not for my single mistake, I might have been doomed to obscurity. "Do you like cream in your coffee?"

"Absolutely."

Normally, interruptions irritated me, but I was not the least bit put out. I would not say I wanted to make a habit of all this, but it was a welcome respite.

The crisp strike of my heels clicked double time to the steady clip-clop of Margaret's clogs as we moved into the kitchen. She set her bag on the marble island, and I moved toward the nearly full coffeemaker.

"The letters I read were spellbinding. Patience did an excellent job of sharing some of the hopes and dreams of each young woman, when they arrived on the shores of the Virginia Colony. The doctor's wife, Mistress Goodwin, dreamed of a new life free of shame. The sea captain's wife, Mistress Smyth, wanted distance from a tainted past in Scotland. And Patience, the farmer's wife, wanted to escape the pain of losing her children."

"All this is in the letters that Patience wrote?"

"Yes, in the letters dated around the 1750s. She was quite the historian. Her attention to detail was fascinating." She dug out a large spiral notebook covered with stickers and crammed full of extra papers. She flipped toward the end.

"You actually read all the letters?" I did not try to hide the fact that I was impressed.

Margaret drummed her fingers on several pockets until she found a pair of purple reading glasses. "I'm not much of a sleeper when I get on a roll."

The machine dripped out the last bit of coffee and I dug

two mugs out from the cabinet as she opened the bag of cookies.

"We're in luck. Fresh sugar and chocolate chip cookies at the bakery today. My sister, Rachel, bakes when she's stressed."

Normally, I would not have asked about the state of Rachel's stress levels, but Margaret fostered an openness that invited questions. "Why is your sister upset?"

She bit into a sugar cookie. "Kids, the business, and her French beau finally called it quits. I wanted her to kick him to the curb when he moved back to France. Hard to keep love alive with four thousand miles between the love birds. But Rachel is loyal to a fault."

I set two plates on the counter along with a small pitcher of milk and the sugar bowl. "I'm sorry to hear about that. But you're right. Distance, compounded with long periods between visits, don't bode well for a successful relationship."

She poured cream and sugar into an empty cup in anticipation of the coffee. "Blind man could see that coming. And she's been through much worse when her husband died."

"He was young when he died?"

"Twenty-nine. Brain aneurysm."

For Jennifer, I would have bargained with Satan himself for a different outcome. Think how different all our lives would have been had she never been killed. We would have been no less devastated when she died at twenty-nine, but how different would all our lives be had she lived a while longer? I filled Margaret's cup and mine with coffee. "I made an effort to review some of the old farm ledgers but couldn't decipher the handwriting. I assume the handwriting in the letters you have is just as challenging."

"I've been reading that stuff for years, so it comes a little faster to me. Patience's handwriting is a bit odd, but I've developed an eye for her lettering quirks."

"That's talent."

"Again, one of those talents that won't make me rich." She sipped her coffee, closing her eyes as she savored the taste. When she opened them again, they were sharp with excitement. "Do you know why Patience McDonald still had all those letters addressed to her mother? Stands to reason the letters would have been with her mother's belongings back in England."

"As I said yesterday, I always assumed they were shipped back to Patience at the time of her mother's death."

She tapped her finger on an illegible word she had circled multiple times in her notebook. "That was my original theory, but as it turns out, it's incorrect."

She enjoyed the slow tease of a story. "But you know the real reason," I prompted.

"I do." She grinned, clearly proud of her detective work. "Her mother died prior to Patience's move to the Virginia Colony. Patience never mailed the letters to her mother. She knew she was writing to a dead woman."

"Really?"

"I suppose those letters were her diary, her confessional—her way of pretending that she still had her mother. Like most of us, she felt safe talking to her mother and didn't want to lose it."

"It's a natural response, I suppose." How many times did I try to connect with my mother after Jennifer's death? How many times did I fail before I gave up?

"I still have my mom," Margaret said. "She drives me crazy and I know I do the same to her, though it's all normal in a good kind of way. I'm not sure what I'd do if she were gone."

Words and emotions unexpectedly bubbled up, but as quickly as they rose, I suppressed them. No need to open the lid of Pandora's box. I learned long ago that hope was not waiting to flutter free and ease pain and suffering. "What did Patience have to say to her mother?"

"Lots of loss. As we know, she lost children. Tough life. But what I find very interesting is that she chronicled the day Faith Shire Talbot moved back to their farmhouse."

"Ah, Faith, the witch, mother of twins, and healer."

"The very same. Patience refers to Faith along with her twin sons taking up residence. She fears and resents Faith but is very drawn to Faith's son Cullen. A year's worth of letters later, Patience mentions out of the blue her own son Patrick is thriving."

"Why is that odd?" I asked.

"On the day Faith arrived, Patience mentions her aching heart."

"She could have been upset about many things."

"I don't think so. I think her baby boy died shortly before Faith arrived," Margaret said. "I believe she thought documenting his death in one of the letters would somehow make it all too real."

"Why do you think he died days before Faith's arrival?"

"She mentions nursing Faith's baby, which means her milk never dried up."

"What exactly are you suggesting?" I said.

"Patience's child, according to earlier letters, is sickly. However, after Faith arrives, he becomes strong and vibrant."

"You said yourself, Faith was a healer. Maybe she helped the boy."

"No mention of that in the letters." Her eyes narrowing, she nodded. "You're a good devil's advocate, Rae."

"I only analyze facts."

Margaret sipped her coffee. "If these were letters to her mother, then you would think she'd mention the adoption," she said.

"Maybe she was so afraid of the secret she didn't dare write it. Secrecy is a common traveling companion with adoption. A very charged subject," Rae offered.

"Point taken. Daisy's birth mother, Terry, told her current husband about Daisy only a few months ago."

I held my breath for a beat. "She kept her daughter's birth a secret."

"For decades. I think I told you, when Daisy first met Terry, it didn't go so well. Terry was very uptight and cold to Daisy. They've struggled ever since. Daisy wants to have a relationship, but Terry is reluctant."

"You think Terry should have done more," I observed. "But many adopted children think of their birth mothers as fairy-tale characters, instead of the flawed people we all are. It's a natural coping mechanism."

Blue eyes darkened with anger. "Regardless, she could be nicer to my sister."

"It might not be so easy for Terry."

"Playing devil's advocate again?"

"You're looking at this in strictly black-and-white terms. Adoption is emotional and fraught with gray areas that aren't as easy to define."

"Yeah, I get all that on an intellectual level," Margaret said. "But it irks me when I see Daisy wrestle with the rejection. She doesn't talk about it much, but it hurts her. I mean, how hard could it be to return an e-mail?"

The boy's e-mail remained unanswered in my inbox. Coming up on twenty-four hours since I read it. Would he see my silence as rejection?

How could I explain to Margaret that answering letters, e-mails, and questions carried tremendous responsibility? Shame. Pain. Daisy's birth mother was not evil, but afraid. What would the people around her think if they knew she gave away a child? People could be intellectual and talk about adoption as a wonderful act of kindness, but many, in their heart of hearts, would judge the birth mother to be selfish.

I couldn't put all this into words for Margaret. So, I didn't. "Does Patience say what happened to Faith?"

"I'm still reviewing my notes on that issue."

"Wasn't there one more McDonald child?" I asked.

"There was a girl named Hanna. She grew to adulthood."

"What became of Patrick? You said he was a lawyer?"

"A very successful one. And Hanna married a planter. She lived to be sixty-four."

"What else did Patience say about Faith?"

"Patience worried about having the woman in her home, but her husband insisted his wife needed the help due to her fragile health." Margaret flipped through several pages. "Patience noted that Faith continued to grow herbs and mix elixirs that she sold to several of the good wives of Alexandria, who visited her in secret." She held up a finger, peering over the edge of her glasses. "She also makes mention of the witch bottle buried in the stone hearth. '*Gone is the sting of loss,*' she writes. Her heart, and I quote, '*was now coated in a fine sheen of resin.*'"

A heart of stone. As much as we change, we don't. "She made the bottle to protect herself from pain."

"Maybe."

"Did she ever say if she regretted that fine sheen of resin?"

"She never mentioned regret. Only relief. But I'll research it and will keep you posted."

Of course, the bottle had no magical powers. And the trauma of losing children would have hardened her. "I'm wondering if Patience wasn't having Faith mix one of her special elixirs to soften the stress," I said.

"She was self-medicating. Very logical. Certainly possible."

Margaret thumbed through several more pages. "She does comment on her other women friends who made the bottles. Once Faith returned to the farmhouse, the other two women never visited again. Mistress Goodwin had issues with a growing madness that made it more difficult for her to think clearly. Addie can tell you all about the mental health issues that run through her family."

"Genetics."

"Right. And Patience said Mistress Smyth grew more and more nervous around Faith, especially when their time in Aberdeen came up. My guess is that something happened back in Scotland that Mistress Smyth did not want disclosed." Margaret reached for a cookie and bit into it. "A regular soap opera."

"I'm amazed you've uncovered all this in the last day."

She raised the cookie to her lips and paused. "History's my bag. And you have a treasure trove here thanks to Patience McDonald. You really need to think about preserving these letters, Rae. Some are so brittle. It's just a matter of time before they turn to dust."

I thought about the boy. He was a McDonald by birth, and all of this was his legacy, if he ever chose to accept it one day. I would never force it upon him. I had signed away all my claims. But if he wanted to know, I was duty bound to tell him what I could, wasn't I? "Would you be interested in reviewing and preparing a written synopsis? I would pay you for your time, of course."

Her eyes widened. "Really? You would pay me to dig through all this history and write about it?"

"I know you have work to do at the salvage yard. But I could offer you twenty dollars an hour."

"Twenty bucks an hour? What's the overall project cap?" She grinned. "All the projects I've ever had were funded by grants, and we always had a cap."

"How much time do you estimate for a thorough report?"

"A couple of hundred hours." Margaret quickly calculated the total. "That's four thousand dollars."

"Sounds reasonable," I said.

"I could use that kind of change and would love to do the work."

"So, you have time?"

"We're still building the salvage business so it's spotty at best," she said. "But there's always pockets of time in the evening."

"You may continue to have the documents at home and study there, if that would be helpful."

"It would. Why the turnaround?"

"Maybe it's time," I said. "There's also another McDonald that I'm also very interested in learning about. My great-aunt. It's come to my attention she was married to my great-uncle. They had a child before she remarried."

"Really?"

"The child's name was Amelia Smyth Murphy. She was a friend of my mother's and is now in a nursing home."

"Sure, I know Amelia," Margaret said. "Wicked sweet tooth and loves gossip. That one should be easy to trace. When was Amelia born?"

"1942, I think. Amelia Smyth Murphy. She and her husband never had children, and he died about forty years ago."

Margaret tapped a ringed finger on the side of her mug. "Amelia owns the house on Prince Street. We cleaned out her basement and found the third witch bottle there. Her niece is the caretaker living there now."

"That's Lisa Smyth."

She scribbled Amelia's information into the notebook. "Lisa is a wet-plate photographer. Very talented."

"I've heard she's won awards."

Margaret circled the name Smyth a half dozen times. "So, why the sudden family interest, Rae?"

"You've shown me that there's a lot of history behind the

McDonald family. I have a hunch the same holds true for the Smyth family."

"Do I have the same writing and publishing parameters as I do with the McDonald project? And where do you want me to start with the family recap?"

"You choose," I said. "But Amelia is old and ill, and she might not have much time. I think she would like to know more about her birth mother, Fiona."

"I'll take the last two boxes then," Margaret said. "That will get me into the early twentieth century and well past her birth."

"Okay." I reached to help with the boxes.

Margaret dusted crumbs from her hands. "I can get those."

"No reason for you to make two trips."

"They're dusty and you're all dressed up."

"I'll clean up."

"I live coated in the stuff. Barely notice it anymore."

We carried the boxes to an old VW Beetle painted a bright orange. She opened the front trunk and loaded in her box, then took mine.

"Is there anything else I can do for you?" I asked.

Margaret waved her hand and then snapped her fingers. "A favor for my sister, Rachel."

"The widow baker and the beau that moved back to France."

"Right. Rachel. If you come across a stray man worthy of her, give me a call. I'd love to introduce them."

"A stray man? Like a rescue dog from the pound with a good disposition?" I almost smiled.

"A good one who likes kids," Margaret said with a straight face. "I have two seven-year-old nieces and he would have to love them as much as their mom. And if he's super-hot and rich, well, all the better."

"Do you think I have a warehouse where I keep them stocked?"

Margaret laughed. "If you do, I sure would like to see the place. I don't want to keep any of the inventory, mind you, but I wouldn't say no to a loaner now and then."

It was oddly hard to keep a serious expression. "A loaner? Don't you want me to match you up with your perfect mate? That's what everyone else wants."

"Absolutely not. No long-term men for me, Rae. No husbands for Margaret McCrae." She laughed, her words clearly amusing her. "I'm strictly a renter. But Rachel, she's different. She'll want a keeper."

"Loaners and keepers. I get it."

"Well, not all of us want Mr. Forever." She grinned. "You should consider an offshoot of your matchmaking business."

"What would that be?"

"You find Mr. Forever for those that want him, and for those that don't, you find Mr. Until Next Friday."

I smiled. "He might get underfoot if you had to keep him around a whole week.

She winked. "I like the hint of sarcasm in the comment, Rae. You're loosening up a bit."

I squared my shoulders and raised my chin a fraction. "I certainly hope not."

Margaret's laughter burst out of her like a bullet. "Rae, I'm assuming that's more sarcasm."

A Letter from Patience

JULY 6, 1753

Dearest Mother,

My son, Patrick, grows stronger each passing day. He is going to be a stout, healthy boy. A very cautious hope stirs in me as a new baby grows in my belly. Mr. McDonald does not speak of the baby, but I sense that he is thrilled at the prospect of another son. Each time he enters the house at night, he glances at our boy, his eyes heavy with thought. I worry for Patrick for fear Mr. McDonald will favor the unborn baby. Surely one child cannot replace another's in a parent's heart.

My friends from town visit, but they are always nervous and agitated when they see the witch moving about the cottage. Though they do not speak to her in front of me, I see them exchange coin for herbs before they leave. It is difficult to resist the allure of Faith and her magic.

Faith's son, Marcus, is a sweet child, though I see he is a bit of a ruffian. When he plays with Patrick the two boys get into tugging matches that end with one crying, but Faith is always on hand to settle them. She cares for my son as if he were her own.

Yours Faithfully,

Patience McDonald

Chapter Seven

LISA, WEDNESDAY, OCTOBER 5, 2011

The nurse at the assisted-living center read my driver's license. "Lisa Smyth." She handed it back to me. "Silly I have to check this each time you come by, but that's policy."

"Just doing your job," I offered.

"Where's Charlie?" she asked.

"At home tonight. This is just a quick visit."

The sun hung low and sullen in the evening sky as I returned to Amelia's room. Though the air held the late summer's warmth, sunset came earlier as fall began in earnest. Soon the cooler winds would chase away the heat until next year.

When I arrived in my aunt's room, my hands shook a little and my nerves were stretched thin. As I drew in a breath, my eyes adjusted to the dim lights. Amelia liked the heat turned up, and she slept better when wrapped in blankets brought from home. Her doctors said this constant chill was a side effect of age.

When I came into the room, I moved to the foot of the bed and reached for the folded quilt. She said it was made by her grandmother and had cherished it since she was a child. As I fingered the frayed fabric, memories resurfaced. Years ago, in the weeks after the car accident I could not sleep. My body was bruised and battered and my mind full of the sound of screeching brakes and the rip of tree through metal. I could not forget the flames or the screams. Amelia had laid this same quilt over me and told me she loved me.

"How can you love me?" I asked.

"Because you're my girl."

And then, through endless sobs, I told her what happened. Jennifer and I were driving on the George Washington Parkway along the Potomac River that last night. The moon was full and the stars so vivid and clear. It was one o'clock in the morning, and we knew we were breaking curfew. A nameless rock song blared on the radio.

But neither of us felt the least bit of guilt. There was a deliciousness in the freedom. We were soaring. At seventeen, we were all grown up and believed life was ours for the taking.

And then, I made a crack about this guy she liked. A real moron, in my opinion. She took exception. And in a span of seconds the mood turned on a dime and we began arguing. Soon after, it all went wrong.

Later, Amelia kissed me and told me again she loved me unconditionally. She told me old people became wise by making mistakes when they were young. It did not make them bad or evil, just human.

But I would not accept forgiveness. My focus was on the moment the car swerved. The tree. The flames.

Jennifer was dead.

And I was alone.

Tears welled as I straightened and touched the smooth, well-worn folds of the quilt. Pulling the frayed edges, I tucked it under her pale chin. Immediately, her skin looked warmer and her body relaxed, as if she sensed love.

I kissed her on the cheek, then opened the nightstand drawer and removed the baby book. Hugging it close to my body, I whispered, "I'll bring this back once I find out what happened to Fiona."

Amelia did not stir, but I imagined the wrinkles of her brow soothed as my words seeped into her brain and calmed a mind that knew no true peace.

I tucked the baby book in my backpack.

Out in the corridor, fluorescent fixtures cast a milky white light. I waved to the nurses at their station and took the elevator to the first floor. As I got into the car, my phone buzzed. The number was local, and I didn't recognize it. It was likely about Amelia's home and the parade of folks that would have to become involved in getting it sold.

"Lisa Smyth."

"Hey, Lisa, this is Margaret McCrae with Shire Architectural Salvage. We cleaned out your basement about a month ago."

"Right. What can I do for you?"

"We found this bottle in your basement."

"Okay."

"It's a pretty unusual bottle, and I'm doing a little historical research on it."

"There's not much I can tell you about anything in the house," I said. "It all belonged to my aunt, and since her hospitalization, she has a hard time with details."

"I'm sorry. I like Amelia. I was hoping to find out more about your family's history," Margaret said.

"Like what?" I asked.

"Specifically, the relationship between the Smyths, the Goodwin's, and the McDonalds," Margaret said.

"I don't believe I know any Goodwin's."

"Well, the Goodwin name fell by the wayside over the last

couple of centuries. The family branch that survived in that line went by the name of Shire."

"As in your company?" I asked.

"Exactly."

"Margaret, it's funny you should mention the McDonalds," I said. "I'm trying to track a connection between the McDonald and Smyth families dating back to about 1940."

"Really? Small world. I saw Rae McDonald today at her home. I'm doing a bit of family inventory for her."

"And?" I was trying to sound interested.

"She wants me to dig into the story of . . ." I heard the rustling of pages. "Fiona McDonald. I did a little digging after I left her place and identified the woman."

Rae had spoken to Margaret? The Ice Queen stirred. "Margaret, I'm close to Old Town now. I could stop by your King Street shop if you're there."

"I'll be here for a couple more hours."

"See you in about twenty minutes."

"There's parking in the side alley behind the store."

"Great."

I detoured through the evening traffic, winding alongside roads until I passed the tall stone spire of the Masonic Temple and merged onto King Street. From there, it was a straight shot to the Potomac. Traffic slowed to a stutter step as I entered the very heart of the oldest part of the city where tourists and shoppers flocked on warm evenings.

Down a cobblestone alley, I parked beside the white Shire Architectural Salvage van and, grabbing my backpack, walked around to the front entrance. The large picture window that faced the corners of King and Union Streets was filled with a collection of odds and ends, including a claw-foot tub, a crystal teardrop chandelier, a fireplace mantel, lighthouse lanterns, and a wooden chest. The store had been here for longer than I could remember. I had come here with my mother when I was about six or seven. She was looking to fill a long summer afternoon. I spent our time at the warehouse sneezing and avoiding the darkened corners and the old unsmiling woman who lingered behind her cash register. To my amazement, my mother was glad to see this shopkeeper and they laughed and joked, leaving me to stand and wonder how my mother knew so many odd people.

After that day, I never paid much attention to the shop because it held onto the past. As far as I was concerned, the past held only sadness.

Bells above my head jingled as I entered. Bright lights illuminated once-darkened corners and highlighted a half dozen neat rows with bins filled with all sorts of history. I heard a baby fuss, followed by the soft voice of a woman who sang quietly to the child.

"Be right there," the woman said.

"No rush." I moved toward a collection of furniture created from repurposed items: a desk fashioned from an old pie safe, a bench made from reclaimed timbers, and an iron gate fashioned into wall art.

Seconds later, a woman rounded the corner. She had curly brown hair tied up into a topknot and wore jeans and a T-shirt that read *Shire Architectural Salvage*. She had a baby front pack strapped to her chest and carried a small box filled with an assortment of doorknobs and keys.

"Oh, hey," she said. "You're Lisa, right? I'm Addie." Addie set the box on the front counter next to an antique register, wiped her hand on her jeans, and extended it to me.

"Right." Addie had come by the house with Margaret. "I was a little overwhelmed when you came through."

"Do you have a sister named Janet Morgan?" I asked.

"I do. Where did you meet her?"

"At a church meeting." I openly talked about attending AA meetings, but not everyone was as forthcoming.

"Janet attends an AA meeting in the church."

"So do I."

Addie grew still. "Well, I'm glad to meet you."

"Likewise. Your sister seems nice."

"Yes."

No missing the rippling tension. If Janet was only five weeks into the program that meant her family was holding their breath, hoping she would make it work. The first twelve to eighteen months was such a fragile time. Failure was common. Me included.

When Addie did not expound, I decided to drop the line of conversation. I cleared my throat. "I'm here because I got a call from Margaret about a bottle."

"Ah, the bottle. Margaret is my new business partner and she's now on a mission to find out all she can about three witch bottles."

"Witch bottles?"

"You haven't heard the story about them?"

"No, but I'm intrigued."

Shaking her head, Addie began to rock back and forth while patting the baby's back. "Basically, there were three women who lived in Alexandria around 1750. They each made these bottles as a kind of protection spell against a woman who they thought was a witch."

"Wow, that's a story."

"Margaret is determined to dig up every detail she can about the three women. She has reached out to the McDonalds and now you."

The bells jingled and I turned to see a woman with strawberry-blond hair enter. She wore jeans, a loose-fitting shirt, bracelets, and flip-flops. She was carrying two cups of coffee.

"Speak of the devil," Addie said.

Margaret raised one of the coffee cups to her lips and swallowed quickly, her brow rising as she smiled. "Hey, Lisa. That was quick."

"I was close by."

Margaret handed Addie the second cup of coffee and waved her hand around the shop. "Welcome to the past."

Addie laughed. "I can attest to that."

"Now," Margaret said, "if you talk to my sisters who work at the Union Street Bakery, they'll tell you I'm the biggest slacker they've ever met. I haven't met a bakery deadline I could keep."

My blood pressure eased as I stood here listening to Margaret launch into a story about boxing mail orders through the bakery and how Satan invented the clear packing tape that always ended up in a useless wad. Honestly, I was happy to be here and away from the solitude of the Prince Street house.

Margaret clapped her hands together. "But you don't want to hear me go on and on about shipping labels and box sizes. What do you have for me?"

Moving toward the front counter, I pulled out the baby book. "My aunt, Amelia, told me about it. She says her birth mother made it for her." Hesitating, I wondered if I had spoken out of turn, but knew if I did not share, we might not ever find out about Fiona. "The other day Amelia told me for the first time she was adopted. But you should also know my aunt has the onset of Alzheimer's but was having a really good day when we had our visit and discussed this book."

"Fiona McDonald was Amelia's birth mother?" Margaret asked.

"It appears so."

"And you and Rae have talked about Fiona?"

How to explain without all the drama? "Our families go way back. She asked about Amelia and I told her about the book."

Margaret stilled. "Did you know Jennifer McDonald?"

"I did," I said, cautious now.

Margaret offered, "After I left Rae's today, I got to thinking and remembered her sister who died in a car accident when she was a teenager."

"It was sixteen years ago."

"Right. I must have been away at college and recalled Mom talking about it." Margaret focused her attention to the worn, faded silk binding of the book. "What can you tell me about this?

"Not that much, other than what I saw when I leafed through it," I said.

Margaret tugged on white gloves and carefully opened the front of the book with deliberate slowness that belied her crazy curly hair pulled up in a ponytail and her brightly colored peasant top. She closely studied the book. "I can tell Rae's a smart woman. Though I'll never understand how she got into matchmaking."

"McDonald women never admit to being matchmakers."

"So, it's true?" Margaret asked.

"It's just known," I said. "Every woman in the McDonald family was a matchmaker. They never really had to advertise it."

Addie moved closer with her head cocked with interest. "A family of matchmakers."

Margaret lifted her gaze. "I've been reading her ancestors' letters and there's no mention of matchmaking, though she often mentions the marriages of local couples. One letter goes into great detail about a lavish wedding."

"Which generation are you reading about?"

"Oh, Patience McDonald, the first McDonald woman to arrive in Virginia. In fact, she knew your ancestor, Mistress Smyth. You said you didn't know much about your family?"

"Afraid not," I said. "I damn near failed history in high school."

Margaret's eyes widened. "My God, woman, how could you come close to failing history? It's ripe with gossip and intrigue."

Spontaneous laughter rumbled in my chest. "I was not as studious as I now realize I should've been. Art was my passion."

"Really?" Addie asked. "What kind of art?"

"Photography."

"Cool," Margaret said. "When we were cleaning out your basement, we saw the images. You use a bellows camera."

"I'm impressed. I do."

"Now, if you must forsake your history studies for a bellows camera, I might be willing to forgive you. I love the richness of the prints created by that kind of work. Would you take my picture sometime?"

"You figure out what happened to Fiona and it's a deal." I then gave Margaret a quick recap of Fiona's two husbands and the infant she gave away.

"Like I said on the phone, I did a quick search after I left Rae's," Margaret said. "Fiona lost her first husband, moved to D.C. for a few years and sang in nightclubs. When she returned to Alexandria, she was married to a gentleman named David Saunders. They lived on Washington Street and had one daughter, Diane, who very oddly, would have been Rae and Jennifer's mother."

"That's right," I said, feeling random pieces assembling. "Rae is so much like her."

"Rae's mom was a bit cold as well?" Margaret asked.

"Yes. She always kept her emotions under lock and key."

"And she was a matchmaker like Rae?"

"So, the legend goes."

"Wow." Margaret studied the pages of the book and

reached for her phone. "Mind if I photograph it? I'd like to keep a record handy while I do some searches, and may I divulge the adoption?"

"At this point, sure. Better my aunt knows the full story of her life."

"Great."

Meanwhile, Addie was studying the keychain dangling from my finger, and I realized she recognized the sobriety chips. "You said you met my sister, Janet, at a meeting?"

"Yes. I'm an alcoholic." I had stopped hiding my disease long ago. It was easier to be open about it than carry the weight of half-truths and lies.

"How long have you been sober?"

"Over eight years."

"Damn, you developed a problem fairly young." Margaret didn't hide her surprise.

"I did." I slid my hands into the front pockets of the jeans. "No sense beating around the bush. I was in the car with Jennifer McDonald when it crashed. She died and I couldn't handle it. I started drinking heavily."

"How have you kept with it so long?" Addie asked.

Having stepped back from the brink of total failure only hours ago, I didn't feel like a success. "One hour at a time."

Addie's smile was sincere. "I hope you and Janet will get to know each other. You would be an inspiration to her."

Margaret scribbled several names as she studied the book. "The initial handwriting is bold and dark, suggesting a man. Halfway through, the handwriting becomes distinctly feminine. That would support that Jeffrey stopped participating when your aunt was about five months old."

Margaret turned a page, studying the woman's handwriting. "There's a notation here: *Can a woman and baby alone make a home?*"

Addie rubbed Carrie's back. "Good question. I worry about that all the time."

Margaret shook her head. "*You're* all the *home* that kid needs. But Fiona would have been a single mother in the early 1940s. If you didn't have money or strong family ties, it was a great deal harder. My question is, why didn't the McDonald family embrace her? She was married to their son and she gave birth to his child. And where was her family?"

"I don't know any of that," I said. "And Amelia's mind is no longer sharp. The fact we had any kind of conversation about this is nearly a miracle."

Margaret nodded. "Not to worry. I'm on the job. I'll figure it out." She carefully closed the book. "May I hold on to this for a day or two?

"Sure. Any information you can find out about Fiona would be welcomed. It would mean a lot to Amelia and me."

The corner of Margaret's mouth hitched into a grin. "I'm on it."

A Letter from Patience

AUGUST 1, 1753

Dearest Mother,

A stranger came to visit today, a traveler headed to Alexandria. He had heard of Faith's healing powers and asked her to make an elixir for his gout. When he spied the children in the cottage, Mr. McDonald introduced Marcus as Faith's son and Patrick as our son. Faith directed an angry glare toward Mr. McDonald, who looked back at her, unflinching. Faith didn't speak up, but she turned sullen. I do not understand what transpired, nor do I care. It was such fun to have a visitor and hear of news from the city. The price of tobacco is on the rise and the Alexandria city leaders are building a large pier that will allow the tall ships to dock at the shore. The Indians continue to cause trouble in the west and there is talk that the king will send troops to put down the troublemakers. Mr. McDonald was pleased by the news about the dock and spoke of one day building a bigger, grander house that will stand as a testament to the McDonald clan.

Yours Faithfully,
Patience McDonald

Chapter Eight

RAE, THURSDAY, OCTOBER 6, 2011

The rain cleared, but the air remained heavy with moisture when I rose from my desk overlooking the bare spot in my backyard. I had just completed several reports for my family practice clients that capped off a highly productive day. But I still had not summoned the courage to write a response to Michael's e-mail.

Margaret's words rattled in my head. *Daisy doesn't talk about it much, but it hurts her. I mean, how hard could it be to return an e-mail?*

Was Michael waiting by his computer, wondering if I cared? Was he disappointed with me?

The idea of his pain sent me shrinking deeper and deeper into my work. He had a mother who loved him very much. I had met Susan and her husband, Todd, when I was pregnant. Knowing adoption was my only choice, I insisted on meeting the couple who would raise my child. My mother thought it was a bad idea and did not want to deal with the child's *real* family, as she called it, but I insisted.

I remember Susan was nervous. Her smile was bright and

welcoming, but her hand shook a little as she extended it to me. Her grasp was firm and warm.

"The prenatal checkup went well." My mother spoke clearly to Susan and Todd as I sat, nearly unable to speak. "She didn't see a doctor in the first trimester of her pregnancy but has since been examined completely and the child is in perfect health."

Susan observed everything she could about me. Maybe documenting it for the boy one day. Several times she looked at my very round belly but did her best to engage me in conversation, so I felt included, rather than just an incubator.

"As you know, the child is a boy," Mom said.

Susan grinned, her eyes moistening with tears as she took her husband's hand.

I rested my hands over my belly. My child. My flesh. My son.

"Rae," Susan said softly. "I brought you a gift."

"A gift. Why?"

She pulled a scrapbook from her purse. It was covered in rich leather and embossed with strands of ivy in each corner. "It's not much. It's a scrapbook that has a few pictures of Todd and me."

I opened the book to a picture of the smiling couple with a large black Labrador retriever sitting between them. The sun shone behind the trio. Their life appeared so blessed.

Carefully, I turned the pages, viewing one happy scene after another. It was bittersweet. I was happy for them and Michael but wondered why it could not have been me. I closed the book and absently traced the ivy corners with my fingertips.

"That book is full of pictures of us and our house," she said, pulling out a second scrapbook. "But this one is empty and will be filled with pictures of the baby as he grows up. I promise you I'll send pictures as often as you like. I want you to know that we'll love him with all our heart. You are also now a part of our family."

I opened the book and leafed through the empty pages. Memories I would never experience. "Why do you want him?"

Todd took Susan's hand. "We can't have children."

Susan's lips did not tremble when she smiled, but I sensed the nervousness. "We tried and tried. In vitro. It all failed." She leaned forward, taking my hand again. "The chances of me carrying a baby to term are nearly impossible now."

And I had gotten pregnant without a single thought.

"I want to be a mother, Rae. Genetics doesn't matter to me."

The baby was mine and I was giving him away. I cleared my throat. "His name will be Michael. They told you that, right?"

"They did," Susan said, wiping away a tear. "And it's a great name. I think I've practiced it about a thousand times in the last few days."

I smoothed my hand over my rounded curves. "You really think you can love Michael?"

Susan raised clasped hands to her heart. "I already do, Rae. There are moments when I think I've been waiting for him for a lifetime." Emotions choked her voice. "And I want to be a mom so badly. I'm sorry if I sound a little emotional."

Outside, the crunch of truck tires on gravel pulled me from the past. I blinked, chasing away the memories and grabbing onto the present. A car door closed. That would be Zeb to discuss the new office. Only now, I was not so sure it should be an office. A guest cottage might make more sense.

My doorbell rang, the chime vibrating through the house. Straightening my shoulders, I moved down the center hallway to the door and opened it.

Zeb stood in the doorway, one handheld a roll of building plans and the other on the shoulder of a young boy standing beside him. The boy could have been Zeb as a child. Dark hair the color of coffee, square shoulders, and curious dark eyes that stared up at me with a boldness uncommon for a child that age.

"This is my son, Eric," Zeb said. "I hope you don't mind, but he's running errands with me this afternoon."

The boy was about seven, and immediately, I compared him to Michael. What had he looked like at that age? Though Michael's mother had faithfully mailed me the promised updates, I never opened one envelope. As curious as I was, I always sensed if I really understood what I was missing as a mother, my heart would break, and I would never be able to recover. But I also dared not throw them away. So, I carefully filed all the unopened letters in a box and stored them with the scrapbook in the top of my bedroom closet.

"No, that's fine. Please come inside."

At the threshold, they carefully wiped their feet before entering.

"Why don't we sit in the kitchen?" I asked. "Margaret McCrae brought by cookies, and I doubt I'll ever be able to eat them all."

Eric glanced up at Zeb and grinned.

"That sounds great," Zeb said.

"I like cookies from the Union Street Bakery," Eric said. "Dad and I go there a lot on Saturdays. Margaret is funny."

"She's very entertaining," I said.

"And I play with Anna and Ellie sometimes."

Ah, Margaret's nieces. And the single sister, Rachel, was it? I wondered how Zeb and Rachel would fare if paired. Two single parents. Business owners. Well liked. They aligned without much effort.

We moved to the bright lights of the kitchen. I retrieved the bag of cookies as well as the half quart of milk. "Do you drink milk, Eric?"

"I do."

"Have a seat on one of the stools and I'll pour you a glass." In the reflection of the cabinet, I saw Eric hop up on the stool.

"The kitchen looks good," Zeb said. "Had any issues with it?"

"No. You did a great job." I set a plate and a glass of milk in front of Eric.

Zeb ran his hand over the white marble of the island. "I remember this gave us fits. We had a heck of a time finding a slab big enough but also with the right shades."

I set up the coffeemaker and turned it on. "I never knew there were so many decisions."

"But you got what you wanted in the end."

"Of course." I did not bother with sugar because I remembered Zeb never took it in his coffee. He and his crews had worked in this kitchen for months two summers ago. Many a morning during the construction phase I brewed coffee for him and his men in a makeshift kitchen in the dining room.

Eric reached for a chocolate chip cookie and took a big bite. "Margaret says you should start every day with a cookie. She says she could eat cookies for all her meals."

"Cookies aren't a major food group," I said.

Zeb grinned. "That's what I keep trying to tell Eric. But so far, Margaret's winning the argument."

Margaret traveled from job to job like a gypsy and would be the first to admit she made a meager income. Dizzying professional highs and lows were the norm for her, but as much as I searched for a fault in her approach to life, she squeezed so much joy out of living. It was a talent I had long ago forgotten. And now coveted.

I poured Zeb a cup of coffee and set it in front of him. "Those the plans?"

"They are."

"I might have some changes."

"Really?" I sensed a touch of frustration. He liked his timetables.

"I've been back and forth on ideas for a couple of days now."

He took a sip, contemplating the possible changes. "You make the best coffee." He rolled out the plans on the cool marble and anchored them with the salt and pepper shakers. "As you can see, I've redrawn the upstairs plan and you now have rough-ins for an office. The downstairs is still dedicated garage and storage space." His weathered, tanned finger pointed to several symbols that represented what looked like a bathroom and kitchen.

"That's exactly what I asked for."

He stared across the wide counter at me. "But."

"I didn't say a *but*."

Frowning, he sipped his coffee. "There is a *but*, Dr. McDonald."

He'd done exactly as I asked and still, as I stared at the plans, it all felt wrong. "I'm generally very decisive."

"But."

"I don't know."

"Are you a real doctor?" Eric asked.

Grateful to shift attention from Zeb, I looked at the boy. "I'm a psychologist."

Freckles splashed across the bridge of Eric's nose in a very appealing way. I made a point not to notice children, but even I could admit he was cute. He cocked his head, studying me closely. "Dad said they aren't real doctors. You can't make sick people better."

Zeb sighed his exasperation. "Eric. Oversharing."

The boy looked up at his father, confused. "But you said—"

Zeb shook his head, a raised finger to his lips signaling silence. "Eat your cookie."

"I finished it."

A frustrated smile tweaked the edges of his lips. "Ask Dr. McDonald if you can have a second."

Eric looked up at me. "Can I?"

"May I?" I asked.

Eric shrugged. "May I have another cookie?"

I pushed the plate toward him. "Yes, you may."

Seconds passed as he studied the collection of a half-dozen cookies. "Are you eating one?"

"I don't eat sugar."

After careful scrutiny, he chose the largest chocolate chip cookie on the plate. "Then why do you have cookies in the house?"

"Margaret brought them by for me. I couldn't throw them out."

"Why?"

Good question. I wouldn't allow myself to eat a cookie, and yet I could not throw them out. "It would be a waste."

Chocolate smeared the edges of his lips. "But no one is eating them."

The child's logic was on target. I wasn't making sense. I couldn't open and enjoy the letters from the boy's mother, nor could I enjoy or discard the cookies.

I handed him a paper towel. "You're eating them, now."

Eric studied the large chocolate chip cookie in his hand. "Yeah. Thanks."

As the boy bit into the cookie, Zeb cleared his throat as he scratched his head. "My mom always said little pitchers have big ears."

"Eric is very astute."

Zeb traced the handle of his cup. "I didn't mean you weren't a real doctor."

I laid my hands on the counter. Smooth. Cool. Calming.

"Yes, you did. And you would not be the first to say it. But I know what I do is valuable."

"You have a lot to be proud of here. I meant no offense."

"Dad said you can't operate on people either," Eric said.

Zeb rubbed the back of his neck. "Eric, enough sharing."

"He's right," I said. "I'm not that kind of doctor."

"What other kinds are there?" Eric asked.

"There are dozens of kinds."

"Like what?"

"Doctors who care for children. Doctors who fix broken bones. Doctors who examine eyes."

"Is that all?"

I looked at Zeb. "I've landed in a maze. I don't think there's any way out."

The edges of his eyes crinkled when he smiled. "There's no escape. And the more questions you answer, the more he'll have. It never, ever, ends."

"Then I shall cut my losses and worry about the building out back." I studied the plans again. "I thought when I cleared the land that I knew what I wanted. Now, I'm not so sure. That's a poor excuse and does little to help you with your job, but I'm still struggling with what to build on the spot."

He slowly rolled up the plans, tugged the rubber band from his wrist, and wrapped it around the papers. "Why don't I leave these with you? You can take a few days to look over them and think about it. The rains have slowed, but your ground won't be dry for another week. Until then, I can't lay the foundation. I have other work, and I'll shift my focus to that."

"A week should be enough time." That was the reasonable response, but I had no idea if I would ever commit. A part of me was sorry I had cleared it.

I reached into a drawer, pulled out a large Ziplock bag and

filled it with the remaining cookies. "Can I give the extra cookies to you and Eric?"

Eric sat straighter and nodded approval.

Zeb realized this was a battle for another time. "Sure. But no more cookies today, pal. You'll be bouncing off the walls if you have another."

He waggled his head from side to side. "I don't bounce."

"Oh, yes you do." He pushed the milk toward his son. "Finish up. We've used up enough of Dr. McDonald's time."

"I'm the one wasting your time." Though having them here did not feel like a waste. There was a warmth about the moment that I could not ignore.

As Eric gulped the rest of his milk, Zeb said, "I'll try to keep my schedule open for you, but if you don't have an answer soon, I'll have to move this project down the priority list."

I did not want to lose my place on the list. "I'll decide."

He sipped coffee, relaxed and unconcerned. "I hear from Addie that you gave Margaret some historical documents."

"She's helping me catalogue some of the earlier letters."

He rubbed the back of his head again. "No doubt, searching for information on her witch bottles. I hear about them every time I stop by the salvage yard."

"I suppose you're there a lot."

"Eric likes to visit his sister."

"That's Addie's baby?" I asked.

"It's complicated."

Eric shrugged. "Mom is Addie's sister. But Mom is sick and can't raise me or Carrie."

Ah. I understood. "I'd say your dad is doing a good job with you."

Eric shrugged. "I like seeing Mom, too."

Zeb tussled the boy's hair. "And she likes seeing you."

Did Zeb like visiting with Addie? His personal life was

none of my business, but I still asked, "I thought you and Addie were close."

He squarely met my gaze. "We're good friends. We both love Eric and Carrie."

But not each other.

I cleared my throat, oddly glad about the unspoken meaning humming under his words. "The children are lucky to have you both."

"I guess you could call us an unconventional family."

"Unconventional can work." Zeb was a man who thrived on convention but was doing his best.

Eric hopped off his stool as his dad rose and moved toward the front door. Forgetting the bag of cookies, I scooped up the bag and followed. At the front door, I asked, "Eric, did you forget something?"

He took them, his hand brushing mine as he grinned up at me. "Thanks, Dr. McDonald."

"You're very welcome."

Before I realized it, the boy leaned forward and hugged me. His arms were strong as he squeezed tightly. For a moment, I couldn't breathe, and I felt my heart pounding hard against the sheen of ice coating it. My hands stretched out, but I did not know if I should hug him back or not. I simply stood frozen in place, as invisible shards of ice cut my insides. I wondered how many thousands of hugs, kisses, and questions I had missed over the last sixteen years. A lot.

When he released me, it took effort not to stagger back a step. "Thanks!"

Zeb laid his hand on the boy's head, glancing at me, trying to decipher my reaction. "Thanks for the cookies."

I liked Eric and was glad I'd made him happy. "Of course. Thank you."

Zeb studied me an extra beat, picking up on the sudden

jab of sadness that leaked into my tone of voice. "We'll talk soon."

"Yes."

When they left, I closed the door gently and locked it. As I leaned against the hand hewn mahogany, my breathing slowed and I closed my eyes, willing the sadness and regrets away like a curse. "I did the right thing. Didn't I?"

But doing right did not always foster good feelings or well-being. Doing the right thing could cause so much pain.

The engine started up and the red pickup drove off. Pressing my palms to my flushed cheeks, I resolved to bring up Rachel again with Zeb. He could use a woman in his life, but he especially deserved one who understood motherhood and how to hug a child.

I slid my hands to my belly, still able to imagine the feel of Eric's hug. Emotion swirled, and like a rogue wave, this swell of emotion came out of nowhere and settled in my chest. Sitting back, I pressed my fist upon my heart as I imagined all the moments lost forever with my boy. I had never been able to bake cookies for him, share a birthday or read him bedtime stories. So much had been tossed away with the stroke of a pen on the adoption papers. Was I dead to him?

Swallowing through the tightness in my throat, I rose with hands on hips and paced the room. Tears burned my eyes, forcing me to tip my head back so that they did not spill.

"What is this nonsense?" I whispered. "I don't cry. McDonald women never cry. You're not done."

But whatever it was that gripped in my chest would not release its hold. In fact, it squeezed tighter, robbing me of breath.

I strode from my office into the kitchen and filled a glass with tap water. Drinking slowly, I focused on the cool water. "I'm not upset. I made a calculated decision sixteen years ago that was best for everyone."

And on an intellectual level I understood that at sixteen I was not in a position to raise a child. I was a child myself. There was high school to finish. College. My PhD.

For the first time in sixteen years, my beating heart echoed loudly, drowning out the logic and not heeding the consequences of the drama it stirred.

"Which is why you, Madam Heart, are not welcome in my life." I set the glass down hard on the counter. "I don't have time for drama."

And still the tears pushed, begging to be freed. I stared out the window toward the raw scar of land. "It was a pile of stones and an eyesore with a questionable history that took up far too much valuable yard. The garage makes sense. A pile of rocks, hell no."

Needing to prove the hearthstones did not matter, I turned from the window and stormed toward my computer, ready to fire off an e-mail to Zeb telling him to proceed with the current plans. At this point I could not care less what he built. Finish the job and move on.

As my fingers were poised over the keyboard, raw emotion gripped my throat. Burying my face in my hands, I wept, allowing the sobs to rise up through my body. I searched for the tissue box I reserved for clients and pulled several sheets to staunch the tears.

"Stop," I said. "I can't do this. I don't want this."

But the sadness continued to rack my body.

The last time I cried was the day I laid Michael in Susan's arms. My breasts had ached from the surging milk and my arms felt so empty. The tears flowed unchecked until sleep finally took me. When I awoke the next morning, my eyes were puffy and red. I rose and moved to the small bathroom off my hospital room and showered, trying to wash away my guilt and pain. By the time my mother arrived that afternoon, I was fully dressed, my hair and makeup in place.

She took one look at me, but I could not tell if I sensed relief or sadness. She commented on how lovely I looked and picked up my packed suitcase. The two of us left the hospital and never spoke of it again.

Why had she not at least asked me about the boy or said a kind word?

On the heels of sadness came anger through the tears. This roller coaster ride was maddening. The past did not rule me, but did it have some control over me?

Now as I moved up the center staircase to my bedroom, I grabbed a stool and carried it to my closet. Climbing up, I reached for the top shelf and found the box that contained all the letters the boy's mother had mailed me so diligently over the years. She had kept her word.

I moved to my bed and kicking off my heels, sat on the neatly smoothed comforter. Slowly, I opened the lid and thumbed my index finger over the sixteen envelopes, each thickly packed.

Removing all the envelopes, I laid them out in chronological order, beginning with Michael's first birthday and ending with his most recent sixteenth. I picked up the first envelope and tried to imagine what was waiting for me. I turned it over and ran my thumb under the back flap and carefully tore the paper.

Inside was a note from Susan.

Dear Rae,

Michael is our light and joy and we thank God every day for him and you. As you can see from the pictures, he has your hair and eyes. He's so smart. Never met a cabinet he didn't want to climb into and recently discovered the taste for sugar cookies. He loves them. You are always in our thoughts and prayers.

Love,

Susan

I dropped the letter to the bed as if it were electrified. Energy snapped through my fingertips. And the anger that had spurred me up the stairs vanished. For a moment I sat, unable to leave but barely able to stay.

Drawing in a breath, I reached for the pictures, hesitating before I looked. The first picture was taken of the boy when he was a month old. My breath caught. Immediately, I saw the baby I remembered in such vivid detail. His face was a little fuller and his hair thicker but had the same upturned nose and the same ears. They were my ears.

I flipped through the next eleven photos, each documenting another month in the first year of his life. He grew so quickly, becoming so chubby that he had rolls of fat at his elbows and his knees. By about his ninth month, the rolls of fat were gone, and he balanced on hands and knees, poised to crawl while flashing a drooling three-tooth grin. By his first birthday he stood straight, his small hand wrapped around his father's index finger.

In the last image, he sat in a highchair, a round cake reading *Happy Birthday* and sporting a green-and-white candle shaped into the number *one*. Chocolate icing and cake smeared across his face, hair, and hands. Clearly, he had dunked his fingers into the cake and attempted to feed himself. This time, he sported a lopsided six-toothed grin, unmindful of his mess.

As I traced the creases around his wide grin, laughter bubbled up in me. He was pure joy.

In the background, I noticed a collection of laughing adults, totally enamored with him.

By his first birthday, I had secured enough credits to finish high school early and leave Alexandria by the fall to attend college. This letter arrived shortly after I returned home from my freshman year. I sat in my room for a long time, holding the envelope to my heart, fearing if I opened it, I would not be able to function. To keep moving. To live. So, I tucked it carefully in this box.

Each year, I anxiously awaited the envelope, only to hold it close to my heart before again placing it unopened in the box.

Instead of replacing these first-year photos back in the envelope, I laid them out in order on the bed and then reached for the second envelope. This one did not have twelve pictures, but seven. As I examined each one, I could see the boy did not change as radically as he had the first year. He was healthy and happy.

And so, it went. I displayed all the pictures, studied them before moving onto the next year. The first day of preschool. His first ride on the school bus. His graduation from elementary school. The awkward middle school picture with braces that reminded me of the ones I had worn at that age. The narrowing of his face. The deep blue of his eyes that looked like my father's.

Over the next several hours, I filled my bed with images and catalogued every bit of him.

He was a McDonald, and yet he was not. And he wanted to know more about his biological roots. I owed him that much.

I found the old scrapbook that Susan gave me when we first met, and I filled it with the pictures of Michael, along with her letters. I owed a debt to Susan, who wrote so faithfully, even though I continued to ignore her each year. God, what had I done?

What had she told Michael about me? Did he know she dutifully sent his pictures, only to have me not respond? She must harbor terrible thoughts of me.

After the book was filled, I rose off the bed, slipped my heels back on, and moved to my office. At the computer, I retrieved the e-mail from Michael and reread it several times. I pulled up a blank message, waiting for the words to come. What was I supposed to say?

Answer his question. Tell him he can to talk to me any time.

And that was what I did. I wrote, erased, and rewrote my response more times than I could count until finally I could lean back and read it and feel somewhat good about myself.

Then, it was the matter of clicking Send.

One tap of the key would have major consequences.

My finger hovered over the mouse. My heart raced and sweat dampened the back of my neck.

Send the damn e-mail!

I pressed the mouse button and immediately heard the whoosh of the message jetting off into cyberspace. There was no un-ringing this bell.

Rising, I paced in front of the computer, expecting a response from him to pop back almost immediately. The grandfather clock in the hallway ticked while I paced.

When my front doorbell rang, I jumped. For a heart-stopping minute I pictured Michael, as if he had been magically transported to my doorstep. And then reason prevailed and shoved the thought aside.

I had a one o'clock appointment today with Samuel and Debra. According to Debra, they had spoken their dark truths to each other, and all was well. But they wanted to have one final visit with me.

I checked my face in the mirror, wiping away the extra mascara smudged by my crying and checked my hair. I was back in my element. This I understood.

Opening the front door almost with a sense of relief, I greeted the couple with a smile.

Only Debra stood on the stoop. She clutched her purse in hands tucked close to her waistband. Her brown eyes were wide and a bit red like her nose. She had been crying.

"Debra. Are you all right?"

"No. No, I'm not."

I stepped aside so she could enter, feeling no sense of judgment, but rather empathy. Secrets were indeed a powerful force that swept through the strongest of lives.

She took a seat in my office and set her purse on the table. "I can see the *I told you so* in your expression."

Unexpected hints of pity flickered like bird wings in my chest. "Would you like coffee?"

"Can you put some whiskey in it?"

"Not if you're driving." Normally I did not invite clients into the kitchen, but I beckoned her down the hallway. Glad to follow, she wanted someone right now to tell her exactly what she should do so she did not have to think.

"I drove."

"Then plain coffee it is."

She sat quietly as I made the pot and set out cups, milk, and sugar. "You were right," she said, after she took the first sip of coffee.

"How was I right?"

"Samuel showed me his piece of paper. He was almost proud to share his deepest, darkest secret." She pinched the bridge of her nose. "Do you know what it was?"

"It's not relevant."

"Oh, but it is. His secret was that he streaked at a college football game on a drunken dare. She shook her head. "My God, if streaking counts as a sin, then I'm burning in hell, twice."

She tapped the side of her coffee mug with her fingertip. There were times I should weigh in on a conversation, and other times it was best to let the silence coax out the words. This time I let the silence do the heavy lifting.

"His next question, of course, was to ask me for my secret. He must have thought it was along the lines of jaywalking or trespassing." Her eyes filled with tears. "It was much, much worse than any of that." A tear fell and she wiped it away. "I don't think I can even tell you."

I thought about my own secret and how very carefully I guarded it. "I don't expect you to. The exercise was meant to pull you two together. It was about ensuring that you two were completely honest with each other."

A bitter laugh rumbled in her chest. "I grew up believing that honesty was not necessarily the best policy. No good deed goes unpunished."

It had been a long time since I had met someone as guarded as me, I realized I was staring at a version of myself. Like Debra, I had so many locks guarding my secret, but no keys.

"What happened?" I asked.

"I tried to make light of it. I told him the past didn't matter. At first, he agreed, but as the hours and days passed, he became more curious. He kept asking. Kept pushing. And the harder he pulled and prodded, the more closed and resentful I became."

"Perhaps if you told him the truth he would understand?"

"If I promise to call a cab, will you pour me a stiff drink?"

"That won't help. It only masks and delays."

"I'm fine with that right now. I want this stabbing pain in my chest to stop."

"Be careful what you wish for." Then, before she could respond, I said, "It's better to acknowledge and work through the pain. Don't push it away."

"You're always so calm and cool. How do you do it?"

An hour ago, raw sadness had cut and scraped against my insides. "I don't matter here. You do."

She sipped her coffee. "Well, my story doesn't have a happy ending. I couldn't tell Samuel the truth and he became incensed. He said if we couldn't be honest, we shouldn't get married. We're over."

"Your life is not over."

"The life I thought I had with Samuel certainly is."

"Perhaps. Or maybe he'll cool off and understand that he must allow you to tell your story in your own time."

"And when I do, he'll really hate me."

"You don't know that."

"The hell I don't." A sigh shuddered through her. "I really do love him. I know you said what we had was mostly hormonal, but I love Samuel."

"But you aren't being honest with him, Debra."

She looked up at me with eyes filled with pain, sorrow, and failure as she wiped her nose on a tissue.

"I'm not judging you, Debra."

"It sure feels like it."

"I promise, I'm not."

"I love him so much that I can't bear to see the pain in his eyes when he looks at me."

"You're so sure?"

I thought about Zeb and how devoted he was to Eric. What would Zeb think of me if I told him I had a son and gave him away? Would he still look at me with kindness? Somehow, I doubted he would ever fully accept me. And that thought troubled me far more than it should.

"Yes, I'm sure."

Tears pooled in her eyes and spilled freely. The marble counter stood between us for an awkward moment. I am not sure what prompted me to walk around the counter, but I did, and wrapped my arms around her. Immediately, she wept, clinging to me like I was her last friend.

An hour ago, emotion had overwhelmed me. And now, as sobs racked through Debra's body, I could only stand stiffly, on guard against my own emotions. The mythical Pandora had opened her box and invited sin and sorrow into the world. There was no sign of hope.

I had been lucky so far. But was it the calm before the storm? I had regained control, but what would happen when Michael returned my e-mail?

A Letter from Patience

SEPTEMBER 1, 1753

Dearest Mother,

My unborn child is due near New Year. Faith and Mr. McDonald pray for a boy, but I do not. A girl would be nice and then I would have a son and a daughter. Mother think of it. Two healthy children? Dare I hope for such a miracle? Faith continues to dote on Patrick, and he is content to be in her company. I don't enjoy these moments, but there is little I can do about it.

Yours Faithfully,
Patience McDonald,

Chapter Nine

LISA, FRIDAY, OCTOBER 7, 2011

More than three months had passed since I settled my bellows camera on its tripod and took a picture. That was the very day I received word of Amelia's Alzheimer's diagnosis from Mr. Colin West and began the long drive back to Alexandria.

At first, it was easy to justify my absence from the camera. I was too busy with Amelia. There was the basement cleanup to coordinate. There was always a handy excuse to find.

But this morning, none of those excuses had merit. I did my best to revive any reason that would justify me not working, but my efforts fell flat. I watched Charlie as he devoured another chew stick. "What do you think, boy? Too overcast outside?"

Use the basement.

"The basement has dark walls and no light."

Get a lamp.

"I don't like the basement's energy. It's too heavy and dark."

Jesus, stop stalling!

All the excuses were lame, and I knew it.

Of course, I could have used my digital camera, which captured the sunflowers so beautifully. But though the end product was lovely, I craved the hands-on challenge of the glass negatives. The bellows camera satisfied a need in me that nothing, including booze, ever did.

After spending a disjointed and confused morning with Amelia, I decided to use the bellows camera to capture the Prince Street house. She had majestically stood here well over centuries and deserved to be not only acknowledged, but especially remembered.

Perhaps I could create a collection of prints and decorate Amelia's hospital room with them. Maybe the pictures would help jog her memory by letting her know that her home was never far away.

Charlie watched me from his dog bed in the corner of the kitchen as I screwed up my courage and went to Amelia's basement where I stored all my supplies.

The bellows camera stood in the center of the room on its tripod, covered with canvas. Gently, I closed the three legs of the tripod and carried the sixty-pound camera up the stairs. I left it in the entryway, and I made several more trips to collect all the chemicals and blank cut squares of glass that would soon join together to create the camera's negative.

When all my supplies were in the foyer, I opened the front door. Charlie rose from his bed, his chew stick casually dangling like a lit cigarette, and he followed me to the front porch where he sat down. The clouds were gone, and the sun shone brightly, creating all kinds of spectacular contrast on the tree-lined street. The bricks and wrought iron of all the houses along this street, known to all as Captain's Row, were beautifully textured and vivid.

The dog, content to bask in the warm sun, settled as I moved to the street and studied the house. It took me a half hour to decide if I wanted to angle the camera directly toward the old home or turn it slightly toward the river. Without the Potomac, there would be no house. The river it was. The view from Prince Street showed Old Town Alexandria at its very best.

Deciding the best vantage point lay in the middle of the street, I glanced up the ribbon of cobblestones, wondering how much time I had before a car drove past or a neighbor or tourist wandered down the brick sidewalk. I could not simply set up the camera and then process the negatives without fear of my camera ending up as roadkill.

Initially, all I could do was sit on the front stoop with Charlie, absently rubbing his head, as I waited for a parking spot to open. As several cars pulled away, I set out orange cones to reserve the spots while I ran around the block, got my SUV, and parked in the center of the street, inches out of camera view. Charlie watched with mild interest as I turned on my emergency flashers and then opened the back of my SUV and laid out the bottles and trays that would hold my processing chemicals.

If someone attempted to drive down Prince Street, they would be forced to stop and wait until I moved my car. Not ideal. Maybe a little inconsiderate. But the images I would create would make up for it, and then some.

I hurried over to Charlie and tugged his collar. "Come on, boy, I'm putting you in my car for a few minutes." The dog looked up at me. "Ride in the car?"

His tail wagged and he followed, happy to jump into the front passenger seat. I turned on the engine, cranked the AC. "Be right back, Charlie."

The first step of the development process required that I pour collodion, an alcohol-acid mixture, onto a piece of black glass. It took skill to coat the glass up to each of its edges without spilling the excess. Satisfied the glass was fully covered, I tipped the edge and poured the excess back into the bottle.

Next, I dunked the plate into a black tank that was filled with silver nitrate for five minutes, which made the silver sensitive to light. Once it was dry, I loaded the glass negative into a metal case that fit into the camera.

With a negative clicked into place, I picked up the camera along with a cone and moved to the middle of the street. After setting the cone behind my car, I adjusted each of the tripod's legs until the camera was steady.

I lifted the black flap that covered the ten-by-ten-inch viewfinder and looked past the camera to the grand old house.

A Smyth had built the house in the eighteenth century, but the property subsequently fell out of the family's hands. When Amelia was a young woman, her father, Sam Smyth who made a fortune in the railroad business, repurchased the house. When my grandfather died, he left it to my father, not Amelia. When the house passed to me from my father's estate, I deeded it to Amelia. It never occurred to me at the time that my grandfather had slighted his only daughter. He left the house to the son he considered a real Smyth. However, Amelia had never spoken a word of anger or disappointment to me. She graciously accepted the house, swearing that at her passing it would revert to me.

I moved to the side of the camera and focused the edge of the lens. I had found my camera at the estate sale of a photographer who lived his last forty years in Roanoke, Virginia. I was traveling with my mom to one of her class reunions when we stopped to grab lunch. The camera was perched in the window of the antique store across the street from the restaurant. Immediately, I was drawn to it and made an offer before I asked my mom's permission. When the store owner sealed the deal, I did some serious begging with Mom, trading the next two birthday, Christmas, and graduation gifts for my latest fascination. She had been sick then, guarding her secret closely, and agreed without much hesitation.

I found out from the store owner that the camera's lens dated back to 1849, predating wet-plate photography by two years. The lens, originally used for daguerreotypes, captured the images of young men attending Virginia Military Institute in Lexington, and later the ravages of the Civil War and the Reconstruction Era. To date, this lens had captured over a century and a half worth of history. If only it could talk.

Glancing to my left and right for traffic, I ducked under the black cape and reached for the slide lever, which opened the viewfinder. When I was sure I had the right view of Prince Street in my sight, I reached around and pulled the cap off the lens.

I slid out from under the cape and checked my watch. Five minutes in this sunlight would do nicely.

Two minutes passed when a black BMW pulled onto Prince Street and stopped a dozen feet behind the SUV. Its dark exterior's polish caught the light, glinting like a black diamond. The driver's sunglasses obscured his face as he shut off his car and got out. Bracing for an earful, I noted that the driver was tall and lean and wore a dark tailored suit, cut to fit his wide shoulders and trim body. A white shirt set off a red tie. He removed his shades, revealing an angled face framed by short black hair brushed back. He moved with a clipped, annoyed gait. Mr. Colin West, aka Mr. Stiff and Proper.

"You're in the middle of the street," he said.

"You're very observant."

Mr. West was in his late thirties, but some would say he was an old soul. He was not exactly handsome, but the sharp angles on his face and the gray feathering through his hair would have translated nicely into a photograph. Lots of contrast and shadows.

"Here comes trouble," Jennifer whispered close to my ear.

"Don't you think you should move?"

So many smartass comments sprang to mind. So many.

But I let them go, accepting that a pissing match with Jennifer or Mr. West required more energy than I was willing to spare. “I need about three minutes.” Smiling, I fumbled with my watch, willing time to go faster. Waiting and patience had never been my forte. I hoped a few minutes would not signal the end of the world for him. “Why are you here, Mr. West?”

He cocked his head, studying me for any hints of delusion. “I came to discuss selling the house.” He looked toward the car. “Charlie is not in the picture?”

The dog’s ears perked, and he rose, wagging his tail as he barked. Mr. West walked to the car and tapped on the window with a smile. The dog barked again.

Mr. West had a genuine affection for the dog. “He’s looking good. You still feeding him table scraps?”

“Charlie has a taste for the finer things in life.”

“That’s not good for him.”

The dog barked at Colin, and the pure adoration in the pup’s gaze annoyed me just a little. I had been the one taking care of him for almost three months now and as soon as Mr. West arrived, I was invisible.

“Traitor,” I mumbled. Glancing at my watch, I didn’t budge, but inside, a cold knot formed as I wrestled with the sale of the house.

He straightened as the dog settled back on the car seat. “I thought you’d have it on the market by now.”

Photographers were generally introverts and liked remaining unnoticed. They were the observers. The visual scribes. “I know I should be calling agents and getting the process rolling, but I’ve been busy with Amelia.”

“If you need an agent, I have a suggestion.”

“Really?”

He took in my Birkenstocks, knee-length jean shorts stained with photo chemicals, pink tie-dye T-shirt, and ruler-straight blond hair twisted into a ponytail. For whatever reason, I was thankful I had at least showered and shaved my legs this morning. The sight of me, I suspected, confirmed his expectations of an itinerant starving artist squatting in the house.

"Our firm has used this particular agent several times. She's highly recommended."

"That's great. I have no idea where to start. If you text me her information, I'll call her."

"He's hot in a Men in Black *kind of way. Not your type, but then again, your type isn't much to write home about."* Jennifer was officially annoying as hell. I smiled, wondering how to elbow aside a voice inside my own head.

He shifted his attention to the camera. "This is the camera that Amelia talked so much about. She's very proud of your work."

Amelia was always encouraging, but I assumed that came with the family-must-be-supportive package. Interesting that she talked to others about me. "I know this looks a bit quirky and cumbersome, but it creates a striking image when I'm on my game."

He moved closer, bringing with him the faint scent of an expensive aftershave. "Amelia said you've had a good bit of artistic success."

A cloud crossed in front of the sun, dimming the light a fraction. The dimming light meant I would need more exposure time. A minute, maybe two. More time with Mr. West. "I've won some awards, but I have yet to cash those wins into a living wage. I'm your classic starving artist." I had used the last bit of prize money to buy my SUV that had more than once doubled as a home and a studio.

"She says you travel around a lot."

"I'm about capturing the images, and as much as I'd like them to come to me, they have not cooperated."

"How long is the total exposure for a photograph?"

I looked up at the clouds, sensing they carried more rain. "Depends on the light. Take today, for example. I first thought I'd need about three minutes, but I'm thinking now it will take every bit of twice that or seven minutes." I pointed toward the sky.

"How do you know when it's enough?"

"I don't, exactly. It's as much art as science with these old cameras. Over time, you develop a feel."

He scanned the street, checking to see if we had blocked traffic yet. No one was waiting on us. He worried about the details. "Amelia showed me a couple of your earlier works. Very nice."

"The prints in the house. I took those in Utah. I call that my Ansel Adams phase." I slid my hands into my pockets.

Until now, Colin West and I had only traded e-mails. His responses were curt with no wasted words. *Amelia is ill. Suggest you return to Alexandria. Matters to discuss.* My responses were as brief. *On my way.*

"I saw Amelia yesterday," he said. "She was sleeping."

"She's sleeping more each day."

"The nurses tell me you're there every day, but we seem to keep missing each other."

"If she's asleep, I don't stay long," I said. "And I mix up the times of my visits. Keeps the staff on their toes."

A smile tweaked the edge of his lips. "Unexpected is a good thing."

"So cute." Jennifer giggled.

"You said you had the name of a realtor?"

"Yes. Her name is Rebecca Tuttle. I can have her here tonight if you're free."

"Is there a rush?"

His mood shifted, signaling that the obligatory time for polite conversation had ended. "It requires money to keep her in assisted living. And the only source is the house."

"I thought she was set financially."

"I thought she was too until I opened her files late yesterday and started reading. When she accepted ownership of the house, she had to refinance it with a home equity loan to cover some of the renovations and her living needs. She's managed it all until now, but there's not enough capital to keep up the house and care for her."

Bracelets rattled on my wrist as I pushed a stray strand of hair out of my face. "Debt. My father racked up quite a bit of it."

"It looks like he used the house as collateral against loans that mostly remained outstanding when Amelia agreed to live there."

"Amelia never told me the house was so leveraged."

"She thought if she could keep the house in the family and in good condition, you would eventually have enough equity in it to pay off the loans and sell it for a tidy profit...if you wanted to leave Alexandria.

"I never wanted this house. I told her that."

"How old were you when you told her?"

"Seventeen."

"She likely didn't think you knew your own mind."

"I did."

He remained silent for a moment. "This house has a ballpark value of $1.2 million dollars and just over seven hundred thousand worth of debt against it. You should clear over four hundred thousand after fees but before taxes. I can help you with the taxes."

"Jesus, Amelia has less money than I originally thought."

"Five years ago, she did a major, but necessary renovation on the house, which was financed against the equity."

"I never understood why she wanted to fix this place up."

"She knew one day this house would be yours and she wanted it in better shape than when she got it."

"I never asked her why," I said, more to myself.

He pushed his hand into his pocket and rattled some change. "But if you sell the house now and settle the outstanding liens, she'll have enough for five or six years of expenses."

"What prompted you to look into her finances?"

"I'm her attorney, and I always want to know what my client's risk is."

I pinched the bridge of my nose. "Mr. West, she may outlive her money."

"Sadly, I see this quite a bit."

Frustration sparred with anger. "You're not making my day, sir. Not at all."

"Better to know the bad news sooner than later."

"I agree."

Panic tugged at my sleeve, but I shooed it away. A few bottles of wine would not help the situation, but Lord did it tempt. But I did not need guilt ladled on top of fear and worry.

"Hey, what happens to me if you leave the house?" the voice whispered.

The house somehow looked different than it had moments ago through the viewfinder. "It's stood for centuries but may be lost by the Smyth family for good this time."

He stared at me for a long moment. "I anticipate a solid bid in a matter of weeks given the location and its condition. Where will you go?"

"I'll manage. Sell it as quickly as you can."

"And Charlie?"

"Charlie will be fine with me. Sell it."

"It's been in your family for years. You have no attachment to it?"

"I do, but I have to be practical." My shirt smelled of

chemicals, my hair needed washing, and I could use a manicure. "Besides, do I look like the lady-of-the-house type?"

"I'll tell the agent to come by tonight."

"Thanks. Give me a time, and I'll be here." I wished I could control this mess as easily as I could my negatives. "Have you any more news for me, Mr. West? Fire, plague, or famine?"

West simply smiled as he seemed to size her up.

The problem of Amelia had morphed from crisis management in the beginning to the slow daily grind of watching her deteriorate. Amelia had done right by me, and I would now take care of her. I would not panic and drink. I would have to find a way to fix this.

"Why did you drop the baby book off at Amelia's room, Mr. West?"

The abrupt shift in conversation caught him off guard. Clearly, he expected more drama and discussion from me. "She asked me for it. She was having a good day and wanted to show it to you. I assume she did?"

"She did. But how did you get it?"

"She left it with the firm about two years ago. Asked us to keep it safe."

I stepped closer as clouds hovered around the sun. Mentally, I added another minute to the exposure time. "She never asked you to dig into her past."

"No. I offered, but she refused. Said it didn't matter."

The Alzheimer's had stripped away her pretense and exposed raw feelings. She did care. Very much. "I just dropped it off with a local historian who is digging into the history behind it."

"Did you know she was adopted?" he asked.

I checked my watch, and seeing I had only twenty seconds left of exposure time, readied the lens cap. "It was news to me. But it makes sense. She was different from my father."

"How so?"

"She was open. Funny. Never kept secrets." I gently replaced the cap on the camera lens. "Though her finances make me realize she learned how to keep secrets. If you don't mind, I need to keep moving with this negative if I want it to turn out. Seems even more important now than ever that I capture the image."

"Of course, go ahead. Mind if I stay and watch?"

"Not at all." I pulled out the negative cartridge, grateful that Mr. West's car blocked the street, I hurried to the back of the SUV.

He followed in no rush to kept pace with me. "May I ask what you're doing next?"

"I'm pouring developer over the glass plate and then the negative should materialize. You may want to stand back so that this doesn't splash on your suit." I reached for a glass bottle and uncorked it. And then, holding the glass over a shallow bin, I poured the clear liquid onto the exposed glass surface.

The acrid smell rose, but it did not seem to deter Mr. West. He watched with fascination as the liquid developer slowly coaxed out the black-and-white image on the glass. The negative space was light and the positive space dark. It was a view of the house, angled slightly so that portions of the river drifted in at the edge. I was pleased by the contrasts, especially since the sun had run for cover mid-exposure.

"It's backward," he said.

"It will flip around when I actually develop the picture."

"And the streak of white in the upper right corner?"

Frowning, I looked at the glass and then up at the house. "Maybe I didn't disperse the chemicals correctly. I'll know better in the darkroom."

"Your timing is perfect. No cars are blocking the view. It looks like it could have been taken hundreds of years ago."

"In the last six weeks, I've noticed most cars on this side of the street are gone about this time of day. And a few well-placed plastic cones buy me the time I need." I laid the negative on paper towels so it could dry.

"A lot of work for one shot." His deep tone carried with it the question many asked. *Who works so hard for just a moment?*

"That's photography. Lots of waiting and watching and then hoping you finally caught the right image at the perfect time."

"You've been doing this a while?"

"Since I was sixteen."

"Impressive."

"Maybe, or perhaps I'm a little nuts." I shook my head, a laugh catching in my throat. "Who spends this much time on work that pays below minimum wage?"

Instead of answering the question with an answer, he asked, "If you're willing to make an extra print of the house. I'd like to buy it."

"Why?"

"I've always liked this street. This town. And a print of that house would fit nicely into my home."

I imagined a house filled with the sleek and modern, and tried to envision the photo hanging on a white sterile wall. "Sure. I've got all your contact information. Seeing as I might not have a house soon, I'll take a few more pictures and after the realtor leaves, I'll spend tonight in the basement developing several prints."

"Great."

I expected him to leave, but he lingered, watching me prep the next glass negative. His quiet, steady energy had me glancing at his left hand for a wedding band. None. I was intrigued.

It had been a long time since I'd had a man in my bed and

in these few silent moments, I was very aware of his presence. My hands trembled a little as I poured the syrupy collodion onto the next glass plate, which would become a negative. The liquid did not quite make it to all the edges of the glass, but I let it go, accepting that the flaw might add interest to the picture.

"Looks like you missed some portions of the glass. Will that mean it won't develop?"

"Correct, but sometimes there's great beauty in imperfection." I dunked the glass into the tank of silver nitrate. "The process isn't precise, but it's like scratching a lotto ticket. I never know when I'll hit it big."

"I can see it's quite technical." His cell phone rang in his pocket and he pulled it out, frowning as he studied the display. "Excuse me, I have to go. But I'm glad I caught up with you. I'll text you the time when Ms. Tuttle will come by this evening."

"The sooner it's sold, the better."

"You're remarkably calm, Ms. Smyth."

"You just told me I'm about to be evicted, and I may or may not have enough money to care for my aunt. I think you can call me Lisa now."

Colin West grinned. "Well then, you may call me Colin."

I pulled the negative out of the silver nitrate, waved it until it dried, and then inserted it into the antique cartridge. "Cheer up, Colin. One door closes, while another opens."

"I'll talk to you soon."

A Letter from Patience

OCTOBER 4, 1753

Dearest Mother,

The baby stirs in my belly and I still feel full of vigor. Last night, I spied Faith under the full moon speaking in low whispers and I know she again prays to her god that I deliver a boy. I see the way she looks at my son, she believes I will forget all about Patrick if I deliver a boy. He is my child. Mine alone. And if she has issue, there is no one in the colony that will not back me.

Yours Faithfully,
Patience McDonald,

Chapter Ten

RAE, FRIDAY, OCTOBER 7, 2011

I received Margaret McCrae's voice mail message after the last client of the day left my office. Speaking in her customary staccato delivery patterns, she said, "Rae, I've got information about your family and want you to come by the salvage yard this evening at seven, if you can. Thanks." I texted her and told her I was available.

Before leaving, I checked my e-mail one last time in case Michael had responded in the last thirty minutes, and then headed into the city. The drive up the George Washington Parkway was always pretty this time of day. With the sun hugging the horizon, the treetops glowed with a delicate orange and the waters of the Potomac River shimmered. Traffic was light—most of the commuters were safely home and sitting down to dinner at this point.

In town, I drove along Union Street and turned left on King Street. With no street parking to be found, I circled the block and eventually found a spot. Once out of the car, I headed straight toward the salvage yard. On the way, I looked up and saw the Union Street Bakery sign. Slowing, I was surprised to see the *Open* sign in the door. From what

Margaret said, the bakery now only maintained storefront hours on Fridays and Saturdays due to their growing online business.

The picture of Baby Michael eating a sugar cookie flashed and made me wonder if any sugar cookies had been baked here. A bone-deep craving took hold. I did not believe it was for something sweet, but a missed moment with my baby.

I stopped at the brightly painted front door. Elbowing aside rational arguments, I pushed open the door and entered. Bells jangled above my head. Immediately, the soft scents of cinnamon and chocolate greeted me with a warm embrace.

The walls were painted a cheerful yellow and decorated with a collection of black-and-white pictures featuring the bakery over the decades. The storefront appeared the same in all, whereas the city around it moved forward with the passing decades. Horse-drawn carriages, women in long skirts. Model T Fords. Fedoras. Tie-dyed shirts and bell bottoms. The bakery had steadfastly stood its ground for nearly a century, a sentinel in a world that hinged on change toward modernization.

Huddled close to the back wall of the bakery was a large spotless glass display case. On its white shelves were two different types of heaven, chocolate chip and sugar cookies. A sign read *Get 'em While They Last.*

A small woman with rosy cheeks and strawberry blond hair tied up in a topknot pushed through a set of saloon doors. She wore jeans and a white shirt under a full length apron that was double knotted at her waist. "Welcome to Union Street Bakery."

Her coloring matched Margaret's and their similarities were clear. Margaret was taller and sturdier, whereas this woman was petite and trimmer. This was Rachel, the widowed sister with two children and an ex-boyfriend from France, who was in need of a good man.

"I'm Rae McDonald," I said.

Her head cocked. "Rae. The lady with all the family papers." She wiped her hands on a towel tucked in her apron before extending her hand over the display case. "I'm Rachel."

Accepting her outstretched hand, I noticed her grip was firm. I thought about Margaret's request on Rachel's behalf. It was doubtful that Rachel knew about this. "Your sister is studying quite a few documents for me."

Rachel hitched her hands on her hips. "And might I say, she's having a ball. Anytime she discovers new details on this city, she's in heaven. I suppose she told you all about the witch bottles."

"I've heard about them. In fact, I'm headed to the salvage yard now to hear her latest update. Margaret sounded very excited on the phone."

"She is, but she won't tell any of us what she's discovered until she tells you first."

"I've never given much thought to my family history, but I'm very intrigued."

"My sister has already left for the salvage yard."

"I know, but I saw your sign in the window and heard good things about the bakery."

"Can I interest you in some cookies?" Rachel asked. "I'm testing new recipes and when I have too many extras, I flip the sign to *Open* for as long as they last. You're in luck because I just put these out."

"What do you have?"

"A very chocolate chip cookie and a sugar cookie made with lemon and polenta. I'm considering both types for the online business. My sister, Daisy, always says I'm throwing too many recipes in the mix, so I thought some informal market research might sway her."

Ah, Daisy. The adopted one. "How about a dozen of the lemon polenta."

"I can do that." She reached for a pink box and lined it with white parchment paper.

"How is the online business?"

"Great." She smiled. "We were hoping it would be an extra source of income, but it has actually surpassed our in-store sales. As a matter of fact, Daisy is out today with a realtor scouting locations for a larger setup outside the city to help meet the growing demand."

"That sounds promising."

"Terrifies me to stretch beyond these walls, but she feels it's a risk worth considering. If she gives the thumbs up, then I'll head out and see the site." Rachel carefully folded the paper over the cookies, closed the flap on the box, and sealed it with a gold sticker.

I reached for my wallet. "How much do I owe you?"

"On the house. You've made Margaret the happiest I've seen in a while, and that's easily worth a box of cookies."

I fished out my wallet. "Thanks, but I'm paying Margaret for her time and expertise."

She waved away the bills I extended toward her. "Believe me, she would have paid you to do the job. Take the cookies. It does my heart good to see her smile and chatter so happily about her work."

Reluctantly, I tucked the bills back in my wallet. "You seem like a very close family."

She laughed. "We're not perfect, but damn close."

Her positive energy and attractive looks made her an easy candidate for a relationship if she were truly open to a union. I decided to drop a line in the water. "Margaret brought by some of your cookies the other day, and I served several when my contractor, Zeb Talbot, came by with his son, Eric. The boy loved the cookies."

Rachel's smile was as warm and genuine as her bakery. "Eric's a great kid. He goes to the same school as my girls."

About the same age. Common interests. Children. Self-employed. Some matches came together with almost no effort. Clearly Rachel and Zeb thought well of each other, so why had they not connected? Could it be both were too busy with their lives and children to go after love? Perhaps it was fear of being hurt? Both were attractive, so the chemistry should not have been an issue. Was it a matter of a nudge or was there a piece of this puzzle I was missing?

"Mr. Talbot did a top-notch job on the renovation of my kitchen a couple of years ago, and he's building a garage for me now."

"The spot of the infamous hearth of stones."

"The very same."

She handed me the box. "So why after all this time, did you decide to remove the hearth?"

"Seemed logical. It was either the hearth or the new addition. There was no other space on the property that made sense."

"Land here is scarce, so I can appreciate the need to put it to use. If we had more, we wouldn't be scouting new locations outside the city."

"I suppose an expansion in town is out of the question."

"Unless we could get into one of the empty warehouses on the river. And then there's the issue of parking. Growing also means more people to hire, and they need to have a place to work and park."

"Sounds like good problems to have."

She tugged at the strings on her apron. "I'm not complaining. Two years ago, I thought we were losing the bakery and was in a panic. Now we're growing by leaps and bounds."

The scramble of little footsteps thundered down a back staircase. My back stiffened slightly, but Rachel took the disruption in stride.

"In seconds you're about to meet the two little tornados that are the center of my life," she said.

No sooner were her last words spoken than two little girls burst through a side door. They were about seven and while one had strawberry-blond hair like her mother, the others was a dark brown. They each wore their long hair in ponytails and were dressed in matching jean shorts, red T-shirts, and sneakers.

The girls didn't notice me as they scrambled toward their mother and elbowed each other for her attention. The child with the dark hair grabbed Rachel's left hand first, but the other was only a split second behind her, tugging on the other.

"Mom!" one shouted. "She's being mean to me."

"Not true!" the other shouted. "I did not call her a bad name."

Over the rumble of an argument that I did not fully follow, Rachel said, "Rae, meet Anna and Ellie. Girls, turn around and say hello to Dr. McDonald."

In unison, they each delivered a high-pitched "Hi" before quickly re-engaging in their squabble.

Rachel shook her head and turned each of the girls around to face me. "Look Dr. McDonald in the eye when you address her."

This time they each looked up with eyes filled with laughter and excitement, and giggled. "Hi, Dr. McDonald." Again, the address came in unison.

"Good evening, ladies," I said.

Whereas Eric had a calm energy, these two children fed off each other. Jennifer and I must have been like these kids because Mom often reached for the aspirin bottle after a long day.

Rachel patted each on the back. "Go upstairs. I'll be there in a minute."

Ellie shook her head. "But Mom, we need to talk to you about our teacher."

"In a minute. Go."

The girls puffed out bottom lips but turned and scurried up the back staircase. Rachel brushed back her bangs with the back of her hand. "My mom raised three girls who were all close in age. I don't know how she did it."

"I have vague memories of Mom needing a nap after a long day with my sister and me."

"I could use one nap. Does your sister live in town?"

Dark emotions shifted in the shadows. "Jennifer died in a car accident when she was seventeen." I had not shared the story in a long time.

Rachel's expression softened before understanding dimmed her brightness. "God, Rae, I should have connected the dots to you and Jennifer McDonald."

Hundreds of people had attended Jennifer's funeral. "It was a long time ago. Life moves on."

"I was a year ahead of Jennifer, but we were both in the cheer squad together. I was dating my late husband, Mike, then and she was dating a boy named Jerry Trice?"

"I haven't heard that name in a long time."

"I hear he moved to California and opened a wine shop," Rachel said. "He made it back to town for a high school reunion. Still looked good."

"I didn't realize Jerry came back to town." After Jennifer's death, Jerry came by the house to visit, but the meeting was awkward and too painful for us both. His connection to us severed with my sister's death.

"He didn't stay long. A day or two and then he had to get back to the West Coast."

"Ah." More emotions rattled below the ice and bumped up against its underside, testing its strength.

Rachel's brows knotted. "Does it bother you when I talk

about her? After my husband, Mike, died, everyone avoided talking about him. They were afraid that mentioning him would upset me, so they ignored him. But forgetting someone only makes it worse."

"I haven't talked much about her in years, so it's nice to hear stories about her. Easy to forget there was a lot of fun in her life."

"Same with Mike."

"You must miss him very much."

"I do. It's been two years and there are still moments when I swear, he's standing right beside me. Moments when I'm laughing, and I want to share. And moments when I'm angry and want to blame him."

Imagining her with Zeb just did not feel right. They made perfect sense as a couple on paper, but now that I had met her, I was not so sure. Perhaps the problem was they were too much alike. No friction to make a spark.

There was someone for her, but his name danced out of reach. It would come to me soon. "Rachel, it's been a pleasure, but I need to hurry along to meet Margaret."

"She'll bust if she has to wait too long." Rachel flashed a smile, but it did not quite hide the sadness. "Don't be a stranger, Rae. I'm glad we got a chance to meet formally."

I extended my hand and she accepted it easily. Her hand was slightly callused, but her touch was gentle. "It was a pleasure," I said. "And I'm certain we'll meet again soon. Good luck with your business."

Rachel crossed her fingers. "From your lips to God's ears." She leaned forward, her eyes dancing with curiosity. "Are you really a matchmaker?"

"No, I'm not. I've made a few introductions that have led to marriages, but it's very informal."

"Your phone must have been ringing off the hook since that article."

"There have been a few inquiries. All are disappointed to find I'm not what they envisioned, but a mere counselor."

Laughing, she shook her head. "Good families begin with good marriages."

"True." Since she had brought the matchmaking up, I said, "Your sister, Margaret, asked me to find a suitor for you."

Her face blushed as her expression warmed with laughter and slight annoyance. "You're kidding?" She shook her head. "You don't kid, do you?"

"I do not."

"Well, don't listen to Margaret. I'm doing fine. My life is complete."

"Margaret never implied it wasn't."

Nervous laughter bubbled. "I might have to strangle her."

"Consider yourself lucky to have a meddling sister like Margaret. Thank you again for the cookies, Rachel."

She weighed my comment against her annoyance. "Sure, Rae."

Outside the shop, I savored the warmth of the evening air as it chased away a chill from my bones. I moved quickly toward the salvage yard, my heels clipping on the slightly uneven brick sidewalk as I made my way past a collection of restaurants and pubs toward the corner of Union and King Streets, the location of Shire Architectural Salvage Company.

The building, like many of its kind in this part of town, was originally a warehouse that stored goods transported in and out of the Alexandria harbor via the Potomac River to the Chesapeake Bay. Faint white-and-red lettering across the top floor read *R & C Dry Goods*.

Through the front display window was an odd collection of items rescued from various homes, churches, and schools within a fifty-mile radius. A church pew occupied the bulk of the display space and on top of a bench set a pair of old brass lanterns, an old bicycle wheel, and stacked cigar boxes. Three stained glass windows that depicted scenes from the Bible leaned casually against the wall. Beside them lay a scattering of brass doorknobs. Above it all hung a trio of industrial lamps casting a warm glow.

As I pushed open the front door, a small bell above announced me. Inside the warehouse the ceiling supported a collection of light fixtures and industrial pendant lights. The front reception area was packed with mantels, windows, and wrought iron fence sections. This hodgepodge of random items should have amounted to chaos, but somehow, among the old and discarded, was a sense of a new beginning.

I did not see anyone at the front counter but heard quite a bit of clanging and banging echoing from the back of the warehouse. Following the sound, I moved deeper into the center aisle, which was stacked with old doors.

"Hello," I said.

Clang. Bang. Clang.

I approached the back of the row slowly. "Hello, Margaret? Addie?"

A shadow shifted and then I saw a woman's figure, silhouetted by the light from a dangling ship captain's lantern. I hesitated and then realized I was not looking at Addie or Margaret, but Lisa Smyth. Standing beside her was Charlie wagging his tail.

Seeing her at the gravesite had been jarring. I knew she was back in town, but seeing her hunched close to Jennifer's gravestone, talking, was reminiscent of teenaged Jennifer and Lisa huddled together, whispering and giggling. In those days, I wanted so much to be included, but interruptions were always met with them shooing me away like an annoying fly. They always kept me at arm's distance.

Unlike all their relaxed chatter in high school, I could see this conversation was not easy. Whatever Lisa had been saying was painful, judging from her white-knuckled fist and unshed tears. Only Jennifer and Lisa were in the car at the moment of impact. Only Lisa knew the last words my sister spoke. She saw it all.

The difference between Lisa's life and Jennifer's death was a seat belt. Lisa wore hers. Jennifer had not. Mom had cautioned her about this, but Jennifer had clung to her tiny rebellion.

Did it bother Lisa that she had been wearing a seat belt and Jennifer had not? Was she forever replaying their last words, wondering if she had changed one syllable or one phrase, the entire sequence of events could have been changed? I had certainly played that game many times. If only I had told Mom that the girls were leaving. If only.

Too many *what ifs* always led to Jennifer's life being spared and the boy never being born. As much as I wanted my sister spared, I could never, would never, wish the boy away. I never rewrote his birth, only the moment I'd laid him in Susan's arms and said good-bye.

"Lisa," I said. "I didn't realize you were here tonight."

She flinched, not expecting the sound of my voice, and rose from a bin filled with random junk. Charlie barked as she slid her hands into the front pockets of her jeans, and a tentative, if not apologetic smile tweaked the edges of her lips. "Margaret called me. I rescheduled for Saturday."

"Stands to reason we'd both be summoned. Our families have crossed paths for centuries."

"What're you doing back here rooting in the junk bin?"

"I was milling around when I found this box." She shoved aside a few more odd items and removed a midsized wooden box. Charlie yawned. "There are glass negatives in here."

"Glass?"

"Taken by me when I was in high school. Addie and Margaret must have taken them when they cleaned out Amelia's basement." She set the box on the floor and pulled out one sheet of five-by-five glass. Holding it up to the lantern light, she inspected it. "I took these the summer between my junior and senior years."

"Perhaps you could develop them."

"I might." Lisa gently set the negative back in its box. Hefting it in both arms, she blew a stray curl from her eyes. "Can't wait to hear what Margaret has to say."

"I'm fascinated as well. There was a time when history bored me."

"And now?"

"I don't know," Lisa said. "It may have relevance."

"I'm not fond of the past. Half the time it's an albatross around my neck."

"We're not talking about witch bottles, are we?" I asked.

"No." She dropped her voice a notch and pulled in a breath. "Rae, you and I have never talked about Jennifer. And we need to."

I tightened my hold on the cookie box. "Now is not really the time."

Lisa struggled with the box of negatives as if juggling the weight of the past. "There will never be a good time."

Lisa wanted to share her burden with me. "I don't know what there is to say."

She swallowed. "You never asked me about the accident."

"Jennifer's dead, Lisa. She's gone. What is there to discuss?"

"Are you crazy? There's so much that has never been said." Realizing her voice rose, she drew in a breath. "Don't you want to know about that last day? What we were talking about in the car? Why we wrecked?"

Ice around my heart cracked under her heated words, driving me deeper within so that I could shore up my defenses. "I came here to talk about Margaret's discovery, Lisa. That's the only history lesson I care to learn right now."

Tears glistened before she blinked. "I owe you a confession."

Holding up a hand, I stiffened. "Don't do this."

"I think it could be healing."

"Maybe for you. I'm fine."

"You're wrong," Lisa said.

"I heard along the way that you joined AA and I'm glad for you. I know facing the past is part of your process, but I'll not be a part of your atonement." The sharp edges of each word surprised me.

"That's bullshit and we both know it." Charlie's ears flattened.

"I'm not doing this now."

She readied to fire back when we heard voices mingling with footsteps. Seconds later, Margaret and Addie appeared, and I was truly grateful.

"Margaret," I said, clearing my throat. "I understand you have news for us."

"You bet I do!" Margaret rubbed her palms together.

Addie rolled her eyes. "She's about to burst. I've never seen her so excited."

Lisa set her box on the counter. "Addie, I want to buy these negatives."

"Those came from your basement. I can't charge you for those."

Lisa fished in her front pocket and pulled out two rumpled twenties. "I gave it all away, fair and square."

"No, keep the negatives," Addie said. "I really do insist."

"I pay my debts," Lisa said.

"Fine. Take a picture of Margaret and me some time. We'll hang it out front. That would be fun."

"Done."

"Now that that's settled, let me tell you about tonight's main attraction." Margaret's grin was electric and held a satisfaction that came with solving a difficult puzzle. "I have pieced together the story of three women who arrived in Alexandria circa 1749. Why don't we go upstairs? Addie has coffee."

I held up the box of cookies. "I stopped at the bakery. Your sister had the doors open because she's selling some of her test-kitchen creations."

Margaret's eyes widened with excitement. "Tell me you bought the lemon polenta. OMG. So good. She's been tweaking that recipe for days. It's perfect, but she keeps playing with it and somehow making it better. My ass is going to be the size of a barn if her baking skills get any better."

Addie laughed. "Inside thought, Margaret."

"I know." Margaret shrugged. "Please, you all know there's no filter between my brain and mouth.

Lisa accepted Margaret's self-deprecation as a moment to regroup and find an easy smile short of genuine. "I like the honesty. It's refreshing."

Margaret crossed her arms and glanced at Addie. "See. Refreshing. I'm refreshing."

"So is a bucket of ice water, Margaret," Addie countered.

As Margaret laughed, I found her openness as endearing as it was frightening. What would it be like to embrace such honesty? "I'm anxious to hear your story, Margaret."

"Good. Let's do this."

"We started up a side staircase that led to a second-floor apartment where Addie, her aunt Grace, and baby Carrie lived. The living room space was large, with a large hearth capped with an ornate marble mantel that sported a collection of pictures ranging from the very recent digital to grainy black-and-whites that spanned over a hundred years. The room was furnished with an assortment of furniture that, like all the other pieces in this space, was enjoying a second chance. There was an overstuffed club chair covered with a dark quilt, a Victorian sofa, a stone coffee table that had once been a miller's stone, and a well-worn oriental carpet with wear patterns that left it faded and thin in spots.

"I've got coffee and beer," Addie said.

"Both pair really nicely with the cookies," Margaret said. "Beer for me."

"Coffee works for me," Lisa said.

I handed the box of cookies to Addie and she led us to the kitchen. More vintage: an oval table trimmed in chrome and surrounded by four chairs with red seat covers; a refrigerator with rounded edges and a long silver latch; dented, well-used pots and pans hanging from a rack next to cabinets from various homes and eras, all pieced together in an eclectic way that was charming.

The silver coffeepot did not drip but perked its brew into a clear glass dome, signaling that it was ready. Circled around the pot were four mismatched mugs.

Margaret scooped up a cookie. "Is it rude for us to serve beer with you here? And should we keep it on the down low that you attended AA with Janet?"

Lisa sipped her coffee. "Beer's fine, but some folks don't want others to know about their meetings."

"So, you're okay talking about this," Addie said. "I'm always relieved to hear when Janet attends."

"Good. Encourage her to talk," Lisa said. "I talk about my experiences at the meetings to anyone who appears interested. You never know who's listening and might benefit from my experiences."

"That's good." Addie fished a platter from the cabinet and arranged the cookies in a neat circle. "Better get started. Carrie is down for the night. That gives us plenty of time."

I accepted a Nationals Baseball Team cup and declined cream and sugar. "I understand she's your sister's child."

"We're working with a lawyer now. I'm formally adopting her." She handed Lisa a cup of coffee that sported an American flag with thirteen stars and *1976 Bicentennial* written on the side.

"Does she have much contact with the baby?" I asked.

"She comes by about once a week and holds her for a short visit. She loves Carrie, but the day-to-day responsibilities are too much. She struggles daily with mental illness and is working to keep herself balanced."

I couldn't help but sympathize with Janet. Although unable to care for her child, she had given Carrie a promising life by laying her in the arms of a caring mother. I hoped Michael would also understand my decision one day.

Margaret reached beside her seat to a backpack from which she pulled out a tattered notebook covered with flower stickers, endless notes, and scribbles in all colors of ink. She flipped through the pages until she was almost to the end. "Thanks to Rae, I was able to piece together the connected lives of our three ancestors. Lisa is descended through Imogen Smyth. Rae is a direct descendant of Patience McDonald, and Addie is descended from Sarah Shire Goodwin on her mother's side and on her father's side through Faith Shire."

Addie paused as she raised the cookie to her lips and grinned. "My descendants are kissing cousins? That can't be good."

"Your mother and father were third cousins. Perfectly acceptable in the world of healthy genetics, but each did come from the same line of mad Shires that hailed from Aberdeen. Sarah and Faith were half-sisters." Margaret peered over her glasses. "Seems Daddy Shire had a dalliance with a local widow, who birthed Faith. Faith, born out of wedlock, lived on the fringes in Aberdeen until she was in her late twenties. She was described as a beautiful woman with red hair, and from what I can gather, was very outspoken. Around 1747, she was put on trial and convicted of witchcraft in Aberdeen. She was sentenced to indentureship in Virginia."

"I still can't believe they would send a woman here on such bogus charges," Addie said.

"They could and they did," Margaret said. "She was said to be pretty and that would have caught the attention of many an older man. She could have served her time in a Scottish prison, but I wouldn't be surprised if the unscrupulous traders who trolled the prisons for new indentured servants didn't cut a deal somewhere along the way to commute her sentence in exchange for indentureship in the colonies."

Lisa sipped her coffee. "Collecting the downtrodden and ferrying them into indentureship is a soulless job."

Margaret tapped the table in front of Lisa. "As a matter of fact, it was Captain Cyrus Smyth and his young wife, Imogen, who did this very work."

"How would you know that?" Lisa asked.

"Because Imogen confessed it to Patience. Imogen told Patience that Faith was cargo held in the hull during the voyage that brought Imogen to the Virginia colony." Margaret retrieved a stack of copied letters. "These are the letters that Patience McDonald wrote to her mother, but she never mailed the letters because her mother was already dead."

"Wow," Lisa said.

"Imogen was only twelve when the captain first met her. She was not as highborn as she pretended but very beautiful. He married her when she turned fifteen, and she set about putting distance between herself and her old life."

Lisa tapped a finger against the side of her cup. "Reinvention is not a crime."

"No, it's not. Neither was spiriting people away to the New World. But the lengths Imogen and Cyrus Smyth went to so that he could fill the hull of his ship was shameful. She mentioned taking women and children from the streets. Of luring men onto the ships with the promise of ale and bread. A cunning woman."

"So," Addie said. "Imogen ends up in a town recognizing Faith, a woman who could expose her sordid past."

"That's exactly right. And I would bet her best solution was to discredit Faith as mad, or better yet, accuse her of witchcraft," Margaret said. "Discredit Faith and neutralize her as a threat. Although, I think Imogen Smyth believed in witchcraft. Otherwise she'd have not gone to such lengths to create the bottles."

"How could three bottles make such a difference in our histories?" I asked.

"Basically, the charges of witchcraft drove Faith out of Alexandria," Margaret said. "Until I read your letters, I didn't know what happened to her. There were no more public records about Faith. I knew her son, Marcus, did well for himself in later years but never knew what became of Faith and her son, Cullen. Reportedly, she was buried in the Christ Church cemetery in 1783, but Cullen vanished."

"And now you do know?" I asked.

"Now I know she moved to the McDonald farm with her twin sons soon after Ben Talbot died. She lived on the farm for over three decades until her death."

"Didn't she start off with the McDonalds, but they eventually sent her away?" Addie asked again.

"You're correct."

"So then why allow her back?" Addie asked.

Margaret spoke about the possibility that the McDonalds lost a third infant son just days before Faith arrived with her twin sons. "Later, records only mention one of Faith's sons. The logical conclusion is one of Faith's babies died. That happened all the time. But."

We all watched as she reached for her coffee and took a deliberately long sip and a bite of cookie for effect.

"And thumbs up to Rae's collection of letters for this theory I'm about to share. The McDonalds actually lost each of their first three sons who died before the age of one."

"That doesn't make sense," Addie said. "Who sired the McDonald line? It didn't die out."

Margaret hesitated, savoring the secret she was about to share. "I believe Faith relinquished, under duress, one of her twins to the McDonalds." Margaret reached for an envelope and pulled out a copy of two old paintings. "This is Patrick McDonald, the only male child of Patience's to survive to adulthood. The other is a portrait of Hanna McDonald Dowd, the McDonalds only surviving daughter."

We all saw a dour-faced man in his mid-thirties with pale reddish hair and green eyes. Gazes then shifted to the daughter's dark hair and brown eyes.

"The two don't look anything alike," I said. "But that's hardly irrefutable proof."

Margaret leaned forward, her eyes glistening while pulling another document from her folder. "This is a portrait of Marcus Shire." Marcus and Patrick shared the same lightly colored eyes. Although Patrick's hair and skin tones were lighter than Marcus's, the resemblance was uncanny. "Granted, these are paintings, but come on, guys. Not identical twins, but definitely brothers."

"Do you believe they knew?" I asked.

"I'd say they did. Neither spoke of a connection, but the next couple of generations of the Shires and McDonalds were close. They had quite a few business ties."

"But there's no way of proving it," I said.

"In my backpack I have three genetic testing kits. They simply involve a cheek swab. I have a lab friend who will test the samples for free. I bet we find markers linking at least Addie and Rae."

"Then why run mine?" Lisa asked. "It's a waste of time."

Margaret shook her head as she nibbled a second cookie.

You never know what will shake out. And what could it hurt?"

"Which brings us back to the bottles," I said. "Why did the good ladies of Alexandria construct the bottles?"

"Because they were deeply afraid of Faith and her powers."

"They really thought she was a witch?" I understood that one person's fear could infect an entire group. "Or perhaps they were afraid she would talk."

Margaret leaned back in her chair and held up an index finger. "Faith had the potential to cause problems for all three women, so it was easy to convince themselves she was a witch. They gathered in secret, cast protection spells, and declared their wishes."

"Unfortunately, their wishes were curses," Addie said. "Sarah wished to be free of her sister, but for generations, Shire women have been bound to sisters stricken with the curse of madness."

"You don't believe that," I said.

"I can't speak for the entire bloodline," Addie said. "But I'll spot you heavy odds that I'm right."

"When Addie's bottle broke, we found a scroll inside encased in candle wax," Margaret said. "Sarah was afraid the world would know Faith was her sister."

"Do the other bottles have scrolls?" Lisa asked.

"Based on x-rays, I think they do. I can't read the other two scrolls without breaking the seal. Otherwise I could tell you what your ancestors wished for themselves."

"I suppose Imogen wished her secret would stay a secret," Lisa said softly to herself.

I could imagine Patience McDonald's wish after witnessing the death of so many children. The agony must have been unbearable. Was it a wonder the women in my family wished to distance themselves from their secrets?

"Should we break the bottles and see what the scrolls say?" I asked.

Margaret held up her hands. "As curious as I am, absolutely not. Breaking them would not be good. They're so valuable because they're intact."

"What are you proposing, Margaret?" I asked.

"I'd like to do an exhibit in town and give a lecture on the families. You've provided so much detail. And the DNA swabs would prove or disprove my theory about Patience McDonald's son. It's all a very fascinating story."

We were tugging at the threads of so many secrets and memories that had remained undisturbed, much like their relatives resting in their graves. Lisa looked at me, and for a moment, I tensed. She was one of the very few people who knew about the boy. Would she blurt out my secret tonight?

There were so many reasons to shut all this down now and simply forget about the McDonald family history. But they were all trumped soundly by the boy.

I held out an open palm toward Margaret. "I'll do it. Give me the swab."

Grinning, Margaret fished out a swab and handed it to me. "This is awesome. You won't regret this, Rae."

I read the instructions and, tearing open the package, swiped the inside of my cheek. This might be a fascinating tidbit for Michael. I then sealed the swab and handed it back to Margaret.

Lisa shrugged. "What the hell. Why not?" She repeated the process and gave her sample to Margaret.

Addie swabbed her cheek and gave the swab to Margaret.

"I'll send this off immediately." Margaret placed the three samples in a padded envelope. "This may be the way to solve the mystery of the missing twin. And who knows, this might help confirm Amelia's birth parents."

"Amelia?" Addie asked.

"My aunt," Lisa said. "She's in a nursing home here in town. She believes her birth father was a McDonald. If I swab her cheek, we could determine if she's related to Rae."

Margaret fished out a fourth test kit and handed it to Lisa. "Have at it."

"You carry spares?" Lisa asked.

"I know you're doing a family search for Amelia," Margaret said with a sly grin.

Lisa accepted the swab. "I'll visit Amelia in the morning."

Addie shook her head. "I'm confused. Lisa's Aunt Amelia is really Rae's aunt?"

I nodded. "Amelia's biological father was Jeffrey McDonald. His younger brother, Stuart, would have been my great uncle. And my mother, Diane, is Amelia's half-sister."

Addie shook her head. "So, that would make Rae and Lisa ...what?"

"Lisa and Rae are connected but it's by adoption and not biological," Margaret said. "Addie and I have completed the job at the church and processed what we salvaged, so I have a day to figure Fiona's story. Digging back seventy-five years has got to be easier than going back to colonial America."

"Famous last words," Addie said.

I left Lisa, Margaret, and Addie at the warehouse and headed home, but as I approached my turn, I felt a tug. Something in me said I needed to see Amelia immediately.

As I pulled into a parking spot, a quick check of my watch told me I had a half hour left before visiting hours ended. Grabbing my purse, I moved across the parking lot. Air-conditioning chilled my skin as I walked through the automatic doors and held up my identification to the front desk nurse.

"Dr. McDonald," the nurse said. "It's been a couple of weeks."

"How's Amelia doing today?"

"Comes and goes."

"May I go in?"

"Certainly."

"Thank you." I slowly walked to Amelia's room thinking about what Margaret had said earlier.

Her door was slightly ajar, allowing a trickle of light into the hallway as I knocked gently. When I heard no answer, I slowly pushed open the door. Amelia was not in her bed but sitting in a chair by the window that overlooked the parking lot. The clouds were thick again, blocking the moon and the stars. The only illumination came from two large lamps that cast light on the few remaining cars and the thin ribbon of woods separating this property from a shopping mall.

I hesitated until she turned and acknowledged me. Amelia's hair was styled in a curly coiffure of soft, bluish white curls that framed her lined face. I knew from the staff that she had her hair done weekly and most days insisted on a hint of rouge to brighten her pale cheeks. The lamp glowed warm and inviting, brightening her clear eyes. She appeared lucid until I spoke her name.

"Amelia?"

She looked away from the window. "Diane. It's so good to see you. It's been ages."

I could have corrected her, explained I was not my mother, but then each time I had, she became upset and confused. So, I simply smiled. "Do you mind if I visit with you for a minute?"

"No, no," she said, smiling. "Always good to see you."

Moving across the room, I pulled a chair closer to her. "I've missed you."

As long as I can remember, Amelia was always a friend to my mother. She was pegged as the vivacious *aunt* who always came by bearing some exotic toy that kept Jennifer and I delighted for hours. I had always assumed the term *aunt* was figurative but now realized it was indeed genuine. No one ever gave a hint to the biological relationship, and it saddened me now to believe Mom had lived her entire life never knowing she had a half-sister.

"Tell me what you've been up to, Diane? How are the girls? Jennifer should be excited about high school. Hard to believe she'll be graduating middle school at the end of this year."

Jennifer had been more than ready to leave middle school by the summer of Amelia's visit. At that time, Jennifer spent a good half hour showing Amelia all the pictures she pulled from the teen magazines showcasing favorite outfits. I had accused my sister later of pandering for money, but instead of getting mad, she shrugged with a laugh.

I continued to play along. "Jennifer would like to go to the Governor's School, but I worry if her grades will be good enough." As it turned out, Jennifer's grades were mediocre at best.

"Rae has the grades," Amelia countered. "She's always had the better report card. That girl is going places. Jennifer is smart, too. But in other ways."

Leaning in a little, I smiled. "It's true."

I took her lined hand in mine and traced a raised vein on her hand. Would I one day end up alone in a place like this with no one to visit me? What right did I have to saddle Michael with my care when I had not raised him?

Sighing, I forced a smile. "Both girls just haven't bloomed yet. I think both will find their own way."

"The girls love you, Diane, and I know you love them."

Emotion tightened my throat. "I know."

"You need to tell the girls how you feel, Diane."

"I will."

"You keep your distance from them. They'll be grown and out the door before you know it."

I leaned forward, straightening a wrinkle on the lap blanket warming Amelia. I wanted to understand my mother and how she could have turned inward from her two children. Why had she always stiffened when I hugged her?

"It's not Jennifer's and Rae's fault your son died."

I froze. "My son?"

"I know it was a terrible blow losing your firstborn. But don't let that shadow what you have with the girls."

My mother had another child? A brother born before me? Suddenly too many pieces tumbled into place. Tremendous love that opened a heart and then grief had torn it to shreds—this I understood. "I don't know how to love." I was my mother. She was me. "I've been this way for so long—I don't think I can change."

Amelia patted my hand with her wrinkled bent fingers. "You just need to try."

"What if I do try to love and still don't feel anything?" If the time came, could I hug the boy and tell him I loved him?

Wrinkles around her eyes and mouth deepened as she smiled. "Don't worry about the emotion. It will always catch the action eventually."

"I think all the good feelings inside me are dead. Atrophied away."

"They'll bloom as soon as you shine a little light on them. They'll open up like flower petals in springtime."

Again, the ice cracked and shifted, and shoring it up took more work than I expected.

Amelia looked at me for a long moment, blinked and smiled. She was back, at least for the moment. "Rae."

I smiled. "Yes."

"Did I ever tell you about my birth mother, Fiona?"

Shifts in conversation were the norm for Amelia now. Her memories were becoming precious few so when one flitted across her mind, she grabbed onto it for as long as she could. "No."

Nodding, she looked relieved and grateful her memory

was validated. "She was a pretty woman. Did you know she was an actress and a singer before she came back to Alexandria to teach after the war?"

"I didn't know that."

"She sang in a club in Washington, D.C. She wore a slinky red dress, long white gloves, and sparkly earrings. I found publicity stills of her. She was a showstopper."

"How did you know that?" I asked.

"I hired a detective once. I wanted to know about her."

"Why?"

She squeezed my hand and sat back in her seat. "I don't think you'd understand."

I leaned toward her and whispered, "I might understand better than you think."

"Girls don't think of their mothers as real women with full lives."

"That's understandable. Many women put the needs of their family before their own," I said.

"I wanted to tell your mother so many times about Fiona, but I never had the courage."

I squeezed her hand gently. "I know Fiona had two daughters, not one. She gave up her first daughter because she lost her husband."

Amelia tugged the threads of her blanket. "Your mother and I were half-sisters."

"That's wonderful. I can't think of a better aunt to have. And I know Fiona must have loved both her daughters with all her heart. I know she loved you."

Amelia shook her head. Tears filled her eyes and when they spilled down her cheeks, she did not bother to wipe them away. "I'm not so sure about that. You see, Fiona could have tried to get me back, but never did."

Time had not healed this little girl's wound. "Fiona did what she thought was best for you, Amelia. She put you before herself and accepted her fate of carrying that burden the rest of her life."

"She never came back for me." Her voice softened. "Never."

"Maybe she was afraid."

"Of what?"

"Of you hating her."

Her watery eyes filled with shattering hope. "I never would have hated her."

I leaned close, staring at her until she looked up at me. "Fiona did what she did for love. It might not have felt like it, Amelia, but she put you ahead of herself. You need to believe that."

Amelia's gaze grew hazy and she looked away, pulling her hand from mine. "I'm tired. I need to go to sleep."

"Okay." Gently, I helped Amelia from her chair and guided her back to her bed. She slid under her covers and I tucked them close to her chin. She closed her eyes and turned her face from mine, embarrassed and hurt. She looked so small and vulnerable.

After kissing her gently on the cheek, I left the room, determined now to find out why Fiona never returned for her child.

A Letter from Patience

JANUARY 12, 1754

Dearest Mother,

My daughter, Hanna, is healthy and carries a lusty cry in her lungs. The witch was my only source of comfort during the long labor, and throughout it, she continued to feed me potions and teas that eased my pain. She was there to catch the babe and when she saw that it was a girl, her face grew pensive. When she told my husband, the child was a girl, he left the house, slamming the door behind him. My milk did not return as it had for the other babes, and when the child grew hungry it was the witch that took her to her breast. Whatever potion or magic flows through her milk silenced the babe. I cried until I drifted off to sleep.

Yours Faithfully,

Patience McDonald

Chapter Eleven

RAE, SATURDAY, OCTOBER 8, 2011

Dr. McDonald,

Can we meet in person? My mom says it's okay, but she wants to be there.

Michael Holloway

As I stared at the e-mail, my heart thundered in my chest, pounding and banging into the ice. I reached out and touched the computer screen, tracing his name. I reached for my cell phone and dialed the only number that made sense.

She answered on the third ring. "Rae?"

"Lisa." I stared at the computer screen. Thoughts raced. Collided. "Can we talk?"

"About what?"

"I'd rather not do this over the phone."

"Yeah, sure. I rescheduled the realtor and she's coming by the house in about two hours. I'm cleaning like a mad woman, so I'm here."

"I can come by then?" I asked.

"Sure. Are you okay?"

"I just need to talk."

"Come on by," Lisa said.

"I'll see you in a half hour."

"Sure."

I barely remembered the drive as I pulled onto the cobblestoned section of Prince Street and found a spot down the block from Lisa's house. I hurried up the street, my head ducked. When I knocked using the brass door knocker, I flashed back to the last time I had stood on this porch. I was with Jennifer who was irritated that Mom had insisted I spend the day with her. Jennifer wanted to see her friend, Lisa, to talk boys and parties, but not be saddled with her kid sister. I'd been excited to hang out with my big sister and her friend.

As I knocked, desperation bubbled to the surface. Inside, footsteps echoed in the hallway and a dog barked. The door swung open.

Lisa had pulled up her hair and twisted it into a loose topknot. The hem of an oversized gray shirt was knotted at her narrow waist and she wore cutoff jeans. Her feet were bare, but a gold ring winked from the second toe of her right foot. Standing beside her was Charlie, barking in a halfhearted attempt to be tough.

She blew a stray strand of hair from her eyes. "It's okay, Charlie. It's Rae."

I relaxed my grip on my purse strap, trying to appear calm. "Is this a bad time?"

"No. Charlie and I were just cleaning." She grabbed the dog's collar and tugged him aside so that I could enter. "Come on in."

I slid past Charlie, who was still sizing me up. "It smells like pine cleaner."

"Yeah, like I said on the phone, I was cleaning up for the realtor. Amelia's attorney is bringing her by at eleven."

"This really isn't a good time, is it?"

"The time is perfect. Coffee?"

"No thanks."

Lisa studied me, searching my reasons to visit. "Okay. Well, come and sit in the parlor."

The house was narrow and divided in half by a center hallway. On the left was a front parlor decorated with pale colors on the walls, sleek window treatments and lovely modern furniture. Most homes in this area drew on the colonial era for their color choices. Dark blues, greens, dark woods. I had never cared for that color scheme that also had come with my house. It was the reason I had repainted several of the rooms, although I had left some—time capsules for the sake of history.

"When did Amelia redecorate? It's lighter than when your parents owned it."

"A few years ago. We'd talked about wiring and plumbing that needed upgrades, but I had no idea how expensive an overhaul can be."

We moved into the side parlor. Lisa settled on an overstuffed couch and immediately curled her legs up under her, whereas I sat on a more angled chair and kept my back straight. Charlie jumped up on the couch beside Lisa and laid his head in her lap.

"It appears she put the redecorating money to good use," I said.

"All her changes were tasteful and should increase the home's resale value."

"You look well. Healthy. I noticed it yesterday. There's color in your skin."

"I was drinking heavily right before I left Alexandria," Lisa said.

"Ah. AA has been good for you?"

"It was a lifesaver."

"The last time we really talked all those years ago was a tough time," I said.

"I remember," Lisa said.

In this room, alone with her, I could speak about what, so few people knew about me. "I was about to give birth."

"Yeah. I have to admit, that surprised me."

"Not what everyone expected of Dr. Rae McDonald."

Lisa's gaze softened. "Who I am I to judge?"

I shifted in my seat, taking a moment to straighten the crease of my pants. "I had a boy."

Lisa nodded. "I wondered but didn't want to intrude. I didn't know who knew what."

"Thank you. Very few people know. You, my mother, and a few others."

Lisa leaned a little closer, her expression so accepting. "You said a boy?"

Tears tightened my throat. "His name is Michael."

"You always liked that name." Charlie nudged Lisa's hand with his nose, and she began to rub him between the ears.

"I wanted to be the one to give the boy his name," I said.

"That's very understandable."

"As you can imagine, my mother was not thrilled with the pregnancy. And I certainly can't blame her, especially after losing Jennifer."

Lisa raised her chin a notch.

"A great couple adopted the boy. A part of me wanted to keep him, but Mother wouldn't hear of it. She insisted I would be ruining both his life and mine."

"You were only a teenager at the time, Rae. Cut yourself some slack."

I plucked at the seam of my skirt. "I always wondered . . ."

"What?"

Clearing my throat, I searched for the right words. "I think

I could have done a good job raising him, if given a little help from my mother."

Nodding, her expression softened. "I've no doubt. You were always the kinder sister."

"Why do you say that?"

"Don't get me wrong, I loved Jennifer, but she and I were very selfish kids," Lisa said. "We did only what made us feel good, and neither one of us gave much thought to anyone else."

"You were seventeen. That's fairly natural."

"Maybe. Or maybe we were just selfish and spoiled and would have continued to be well into adulthood if life hadn't bitch slapped us."

"An odd way of putting it," I offered.

"I've never figured out a nice way to say it."

"No, I suppose not." Normally, I was the one sitting on the other side of a conversation like this. I listened to my clients as they unpacked their burdens. I helped them find a way to feel better, to cope and perhaps mend. And yet I couldn't help myself.

"What brought you here today, Rae?" Lisa asked.

"I went to see Amelia last night. She thought I was my mother."

Lisa rolled her head from side to side. "She often mentions that Diane comes to visit. The resemblance is uncanny, and Amelia gets confused."

"I understood, even expected that."

"But."

"She talked about Fiona. She wanted to know why her birth mother never came back for her."

Lisa studied me closely. "And you thought about your son."

"Michael sent me an e-mail. He saw the recent article in the paper about me."

"You've never had contact with him before?" Lisa asked.

"Not him. His mother has been sending me pictures and short notes about him each year on his birthday. But I only just had the courage to open her letters."

"But you did."

"Yes."

"Does Michael look like you?" Lisa asked.

Pride flickered. "He does. His hair is auburn."

"I bet he's handsome."

"Absolutely."

"Rae, if you don't mind me asking, who is his birth father?"

The direct question caught me a little off guard, but it really should not have. Lisa had always had a painful bluntness that Rae admired.

"His name is Dan Chesterfield."

"I remember the Chesterfield family. Did he have an older brother, Tim?"

"He did. Dan and I hooked up, if that's what you want to call it, shortly after Jennifer died."

"He would have been a senior?" Lisa asked.

"He was."

"Did you tell him about the baby?" Lisa asked.

"I didn't tell anyone about the baby until I was into my third trimester. Classic case of denial."

"The Chesterfields had big plans for their sons."

"Both have gone on to do some very impressive work," I said. "Dan is now an engineer in Fairfax County, with his eye on making a run for the state senate one day. His brother is a surgeon, I think."

"Well, time has been good to both."

"Perhaps."

"And a baby didn't fit into his big plan," Lisa surmised.

"No. My mother spoke with his parents and arrangements were made."

"Did he ever see the baby or contact you?"

"No. I haven't seen him since high school. After we had sex, I was too embarrassed to speak to him and he was not interested in talking to me. He wasn't looking for love."

"But you were."

Looking back at that teenage girl, it was easy to distance myself. "I was so lonely then. Jennifer and Dad were gone while Mom was emotionally distant. We both dealt with grief in our own way."

Lisa was silent for a moment as she fiddled with a ring on her index finger. She allowed a heavy breath to escape between her teeth. "You said the boy wants to see you. That's a good thing, right?"

Nerves twisted and turned in my belly. "It's natural for him to want to understand his biological family."

"It's got to be more than that, Rae. You carried him for nine months. You gave him life. Without you, he would not be here."

"Yes."

"What's the issue?"

"He wants to meet, but I'm afraid."

Her head cocked with disbelief. "What are you afraid of?"

"I'm afraid . . ." Words that echoed Amelia's fears stuck in my throat until I finally wrestled them free. "I worry he won't accept me. That he'll be angry."

"Why would he be angry?"

Again, the words hitched. "Because I gave him away."

"You gave him to parents who would love him."

I shook my head. "Adoption is filled with emotion. Feelings aren't always black-and-white."

"You weren't always so logical, Rae. Serious, yes. But you

used to laugh and cry. At your dad's funeral, your mother and sister didn't shed a tear, but you certainly did."

"And I remember feeling very foolish," I said. "Out of control."

"More like human. Alive."

"Maybe. But I'm not that person anymore. I've become my mother."

"You aren't Diane," Lisa said.

"How can you say that?"

"Because Diane wouldn't be sitting here talking like this. She'd be in denial cleaning a closet or scrubbing a floor."

"I considered doing the same when I first read his e-mail."

"But you didn't." She leaned forward. "Addie said our ancestors' wishes have become our curses."

"Maybe she's right. Maybe I'm destined to be like all the women in my family."

"Can't be that much fun, keeping all your thoughts buried."

"I never thought about it before."

Lisa settled her feet on the floor. "How can I help?"

"Michael." I paused. "I'm still not used to saying his name out loud."

"That's a shame, Rae. It's a great name, and it's okay to love him."

None of this felt okay. "He's not my child. I gave that right up a long time ago."

"You haven't given up anything."

Clearing my throat, I willed my heart to beat slower. "He wants to meet me face to face. His mother will also be there."

"And you need a wingman."

"I'd rather not do this alone."

She fingered a dangling earring. "Why do you say that?"

"I don't know how he'll react."

"He's a kid. He's curious. Maybe a little goofy and awkward. We all were at that age."

Skimming my index finger along my pearls, I nodded.

A sad, thoughtful grin tugged at her lips. "Look, I'd be glad to go with you. Give me the time and place and I'll be there."

"We haven't set the time and place."

"I'd say pick a pizza place. Teenagers love pizza and a restaurant will be public enough so that it makes the meeting a little less stressful."

"I think that's what we're all hoping. Are you sure you can do this?"

"Rae, I'll be there. And I promise if it all gets a little awkward, I'll find a way to cover your back and find a graceful reason why we need to leave."

"Thank you." Hugging Lisa would have been a natural response, but my hugs were always awkward and stilted.

We walked to the front door together. "I'm glad you came to me."

A Letter from Patience

April 6, 1754

Dearest Mother,

My milk remains dry and I cannot nurse my four-month-old daughter, Hanna. The witch cares for all three children, who get along well enough. The best times of the day are spent reading to my son, who adores the written word. I read the Bible to him and can see he is captured by the stories. Marcus, the witch's son, likes to be outside and enjoys rough play. Never were there two boys so different. Baby Hanna spends most of her days with the witch. The child is always irritable, and it suits me fine not to have to deal with her.

Yours Faithfully,

Patience McDonald,

Chapter Twelve

LISA, SATURDAY, OCTOBER 8, 2011

With Charlie at my side, I watched Rae leave and waved when she got into her car. I kept my body relaxed and casual until I saw her drive away. When I closed the door, my shoulders slumped. "I did that to her, Charlie. I'm the one who screwed up her life. If I hadn't been drunk, the accident would have never happened."

I tipped back my head, and a tear trickled down my cheek. Over the last couple of days, my doubts about carrying a secret shame had grown heavier and more cumbersome.

"Stop whining, Lisa. We both screwed up that night. I was drunk before we got in the car. We both know I created the chain of events."

"Doesn't matter how it all started. It's how it ended." I groaned. "Why are you here, Jennifer? Just walk to the light and find some damn peace."

"For now, I'm stuck here in Purgatory, just like you."

"Shit."

"Look on the bright side. Maybe that's why I'm here. Maybe I'm here to help you fix all this."

"How can we fix this? Rae gave up her son and can never get back the time they lost."

"There's so much more time for them, Lisa. I don't want to see her lose that as well."

My head pounded. "I could use a drink."

"You and me both, sister, but that's off the table. I need your head in the game."

Charlie pushed his nose against my hand, sensing something. When I did not look at him, he nudged me again and barked. "It's okay, boy." I scratched his head. "I've lived with all this for a long time. Some days are just worse than others."

The front doorbell rang, startling me from my mood. I wiped my cheeks with my palms and looked into the mirror hanging in the hallway before opening the door. Standing on the porch was Colin, along with a very sleek-looking woman wearing a red suit, crisp white shirt, and black high heels. Pearl earrings matched a necklace and a bracelet. Her manicured hands reminded me a bit of Cruella de Vil.

"You're early," I said.

"Hopefully, this isn't too much of an imposition," Colin said.

Cruella de Vil grinned. "It was my fault. My schedule is insane today."

"No worries," I said.

Colin made a quick sweep of my appearance, taking in the jeans and bare feet, then looking beyond me to Charlie. "I'd like you to meet Rebecca Tuttle. She's one of the best realtors in the city."

I had intended to change before they arrived, but Rae had tossed the schedule out the window. Whatever. I wasn't looking for love or approval right now. I simply wanted the house sold. "Very nice to meet you, Ms. Tuttle. Please come in."

Charlie pushed past me to Colin, who rubbed him on the head. "How are you doing, boy?"

"He's fine," I said, tugging him gently out of the way to allow them to enter. I slid my feet into clogs I kept by the front door. "I'm a little off schedule this morning. A friend just stopped by, but the house is ready for your inspection."

Ms. Tuttle openly appraised the walls, the flooring, and the furniture. "The house has been remodeled. And it doesn't smell like dog."

"Amelia remodeled and Lisa's been taking good care of the place," Colin said.

Praise from Mr. West. I wasn't sure if I should make a smartass comment or accept him as an ally. I chose the latter. "The original finish has been removed from the floors," she said. "That won't help with the value."

Feeling a need to rise to Amelia's defense, I said, "I would think the brighter colors would attract more buyers. These older houses can be a little stuffy."

"Not stuffy," she corrected. "They're traditional and represent a very specific market that will pay for that colonial look."

"The house is in a prime location," Colin said. "Colors can be changed."

As she passed, I gave him a thumbs-up. Smiling, he held out his hand and gestured for me to go first. She moved straight through the center hallway into the kitchen. I was not much of a baker, so there was no cookie aroma to entice anyone, but I had purchased a bundle of irises and arranged them in a crystal vase that now sat in the center of the polished marble island.

Charlie and I followed as Ms. Tuttle ran a manicured hand over the marble and inspected her fingertips. "Compliments to your cleaning lady."

I hitched my hands on my hips. "You're looking at her."

The realtor turned from me, unwilling to give away any hint of what she was thinking.

However, Colin's gaze did not waver. "You've done a good job getting the place ready for sale.

"Rebecca," he said to the agent, "she had the basement cleaned out over the summer. The space was jam packed."

He slid a hand into his pocket, and the joint of his jaw pulsed. Turning, he spotted a collection of my prints on the farmhouse table. "Is that the picture you took of the house yesterday?"

"It is. Not exactly finished, though. I developed a few prints last night, but as you can see, I've experimented with several different types of exposure. Once they're dry, I'll wax them, and that will really make the contrast pop."

He hovered over a print, not touching, but clearly interested. "These are really good, Lisa."

"Thanks."

"Rebecca, you should come and have a look," he said.

Tapping a finger on her purse, Rebecca obliged. To my satisfaction, her focus lingered. "Very nice."

"Thank you."

"So, is this your hobby?" Rebecca asked.

"More like my job."

"A professional artist?" Rebecca asked.

"That's right."

"I'm very active in the art community and know most of the up-and-coming artists," Rebecca said. "I've not heard of you."

"And until yesterday, I'd not heard of you."

"Stick around another few weeks. You'll find I'm very well known in this city, and a good person to network."

I honestly did not care. "Do you want the listing or not?"

Rebecca did not miss the intentional bite snapping behind the words. "I'll list it."

"How long will it take you to sell the place?" I asked.

"Hard to say," Rebecca said.

"I bet you have an idea," I countered.

"The markets are hard to predict," she said.

"You have forty-five days," I said, using her tone. "If you can't move the property at a competitive price by then, you're out."

Colin looked amused but did not interfere. Props to him for that.

A plucked eyebrow arched. "Oh, I'll sell it."

As much as she criticized the place, she knew it was worth good money. Bitchy, but not stupid. "Then it's a win-win for us both."

"I'll draw up the paperwork tonight and have it for you to sign in the morning."

"Drop it by my office," Colin said. "I'll review it first and then bring it by with comments."

"Of course." Rebecca pulled her car key from her slim purse and made for the front door. "Then I'm off. Keep the house in order, and I'll sell it."

Colin closed the door behind her. "She's a top producer."

"Lovely woman."

"No, but she'll sell the place and get you top dollar. She's the best."

"As long as I get the money for Amelia, I'll deal."

He didn't make the hasty departure I expected. Stepping closer, he said, "Your aunt is lucky to have you."

"I could say the same thing about her."

His eyes lingered an extra beat, and I was not so lost in my own world that I did not pick up on his interest. One word from him and we would be upstairs messing up the bed I had so carefully made an hour ago. But Colin West was Amelia's attorney and business came first, especially when helping Amelia.

"Thanks for your help and for finding Rebecca," I said, folding my arms.

He nodded, understanding the evening was over. "Glad I could help." As he moved toward the front door and reached for the doorknob, he paused. "I almost forgot. I found a picture that I thought you might want."

"What?"

He reached in his breast pocket. "I'm still reviewing Mr. Murphy's files, and this picture was tucked in the back of one. I don't know how it came to me."

The three-by-five photo was black and white, and its coating reflected the light. The picture showed a group of high school kids, their teacher, and a couple of parents in front of the warehouse at the corner of King and Union Streets. The printed date on the side read *September 1968.*

I scanned the faces, searching for anyone I knew, and then I saw Amelia, standing in the center. She would have been in her mid-twenties. "Who are these people?"

"That was taken the year Amelia came back to Alexandria and taught high school."

"She taught high school? I thought she was trying to crack Broadway in those days."

He tapped the face of a tall, lean man standing by Amelia. "See that young twenty-something-year-old man next to your aunt?"

The man had warm eyes, and instead of staring at the camera, he was looking at Amelia. "Yeah."

"That's my dad's law partner, Mr. Murphy. They opened Murphy and West in 1970."

"Amelia's husband?" My memories of the man conjured three piece suits, a stern face, and a deep voice.

"Yes."

"I thought they met in New York." I knew the story well. She was waitressing in a coffee shop, hoping for a callback from her last musical audition that she swore would be her last. Distracted, she spilled hot coffee on a young man and when he looked up at her, his irritation immediately melted. That man was Mr. Murphy, Amelia's husband.

"Yes, but apparently when he asked her out there, she said no. Fast-forward a few months and they both found themselves back here in Alexandria."

Behind the crowd stood a tall brick building with a large glass window that was boarded up. "That looks like the Shire Architectural Salvage yard," I said.

"It certainly is."

The corner didn't look as tony or smart as it did now. There were no tourists, and judging by the rubbish on the brick sidewalk, the city had been in rough shape. "I wonder what the group was doing there."

"The city was struggling in those days. Lots of crime and poverty. I have to hand it to your aunt for taking a bunch of kids there."

I pressed the picture to my chest. "Thanks, Colin. It was kind of you to give this to me. I don't have much history on Amelia."

"Glad you like it." He grinned, pleased with himself. "I'll get back to you tomorrow about the contract."

"Sounds good."

When I closed the door behind him, I studied the image again. There must have been twenty kids in the picture. I studied Amelia's smiling face, so full of life and happiness. Her concentration appeared clear and sharp. "So unfair."

A closer look showed she was holding something in her hand. I grabbed my glasses and held the picture up to the light. I realized Amelia was holding a witch bottle.

"I'll be damned."

A Letter from Patience

MAY 10, 1754

Dearest Mother,

I've lost so much to the witch who has an uncanny mind and memory. She grows more beautiful with each year. There is not a gray hair intertwined in her auburn locks nor is there a wrinkle marring her flawless skin. My children love the witch who now reads to them and helps them with their letters and numbers. I also now fear that my husband has fallen under her spell. I am certain the Devil conjured this woman and sent her into my life to taunt me.

Yours Faithfully,

Patience McDonald

Chapter Thirteen

RAE, SATURDAY, OCTOBER 15, 2011

After leaving Lisa's home last week, I exchanged e-mails with Michael as we tried to settle on a meeting date. I suggested next Saturday, but he had morning soccer practice that ended at noon. Would one o'clock work? I agreed and asked him to select the restaurant. The pizza place on Duke Street. Lisa had been right. Teenagers loved pizza. A date was set, and I sent a quick text to Lisa of the place and time.

Done.

Simple, right?

Not even close. The idea of meeting Michael churned up so much turmoil that I could barely concentrate or sleep more than a complete hour the night before.

Finally frustrated with pretending to sleep, I rose before sunrise and went for a jog. My hope was that the run would elevate endorphins and calm my nerves. I sweated out a five mile run along part of the Potomac, but my nerves were just as unsettled as they had been when I first stepped out the front door.

As I finished up the run and turned down the street that

led to my house, the morning sun rose over the horizon, coloring the leaves in a bright shade of orange. I rounded the final corner and jogged down my cul-de-sac. The sunlight bathed over my property, hit the slate roof and cascaded down the sides of the house's worn red brick and glinting off the windows' wavy glass panes. Breathless, I reached down and picked up the morning edition of the *Washington Post* on my way toward the backyard and its barren patch of land, where the stones had once stood for centuries.

The soil remained soft and small puddles of water still pooled, but according to the news, we were due for a stretch of dry weather. Perhaps a string of sunny days to finally dry the earth. I hoped we had turned a corner.

Though the rain had bought me time to hem and haw over the design of the garage, it was now time to decide. Zeb had said he would have to move on to other projects if I could not, and I knew he would do it out of principle. To the back of the line, I would go. Just like in grade school.

I stood at the edge of the neat square of raw dirt, now wondering if my decision to remove the stones had set off a chain reaction, overturning my entire life. That sounded like blasphemy for someone in my line of work.

My mother hated the stones and would have loved to see them gone but would have never actually considered getting rid of them. She could not articulate why they needed to stay but insisted they did. Maybe, she had good reasons.

Kneeling, I picked up a clump of the dark, wet earth and tested the weight of it in my hand. "Mom, what have I started? Where will it lead to?"

Rising, I tossed the dirt down and went inside, toed off my running shoes at the back door, and climbed the back staircase. I took a long, hot shower, tipping my face toward the spray and savored the warmth. If only the stress would melt away as easily as the sweat on my body. Normally on Saturdays, after my morning run and shower, I ate a quick breakfast and worked on patient files. But today, concentration was impossible. Instead of working, I retrieved the photo album of Michael and sat at the kitchen table, examining each picture with careful scrutiny, looking for any clues to help me prepare for my visit with him.

"Please don't be disappointed with me," I whispered as I traced the outline of his round face. This was a picture from his fourth birthday party, where he held up what looked like a red soldier. The caption on the back said, *Michael loves the Red Power Ranger.*

That note from Susan led to an Internet search of Power Rangers, which I discovered had an involved storyline around the main characters. The Red Rangers, I learned, were Jason and Rocky. The Red Ranger was the team leader and carried the most powerful weapons.

"He's nearly sixteen, Rae," I muttered, turning the page. "He doesn't care about Power Rangers anymore."

I flipped to the last image and found him standing at the finish line of a cross-country race. He ran on his high school team, like me. In fact, I had run fall track during my first trimester. The silky synthetic jersey top had remained untucked for the regionals, billowing over my still flat belly.

I searched the cross-country picture for more clues about the boy and saw a silver medal glistening around his neck. I had won a couple of meets, though never really possessed the speed that Jennifer enjoyed. If she had focused, All State would have been in her grasp. My last race marked the end of my first trimester. I came in third, however I could have taken first place if not for the morning sickness.

When the clock in the hallway chimed twelve times, I realized I had lost the whole morning. Quickly, I dressed, slipped on my heels, and straightened my hair. A glance in the mirror should have been quick and cursory, but the image I discovered staring back was not a very friendly looking woman. She looked stiff, beyond her years.

"When did I turn into my mother?" I whispered. I reached for the ponytail band holding back my hair and pulled it free, allowing the long strands to tumble around my shoulders. Practicing a few smiles took some of the edge off, but still, it was Mom's cool eyes that stared back at me.

Where did the time go?

I was thirty-two, but on the inside, I felt twenty years older. Life was not waiting for me to get my act together.

What did I want Michael's first impression of me to be? Without thinking, I fumbled with the buttons of my button-down blouse before quickly peeling it off. I hurried to my closet and stood for a long moment, searching for something that would make me look like a reasonable woman who gave up her son for all the right reasons.

But all the outfits had a similar starchy feel. Nothing created an approachable impression. The ice around my heart shifted and cracked, heated by the anger and frustration churning underneath.

In the end, I settled on a black pair of slacks, flat shoes, and a sleeveless red sweater. The sweater had been a gift from Amelia several years ago, but I never wore it, feeling that its bright color drew far too much attention to me. Feeling exposed, I slid on a black jacket. Not exactly cutting edge, but better.

I hurried to my car, suddenly fearing that the extra time frittered away would be needed for any unexpected traffic that on any given day could easily add another fifteen minutes for no apparent reason.

Racing down the parkway, I quickly ducked into the city and pulled in front of Lisa's house on Prince Street. Immediately, I noticed the realtor's large *For Sale* sign fastened to the front of the house. The agent's bright smile pictured on the sign stared back at me. More change was coming into our lives. Had the removal of the stones caused that as well? Putting the stones back was as impossible as shoving the genie back in the bottle. There was no going back, ever.

I texted Lisa and told her I was outside. "Please don't be late," I muttered.

My hand slid to the horn and before I thought, I tapped it. It blared, making me flinch.

The front door opened, and she appeared, dressed in a dark loose-fitting dress, with a collection of bright necklaces and brown midcalf worn boots. Lisa turned to yell good-bye to Charlie, then closed and locked the door before turning and smiling at me. She looked so carefree, and I envied it.

She slid into the front seat, smelling of fresh soap and apple shampoo. "Sorry. The realtor has a showing today, and I was just wiping down the counter."

"Where's Charlie?"

"In his crate in the kitchen. He's not a happy camper."

"Amelia said he never minded the crate."

"He hasn't seen the inside of it since I arrived. He's feeling a little put out right now."

"Better to be in the crate if people are coming in and out of the house." I started backing out of the driveway, almost before she had hooked her seat belt. "The house shouldn't be a hard sell. Everyone loves this street," I said.

"I hope you're right. I'm not sure how long I can keep it in order. And I suspect it will cost more than chew sticks to get Charlie back in the crate next time." She twisted in her seat and looked at me. "I like your hair down, Rae. You look very . . ."

Flipping on my blinker, I turned left on Union Street. "Please do not say *old* or *like my mother*."

She grinned as she arranged the folds of her dress. "So very not like your mother. You look like the Rae I remember from high school. And the red suits you."

A lump formed in my throat, and swallowing it took effort. That girl—*that Rae*—was long gone. She had been buried under ice and isolation for sixteen years. "Thanks."

"Why the change?"

I turned left on Union Street and then drove up King, knowing I could cut over to the pizza place on Duke in about a mile. "Because I realized today, I dress like my mother. I look like my mother." And with a rising sense of panic, I said, "I am my mother."

"And you only just realized that?"

"Yes. It all hit me this morning while dressing. I dressed like I always do and then I looked in the mirror and saw Mom looking back. I don't want to be Mom. I want Michael to see me, not her."

"He'll like you, Rae. He's reached out to you. He wants to know you."

"But what if he meets me and he's disappointed?"

"Why would he be disappointed?"

I stopped for a red light. "There are a thousand reasons."

"Name one."

"I never answered any of the letters from his mother. Each year she sent me pictures and I never looked at them until last week. Who does that?"

"A woman who's in pain," Lisa said, softly. "A woman who's struggling to set the guilt down but doesn't know how."

"I've been doing so well. My career is booming. I exercise. Eat right. I don't drink hardly ever."

"You act like a woman who's using work to numb pain."

Driving along with the creeping traffic, I was grateful to look away and focus on the road. "How would you know something like that?"

She raised her hand. "Queen of the AA meetings. I've been to meetings in two dozen states in the last eight years. I know all about avoidance and numbing techniques. You'd be surprised what people do. At least you didn't use drugs or alcohol."

"Maybe I should have a drink to loosen up."

A frown wrinkled her brow. "A drink might loosen your control for a short time, but it never solves anything."

"Then how do I loosen up? I have no idea how to let go of the reins." Panic tightened my tone.

"You're about to miss the pizza place."

Glancing to the side, I saw the sign featuring a huge flying pizza. "Damn." Pulling into the parking lot, I found a spot at the very back.

"Just be yourself, Rae. You owe it to Michael and yourself."

I shut off the engine and stared out the windshield for a long moment as I gathered myself. "In my office I know who I am. I know how to act and behave. But outside those walls, not so much."

"I don't know the professional incarnation of Dr. Rae McDonald. She and I have never met. But I knew the other Rae when we were kids, and I liked her."

"But you never wanted that kid to tag along."

"That wasn't on you," she said. "You were a good kid. Jennifer and I were immature shits. There's no nice way to say it. We were so wrapped up in our own stupid dramas, we were rarely gracious or kind. It was all about us. And for that, I'm sorry."

The apology soothed an old wound that I never realized had not healed. "It was a long time ago."

"Sometimes it feels like yesterday with Jennifer sitting right beside me, egging me on just like when we were kids. I can almost hear her."

"She had a great laugh," Rae said.

"Yes, she did. And she could be nice once in a while."

I relaxed back in the seat, willing the tension away. "She could."

Breathe in. Breathe out.

"Do you want to go inside now?" Lisa asked.

"I just need a minute."

We sat in silence for several minutes. I was almost feeling like I could deal with seeing Michael when I saw the green minivan pull up in front of the restaurant. On the back bumper was a cross-country high school sticker as well as a *My Kid Is on the Honor Roll* sticker.

My heart jumped, and I reminded myself to breathe. "I think that's them."

Lisa sat forward, shadowing my line of sight. When the woman got out of the driver's seat, I did not recognize her. She was rail thin, and her shoulders stooped slightly. She wore crisp jeans, a white blouse, a cardigan, and a scarf wrapped around her head. It was the kind of scarf worn by patients undergoing chemo. When she turned slightly, I thought I recognized Susan's profile, but weight loss had made all her features sharper. She was at least fifteen pounds lighter than I remembered. How old was she now? Forty-five?

"Is that her?" Lisa asked.

"Yes. That's Susan Holloway."

"She's sick, Rae."

"I didn't know," I whispered. "All the notes and letters she sent me never mentioned her health. Not one." Guilt jabbed. "She must think I'm such a bitch."

"You don't know that."

"Sure, I do. I am a bitch."

Lisa laid a hand on mine. "She looks like she's a nice lady."

"She is. Nice and kind." My God. Poor Susan. And Michael. How is all this affecting him?"

I counted my breaths as I waited for the passenger-side door to open. One. Two. Three. "What if he didn't come? What if he sent his mom to tell me he can't do this?"

As I shifted to study her expression, the other car door opened. Out of the front seat unfolded a tall, lean boy. There was a splash of freckles across his pale skin, and his auburn hair could have used only the tiniest bit of a trim. Most of his height was already developed, but he had yet to fill out the frame with size and muscle. He was still a gangly kid. I had not missed his entire life.

He studied the pizza place, his brow wrinkling like mine did when I was worried. He looked at his mother and smiled in a way that made me think he was hiding his nerves to protect her.

His mother smiled, extending her hand and motioning for him to come around the car. When he walked, he stood straight. Carried himself with poise. I could see he was an exceptional young man.

"He's cute," Lisa said.

I studied Lisa's expression, searching for any signs that she was joking, but I saw only sincerity. "He's handsome."

"And he looks like you. It's like I'm flashing back to high school. I don't see much Dan Chesterfield."

I couldn't help but feel a little bit of satisfaction. "Is it wrong to be glad about that?"

"Did Dan carry that boy for nine months? How many hours was he in labor? Where was he when Michael was born?"

"Michael was born on a Wednesday in June, so Dan was most likely back from his first year of college and was on vacation with his family."

"How would you know that?"

"I saw him the Christmas after Michael was born. He said

I looked well. Said he loved college and never missed a Wednesday night Hump Party."

"He's an ass," Lisa said.

And yet I could not summon the least bit of resentment for Dan. Not as I watched this near-perfect boy open the door to the pizza place and allow his mother to go before him. "He has manners. Did you see that?"

"He's a good boy." She laid her hands on my shoulders. "Now, why don't you go meet him?"

My gut clenched. "You're coming, right?"

"I've got your back."

"If you weren't here right now, I could very well be running in the opposite direction." I was not being overly dramatic but stating facts. This was a terrifying moment.

She gripped my hand. "I'm not letting you run away. In fact, if you look like you might bolt, I'm taking you down like they do on *Cops*."

"Understood."

We got out of the car and crossed the parking lot. When I reached for the door handle, I could feel the blood rushing to my head, making me light-headed. Drawing in a breath, I yanked open the door to a crowded place filled with kids, parents, and laughter. Scanning the crowd, I did not see Michael or Susan. "I don't see them. What if he panicked and ran out the back door?"

"Then I'll tackle him, too. It will be worthy of an ESPN highlights reel."

"You can't do that," I said in all seriousness. "If he's afraid, that's fine. It's just me that can't be scared."

"Got it. No tackling or choke holds."

"Okay." I continued to scan the room. A group of middle school kids dressed in soccer uniforms rose from a table and in a loud rush of chatter and laughter made their way to the front of the restaurant. A couple of moms followed behind, herding the children like shepherds.

"Loosen up," Lisa ordered.

"I can't."

"Why not? Michael suggested the meeting. That means he wants to see you."

"Good point." Just then I saw Susan emerge from the ladies' room and a second later, Michael from the men's room. A sigh shuddered through me, pulling some of the tension with it. Either way my life would change in the next several minutes.

Susan and Michael sat at a back corner booth and when a waitress came, they accepted three menus. They were expecting me.

The hostess appeared before us, a short, plump teenager with bouncy brown curls and a bright smile. She picked up a couple of menus. "Table for two, ladies?" she asked.

I looked at her and opened my mouth to speak, but nothing came out. Words usually came to me easily. They were my stock-in-trade.

Lisa leaned around me. "We're meeting friends. And we see them in the corner booth."

"Great!" the young girl said as she tucked the menus back under the register.

Lisa nudged me forward. "One foot in front of the other, Rae."

"I don't want to mess this up," I said.

"You won't. Now, march."

Placing one foot in front of the other, I passed several booths that were filled mostly with families. "What if I say the wrong thing?"

"You won't," Lisa said. "I'm right here."

"Okay."

We rounded the final corner and Susan, sitting with her

back to the wall and facing the door, spotted us before Michael. My guess was the decision was deliberate. She wanted to run interference in case there was trouble that needed heading off. A part of me appreciated the gesture while the other resented it.

Susan said something to Michael, and he craned his neck so that he could see me. Eyes that looked so much like mine locked on me, and for a second my heart stopped beating. Sixteen years ago, I was his age, holding him in my arms in the hospital. That had been the last time I had looked into his eyes. I had not felt all that young, but my mother knew I was just a child.

He pushed out of the booth, as did Susan. He simply stared at me, cataloguing each of my physical details, as I did his. Eyes. *Check.* Hands. *Check.* Limbs. *Check.* And on and on went the list.

Susan was the first to speak. "Rae?"

I pulled my gaze from the boy. "Yes. Susan?"

Her smile warmed. "Yes." She came closer to Michael and placed her hands on his shoulders. "Michael, this is Rae McDonald. She's your birth mother."

He stood staring, frozen.

Susan squeezed his shoulders, reminding him that he needed to say something. "Uh, hi. It's really nice to meet you." He stuck out his hand.

Should I grasp his hand and shake or wrap my arms around him and hug him? I thought about the counseling I gave my clients. The first moments of a meeting create lasting impressions. Less is more. Smile.

I smiled and took his hand, which felt warm and a little clammy. Nice to know I was not the only nervous one here. "It's good to see you again."

"Again?" He cocked his head and then nodded. "Right. I guess we did kind of meet once before."

"We did."

Lisa reached her hand around me and extended it to Susan. "I'm Lisa Smyth. Friend of Rae's. I'm here for moral support."

The comment relaxed Susan's tense shoulders a fraction. This close, she looked so pale. So frail. "I think we're all a little nervous. Todd would have been here, but he's overseas and couldn't get home."

"That's okay," I said. "Is he doing well?"

"He's great," Susan said. "Why don't we sit down?"

"Sounds good," Lisa said. She nudged me into the booth and then took the seat next to mine, eliminating an awkward moment of where Michael and I would sit. He and I both looked relieved that she had grabbed the bull by the horns. He slid into the other side of the booth and Susan sat beside him.

The waitress appeared, gave Lisa a menu, and took our drink order. We all read the menus, but I could not process a word. I found myself stealing a peek at Michael. The second time I looked, I caught him staring at me. His face turned a light pink, embarrassed.

I smiled and leaned back in my seat. *Nonthreatening body language*, I said to myself. *Relax. Breathe.*

"You don't look like your picture in the paper," he said.

"It's not one of my favorites." It made me look stern and angry, but of course, the writer had dubbed me the matchmaker with the heart of stone. I suppose the photo fit the headline.

"Why did they write that article about you?" he asked.

"One of my clients is a friend of the reporter. She told the reporter about her experience with me and the reporter was intrigued. I suppose she thought the story would be a light, fun read."

Susan carefully sipped her soda, closely studying me. "I didn't realize you were a matchmaker."

"I'm not, really. I've introduced some people who've ended up married. I told that to the reporter, but she wanted to hear something else."

"The article outlines many of your successes," Susan said. "Several couples had nice things to say about you. They called you a matchmaker."

"I suppose so many people want to believe the perfect match is possible," I said.

"Makes sense." She smiled. "How is your mother doing?" Susan asked. She swallowed with care. Her throat was clearly raw.

Susan had met my mother a couple of times. In fact, it was Mom who found Susan and suggested I look at the Holloways' profile. "She passed a couple of years ago."

"I'm sorry, I didn't know."

Remembering how cool my mother had been to Susan during the adoption process, I felt I owed her an explanation. "You met my mother at a difficult time. My older sister had recently died in a car accident, and she wasn't herself." Not entirely true, but I felt a need to defend her.

Susan's eyes softened with sadness. "I remember that. I felt so sorry for her. And you."

I drew in a breath and looked at Michael. "My sister, Jennifer, died just before her eighteenth birthday."

"That's what Mom told me."

"You would have liked her," Lisa said. "Jennifer and I were good friends."

Susan stirred her straw in her glass and gently shifted the conversation. "I remember your mother telling me the house your family lived in was built in the 1700s."

"It's almost three hundred years old and has always been in the McDonald family. I still live there."

Michael nodded. "Cool. Our house is only three years old, but I guess Mom told you that in her letters."

Heat warmed my cheeks as I nodded.

A silence settled for a few seconds before Susan asked, "So you've both known each other for a long time?"

"Lisa and my sister, Jennifer, met in kindergarten. She was always around the house when I was growing up."

Lisa nodded and sipped her iced tea nonchalantly. "So, Michael, what grade are you in?"

He cleared his throat. "I'm a sophomore."

"So next year you'll begin looking at colleges," she added.

"Yeah."

"Any thoughts on where you'd like to go?" I asked.

"I've good grades," he said. "I like UVA and Virginia Tech."

"He's downplaying his talents," Susan said. "He's very smart. Straight A's and on schedule for AP Honors classes next year."

Michael rolled his eyes. "Mom."

"It's true," she said.

"I took AP Honors," I said. "It's nice getting to college with a semester or two's worth of credits under your belt. Plus, I was able to graduate high school a year early."

"That's what Mom keeps saying." When he realized he had called Susan "Mom" again, he looked at me, worried he had offended me.

There was a lot I had not done right concerning Michael over the years but was not about to mess up this meeting. "That's okay. She *is* your mother."

"But so are you," he said, glancing toward Susan, worried again he had said something wrong.

Susan nudged him gently with her elbow. "She's your birth mother. And I'm proud of that, Michael. Without Rae, there would be no you."

"What do I call you?" he asked me.

The ice around my heart dripped and melted under the heat of his watchful eyes. "Rae works just fine."

He nodded, and again I sensed the rush of relief.

"Thank you for all the pictures," I said to Susan.

Her dark eyes brightened. "Amazing how fast he's grown."

Feeling that I owed her an explanation, I said, "It was hard to look at them, but you kept your word, and I am grateful for that."

"Why was it hard?" Michael challenged.

A lump rose in my throat. I struggled for objectivity and a sense of calm. "It's very emotional for me, Michael." I struggled to corral the words that skidded just out of reach. "Handing you to your mother was the hardest thing I've ever done. And looking at the pictures reminded me of what I was missing. Not a day has gone by that I haven't thought about you and your family. You are so lucky to have each other."

He reached in his pocket and pulled out his phone. He scrolled through several screens before he found what he wanted and turned the phone toward me. "This is a picture Mom keeps in the den next to all the other family pictures."

I took the phone and found a sixteen-year-old me holding Michael. My hair was tied back in a ponytail and the stark hospital gown made my face look sallow. "I remember very clearly when the nurse took this picture. I was physically drained."

"Why?" he asked.

"Sore from nineteen hours of labor. Worried about you." For a brief instant, my eyes stung as tears threatened, but I willed them away. "Of course, I can see I had nothing to be worried about."

"This is what I picture when I think of you," Susan said. "Young. So very young. And now it's nice to see you've become such an accomplished woman."

I studied the picture an extra beat. "Michael is still a tiny baby in my mind. It'll take some adjusting to the fact that he's a young man."

Silent, Michael traced his finger down the condensation on the side of his glass. Susan sat back in her seat, looking exhausted. Overwhelmed, I looked down, needing time to shore up my senses before I looked at either one. My roller-coaster of emotions ranged from exhausted to exhilarated.

When the waitress arrived, the only one able to speak was Lisa, who grinned and ordered two pizzas—one cheese and the other with pepperoni.

"I'm proud of you all," Lisa said, shattering the silence. "None of this is easy and yet you're all here." Susan looked up, clearly ready to focus on anything different. "Without heaping TMI on you, I'm in AA. We talk a lot about secrets. They will eat away at you and make life tough. We drink so we won't feel as much. Talking is a very good thing."

Michael studied her, trying to get a read on her. "I guess."

"Rae, you should tell him about the family papers that you're having a historian study," Lisa said. "Michael, Rae recently had an old hearth fireplace removed from her backyard. It was built in the 1750s."

"Wow," he said.

"It had seen better times." I felt Lisa's elbow nudge me, and I gladly reached for benign facts that were only a curiosity to me. "The first McDonalds in Alexandria came from Scotland in 1749. Their names were Patience and Michael McDonald."

"Is that where my name came from?" he asked.

I shook my head. "Michael is the strongest of angels, plus I liked the name. I didn't know about the first Michael when you were born."

"Oh." Michael said.

"My family has always been good about drafting and saving family papers, and I recently gave the letters to a local historian who studies the city's history. She found letters from Patience that she never mailed. They're quite detailed."

"Turns out," Lisa said, leaning forward like a conspirator sharing a secret, "that there are three families that are connected." She explained that the families all still had descendants in the area. She now had an attentive audience, so she added the story of the three witch bottles for good measure.

"Can I see the bottles?" Michael asked.

"I believe they'll be on display very soon," I said. "If you're interested, I'll send you an e-mail when the exhibit opens."

"Yeah, that would be cool."

I reached into my purse. "You'd also asked about the family's genealogy. This is a printout of all the generations dating back to Patience and Michael."

He scanned the pages. "Wow, Mom, your family only goes back a couple of generations."

Susan shrugged, looking a bit chagrined in the face of the McDonalds' long history. "We came from Ireland about eighty years ago and don't have many records. You're lucky that Rae can trace her lineage back so far."

Lisa tapped a finger against the side of her glass of tea. "My people were here early, but I'm not thinking they were such nice folks. They transported indentured servants and slaves."

I tapped Patrick McDonald's name, which rested under Patience's and Michael's. "The historian thinks he was adopted. There are letters that suggest Patience adopted one of Faith Shire's twin sons."

"Really?"

"The historian has a couple of portraits. One of Patrick and one of Faith's other son, Marcus. They look like they could be brothers."

"Cool."

The pizza arrived and we all welcomed the chance to eat and reflect. Susan nibbled at the crust of her pizza but did not eat more than a bite or two. I wanted so much to ask her about her illness but sensed she was reluctant to discuss it in front of Michael.

When we'd finished eating, we boxed up the extra for her to take home for Michael and made our way out to the parking lot. The wind had picked up and blew a paper cup randomly across the lot, but the skies had cleared, and the sun was warm.

I had feared and dreaded this meeting for years, and now Michael stood before me. Why could it not have been so much sooner? As we stood on the curb, Michael's hands were tucked in his front pockets as Susan loaded the pizza boxes in the backseat. When she faced us, a sense of awkwardness bloomed. Should I shake hands again? Would a hug be out of the question, and if I hugged both, how long was too long? Judging by Michael and Susan's expressions, they were just as uncertain.

Lisa picked up on this and quickly leaned in and hugged Susan first, and then when Michael pulled his hands from his pockets, hugged him. She was our Switzerland. Our safe place. Following suit, I quickly embraced Susan, and cringed when I felt the bones in her back. "I'm sorry," I whispered.

She squeezed me with a surprising strength. "It's okay. Really."

Tears burning my throat, I turned toward Michael. We both hesitated, but I put my arms around him. I wanted to hug him. To feel him. Hear his breath. Just as I had when he was in my arms.

After a not-too-quick hug, I backed away and tucked my hands in the folds of my jacket. "It was really nice to meet you, Michael."

"Yeah, Rae," he said.

I wanted the moment to linger just a little longer. "If you have any questions about those papers, just e-mail me."

"Yeah, sure. Thanks."

Susan smiled. "Thanks, Rae. This really has been great."

There was so much I wanted to thank her for doing. I understood that this moment was happening because she was supporting Michael as he reached out to me. "Thank you, Susan."

They drove off while we climbed into my car. For a moment, I simply sat, completely exhausted, unable to start the car.

"Very intense," Lisa said.

"Did you see his expression? He understood toward the end how heavy this was for everyone involved."

"This is a lot to absorb. Seems there's no easy way to do this."

"As a psychologist, I can tell you that he underestimated the emotions of today. Until now, I've been a curiosity. A fictional character molded anyway he wish or simply tuck away in his subconscious when it suited."

Lisa clicked her seat belt in place. "No one can predict how they'll feel in this kind of situation. I think all in all, it went pretty well."

I sighed, fastened my seat belt, and started the engine. "We're in the honeymoon phase."

"What is that?"

"Where we're polite and everyone was on their best behavior."

"Maybe, but Susan seemed really cool about the whole thing."

A dull headache throbbed behind my eyes. "I had no idea she was sick."

"You think it's cancer?"

"She shows signs of undergoing chemotherapy treatment."

"Shit. How sick do you think she is?"

"I don't know." My head dropped back against the headrest. "And still, she's here with Michael, and so gracious."

"You picked a good mom for him."

"I wish I could take the credit, but that was all Diane."

"How?"

"She never said. But when I met Susan, I instantly liked her." My hands trembled. "Mom was always good at introducing people that got along well."

"I wonder what he would have been like if I'd raised him. I barely knew how to take care of myself then, let alone a baby. He's very together and secure."

Lisa was quiet for a moment. "Where to from here?"

"Unless I hear from him, I'll give him a little time. When Margaret displays the witch bottles, I'll invite him and hope that this whole thing doesn't scare him off."

"You're not a scary person, Rae. You may put up a front, but today the true Rae was there."

"What does that mean?"

"Let's face it, Rae. When you're doing your I-must-be-perfect mode like your mother, you're a little Stepford Wife–ish."

"I am not."

"You *are*, Rae. But when you're like this, you're pretty cool. Kid, you need to loosen your grip on the wheel of life."

Sliding on my sunglasses, I backed out of the parking space and drove toward Duke Street. "Yeah, right."

"See, there you go again, Rae. You're shoring up the defenses."

"Control is not a bad thing, Lisa. You attend your AA meetings in an effort to stay in control, don't you?"

"No argument here. But I also know I can't control everything around me. I can only manage and accept."

"That sounds reasonable."

When we pulled up in front of the Prince Street house, a

white Mercedes was parked in front. The front door was ajar and there was an *Open House* flag planted by the For Sale sign. The realtor, I figured.

"Great," Lisa said. "I was hoping she'd be gone by now."

"You don't like her?" I was now ready to talk about something else.

"She's a little overbearing."

"Like me?"

"Not at all like you. I know you have a heart in there somewhere. Not so sure about this one."

"Do you want me to come in with you?"

"Would you?" Her look of genuine relief surprised me. She had handled the restaurant so well and now Lisa was melting because of a realtor.

"Of course." I parked and we walked into the center hallway. Charlie barked from his crate, clearly not happy with people in his house. Lisa hurried to the kitchen and let him out. He jumped up on her and she greeted him with a quick hug before she hustled him out the door into the yard. She picked up a red chew ring and tossed it as he took off running. She tried to slip back inside unnoticed, but the dog barked at the door. "Rae, I'll be out here with Charlie if anyone needs me."

"No trouble. I'll call out if you're needed."

"Thanks." She turned to wrestle the red ring from the dog and threw it again.

I turned to study the interior of the house. It had been years since I'd stood in this hallway. There had been so many renovations that I barely recognized the place. "I like what Amelia did with the place," I said to Lisa, who was still standing just outside the back door.

"I do, too. She always wanted to give it back to me one day in better shape than when she received it."

Upstairs, we heard footsteps and then a couple appeared at

the top of the stairs. I recognized them immediately. It was Samuel and Debra. Each was smiling and both were equally shocked when they saw me standing at the base of the bull-nose staircase.

"Dr. McDonald?" Debra asked. Her face reddened a tinge, but she summoned a grin.

Samuel was more relaxed, extending his hand. "What brings you here? Are you thinking about buying the place?"

"I'm a friend of the current owner. No interest in buying."

Samuel studied the entryway, admiring the house. "This kind of house doesn't come on the market very often," he said. "When my agent, Ms. Tuttle, telephoned me, I told Debra she had to see the place." He wrapped his arm around her shoulders and grinned. "We told our families that we're getting married. Buying this house will top off the wedding perfectly."

Hormones and ego were driving this couple. But clear thinking? No way.

A Letter from Patience

DECEMBER 17, 1758

Dearest Mother,

My health worsens with this pregnancy, and it doesn't feel like the others.

The girl, Hanna, is nearly five. She is a chubby child, very bright and continues to spend her days with the witch. Patrick is now writing his letters and proves to have lovely handwriting. Marcus is learning the tobacco trade with Mr. McDonald. Marcus loves the outside as much as Patrick loves his books. Patrick is very bright, learns quickly, and rarely needs me to read to him.

As I watch Hanna and the witch tend the herbs in the garden, I feel as if I never knew the girl. She is always pleasant to me but when she falls or needs help, she goes to the witch. Though I am content with this arrangement, I dread the day my son will leave.

As my belly swells, Mr. McDonald is thrilled at the prospect of another child. However, I've felt no quickening in the womb and each time the witch looks at my belly, she slowly shakes her head.

Yours faithfully,
Patience McDonald

Chapter Fourteen

LISA, SATURDAY, OCTOBER 15, 2011

After the prospective buyers left, Rebecca mentioned that another couple might be coming by for a showing. So, I hooked the leash on Charlie's collar, and we made ourselves scarce.

We walked from Prince Street down to Union Street and along the Washington & Old Dominion Trail. A gentle breeze blew off the water and it felt good to exercise. The buyers looked excited and Rebecca had seemed pleased, whispering to me that she expected an offer.

When we left the trail and headed back to the house, I saw Rebecca's car still parked out front, so we turned and headed down King Street. When I saw the salvage yard sign, I remembered the picture of Amelia taken in front of the warehouse and decided to pay them a visit.

The bells on the front door jingled as I pushed through the door. I was not sure if they could help me with the image but decided it was worth a try. Maybe if I knew Amelia's past better, I could help her recall other memories.

Addie Morgan stood behind the front counter sorting what looked like hundreds of keys. Her smile was quick and bright. "Lisa! Did you come in search of more glass plate negatives?"

"No, but if you come across any, keep me in mind. Do you mind if I have Charlie in here?"

She pushed up off a stool and stretched her back. "No, he's fine."

"Where's the baby?"

"Upstairs sleeping. She's been very fussy today and is cutting teeth. We both could use a nap." Addie held out her hand to Charlie and let him sniff it. When he licked her hand, she patted him on the head.

I fished the picture out of my purse and showed it to her. "My aunt's attorney gave me this picture. He found it in her late husband's papers. I was hoping you could help me figure out who's in the picture. The young woman in the center is Amelia."

Addie looked at the image. "She was lovely."

"She taught high school music for a year, and judging by the teens around her, I think this was a photo of her students. And they appear to be in front of your building."

"That's the warehouse. But no sign on the front door." She studied the date. "Taken 1968. We didn't officially become a business until 1969. But I think that's my Aunt Grace to the left." She tapped the face of a midsized woman with long curly brown hair wearing jeans, a tie-dyed shirt, and sneakers. "Grace was quite the hippie. But I don't see my mother."

"Grace's sister?"

"Yes. If this were 1968, it would have been around the time my grandparents died. We should ask Grace."

"You don't think she'd mind?"

"I don't see why not. Let me call up to her. Be right back. Would you man the fort?"

"Will do."

She ran up the stairs, leaving Charlie and me alone to

study the keys laid out on the counter. Most were thick, old, and rusted. How much had each one seen over its years.

"I like this place. Full of so much life," Jennifer whispered.

I almost asked why she was whispering but then realized that answering was somewhat insane. She was not real. She was me. My own thoughts echoing back, I think.

"If it makes you feel better, pretend it's not me talking to you. But it is!" she said, louder. "I've been with you since the accident."

I ignored the voice.

"Oh, you hear me, just like you have before."

I hesitated before asking, "Are you with me forever?"

"That depends."

The sound of footsteps on the staircase sent color rushing to my cheeks. God, I hoped they did not hear me talking to myself.

Addie appeared, with Carrie in her arms and an older woman moving slowly behind her. I recognized the woman immediately as the girl in the picture. Gone were the long brown locks and the tie-dye, but her eyes sparked with the same brightness.

Addie adjusted the baby in her arms. "Lisa Smyth, this is my aunt Grace. Grace, this is Lisa."

Grace extended her hand. "Lisa, how is Amelia these days?"

"She has been diagnosed with Alzheimer's."

The lines around Grace's lips deepened with a frown. "She was one of the sharpest gals I knew. Always so funny. And she had a voice like an angel when she sang."

"Grace, I was hoping you could help me with this picture. Amelia's attorney recently found it in her husband's papers."

Grace pulled her glasses from the pocket of her shirt, settled them on her nose, and studied the image. She chuckled and looked up. "1968. God, that transports me back."

She traced a bent finger over the faces, surprised by the image of herself at such a young age. "Where does life go?" she asked. "I was only eighteen when this picture was taken."

"What was Amelia doing there that day?"

"School had just started, and she was producing *The Sound of Music*—or maybe it was *The Music Man*. I don't remember, but she decided to tackle this ambitious project and told her class that if they wanted extra credit, they had to meet her at this corner."

"Why this corner?"

"Scavenging. My parents died shortly after I graduated high school, and the warehouse was my inheritance. My mother, Lizzie, collected every bit of junk and salvage she came across for years and stowed it all in this building. I was overwhelmed with what I found and decided to start selling it. Out of that eventually came this business. Amelia's parents had owned a house on Union Street then, and she was familiar with this warehouse. She called ahead and asked if she and her students could scavenge. I was more than happy to have them take whatever they could carry."

"Alexandria was kind of a rough place then."

"It's not what it is now, and it probably wasn't smart for either one of us to be on the streets alone, even in broad daylight." A smile tweaked the edge of her lips. "In those days, I was always about taking chances."

The baby in Addie's arms hiccuped. Addie shifted her to her opposite shoulder and patted her on the back. "I like the idea of you being wild and reckless. I'll remind you of that when you tell me to be careful."

Grace waved a hand at her. "You're different. You've got a baby. I didn't have anyone depending on me."

"Where was Mom then?" Addie asked.

"She must have been in school."

Addie glanced at the picture. "You looked pretty composed, considering you'd lost your parents."

"I was terrified. But that's the way it went. Amelia was always so talkative, and she told me about the high school play she was producing and that she needed props."

"I told her she could have whatever she and her students could carry away from the warehouse if they paid me twenty bucks. That was a fortune to me then, and I thought she'd laugh it off, but she agreed."

"Do you remember who was in the picture?"

Grace straightened her shoulders. "Well, let me see. You know that's me and that's Amelia. That good-looking young man is Robert Murphy."

"Amelia's husband," I said.

"Yes. They met that day. One of the schoolgirls saw him passing by the warehouse and asked him for help with a trunk. He came inside and saw Amelia and was hooked. Heard he followed her to New York when she took the train up for one last audition."

"She said they met in New York."

"She might have noticed him in New York, but they met here."

"I wonder if she got the part in the play." I mused.

"She did. Turned it down," Grace said.

"Really? Why?"

"Fell in love with Mr. Murphy." Shrugging, Grace tapped a bent finger on the face of a young girl. "That girl, Diane, she was about eighteen and a senior in high school. She was the one that pulled Robert off the street for Amelia. What was her last name? Saunders. Her name was Diane Saunders."

"That's Rae McDonald's mother."

"I suppose so. In fact, that's Stephen McDonald, the one she ended up marrying, right there next to her. He was also one of Amelia's students."

"Who's the older woman next to Diane?"

"That's her mother. Nice lady. Felicity. Fay. Fran."

"Fiona?" I asked.

"Yeah. That's it. Fiona Saunders."

"Oh, my God. That's Fiona?" I asked. Fiona must have known who Amelia was and never said a word. Did Amelia know she'd stood just feet from her birth mother?

"Who was Fiona?" Addie asked.

"Amelia's mother."

"No, Amelia's mother was Marjorie Smyth," Grace said. "She came to the warehouse several times when she was restoring her house."

The secret did not really need to be kept any longer. "Fiona was Amelia's birth mother. She just told me a few days ago that she was adopted."

Grace rubbed her hand over her chin. "I didn't know that."

"She was having a good day and wanted to set the record straight about her parents. She gave me the baby book that Fiona and her first husband, Jeffrey McDonald, made for her."

"She was married to a McDonald? I never would have guessed it."

Addie shook her head. "What is Amelia holding there? I think I know, but I want you to tell me."

Grace shrugged. "Let me get my magnifying glass." She moved to the front desk and retrieved a large round glass that she held over the picture. "Well, I'll be damned. Addie, look at this."

Holding the baby close, Addie looked through the magnifying glass. "Lisa, you'll never guess what Amelia is holding. It's the witch bottle."

"The one that Margaret and I scavenged from the Prince Street house?"

"It appears so."

"How'd she get it?"

Grace shook her head as she pulled off her glasses. "I told them they could take whatever they wanted, and they all spent hours scavenging the warehouse for chairs and tables and props for their play. Amelia must have picked it up here that day."

"According to Margaret's research" Addie said, "she believes those bottles were likely made in Alexandria."

"And they have all found their way back to the corner of King Street, the heart of the city," Grace said. "I'm not a statistician, but what are the odds?"

A Letter from Patience

JUNE 17, 1759

Dearest Mother,

Mr. McDonald no longer comes to my bed. And in truth I am glad. The children are growing bigger and bigger and my swollen belly aches so badly. The child has never quickened in my belly, and I fear it has been cursed.

The children and he turn to the witch for their care. I should be angry, but I'm not. In the last year, my senses and feelings flicker like a candle in a breeze and soon I believe they will extinguish entirely. Would it be wrong for me to welcome the stillness?

Yours faithfully,
Patience McDonald

Chapter Fifteen

RAE, TUESDAY, OCTOBER 18, 2011

Three days had passed since Lisa and I had met Michael and Susan at the pizza place. Michael and I did not exchange any more e-mails, nor did either of us call or reach out in any way. Susan sent me a short handwritten note thanking me for seeing Michael and her. She said it meant a lot to him. As I tucked the note into the scrapbook now filled with Michael's pictures, I wondered what *meant a lot to him* really said. The words were straightforward, but I kept injecting extra meaning. Did it mean he liked me? Wanted to see me again? Was satisfied he did not need to see me again?

I ran extra miles each day, hoping to exchange fear and insecurity for discomfort and sweat. And though each run gave me a bit of momentary peace, the unease never left.

As Tuesday morning dawned, I found my curiosity for Michael weighing down my thoughts. The pictures and the memories of our lunch were not enough to satisfy me, and I thought if I could just get back into his life, all the questions buried so deep in me would be settled. I went online and searched his name as well as his parents' names but found little more than a few cross-country stats. There was a Facebook page, but I was not a friend, so the page was closed to me.

Greedy for any scrap of information I could find, I kept searching, unmindful of the time that ticked by. Dozens of long-denied questions eased out of the darkness. What did he like to eat for breakfast? Was he a night owl? Did he have a girlfriend?

The questions buzzed like flies and would not be shooed easily away by work, my clients, or Zeb's calls regarding the addition.

Thinking maybe I could visit with Lisa, I drove down Prince Street, but finding no parking, turned left on Union Street. By the time I found a spot, I was steps away from the Union Street Bakery. Margaret said they were closed early in the week, but I found an *Open* sign dangling in the front door.

Surprised and grateful, I parked, grabbed my purse, and got out. The air was warm and the breeze from the Potomac River nudged me up the street. I pushed through the front door, expecting to see Rachel, but instead discovered a tall, lean woman with olive skin and straight dark hair. Judging by Margaret's descriptions, I guessed this was her sister, Daisy.

Whereas openness came naturally to Rachel and Margaret, Daisy, though smiling as I approached, immediately struck me as more closed and guarded. Somewhere on her cellular level, she understood that the world did not always have open arms, and that sometimes it deals a bad hand to good people.

Daisy reached for a towel tucked in her apron and wiped her hands. "Rae McDonald."

"That's right."

"I believe Margaret has told me all there is to know about your family tree."

Certainly not all. I moved toward the display case now filled with a dozen different cookies and pies. "She's a very enthusiastic woman when it comes to history."

She extended her hand over the case and took mine in a very firm grip. "I'm Daisy."

"I guessed. Your sister has also told me a lot about you."

Her laugh was warm and sincere. "Has Margaret totally spilled the beans about the entire McCrae family yet?"

"She doesn't share as much as you might think."

Daisy hitched her hands on her hips. "Good to know. Margaret keeps us all guessing."

"She seems to enjoy her work so much."

"These days, she's consumed by the McDonald papers."

"I haven't heard from her in a few days," I said.

"She and Addie drove out to the Eastern Shore to look at the potential salvage of a light keeper's house. I'm not sure. Could be a big job. And they've had several smaller jobs that have kept them busy."

"Sounds encouraging. I'm glad to see the business growing."

"I thought Alexandria would lose the salvage yard a few months ago, but Addie brought it back from the brink," Daisy said.

"That's what Rachel said you did for the bakery."

She hitched her hands on her hips. "I'm the numbers gal. And that's important, but it's Rachel's baking that brings in the customers."

"She said you were out looking at warehouse space."

"I was. It's a very nice place out in Loudoun County, about an hour commute if there's no traffic."

Loudoun County. "It's a very nice area."

A wisp of hair slipped free and brushed over her eyes before she quickly tucked it back in place. "Has a lot to offer in terms of the location."

"Does that mean you might be moving?" I asked.

"Prices are still a little high, so I need to keep searching. But my husband and I are considering a move. A place in the country means more space for his bike business—he does excursions, so it's easier to launch a tour from Loudoun or Prince William County rather than from Alexandria city roads. We could also afford a bigger facility where he can store bikes. Less traffic. I don't know. Still processing."

"Good luck with it."

She clasped her hands together. "What can I get for you? Rachel has been testing recipes for days. Though I'm afraid nothing is too savory. Margaret says you don't have a sweet tooth."

"I'm thinking about expanding my horizons and thought I'd try your sugar cookies," I said. "Rachel gave me some the other day when I visited but they were gobbled up before I had a chance to eat one bite."

"Must have been the lemon polenta. We don't have those today, but I can hook you up with plain sugar cookies."

"That sounds perfect."

She tugged a piece of wax paper from a dispenser and grabbed a pink box. She inspected the cookies a moment before she chose a perfectly round one. "So, you're enjoying working with Margaret?"

"Yes, I appreciate her directness and humor."

"When it comes to history, she's unstoppable. She really does know her stuff."

I remembered what Margaret had said about Daisy. She was adopted at age three and reached out to her birth mother last year. The reunion had not gone smoothly.

As I watched Daisy arrange the cookies carefully in the box, she reminded me of myself. Control was important. She did not have Rachel's artful knack for making the haphazard look beautiful.

Questions about Daisy's birth mother jabbed at me. She was a year into this discovery process, and I wanted to know more. What had her birth mother done wrong? What could I do to reach out to Michael without pushing him away?

Instead of opening my heart and sharing, I opened my wallet and pulled out a ten-dollar bill. As I creased the bill lengthwise and stretched out any wrinkles, the questions shoved against the ice. *Just ask her.*

All I could manage was, "How much do I owe you?"

She closed up the box and sealed it with a gold Union Street Bakery label. "Seven dollars."

I pushed the bill toward her and accepted the box, almost wishing she could reach into my mind and see the questions clanging around.

She, of course, did not and I was reminded of my advice to my clients. *No one can read your mind. If you have a question, then simply ask it. What harm can come from asking?*

Daisy looked up at me from the register and arranged three bills face side up. "Three dollars change."

"Thank you."

"Are you buying the cookies for a special occasion?"

I tucked the bills away. *Ask her!* For a moment, I imagined Jennifer prodding me as she did when we were kids. "Nothing special."

"You're eating them all?" She held up her hand. "And if you are, I'm not judging. I've crushed a few boxes of cookies in my time. Raises the endorphin levels through the roof. Good for the soul."

"I think you mean serotonin levels."

She chuckled. "Definitely, the feel-good levels."

"Yes." *Ask her!* "Have a nice day."

"You do the same, Rae. Don't be a stranger."

A baby cried from the back room and I hesitated. "Who's that?"

"My son, Walter. He's up from his nap. Would you like to meet him?"

Something primal and feminine clenched inside me. "I would."

"Be right back."

I waited as she vanished through the swinging doors and then reappeared seconds later with a boy that appeared to be about ten months old. His hair was as dark as his mother's, but instead of being smoothed and controlled, it stuck straight up. He popped his thumb in his mouth and though his eyelids were heavy with sleep, he grinned when he saw me.

I pictured Michael at that age. His face was round though the hair was thinner and more red. Grinning, drooling, and sucking his thumb all at the same time. "He's very cute."

She rubbed his tummy and kissed him on the cheek. "Walter Sinclair is the best thing that ever happened to me."

Sadness gathered at my feet like a mist. "I can see that."

Daisy studied me, picking up something in the tone under my words. "Would you like to hold him?"

Shifting, I struggled with the powerful and surprising urge to hold the baby. "I don't have much practice holding babies."

"He's pretty easy. A very laid-back child."

The ice cracked and broke, and disconcerting warmth emerged. "I would like to hold him."

She came around the counter as I set down the cookies and my purse on the display case. I extended my hands to him, and he leaned gently forward until I had his full weight in my embrace. So much heavier and sturdier than I remembered when I held Michael, though he had only just been born when I had cradled him.

"His name is Walter?"

"Yes. Walter Gordon Sinclair."

"He looks like you."

"Good. He should after the stretch marks and twenty hours of labor. I'm still trying to get my shape back."

That was one of the perks of having a baby so young. The body forgave quickly.

Walter looked at me, thumb firmly in mouth, and studied me as closely as I studied him. This close, I could see the cracker crumbs in his hair, the bits of sleep in the corner of his eyes, and the way his earlobe gently rounded. "He's very sturdy."

Daisy retied her apron strings, securing them with a tight bow. "He's a tank. You should hear him when he's working his way through the lower pantry, pulling pots and pans from the cabinets. I tried to keep him out of the cabinets at first, then just decided to move the dangerous stuff up high and leave the fun stuff within his reach. He won't be this age forever, and I enjoy watching him wreck the kitchen."

I tugged down his blue T-shirt, which had inched up over his round belly. The ice splintered more, and this time, I did not even try to shore it up. This was a moment of pure joy, and it had been so long since I had felt anything like *this* that I could not shut it out.

"You're a natural with him," Daisy said. "Do you have children?"

And there was the opening. *Just tell her!*

"Only a few people know this. But . . ." Emotion clenched my throat and threatened to cut off the words. "I had a baby when I was sixteen. His name is Michael." Tears stung the corner of my eyes. God, I'd said it out loud. "I gave him up for adoption."

Daisy stilled, staring at me and searching for answers to questions she had so carefully walled away. "Oh, Rae."

I smiled, keeping my focus on the baby's face, unable to speak with a steady voice.

"Have you seen him since?" she asked.

Walter pulled his thumb from his mouth and grabbed my

lower lip as if he were waiting for my answer. Grinning, I gently pulled his tiny hand away. "For the first time last week."

She straightened her shoulders and shifted. "How did it go?"

I looked up at Daisy. "I think it went well. But we were both so nervous."

"Did you reach out to him or did he contact you about the meeting?"

We both had answers to questions that the other one wanted so badly. I studied Walter's sweet face, drawing the warmth my heart needed to speak. "He e-mailed me a couple of weeks ago. It took me a little time to get the courage to respond, but I did."

She cleared her throat. "Why were you afraid?"

Daisy's expression was almost childlike. It reminded me of Amelia when she spoke about her birth mother. "I didn't want him to hate me."

"Why would he hate you?"

I kissed Walter on the cheek and handed him back to Daisy. "Because I gave him away."

She held her son tightly. Most in this situation would have said, *What you did was the best for you both. Giving him away was an act of love. You should be proud.*

Though all true, those words described only one side of the coin. The other, the one few discussed, was the loss, the unnatural separation, and the sadness that always lingered in the shadows.

With Walter gone from my arms, so went the warmth in my chest. A chill snaked up my back, circling over my shoulders, and crept toward my heart. "That's a hard thing to forgive, even under the best of circumstances."

A wrinkle furrowed her brow. She no longer saw her birth mother now, but me. "It sounds like you did it out of love," she said.

"I'd like to believe so. I was sixteen and scared. I just didn't think I was brave enough to raise us both without my mother's support. And my mother was very clear she wouldn't help." The anger that had stirred in the last couple of years glowed. "Michael is with a great family."

Daisy chewed her bottom lip. "How is your son doing?"

I reached for my purse and the box of cookies. "Very well." Susan's pale, drawn features and the wispy strands of hair peeking from her headscarf troubled me.

"Does he look like you?"

A sigh shuddered over my lips and I said with no small measure of pride, "He does."

"I'm glad for you, Rae." She kissed Walter. "No guarantees in life, Rae, but here's hoping you and your son can become good friends."

Never a mother. I'd signed away that right. But a friend . . . "That would be nice." I raised the box of cookies. "Thank you for these. Please tell Rachel I said hello."

"Sure, any time." She shifted Walter to her other hip. "Come back soon, Rae. I like talking with you."

I raised the box of cookies. "Me, too, Daisy."

Twenty minutes later, when I arrived home and saw the Shire Architectural Salvage truck in front of the house, I did not tense up or resent the intrusion. I was actually grateful for it.

As I parked, Margaret swung open the driver's-side door and hopped out. "Rae! My wo-man! I have news from the past!"

Always excited. Always ready to grab life by the fistful and run with it as fast as she could.

"Margaret. You must be psychic. I just bought cookies."

She stretched and rolled her head from side to side. "USB cookies, I hope!"

I held up the pink box. "Is there any other kind?"

Nodding, she grinned. "I'll trade coffee and cookies for a data dump."

"Sounds like a fair swap." The sky now was a deep blue and so blissfully cloudless. No rain in sight for now. "Let's eat on the back porch. I could use a little sunshine."

"Done!"

And so, I made coffee, and within ten minutes, the two of us were sitting on black wrought iron chairs on the brick patio.

"At one time," Margaret said, "this very spot would have offered us a panoramic view of the river."

For as long as I can remember, houses crowded the land between my current property line and the banks of the Potomac. "The family began selling off parts of the property a hundred and fifty years ago."

"That would have been right after the Civil War," she said. "The family's finances were decimated. Your great-great-grandfather was one of Mosby's Gray Ghosts. Basically, the cavalry special forces of the Confederacy. They did a lot of damage not far from here and made the Union very unhappy. Union soldiers burned all the McDonald's crops. That generation of McDonalds lost three sons in the war."

"I didn't realize."

"One son survived. He ended up being your great-great-grandfather," Margaret said.

"We seem to barely survive each generation until now. No more sons in my generation to carry on the name."

"Then you keep the name. You pass it on to your children."

I reached for a cookie but did not bite into it. I had never considered that I could have more children. It was almost as if fate gave me my chance and I blew it. Now, especially after holding Walter, at least a door to the possibilities had cracked open. "Maybe."

Margaret tucked her feet up under her as she bit into a cookie. She pointed to the square patch of dirt. "So, have you finally decided what'll be on that spot?"

"I asked for a garage with an office. But now, maybe an apartment."

"Sounds a little indecisive, Rae. First you buy cookies and now you can't decide on a construction project. What's next? No high heels and pearls?"

A smirk tugged at the corners of my mouth. "I'm never indecisive. But for whatever reason, I can't make up my mind on this."

"That hearth was there for nearly three centuries. It must be hard to imagine something else in its place."

"I was told by my mother and grandmother never to remove the stones. The stones were supposed to bring us good luck."

"Then why'd you tear it down?" Margaret asked.

"I wasn't feeling like the McDonald family had seen much good luck."

"Why?"

"I decided to remove these stones because the hearth felt like a monument to the past, and for me to move forward, the hearth would need to go."

Margaret reached for a cookie. "I can see that."

"I just didn't realize that once it was gone, choosing what is to come next would be harder than I ever imagined."

Margaret inspected her cookie as if it held the answer. "Too many people assume the past, present, and future are separate. When will they learn?"

"What do you have for me, Margaret? Something about your witch bottles? Or maybe Fiona McDonald?"

Margaret glanced up. "As you have already guessed, the McDonald women have had a very rough time of it over the generations here in Alexandria."

Needing a distraction, I bit into the cookie. The taste caught me by surprise. It was the perfect blend of butter and sugar, with a hint of lemon.

"Pretty good, right?" Margaret asked, grinning with a wink.

One bite created a longing for more . . . "Very good."

"Dare you to eat just one."

As much as I wanted to prove her wrong and set the cookie aside, I could not. Not only would it be a waste to toss away what was clearly made with such love and care, but also did not want to deny myself the pleasure.

It was only a moment before I could say, "Rachel is a genius."

"I know. She's the cookie master." She gobbled the last of her cookie and reached for another. "You can taste all her emotions she puts into her food."

"After her husband died," Margaret said, "she went through a phase where everything was too salty. Then there were the months she dated that French baker. Too sweet. She's still trying to find the perfect balance."

"I remembered reading the obituary notice for her husband in the paper," I said. "The young ones always remind me of Jennifer. I know that was a very difficult time for her. And the kids."

Margaret shook her head. "It was a tough time, but Rachel is stronger than she gives herself credit for, and we were all lucky when Daisy came to the rescue. It always seems to work out for us."

"Really?" I reached for a second cookie.

"They say my great-great-grandfather had the luck of the devil. He won the Union Street Bakery in a card game and found the love of his life when he was in his late forties. He and his wife, Sally, raised seven children, and all survived to adulthood."

"All? That's something."

"We also have a wanderlust in us. Most of the McCrae's are now scattered, but from what I've been able to piece together, that thread has followed us."

"Very fortunate."

She dug her worn spiral notebook from her backpack. "But not so much for the McDonald women."

"I've done well enough in my career."

She shook her head. "I'm not talking financially, Rae. I'm talking in matters of the heart. All the generations of McDonald women have suffered terrible losses."

"True."

Margaret finished off her cookie and reached for another. "Are you dating anyone?"

I laughed, surprised by her forwardness. "No."

"Not ever?"

"Not in a long time," I said. "It's odd that the McDonalds were so unlucky in love when we have had a knack for introducing people who went on to find love and marriage."

She slapped her hand to her thigh. "I knew you were a matchmaker!"

"I'm not a matchmaker."

"You keep telling yourself that, Doc. I've gotten to know your family pretty well. Excellent journalists and scribes. From what I've gleaned, love is very aloof, and that's putting it delicately."

"Perhaps we're smart women who simply make bad choices."

"Generation after generation. Come *on*," She finished off her cookie and dusted the crumbs from her hands. "What are the odds that ten generations of women would struggle with happiness so much?"

"Ah, I think we're back to the witch bottles. Are you saying we're cursed?"

"The Shires called their ailment a curse," Margaret said.

"They suffer from mental illness. Genetics are not curses."

"That's what Addie used to say before her witch bottle broke. After it shattered, her sister seemed to improve."

Relaxing back in my chair, I stared at the spot where they had found the witch bottle. "So, it all goes back to those bottles."

"Appears so," Margaret said, "Addie told me that Lisa brought an old picture by the salvage yard. Dated 1968. In the picture were Grace, Amelia, Fiona, and your mother."

"Really?"

"And you know what Grace said?"

Again, she paused, ever the performer. "What?"

"Grace said your mom, who was about eighteen, saw a young guy passing by the yard and asked him to come inside and help move a heavy piece. That guy was Robert Murphy. He saw Amelia and was smitten right away. They were married six months later."

"Mom, the matchmaker."

"Also, super weird that Fiona was in the picture. Amelia is with her birth mother and half-sister and never knew she was in the middle of her own family reunion," she said. "Amelia found a witch bottle that day in the yard. It's the one we found in Amelia's basement over the summer. It's all so full circle it gives me goose bumps."

"Lots of coincidences."

Licking the tip of a finger, she flipped through her notebook pages. "I got the DNA test results back. Doc, you may want to retract your last statement."

"That was very fast."

"I have friends who helped."

My mood had been somber when she arrived, but Margaret McCrae had a way of uplifting my spirts. "Tell me what you found."

She tapped her finger on her dark, almost illegible handwriting. "All three families share similar genetic markers."

"All three? I wasn't expecting that."

"The Shires and McDonalds seem to originate from the same genetic line."

"Meaning Faith and her twin sons?"

"Yes. Addie is descended from Marcus and you from Patrick. I truly believe now that Faith's son became Patrick McDonald. Faith and the McDonalds never told anyone. It would explain why Faith never left the McDonald's farm."

I had not given Faith much thought since Margaret had brought her to my attention, but now I wanted to know more. The witch and I were not so different from one another.

"And you have nothing else on Faith?" I asked.

"Patience speaks often of the witch, but Patience died in 1770, thirteen years before Faith passed."

"What does Patience say about her?"

"That women sought her out for her healing powers. Faith was very close to Patience's daughter, Hanna, whom she practically raised."

"And Patience's husband?"

"Mr. McDonald died a few months before Faith."

"So, they were here at the house alone for thirteen years."

Margaret grinned. "And he never remarried."

"Do you really think there was something between them?"

Margaret shrugged. "Sure, makes sense, but who knows."

"Funny that Patience's letters would survive. If Mr. McDonald didn't want the world to know the truth about Patrick, why would he not destroy the incriminating letters."

"Very likely he never knew about them. And if Faith knew, she would have saved them to prove Patrick was her son and Marcus's fraternal twin."

Shaking my head, I asked, "What about Lisa's genetic markers?"

"Would you believe she's related to my tribe?"

"The McCrae's? How?"

"That, I don't know yet. But rest assured, I'll figure it out."

"Is there anyone in Alexandria who's not related?"

Margaret laughed. "Stay tuned."

A Letter from Faith

MARCH 17, 1769

My Dearest Children,

The farmer's wife no longer writes her letters and remains bedridden. She rarely speaks, and when she does, it's always about Patrick. As much as I hate the lie, I see that the boy will have far more than I could ever give him. Marcus, the oldest of my boys by minutes, will take over his own father's lands when he turns eighteen. He now lives in Alexandria, where he apprentices for the owner of Gadsby's Tavern. Patrick is away at school and will go to the university in Williamsburg to study the law.

Forever,
Faith

Chapter Sixteen

RAE, WEDNESDAY, OCTOBER 19, 2011

The next morning, I rose early and was restless. After my morning run and my client appointments, I still could not calm my thoughts. I decided to go see Michael's birth father on a long shot he might know something. We had not seen each other in over sixteen years.

Of course, I had kept tabs on him over the years, but we did not speak. But now after meeting Michael, I needed to know what he was doing. I needed to see what genetics he and the boy shared. A year older than I, Dan had finished college at Virginia Tech and gone on to become an engineer and joined the family firm in Fairfax County. He married. Had two more children. Girls. No boys.

I needed to talk to him and tell him about my meeting with his son. I needed him to acknowledge that Michael's birth, which had changed me so deeply, had left some kind of lasting impression on him. Something. Anything.

I found the engineering offices in Fairfax easily enough and parked. The building his company owned had the look of old money, just as his family had been. There was a time I would have been terrified by all this raw emotion, but now I did not worry about who I upset or how it made me feel as long as I felt something.

I needed to know.

Inside the lobby, I walked to the receptionist with my shoulders back. She was young and pretty and wore a blue dress. When she looked up at me, the smile reached her expressive blue eyes. "Can I help you?" she asked.

Quickly, I shored up the ice, hoping it would protect me a little longer. "I'm here to see Dan Chesterfield."

"Is he expecting you?"

"Yes," I lied. "My name is Dr. Rae McDonald. We grew up together in Alexandria."

Let the name from the past jostle him if only just a little. I needed to know I was not alone in this boat.

She cradled the phone under her chin as she pressed his extension. "I'll buzz him."

"Thank you."

I did not sit but turned and moved to the window. The view did not match the grand interior. It was a busy side street that butted up against the parking lot. At two o'clock, the traffic was already growing heavy and would make the trip home twice as long.

Suddenly, my reasons for coming seemed silly and selfish. In fact, I felt foolish. What did I hope to prove by coming?

"Rae?"

I turned at the sound of his voice. He was as tall as I remembered, but that thick hair had thinned just a little and his face was rounder. He wore a crisp, monogrammed white shirt, red tie, and suit pants that looked custom tailored. He also wore a wedding band.

I was not sure how I would feel when I saw him, but there was no animosity. "Dan. Thank you for seeing me."

He nodded toward the inner office door. "Why don't you come into my office and we can talk?"

"Of course."

Neither of us spoke as we walked down the carpeted hallway past beautiful color pictures of buildings that I assumed his company had done the engineering work on.

Inside his office, he closed the door quietly and held out his hand toward a chair. "Why don't you have a seat, Rae?"

A part of me wished I could summon a witty quip or something to draw the pure awkwardness out of this moment. But I had nothing, and I could see that he was a little nervous. So, I simply said, "Thank you."

Dan took the seat to my right instead of behind his desk. I took that as a good sign. He was not going for the power position. In this, he saw us as equals.

"How are you doing?" he asked. "You look great, by the way. You've barely aged at all."

"You look good as well, Dan."

"I try." He tugged at his cuff and sat a little straighter. "Not possible to look like the eighteen-year-old track star these days. A thriving engineering practice and a couple of kids running around the house makes it hard to find the time to work out. I only run a few days a week at best."

I raised my chin a fraction at the mention of children. "How many children do you have?"

"Two girls. Alexa and Madison. They're ten and seven."

"I bet they're beautiful."

On the credenza behind his desk were pictures of his wife and their two daughters. Michael did not look like his half-sisters. He looked like me, and the girls favored their mother. For some reason, I was glad he did not have a son.

"Are you married?" he asked. "Do you have more children?"

More children. The subtle acknowledgment of Michael did not spin me into a panic as it might have years ago. "No, to both."

He let a sigh leak over his lips. "I've thought about you over the years and wondered how you were doing. Susan sends me pictures of Michael every year. He really looks so much like you, Rae."

He had opened Susan's envelopes and had gotten on with his life. I cleared my throat. "The pictures are amazing. I really do appreciate her."

"She's been great. You did a fantastic job choosing her." He cleared his throat. "The older I get, the more I realize how much I dumped on your shoulders back then. I was so scared that I didn't think about anyone but myself."

"We were both so clueless."

"Yeah, but I could have done a hell of a lot more."

There was some comfort in knowing he was affected by the boy's birth. "Michael sent me an e-mail a few weeks ago. He wanted to meet, and I agreed. I met him and Susan in a restaurant a few days ago."

His smile was genuine, warm. "How did it go?"

"Initially, it was hard facing him."

"Why?"

"Because I gave him away."

"Rae, you were a kid."

"He was my child." My tone sounded defensive. Maternalistic.

Absently, he twisted his wedding band. "We did right by him, Rae. Neither one of us was in a position to give him what he needed. You were at least enough of a parent to see he had good people to raise him. You stood your ground while I ran away."

"Do your wife and children know about him?"

"My parents do, of course, and so does my wife. We'll tell the girls when they get older." He shifted before looking at me. "You okay, Rae?"

"Did you know Susan was sick, Dan?"

A wrinkle deepened across his forehead. "No."

"I think it must be cancer, judging by her pale skin and hair loss. I didn't ask her about it because Michael was present."

"I'm sorry to hear that."

I moistened my lips. "I hate the idea of him losing her."

"Rae, medicine is pretty amazing these days."

"It doesn't look good, Dan."

He drew in a deep breath. "She's still married?"

"Yes."

"Good. They aren't alone."

"But the boy still needs his mother."

He studied me. "Are you sure you're okay?"

"Why wouldn't I be?"

Dark eyes studied me with a maturity absent from my memories of him. "I haven't seen you in over sixteen years, and now you're here."

Fine was the first word to spring to the tip of my tongue. I *was* fine. Right? The ice was cracking. Emotions were bubbling up. I could feel my life's direction changing whether I liked it or not. "I just thought you might like to know I saw him. And that he's doing well."

"That doesn't answer my question."

"I don't know how to answer the question. I thought I had my life figured out and now, I'm not so sure." I drew upon a smile I used for emotional patients. "Once I have the emotions sorted and put back in their boxes, I'll be fine."

"You didn't use to be so careful. You used to laugh and have fun. That's what I always liked about you. You were never afraid to try or do things."

My breath caught in my chest. "That was before I handed Michael over to Susan."

His eyes now showed a surprising sadness. "I thought you wanted the adoption, Rae."

"It was practical. Made sense. My mother wanted it. You and your parents wanted it. I don't think I did." I turned the wattage up on the smile. "But what's done is done."

The lines feathering from the corners of Dan's eyes deepened. "I didn't realize you wanted him. When I saw you sixteen years ago, at that Christmas party, you looked so in control and back on track. I was your typical eighteen-year-old male. Drunk. Foolish. Selfish. And relieved I hadn't lost my future. But now that I'm older, there are times I wonder what it would have been like for you and me to raise our son. He looks like a great kid."

"He is. We missed out on a lot." There was comfort knowing this had not been easy for him.

"No, it's good to talk about it, Rae. I don't talk about him much and that seems wrong."

"If I have more updates, would you like me to send you an e-mail?"

"That would be great. I sincerely do."

I extended my hand. "Thanks for your time. I know this visit is the last thing you ever expected."

"I'm glad you came by." He took my hand and shook it as if we were business associates. "Take care, Rae. Any time you want to talk. And if you or Michael or his parents ever need me, let me know."

"Thank you." But of course, it was not likely I'd ever visit him again. I had allowed emotion to drive this entire scene and felt weak and foolish for it.

My fingertips prickled, as if warming from frostbite. "Best of luck to you."

"You too, Rae. Let me show you out."

"No. That's not necessary. Really."

He nodded. He understood.

I left Dan standing in his office, with the pictures of his lovely children and wife smiling back at me from the credenza.

A Letter from Faith

MARCH 30, 1769

My Dearest Children,

The crops have been bountiful for the last decade and Mr. McDonald has profited handsomely. Mr. McDonald works even harder on the foundation for the fine brick home near the cottage. The hard labor seems to ease his sadness. He seems to accept that his dreams for a son have ended with his wife's illness. The growth in her belly is not a living creature, but something dark that drains life from her.

Hanna is now almost sixteen, and she is very pretty. Many of the young men in Alexandria have taken notice. We spend most of our days together and I am now teaching her the magic of the herbs. She is an apt student and may one day be a better healer than I. The farmer speaks of her making a fine marriage one day soon, but I rarely dwell on any notion that leaves me with no children in my care.

Forever,
Faith

Chapter Seventeen

LISA, WEDNESDAY, OCTOBER 19, 2011

Since I retrieved the box of glass plate negatives from the salvage yard, I had not looked at them. Common sense told me they would not be as technically sound compared to the work I was doing now. And so, I allowed myself to believe it was my artist's ego that kept me from inspecting them. I looked up from the computer, glanced over at a sleeping Charlie, and then studied the dusty wooden box at the end of the table. It looked as if it belonged in another time and place.

"If you walk that dog much more, his legs will fall off. And I swear, if you watch any more astrology on YouTube, I'm screaming."

"It's either that or drink."

Charlie opened his eyes and stared at me.

"What happened to work? You used to work all the time. And you've got a whole box of negatives that must be a real trip down memory lane."

"I can't mess up the house. And I'm not developing more negatives in the alley. That was maddening trying to keep the dust off the prints."

"The basement, duh."

"I hate the basement."

"I hate the basement." The inner voice mimicked a child's voice.

Irritated, I shut the laptop and rose. I opened the refrigerator. All that remained was a carton of milk and Chinese food from last night. Charlie stood and walked toward me, his tail wagging.

"Keep eating takeout and you'll get fat."

I shut the door. "Why do you care?"

"You know how I loathe shopping, and if your ass gets fat, we'll have to shop for new jeans. Just the drama of that moment makes me want to cringe."

"I'm not getting fat."

"Fatter. Go to the damn basement and make some pictures." She giggled. "You know you want to."

Rolling my head from side to side, I realized I did want to make prints. The few I had developed the other day in the alley had whetted my appetite and reminded me why I loved photography.

Grabbing a water bottle, I headed to the door that led downstairs. Flipping on the light, I stared down the shadowed steps, wondering why the space bothered me so much. Charlie stood beside me. I was fearless until my return to Alexandria. Grabbing my phone, I plugged in my ear buds, cranked the music, and tucked it in the waistband of my yoga pants. Charlie barked and looked as if he would follow, but I ordered him to stay.

My spirit lifting, I headed down the stairs, feeling the old planks creak under my steps. I moved toward the large, deep sink, which must have been used for washing clothes back in the day. The rusted hot and cold water knobs groaned as I twisted them. The pipes shuddered, as if shaken awake, and reluctantly spat out water. I dipped my fingertips under the stream to eventually find clean hot and cold running water.

With a determined purpose, I moved toward the other lights dangling from the ceiling in the basement and tugged their strings, waking them up. "It's still too dark."

"Lamps upstairs, dumbass."

"Right."

Back upstairs, I unplugged a floor lamp from the front sitting room and lugged it down the steps. Its light helped, but not enough. Three more trips up and down the stairs created a collection of fancy lamps that had no place in a basement, but the aggregate light chased the shadows from the space. No scary corners where danger lurked.

On the next trip up the stairs, I retrieved two folding tables from my SUV, which I set up along the wall. Next came the tubs for the chemicals. The entire process took me almost an hour, but by the time I was done, I had a workable darkroom.

On the first table I arranged three boxes of glass negatives I had shot in the last year. I had made one set in the Dakotas during the summer and the others while driving back to Virginia. As I thumbed over the rough edges, I could picture each and every image: The Rocky Mountains, the musicians in Austin, and a singer's cowboy boots in a Nashville honky-tonk.

Restless, I retrieved the negatives from the kitchen. These were the images I had captured before Jennifer's death. "I thought I lost these."

"I guess Amelia saved them along with all the other stuff she couldn't bring herself to toss."

"The same stuff I tossed without any thought the day Addie and Margaret were here."

The first image I pulled out was a view down Prince Street toward the Potomac River. "When I left town after you died, this was my last view of the city. I swore I would never come back."

"You used to say *never say never.*"

"I know." I held up the glass negative, allowing the light from a brass floor lamp to stream through the contrasting blacks, whites, and grays. "I wasn't patient then and didn't realize it could take hours of waiting to catch the right light. As I went through the collection, I realized only two were good enough to keep. The view from Prince Street, and the stoic picture of a young woman with long auburn hair. Jennifer.

"Maybe the universe is sending you a message."

I traced the outline of her eyes. "You look so much like Rae."

"Thanks. That's a good thing."

It was. "Do you think she'd be my friend if she knew the truth?"

"I know the truth and I'm still sticking around."

"But you're dead."

"And your point is?"

Pinching the bridge of my nose, I smiled. "You're such a pain in the ass."

"Shut up and make some pictures."

Even in negative form, I could see Jennifer staring boldly into the camera. She was not smiling, but there was a spark in her. She had agreed to be my guinea pig that day. It had been a chilly spring Saturday and I needed a model.

"You ruined the first couple of attempts because you kept moving."

"Sitting still has never been my style."

"It's as good a place as any to start. Rae might like to have it."

Time has a way of stopping when I am in a darkroom.

The outside world fades and I do not get hungry or tired. It's just me and the process. When I finally stepped back from the collection of prints fastened to a dangling clothesline, it was the early hours of Thursday morning. All the prints I had done were of Jennifer, in varying shades of light and contrast. It had been so long since I had seen her. For a moment, she was alive.

I moved back to the box and was about to stop when I found a negative of Jennifer and Rae. They were sitting close to each other, their heads tilted and touching. Both wore solemn expressions.

Excited, I made several prints. Despite all the skills I had learned over the years, I could not quite compensate for the negative, which showed my novice status. Drips, uneven edges, and a smudge were impossible to fix, but after a few tries, I accepted that my inexperience added to the charm of the picture. Two young sisters and a novice photographer.

Feeling an acute sense of satisfaction, I climbed the stairs and let Charlie into the backyard, and when he returned, I took a quick shower before falling into bed. Charlie jumped up on the bed and settled beside me. My eyes closed, I dropped into the darkness.

Colin West called at half past seven that morning. I started up in bed, sure that something terrible must have happened to Amelia for anyone to call me at this ungodly hour. Blinking, I shoved hair out of my eyes and reached for my phone. "Hello." I cleared my throat. "Hello?"

"I woke you." Colin's voice was far too alert and cheerful this early. It was wrong on so many levels.

"Is there a problem?"

"I woke you, my apologies"

"I was up until four a.m. developing pictures." Charlie stretched but did not open his eyes.

"Do you often work through the night?"

The question irritated me. "I try not to, but when inspiration strikes, I answer."

"More photos of the Prince Street house?"

"Some, yes." I swung my legs over the side of the bed.

"Well, I've good news."

I yawned. "I won the lottery."

"Not exactly. But the realtor has a very good offer on the house. I wanted to show it to you."

"That's great. When?"

"Twenty minutes. It's the only time I have today. I've got to be in court."

I pinched the bridge of my nose. "Sure. That should give me enough time to pull my hair into a ponytail."

He laughed as he hung up.

Ten minutes later, I was resting my head on the kitchen's marble countertop, waiting as the coffeepot gurgled out a fresh brew. Charlie climbed back onto his dog bed and drifted off to sleep.

Though I had no idea where I would live after the place sold, I was glad to be leaving. The past was not my favorite thing, and here I was surrounded by it. The doorbell rang before the pot finished brewing. Charlie scrambled to his feet and barked.

Casting a wistful glance at my yet-to-be filled cup, I moved down the center hallway toward the door. I opened it to a very bright and energetic Colin.

"Stop smiling so much," I said. "That kind of cheeriness is wrong on so many levels this early in the morning."

Charlie pushed past me to greet Colin, who rubbed him between the ears and patted him affectionately on his side. "It's the middle of the day."

"Right, if you're a farmer. Come on in. I've got a pot of coffee that's brewing particularly slowly this morning."

He closed the door behind himself, Charlie's paws

matching his clipped steps. "You look pretty good for only a few hours' sleep."

"It's a façade. I'm weeping inside. Black?"

He chuckled. "Any sugar or milk?"

"High maintenance," she teased. I filled his cup and set it on the marble island, and Colin took a seat on one of the bar stools surrounding it. I set the milk carton and the entire sugar canister on the island. Rae would have done a fancier job of serving. She would have used the right kind of milk pitcher and probably had those little sugar cubes like her mother used to keep on hand. I was just grateful the milk was fresh.

Charlie sat beside Colin as he splashed milk into his mug. I did the same and added a heaping teaspoon of sugar. Alcoholics who have stopped drinking gravitated toward sugar, and I was no exception. The craving had something to do with the receptors in the brain, I was told.

I sipped. Added another teaspoon and then sipped again. If he had not been there, I would have added another spoonful, but decided to pretend I had no overpowering addiction to sugar. "So, you have an offer."

"I do." He tugged a folded piece of paper out of his breast pocket and slid it slowly my way. I was impressed. "That's about ten percent over asking."

"Rebecca's good at what she does."

"How much of that does Amelia get to keep?"

He tapped a finger on the countertop. "Enough to keep her in her current situation for about five years."

"Five years."

I had no way of knowing if she would live six days or ten more years. "Okay. Well, at least that gives me time to figure out how to best help her."

"What will you do?"

"Not exactly sure. Maybe I'll finally get serious about my photography and find a way to support us."

His stare was bold, direct. “I looked you up online. “You had some good reviews.”

“I never did much with them. I could have traded them for more gallery showings and better exposure, but I didn’t.”

“Why not?”

Because there was a part of me that believed I did not have the right to a full life. My stupidity cost Jennifer her life, so as long as she was dead, so was I. “Who’s to say?”

“Been my experience that when people get vague, they have an answer. They just don’t want to share.”

I tapped the tip of my nose. “You’ve got good senses, Detective.”

He sipped his coffee. “What do you think of the offer?”

“Take it. Just let me know where to sign and when I need to be out of here.”

“You sure you’ll be fine?”

“I always land on my feet. I’m like a cat.”

“Can I see the pictures you developed?”

“Sure.” I pushed away from the counter with the cup in hand. “In the basement.”

“I didn’t see equipment down there during the tour.”

“Don’t tell Rebecca, but I set it up last night. Nothing that can’t be broken down in about an hour.” Moving to the small side door by the kitchen, I opened it and switched on a light. I ordered Charlie to stay, but he tried following anyway.

Colin looked at the dog. “Sit.”

The dog sat, ready for his next command.

“Wow,” I said.

“You’re too soft on him.”

“Right.” We stepped down the stairs. I turned on the collection of floor lamps brought from upstairs.

“Looks like you raided every light in the house.”

“If I could carry it, I brought it down. Though I did discover that too many lamps blow a fuse. It’s a little disconcerting finding yourself in a dark basement all of a sudden at night."

"You're not afraid of shadows?"

"Why should I be?" I moved toward the clothesline, where I had pinned up a collection of glass plate prints. They would dry for several more hours before I coated them with a fine sheen of wax.

He leaned in, studying the pictures, moving down the line slowly and carefully. To his credit, he seemed genuinely interested. "These are very good."

"This is one thing I do particularly well."

"You should consider having a show in town. The locals would love it. I'm sure Rebecca would help."

"It's not quite that easy. It's a lot of work making inroads with the art dealers."

"The D.C. market has a fair number of galleries."

"I would still have to create a portfolio and get my act together." I took a sip of coffee. "But you're right, I do have to do something. My gypsy days are over while Amelia is sick."

He moved to the pictures of Jennifer. "Who's this?"

The quality of the negatives was poor. I had only just begun learning the art of coating the plate with chemicals, and consequently there were runs and untreated spots that would never develop. "I took those in high school. That's my friend, Jennifer."

"She's pretty."

"She was."

A frown furrowed his brow. "Jennifer McDonald. Amelia told me about her. She died in a car accident."

"We were kids."

"That couldn't have been easy."

I wasn't allowing self-pity today. "Never is."

"These prints are not as polished as the others, but I really like them."

"Thanks. My developing skills have grown, but I can only do so much with a novice's negative. I was thinking I'd give the prints to Jennifer's sister. She might like to have them."

"I'm sure she would." His watch beeped. "I've got to be in court in a half hour, so I'm off."

"Thanks for delivering the good news. Let me know when I need to hit the streets."

"Will do." He climbed the stairs and paused at the front door. "Would you like to have dinner?"

"Dinner? You mean like a business dinner or a date?"

"A date."

"Wow."

His hand on the door, he looked amused by my confusion. "You sound surprised."

"It's been a while since I had a real date."

"Then we'll keep it simple. There's a pub on Union Street."

Considering all I had were jeans and maybe one nice sweater, it would have to do. Though pubs meant alcohol, I could be surprisingly controlled when I was not alone. "Sure. That might be fun."

"I'll pick you up at seven on Saturday night."

"Okay. Looking forward to it."

When he left, I stood in the hallway, allowing the silence to fold around me. The moment's exhilaration faded, and I was left with an overwhelming sense of guilt. I was going on a date. Living my life.

"If you back out of this, I'll scream."

"I'm not supposed to have fun."

"Bull."

"The deal was as long as you couldn't have fun, neither could I."

"Who says I'm not having fun? I haven't seen you squirm like this in years."

"Go away."

"It's just getting interesting. No way."

A Letter from Faith

JULY 12, 1769

My Dearest Children,

The boys have long left. Hanna is betrothed to a young man in the city. He is a master carpenter and he hail from Scotland. Their wedding will be right after the harvest. I spend most of my days helping her sew clothes that she will carry into her new life.

Mr. McDonald's wife rarely gets out of her bed now, and when Dr. Goodwin visits the farm, he leaves her with a fresh bottle of laudanum to help her with pain. The wife is too sick to notice that the boys are gone, and Hanna will soon follow. Both Mr. McDonald and I mourn their absence. We speak fondly of the days when we had three lively children bustling about the cottage and of the nights, we sat by the stone hearth while his wife read to us.

Unable to sleep, I prowl the nights often. I fear with my long fiery red hair billowing about my shoulders that under the moon I do indeed look like the witch whom many still believe me to be.

Forever,
Faith

Chapter Eighteen

RAE, THURSDAY, OCTOBER 19, 2011

There was a time before Jennifer died when I had hope for the future. But when she died and I gave Michael away, hope abandoned me. Now after all these years, I thought maybe it would be possible again.

According to Margaret, the local media were very interested in her witch bottles and wanted to interview the surviving ancestors. We would all meet at the Shire Architectural Salvage warehouse tomorrow at four.

When the doorbell rang and I saw Zeb's truck in the driveway, I was oddly excited. I am not sure why I walked a little faster toward the door, but I did. Maybe it was the break in the rain or the idea of seeing Michael again. Whatever the reason, it had been a very long time since I had believed that life could truly get better.

Opening the door, I actually smiled. "Mr. Talbot. Thank you for coming so soon."

He studied me an extra beat, clearly trying to figure out what had changed. "Dr. McDonald. Are you okay?"

"Yes, why wouldn't I be?"

"You don't usually smile like this."

Did the smile make me look more than a little demented? It had been a long time since I actually tried smiling. "You can call me Rae."

His head cocked. This *happy me* was not at all what he expected. "Call me Zeb."

"Great, Zeb."

He twisted his hands around a set of rolled-up engineering plans. "You've never called me Zeb."

"Maybe it's about time." I stepped back from the door. "Please come in."

He paused and wiped his boots on the mat before entering. "You said you made a decision about the garage."

"I did. I realized I've been overthinking it and should stop worrying. Let's go ahead and build it with the apartment on the second floor. No need for an office or storage space."

"Thinking about rental property?"

We stepped into the front parlor overlooking the site of the new building. It no longer looked like an angry scar but a sign of better things to come. "No. But you never know. It will be nice to have the space. Do you know when you can start?" I always forgot about his towering height until we stood side by side. He was solid, and perhaps that was what I'd always liked about him. I pictured him with Rachel. They certainly had all the makings of a successful match. They were the logical choice. And yet it didn't feel right. Hardly scientific, but I did not question

"We can start first thing next week."

"Great."

He held up the plans. "Do you want to go over them one more time? I actually have two sets of designs. One for an office and one for an apartment."

"The apartment design is fine."

"Let's just go over it one more time."

There was no missing his hesitation. How many times had

I said I knew what I wanted and did not? "Sure. One more time."

He crossed to the conference table and spread out the plans. He reached for a tape dispenser, a small vase, a stapler, and the stone heart and laid each on a corner. "As you can see, we're still creating the two-car garage. And the upstairs will have one bedroom, a kitchen, a bath, and a small living area."

Standing close to him, I felt energy snap. I recognized the feeling. It had been a long time, but I knew. It was sexual attraction. Clearing my voice, I smiled, and this time it felt a bit more natural. "It looks great."

"It will be. And if you decide to rent, you'll get top dollar."

"Good to know."

He slowly removed the objects from the plans, pausing as he held the heart-shaped stone. "I hope you didn't take offense at this."

"I did, but not anymore. I know I can be cold."

"Not cold." He closed his powerful hand around the stone, warming it. "Just reserved. Eric likes you and he's a good judge of character. The cookies were a big hit."

"He's a good kid. You've done a solid job with him."

"Thanks."

"I can't assume credit for the cookies. Rachel has a magic touch when it comes to baking." I dangled the fishing lure in the water. "She said her girls and Eric go to the same school."

"Yeah, she's great. I've always admired the way she kept it all together after Mike died. She was like a kid sister to me. Mike and I were pals in high school."

Well, that was something as I reeled in the fishing lure.

"I didn't know that."

What the heck was I digging for? All the facts I'd listed regarding a match between Zeb and Rachel proved they would be a good fit. He did not act particularly interested in her as a partner, but then men did not always know what was best for them.

The conversation was petering out quickly, but I was not ready for it to end. “Margaret is having a meeting with a local newspaper writer about her witch bottles,” I said.

“Eric and I hear a lot about those bottles whenever we’re at the salvage yard. Margaret’s passion for history is infectious.”

“She’s doing a small presentation, and I thought you and Eric might like to come. It’s a bit of a history lesson, and well, it’s different.”

He studied me a beat, still wondering what had changed. “Sounds good. When?”

“Tomorrow afternoon at four.”

“We’ll be there.”

“Great.”

Carefully, he rolled up the plans and then straightened. “You’ve changed. And I’m not quite sure how.”

“I feel a little like I did before . . . before my sister died. *Whole* comes to mind.”

His eyes darkened. “I can’t imagine what you and your family went through.”

“It was a dark hole, but it’s time to climb out. I know Jennifer wouldn’t want it.”

He cocked a brow. “Think Margaret’s witch bottle has anything to do with the change? Addie’s aunt Grace swears their lives all changed for the better once her bottle was broken.”

“I think the MacDonald bottle is still intact, unless Margaret dropped it and didn’t say.”

“You would have heard the scream up and down the Potomac if she had.” Zeb chuckled. “She handles the thing like it’s a newborn.”

“It’s her baby.”

"Margaret's fun but she needs a life. Maybe you could make a match for her."

"She asked me just that for Rachel. Wanted to know if I had any spare men lying around."

He shook his head slowly and laughed at the thought.

The heat radiating from him warmed my face. "I think everyone expects me to have a fully stocked warehouse of specimens. Or perhaps mail order like the bakery."

He twisted his hands tighter around the plans. "Hey, you might have something there." His phone vibrated on his hip. Frowning, he unclipped the phone and checked the number. "Job site. I'll need to take this."

"Sure, go ahead. I'll see you tomorrow?"

"You bet."

Normally, when a patient was a couple of minutes late, I became irritated. But today, I could not cling to anything other than hope. The rains had stopped. The project was moving forward. And tomorrow I would see Michael. Life was looking up.

When the doorbell rang, I rose, walking down the hallway with a softer clip of my heels than usual. Opening the door, I found both Debra and Samuel standing on the threshold. They were holding hands. Smiling.

I returned the smile. "You two look very happy today."

Debra grinned. "We bought a house."

I stepped aside so that the two could enter. "The house on Prince Street?"

Samuel rattled the keys in his hands before tucking them in his side pocket. "That's the one. Houses like that don't come on the market that often."

"You've bought yourself a lovely home," I said. As hopeful as they looked, I feared they would not be a couple in that house for very long. "I visited there several times as a child. And I'm amazed at the renovations."

"We're paying for move-in ready," Debra said. "We're too busy with our careers to tackle a renovation. The basement will need work, but we'll deal with that after the wedding."

We settled into the front room. "So, what has changed between you two?" I asked.

They smiled at each other and Debra nodded, giving Samuel the go ahead to speak. "I was pretty mad at Debra when we left here. She wouldn't share her secret and it bothered me. I couldn't be with someone who was not forthcoming. We spent some time apart." He held her hand. "I really missed her."

She smiled and clasped his hand. I understood body language enough to know she was still hiding a whopper and was not even willing to tell me. "I'm sure you did." I hoped she would share more.

Debra's smile did not quite mask her trepidation. "I love Samuel. I want to marry him and have a family. I went to see him, and we talked. It wasn't easy."

I wanted to dig deeper below the surface, suspecting she had only slapped a small bandage on a wicked wound. But as I searched for the right question to delve deeper, I hesitated. Honesty was the best policy, but if Zeb and I became closer, could I tell him about Michael? It seemed that was exactly what I would be doing tomorrow at the salvage yard. My past and present would collide when Michael and Zeb met. I had made a strong argument for truth, but now it was time to back it up. "And you two were satisfied with the conversation?"

"She told me everything," he said. "I know all about the drugs she used in college."

"Drugs," I repeated. As much as I wanted to believe she had been honest with him, I could not. The explanation was too easy and convenient.

"Yes," Debra said. "I told it all to him. It was a bad time for me. I made a lot of foolish choices that I never talked about."

"How do you feel about what you told him?" I asked.

She crossed her feet at her ankles. "I didn't like doing it, but I'm relieved to have this behind us. I don't want to look back. What purpose would it serve to dwell on it?"

Samuel nodded. "We're glad you made us look inside ourselves. There were clearly things between us that needed airing, and better now than later."

Debra tightened her hold on his hand. "We love each other."

And this, I believed. Debra wanted this to work, but she was not being forthcoming.

I only hoped the future would be kind to them and that they never were forced to look back. "I wish you two the very best. If you ever need me, know that I'll be here."

Samuel straightened with pride. He was on top of the world. "We're good now, but thanks."

A Letter from Faith

DECEMBER 13, 1769

My Dearest Children,

The farmer's wife lies in the new fancy four-post bed on the first floor of the recently completed brick home. In the spring, the farmer will begin on the second floor. But she does not notice the new home with its white plaster walls, freshly hewn floors, and grand hearths. All she knows now is the pain that grows worse by the day. All the color has faded from her face, her hair now thinned to faint wisps.

As I tended her with a compress to her fevered brow, she confessed she and the other women had made witch bottles to cast a spell against me. I bade her to tell me where the bottles were hidden. I would smash them, for wishes can easily turn to curses. She refused to tell me. They know not what they've done.

Forever,
Faith

Chapter Nineteen

RAE, FRIDAY, OCTOBER 21, 2011

I was nervous when I arrived at the Shire Architectural Salvage yard the next day. Once again, choosing what to wear was a headache as I thought about seeing Michael. I finally settled on dark pants, a matching fitted jacket, and a white shirt. Hardly a fashion statement, but this was my go-to suit that made me feel confident and comfortable. And more than anything, I wanted to at least appear relaxed and confident around Michael.

Pushing through the front doors of the King Street warehouse, I noticed that Margaret, or more likely Addie, had arranged a collection of mismatched chairs in a theater style. They faced a long, makeshift table made of a reclaimed door and two sawhorses. In the center of the table stood a tabletop lectern that looked like it had come from a church.

A baby's cry echoed from the back of the warehouse, and as I heard footsteps, I expected to see Addie with Carrie bundled in the front pack. But it was Margaret who rounded the corner with the child tucked in a sling. The baby was awake, bright eyed, her fists balled up with energy and excitement.

Margaret raised a hand. "Rae. Are you not thrilled about this event?"

"I am. I hope you don't mind, but I invited Zeb and Eric as well as a couple of friends of mine."

"Wonderful. My lectures are not typically well attended. I have a talent for developing a great fascination for things few care about."

Around Margaret, my blood pressure dropped. Even the baby, normally fussy, appeared content.

"The local reporter did say she might come," Margaret added. "Though, I'll warn you, I think it was the same reporter who gave you the 'heart of stone' moniker."

"Even better." I moved forward and took the baby's foot in my hand. "I didn't expect to see you with a baby."

"Addie had to deliver a 1910 hand-carved mantel to a client and Grace was too tired to watch the kid." She rubbed Carrie on top of her head. "And I'm fairly sure that Carrie is not a real baby. I think she's a thirty-five-year-old woman trapped in a baby's body. I find the more I talk to her like an adult, the calmer she becomes."

"Really? What makes you say that?"

"When I speak, her eyes are always open and studying me. And yes, she can be a crier, but this kid knows what she wants. You've got to admire a woman who knows what she wants and then promptly demands it in full. I've been running through my presentation, and she's been offering her opinion freely. She's quite the critic."

It was hard not to grin. "What's she saying so far?"

"Well, that depends on how you interpret burps, grunts, and a little gas. I'm thinking it means, 'Good job, Margaret. You're brilliant.'"

"That's how I would interpret it."

"Good, because there have been lots of it." Margaret checked her watch. "Lisa should be here soon."

"Great."

"I did find out a few tidbits on Fiona that I'll share after the meeting if that's okay."

"Perfect."

Lisa pushed through the front door. She was dressed in dark jeans, a black T-shirt, and a lightweight gray jacket. Her blond hair was twisted into a loose topknot and secured by two bright red hair sticks. Silver feathers dangled from her ears, and though her makeup was slight, there was just enough to accentuate her blue eyes. She was only two years older than I but looked hip and cool, whereas I felt a little stiff. I considered popping the collar of my shirt or pushing up my jacket sleeves, but in the end, it just was not me.

Tucked under Lisa's arm was a leather portfolio case. "Rae, I'm glad you're here a little early. I have something for you."

"You brought something for me?"

Lisa set the portfolio on Margaret's table. I approached as she unwound the string that was holding the top flap closed. "When Addie and Margaret cleaned out Amelia's basement, I didn't realize they had found a box of glass negatives. I told them to take everything, and they did. When I was here at the warehouse a few days ago, I spotted the box. Until that moment, I'd forgotten all about it."

Margaret studied the portfolio. "I knew they were glass negatives but assumed they were really old."

"They're only seventeen years old. They were one of my first attempts at wet-plate photography. I cringe when I see all the mistakes I made in my early days."

"I stopped worrying about my mistakes a long time ago," Margaret said. "It's about the only kind of history I care to ignore."

So much of me wished I could be like Margaret. I meticulously catalogued every error I made. I had become so focused on making no missteps that I could not move forward. I was a dowdy thirty-two-year-old who had not been on a real date in more than two years. But I was realizing that to wish away my mistakes would also cast off Michael. Something I would never do. "It looks like you developed some of the negatives."

Lisa reached into the portfolio. With her fingertips barely touching the print, she hesitated. "I made this of you and Jennifer, Rae."

Slowly, she pulled out the image, its white backing facing me. "It's not the best photography I've ever done. In fact, the negative had technical mistakes that I couldn't fix. However, I was able to capture a great moment."

Drawing in a breath, she turned the picture around and I found myself staring into Jennifer's face. For a moment, I could not move. My heart stopped as I studied the image, feeling the last of the barriers splinter and crack. Feelings began to stir.

My hands shook as I accepted the picture from her. My gaze lingered briefly on my young face before shifting to Jennifer's expressive eyes. A lock of her reddish brown hair, which looked darker here, cascaded over her shoulder, thick and full, and a small strand dangled over her left eye. She wore the gold hoop earrings that Mom had given her on her last birthday and the black V-neck I'd given her for Christmas. Her smile was so slight it would have been easy to miss. She possessed a look that suggested to the world she knew a secret.

We were sitting on a bench. She had slung her arm around my neck, and I was grinning. This was the Jennifer I remembered. She was real. I had never liked the formal pictures Mom displayed at her funeral or the last yearbook picture that made her look so prim and proper. The girl looking back at me now was the bossy, sometimes irreverent sister who took all the chances and broke the rules.

Words escaped me until, finally, I cleared my throat and said, "That's her. That's Jennifer."

Lisa released the breath she held. "That's you, too. The kid I remember."

"I'd forgotten we looked so much alike."

"I've had these faces in my memory for so long, but I realized when I saw this picture, I'd forgotten so much." She pointed to a small white scar above Jennifer's lip. "Remember when she got that? We were in the sixth grade."

"You and Jennifer were playing baseball in the backyard. She called you a wimp and you hurled the ball at her and hit her in the mouth."

"Your mom was so freaked out. Jennifer had a cotillion dance that Friday and your mother was certain she would greet her date with no front teeth."

"The doctor said the cut could use a couple of stitches, but Jennifer wouldn't let him get near her with a needle," Lisa remembered. "She said the scar would add character."

"I'll never forget all the blood. She must have made up a dozen stories about how she got the scar. Milked it good."

A flood of memories of the girl we both dearly missed came rushing back.

"Really nice job," Margaret said. "I can see you had the gift, even in high school."

"There are so many technical problems with the negative," Lisa said.

"I see none," I countered. "It's absolutely perfect. I'll frame it. I know exactly where I'll hang it in my house."

The bells of the shop jingled, and Addie pushed through the door. Carrie, hearing Addie, began to kick, fuss, and cry.

Margaret shook her head as she pointed at the baby. "She was not crying while you were gone. Do not believe her."

Addie grinned as she set down her purse. The baby cried

louder and kicked her feet. "Did Margaret not give you everything you wanted?"

The baby cried as Addie pulled her from the front pack and kissed her on the face. Carrie wailed and smiled all in the same instant.

"I'm being set up," Margaret said. "The kid and I were inventorying doorknobs and reviewing my witch bottle presentation. I talked. She burped. She was happy until she saw you. She's a sly one."

Addie kissed the baby in the crook of her neck until she stopped fussing. "I know. Carrie's a little con artist. She does the same when Grace watches her. By the way, how is Grace doing?"

"Sleeping. She babysat earlier today, and the kid wore her out, too. But she's fine. The kid and I held down the fort."

"I knew you would."

"So, do we have press yet?" Addie asked.

Margaret pulled her phone from her back pocket. "The reporter texted and said any minute."

The doorbells jingled, and I turned to see a tall blond woman. She wore skinny jeans accentuating a flat belly, an off-the-shoulder T-shirt, and boots. "Am I late?"

It didn't take a PhD to see the tension ripple through Addie as she smiled. Putting two and two together, I deduced it was Janet Morgan, Addie's sister and the baby's birth mother.

"Hey, Janet," Addie said. "You came to hear Margaret talk about the bottles?"

"Wouldn't miss it." She moved to the baby, grinned, and held out her hands. The baby smiled back as Janet reached for her. Addie allowed her to go but kept a close watch.

As I studied Addie's body language, my respect for Susan grew. She could have handled Michael's relationship with me a dozen different ways. It would not have been hard to shut me out completely. I'd certainly made it easy for her over the years. But she stepped back and let her son, our son, find his own way. Michael and I were not guaranteed anything. We would both have to want it. Susan loved Michael enough to let him love me. And Addie was doing the same for Carrie.

Janet nestled the baby on her hip, though her hold was not quite as relaxed as Addie's. One baby and two mothers.

I checked my watch and realized Margaret's show was starting in a few minutes, if she stuck to schedule. Michael and his mother would be here soon. Tension banded across my chest as I stole another glance at the clock and door. Maybe they were stuck in traffic. Susan did not live in this area and she might very well have underestimated the time it took to find a parking space. Maybe I should have told her to leave earlier? Should I call and check on them? Or would that be too pushy? Technically, they weren't late, and she could just be circling the block right now looking for parking.

The bells jingled again, and I turned to see Zeb and Eric. The boy's grin was wide, thrilled as he rushed into the room and up to Janet.

"Mom!"

Janet rumpled his hair with her hand. "Hey, baby. How are you doing?"

Eric's exaggerated frown almost made me laugh. "I'm not a baby."

She made a good-natured face at him. "You're my baby."

"I'm not a baby, Mom. Carrie is your baby," Eric said.

Addie took a small step back, fingers tightening on her forearms.

Zeb placed his hand on Eric's shoulder, squeezing gently. Puzzled, the boy looked up at his dad.

Janet was oblivious to Addie and Zeb's tension as she held the baby closer.

Margaret coughed loudly and clapped her hands. "Let's get this show on the road."

The loud noise startled the baby. Her eyes widened and she began to cry. Janet rocked Carrie for a minute or two longer but when the crying would not ease, she turned to Addie, who gladly took the child and rested her against her shoulder.

Janet's hands trembled slightly as she tucked them in her pockets. I studied her more closely and caught the averted gaze and the nervous tap of her toe. No wonder she could not deal with a crying baby. She could barely deal with herself. I did not know exactly what she struggled with, but clearly the burden required all her attention.

Margaret, in a hushed voice, said, "I've a lot of good information on Faith and the witch bottles."

Glancing toward the door, I wanted to ask Margaret to wait but caught a glimpse of Addie's stone face. Carrie was Janet's child by birth, but Addie was the child's mother in every other way. "Your reporter isn't here, Margaret."

"She said she would be here any minute, and I've e-mailed her all the facts." She rubbed her hands together, more quietly this time and grinned. "Let's talk witch bottles."

We all took our seats, Janet sat in the front next to Eric with Zeb, flanking the boy's other side. Lisa and Addie took the second row while I opted to sit in the back saving the empty seats beside me for Susan and Michael. I looked at the door again and, when I faced front, found Zeb looking back with a puzzled look. When Michael and his mother arrive, he would learn more answers about the McDonalds than he ever bargained for.

Eric turned around. "Hey, Dr. McDonald."

Hard to fret around that boy. "Eric. Are you excited about all this family history we're learning?"

He nodded yes and in a small whisper said, "Witches are pretty cool."

Zeb ruffled his boy's head and turned it back toward the center of the room. "Margaret has a new fan."

"Can't fault him for that."

I settled in my seat, refusing to look anxious. Checking my watch, I calculated that Susan and Michael were now fifteen minutes late. This was normal with Beltway traffic, but it felt like fifteen years.

Margaret set three boxes on the table and opened each. She removed the shattered pieces of the Shire/Morgan family's bottle and then the very intact bottles created by a McDonald and a Smyth.

"This has turned into a very interesting story, not just about three bottles, but three women and their dire circumstances that brought them together to create a pact that bound them for a lifetime."

A Letter from Faith

MARCH 2, 1770

My Dearest Children,

The farmer's wife died on a snowy Wednesday afternoon. She was forty-nine-years-old. Mr. McDonald and Patrick were at her side. Neither of the men wept but stood solemnly.

We buried her in the back field and the three of us stood over the grave, silent, not holding hands or giving comfort. When the farmer turned and walked back to the main house, Patrick took my hand in his, but did not look at me. "Thank you," he whispered. He pulled free and went back into the house. Marcus, at my invitation, joined us that evening for dinner as we ate in silence. As I sat in my rocker by the fire, both boys sat close, talking in hushed whispers. This was a rare and precious moment, and I should have savored it. But I could only think about the thousands of moments just like this that had been stolen from me by the woman we buried today.

Forever,

Faith

Chapter Twenty

RAE, FRIDAY, OCTOBER 21, 2011

A *pact that bound them for a lifetime.*

Margaret's presentation did not register with me. My focus remained on my phone, the back door, and Michael and Susan's arrival. As the minutes ticked by, the sharp edge of my excitement dulled. I watched as Margaret flashed slides of the contents of Addie's bottle. Nails. Shards of glass. A strip of cloth. A lock of hair. She explained the meaning and the context, but I was not there. I wanted to see Michael, if only for a few minutes. Had he changed his mind? Was he angry with me?

When my cell buzzed in my hand and I saw Susan's number, I rose immediately and moved out the side door to the alley. Pressing a finger into one ear to block out the noise of the street, I clutched the phone closely. "Susan. Is everything all right?"

"No. I should have called you earlier, but this is the first time I've had the chance to get to my phone." Her voice shuddered with worry.

"What is it?"

She hesitated, drawing in a ragged breath. "There's been a car accident. Michael was injured."

The world around me shifted and I felt the ice cascade over me, freezing every cell in my body. "How bad?"

Her voice wavered. "It's serious."

"Where is he?"

"He's in surgery at the hospital in Alexandria. We were on our way to your event. We were broadsided at an intersection just a few blocks away."

As I looked to the setting sun, the vibrant oranges and yellows shattered like glass. "Susan, may I come to the hospital?"

"Yes. In fact, I was hoping you could donate blood. He's AB negative, like your medical record stated."

"I'm leaving right now." I mapped the journey in my mind. "I'll be there in fifteen minutes."

A sob escaped. "Hurry, Rae."

When I turned, Zeb stood by the door, his face etched with concern. I had done my best to keep my emotions in check, but he knew something was wrong. As much as I wanted to hide all this, I was overwhelmed. "I've got to go."

He stepped in my path. "What's wrong?"

Whatever locks I had fastened to the past had broken with Susan's call. "I have a son, Zeb. I was sixteen when he was born, and I gave him up for adoption. I just got off the phone with his mother. He's been in a serious car accident here in town. I need to go now."

Without looking away, he reached in his front pocket and pulled out car keys. "I'll drive."

"What?"

"You focus on what needs to be done. I'll drive. We'll get through this."

"What about Eric?"

He went up to Addie and whispered something in her ear,

and she got up and moved directly behind Eric. "Addie's got him."

Tremors rattled deep under the ice. "You don't have to do this."

He pressed his hand to my back. "We've got to move. Stay positive. The boy will need it."

I was always in control. I ran my own show. It had been a long time since I had accepted help, but right now, I was so grateful for it. "It's Alexandria Hospital."

"Understood."

He grabbed me under my arm and nearly lifted me out of my shoes as we sprinted to his truck. He slung open the passenger door and pushed me inside. I clutched my purse to my belly that now ached with a sensation I had not felt in years. Worry. Fear. Dread. Sadness. It was all there.

"Buckle up," he said.

Frantically, I clicked the buckle in place as he slammed the door. Seconds later, he was behind the wheel and we were in route. He did not ask me any questions as we drove across town. He did not prod or pry. He did what he did best. He acted. No hesitation or doubt.

We both hurried through the emergency room doors and I rushed up to the nurses' station. "My name is Dr. Rae McDonald. I'm here for Michael Holloway. His mother, Susan Holloway, just called me."

"Are you family?"

I raised my chin. "I'm his birth mother."

"Ah, you're the one we've been waiting for. We may need you to donate blood if you're a match."

"Where are Michael and Susan?"

"She's in the family center waiting for the surgeon's update."

The paltry details did not satisfy, but I understood that

regulations prevented her from telling me more. Legally, I was not family. "Take me to where I should go."

The nurse studied Zeb, her stern eyes sizing him up.

"I'm with Rae. And I'll go back with her."

"I can only take blood donors back."

Zeb grinned, but there was no humor in his dark eyes. "Then I'm a blood donor."

The nurse handed us both visitor badges. "We can always use blood."

We moved down the sterile hallways, the fluorescent lights buzzing as monitors beeped, gurneys rolled, and people talked in hushed tones. We entered a lab where there was a collection of large chairs. They were equipped with adjustable armrests.

A nurse looked up from a clipboard. "Yes?"

"I'm Dr. Rae McDonald. You're expecting me."

"Especially if you're AB negative today."

"My blood's not a match," Zeb said. "But you're welcome to it."

"Great. You can sit next to your wife."

I would have been slightly chagrined by the comment given a different set of circumstances. Both Zeb and I let the comment pass.

Without a thought, Zeb took the seat beside me. "I'm O positive."

The nurse nodded. "We're short all types right now, so glad to have you."

I tipped my head back against the seat, and as tears brimmed, I closed my eyes to stop them. When I thought I could trust my voice, I said, "Thanks, Zeb."

His dark eyes softened with a tenderness that stirred more emotion than I could handle. "You would've done the same, Rae."

That startled a nervous laugh and I opened my eyes to find him staring at me.

As the nurse readied to insert a needle in my arm, I asked, "Do you know where Susan is? I'd really like to speak to her."

"She's waiting for the surgeon's update and said she'd find you as soon as she could. From what I understand, the operation is nearly finished."

I instinctively drew my arm back. "And he's okay?"

She eased me back in the chair. "I'm not supposed to say." She winked and smiled, suggesting the outcome was good. She pushed up my sleeve and traced the deep blue vein on my arm. "You're in good shape. You work out?"

"I run most days," I said, more to myself than to her.

"How far do you run?" She positioned the needle over the vein.

"I know what you're doing. You're trying to distract me. I promise I'm fine. Just stick the needle in me."

The nurse regarded Zeb, as if she had something important to say. For an instant, I looked at him, and the nurse slyly slid the needle into my arm with little pain. She quickly taped it in place and asked me to squeeze the rubber ball in my hand. "I heard you were a psychologist, but nurses also have a few tricks up our sleeve."

"Well played," I said.

Within minutes, Zeb too was attached to a bag and we had nothing to do but wait.

I was amazed that the clock's second hand now crawled around the face of the dial.

Zeb tracked my gaze and said, "The nurse said he was going to be fine."

"But what does *fine* mean? It's one of those words that really doesn't say all that much when you think about it."

"You're thinking too hard. *Fine* means he'll be okay. I could tell by her expression that she meant *fine* in the best way."

I knew he meant well but his reasoning grated against my

fears and left me annoyed. "You're a psychologist as well?"

A chuckle rumbled in his throat. "You don't run a successful construction business without learning a thing or two about people. You should meet some of my clients."

I stared at the rubber ball in my hand. "We can't be sure of anything regarding Michael at this moment."

"Take you, for instance," he said, as if I had never spoken.

"What about me?" Annoyance sharpened the words.

A smile tweaked the edges of his lips as he leaned his head back and paused a long moment, until he was satisfied, he had my attention. "You don't like your house."

"What? Of course, I like it. It's been in the family for hundreds of years."

"You stay there because it belongs to your family, but deep down you don't like it."

"It's a wonderful house."

"For whom? You've been slowly dismantling it for the last couple of years since your mother passed. First, you had me gut the kitchen, and then you hired me to redo your room and the suite. Then your office. You've transformed the spaces. Now, the addition."

"The house needed it."

"And the stone hearth. You've been eyeing that for a couple of years."

"How do you know?"

"While we were working on the kitchen, I'd watch you go outside and stand in front of it and just stare."

"It was an unsightly pile of rocks."

"That you were told never to remove."

She shook her head. "Maybe my mother was right. I've seen more change in the last six weeks than I've seen in the last sixteen years."

"Is that so bad?"

"No. It's not that bad." I relaxed back against the headrest, energy fading. "Thank you for being here. But a part of me felt as if I had the right to be here and another part told me this was not my place."

"You've a right to be here," Zeb said, reading my thoughts.

I searched his steady, determined expression. "Do you really believe that?"

He shoved out a breath. "I've had a lot of issues with my ex-wife. I resent the hell out of the way she just took off and abandoned Eric. I know she's sick, but the facts don't lessen the anger. But one thing I have admired about Janet is that she gave Carrie to Addie. That little girl is better off with Addie, and Janet knows it."

Secrets. Was I willing to shine a light into the darkest corners? "The last time I was in a hospital, Michael was born. The place was so huge and frightening to me."

Zeb studied me a long moment. "Were your parents with you?"

"My dad had already passed. I was staying with a friend of my mother's in Winchester and when my labor started, she was called. Mom drove out to get me and helped me pack my bag. As she drove me to the hospital in Winchester, she never said one word." The rolling landscape had raced past me as contractions gripped my belly. "I just did my best not to cry."

His frown telegraphed his disapproval. "She didn't support you very much."

"I can't blame her. My father died three years before my sister. Mom always struggled with emotion, and their deaths shut her down completely."

"It's okay to be angry with her, Rae."

"I'm not angry. Or at least I wasn't." I tipped my head back. "That heart of stone you gave me pretty much sums it up."

"That's not true. Not at all. You wouldn't be here if you

didn't care, Rae. And adopting out Michael explains a lot about you."

Unwanted tears burned and I pressed my fingertips to my eyes. "Only a few people know, including Lisa, and she only found out by accident. She was a good friend of my sister's and she happened to see me right before Michael was born."

He took my cold hand in his and gently squeezed. "No one will know about this from me."

"He's not going to be a secret anymore. He's a part of me, and I can't deny that anymore."

"Fair enough."

His phone dinged with a text and he dug it out. A smile tugged at the edge of his lips and he turned the phone toward her. It was a picture of Addie, Carrie, and Eric peering through the windowpanes of a reclaimed window covered with white, chipping paint.

"Addie is a good soul," I said.

"She is."

"You and Addie have a lot in common."

He tucked his phone back in his pocket. "Trying to fix me up, Dr. McDonald?"

The words lifted the weight off my heart for an instant and I could almost smile. "No."

"Good." His focus didn't waver.

I moistened dry lips. "Margaret asked me to find a husband for Rachel and my first thought was you. You both make logical sense."

His gaze held mine. "Really?"

"You two have a lot in common. Children. Family. Friends. And then you said she felt like a sister."

"I can find my own woman, Rae."

"I would agree."

He traced the back of my hand with his thumb.

Words so long locked away rushed toward a bottleneck. "I like you."

"I like you too, Rae."

I looked at him. "I mean *really* like."

"I know what you mean. You've hired me for four different jobs on a house you're not that crazy about."

Heat flooded my cheeks. "You're a good contractor."

"That, too. But I don't visit my other job sites as much as I do yours."

"You don't?"

"Why do you think I kept revising those plans for you and coming by your house? That's not standard client treatment."

"Oh."

"For a matchmaker, you should have seen through that."

"I'm not a matchmaker." A frown wrinkled my brow. "Ironic. I like you and now I'm telling it all to you in one rush. If it's too much, I understand."

Lines around his mouth deepened with a frown. "Do I strike you as the kind of guy who runs from trouble?"

"No."

Just then Susan entered the room, her face drawn. I wanted to rise but could not get out of the chair. "Susan."

She came up to me and took my hand. Her grip held surprising strength. "He's out of surgery. They had to remove his spleen and he's lost a lot of blood."

I searched her watery eyes. "But he's going to be all right?"

"The surgeon is still worried. I can see it in his expression. He said the next twenty-four hours will be critical."

I had lost Michael once, but to lose him again. "I feel like this is somehow my fault. I thought it would be fun for him to hear about the witch bottles."

"This isn't your fault. I refuse to see you beat yourself up." Her voice caught in her throat and tears spilled down her cheeks. "He was very excited and looked forward to seeing you and learning more about his family history. He wanted to drive so I let him because I was tired. Michael's always taking care of me without one word of complaint. My husband Todd's job requires him to travel out of town a lot."

"Susan, your health is none of my business."

"I have cancer," she said without hesitation, as if she had said it a million times. "Breast cancer. My second bout. The chemo has been rough, but the latest blood work looks hopeful."

"Is there anything I can do to help?"

"Michael has been a champ. I don't think I'd have made it without him." She shook her head. "I've got to beat this, at least until he's a little older."

"You've raised a great kid."

"You made a great kid, and my husband and I will always be indebted to you for your unselfishness." She squeezed my hand again. "He's tough, and I know he'll pull through."

I did not dare voice my fears of the McDonalds' terrible track record for longevity. "I know he will."

As if recalling a memory, a smile teased her lips. "When he was ten, he decided to build a ramp in the backyard. He thought of himself as a stuntman. He propped up boards on my lawn furniture. I remember coming around the side of the house just as he took off. He hit the ramp before I could tell him to stop, and within seconds his front wheel pitched down and he sailed right over his handlebars. Evel Knievel on a bad day. Fell on his arm and broke it in two places. I freaked out. But all he could talk about was how he would adjust the ramp for the next jump. When I pointed out his arm was broken, he was excited about the cast he would get to wear the next day at school. I aged a decade that day."

"In twenty-four hours, he'll be doing handstands for the nurses," I said with a force grin.

More tears ran down her cheeks as she wiped them away.

"I should have taken over driving once we hit heavy traffic, but he was so sure he could drive and didn't want to be late for the presentation. He really wanted to see the exhibit on the bottles."

"There will be plenty of time for you both to visit and see the exhibit."

The nurse came and removed the needle from my arm, and as soon as she put a bandage on me, I rose out of my chair and hugged Susan. "I'm not usually a hugger—or at least I hadn't been for a long time. Where's your husband?"

"He's flying in tonight from out west. I called him. He'll arrive at National this evening and come straight here."

The nurse removed the needle from Zeb's arm. "When does your husband's flight arrive?" he asked.

Susan checked her watch. "In about an hour."

"Let me send one of my guys to pick him up and bring him here."

She pressed her fingertips to her temple. "Normally, his car is at the airport, but it needed an oil change, so I dropped him off. Our other car is at home."

"I'll see that he gets a ride to his auto shop in the morning."

She laid a palm over her heart. "You're so nice. You don't have to."

"Glad to help."

"Rae, thank you for giving blood," Susan said. "Michael not only looks just like you, but thank God, he has your blood type."

I rolled down my sleeve, covering the bandage. "If he needs anything. Anything at all. Let me know. I'll give it."

"You're a good friend." She hugged me close. "I've often thought about what it must have been like for you to share him with me. I never wanted to let you down." Fresh tears streamed down her face. "I don't know what I'd do if anything happened to him.

Losing him once had sealed my heart. I could not bear the idea of losing him again. "May I see him?"

"The surgeon wants you to wait until morning. I could only see him for a minute."

Right. She was his mother. She had the right to the minute I so desperately would have taken. "I can spend the night."

"Go home, Rae. There's no chance of him waking before morning. I have a cot next to his room and will call if there is any news."

I did not want to leave him. "I'll be back in the morning."

After hugging her again, I left with Zeb, who said, "Let me drive you back home."

Nodding, I followed him as we made our way to his truck. Inside, I sat numb and unable to move as he started the engine and turned on the lights. "You both are so lucky to have that kid in your life right now."

Surrounded by the darkness and with only the light of the dash, we drove through the city. "Zeb, just take me to the warehouse. I can get my car."

"I don't mind driving you home, Rae."

"I know. You've been great. Rock solid. But I need to stop by and see Margaret and Addie. I'll be fine."

"I'm checking in on you in the morning."

"I'd like that."

At the warehouse, he pulled up to the curb and through the large display window I could see Addie, Margaret, and Lisa. The cab was warm and with him close, I felt safe. Secure. "Thanks again, Zeb."

He laid a hand on my shoulder. "Any time."

Avoiding temptation was one of my strong suits, but the idea of kissing him now was just too appealing. I leaned forward. When he did not move, I pushed past the halfway point and kissed him on the lips. He tasted salty, rough, soft, and so good. For an instant, he remained still, and then raised a hand to my cheek and kissed me back.

Blood warmed and surged in my veins. My senses sharpened. Time slowed. The tumblers of an old lock fell into place.

Slowly, I drew back. "To clarify, that was not just a thank-you kiss."

The corner of his mouth rose. "Nor was it a you're-welcome kiss."

"You have to go in and get Eric."

He traced small circles on my shoulder. "Addie texted. He's asleep upstairs. I'll get him in the morning. He likes sleeping over."

"Having family close is good for him."

He brushed a small strand of hair from her eyes. "Yeah."

"See you soon."

"Tomorrow," he said.

Outside the truck, the night air felt good on my face. Zeb nodded and then shifted into gear and pulled into traffic.

I pushed through the front door of the warehouse.

Addie, Margaret, and Lisa rose immediately. Both looked at me with worry. "Are you all right?" Addie asked.

"I'm fine," I said.

Lisa shook her head. "Are you sure? You look pale."

Margaret studied me for a long moment. "Rae, you look ragged as hell."

"I gave blood at the hospital. Where are the witch bottles, Margaret? I never got to see the one that belonged to the McDonalds."

"Right over here." She took me to the long table in the back where she had moved the bottles. Two were intact and one in pieces.

"Addie, what happened to the Shire bottle?" I asked.

"I accidentally dropped it a few weeks ago. It shattered the instant it hit the floor."

"What was inside?" I was no longer looking at her family bottle but the dark round one in the center. The McDonald bottle. The neck was not as long as the Smyths' and the base was wider. Judging by the shape, it had held port.

"There were nails, buttons, glass, and a note sealed in wax."

I picked up the bottle and traced my finger around the cork top sealed with wax. "The note. What did yours say?"

"*May I never see my sister again.* Sarah Goodwin was afraid people would realize Faith, the witch, was her sister."

"So, she prayed she would never see her sister again?" I asked, incredulously.

"That's right." Addie ran her hands through her dark, curly hair. "Seems like Sarah's wish became her curse."

"How so?" I held my bottle up to the light. Its brown glass offered no clues about the contents.

"That's what my mother and grandmother used to say. Generations of Shire women have been bound to their sisters by mental illness."

I tipped the bottle, listening to the clink of metal. "You and Janet seem to be doing fairly well."

Addie slid her hands into her pockets puzzled by my sudden change in tone. "We aren't perfect, but it's the best it's ever been in our lives."

My grip on the bottle tightened. "And that's good for Carrie and Eric, right?"

"I would think so."

Holding the bottle up higher, I tried once again to will the light into the darkness and reveal its centuries-old secret. It remained smugly opaque. "Margaret, you said that Faith lived with the McDonalds for the rest of her life."

"That's right."

"Because of her son."

"Yeah. She gave him up, so he had a better chance at a fulfilling life. But she never could bring herself to leave the only home they had known as a family."

"Would you have cursed the Goodwin's, McDonalds and Smyths?" I asked.

Margaret nodded. "In a New York minute."

"I think Faith in fact did curse them all," I said.

"Why do you say that, Rae?" Margaret asked.

"I understand her anger," I said.

"What was Mistress Smyth's involvement with Faith?" Lisa asked.

"I believe it was Captain Cyrus Smyth who convinced the judge to sell Faith into indenture. She was described as a striking woman, and he knew he would fetch a handsome price for her contract in the colonies," Margaret said.

"All three families betrayed her," Lisa whispered.

"Oh, yeah," Margaret said.

"What did Patience McDonald wish for?" I asked.

"No one really knows," Margaret said. "But Patience endured a great deal of loss and pain."

What wish had cursed the McDonald family?

Before I stopped to analyze anything, I opened my hand slowly and let the bottle fall. Almost in slow motion, it drifted through the air, plunging toward the floor. It hit hard and shattered into three large pieces.

Addie's mouth dropped open.

Lisa closed her eyes.

Margaret's eyes nearly popped out of her head. "Holy shit, Rae. What have you done?"

A Letter from Faith

JULY 3, 1782

My Dearest Children,

Marcus came home to the farm today to visit. We spoke of the fine, prosperous tavern he has built. Men of great importance visit his place and talk of politics and the war which we all hope will end soon. Marcus never joined the fighting, but I fear he carries secrets for the rebels and takes great risks with his life. He bade me to leave the farm and move into his home. But I told him I would not. I will stay until Patrick returns from the battlefield. He has been at war for nearly six years and I pray for his safe return. Marcus resented my decision and was angry, but in the end, he understood my resolve.

Forever,
Faith

Chapter Twenty-One

RAE, FRIDAY, OCTOBER 21, 2011

The four of us gawked at the shattered pieces. I was not quite sure why I thought breaking the bottle would accomplish anything. Had I expected a rush of euphoria that would sweep away all the heartache, turn back the clock, and prevent the many mistakes that I had brought upon myself?

There was no crack of thunder. No sudden breeze. No shift in the earth. There were only the broken pieces of brown glass scattered around four nails, a button, several pebbles, and what looked like a scroll, rolled up tightly with a wax coating preserving the ink. Just like the Smyth bottle.

Margaret knelt down with her hands in the air. "Don't anyone move! I'm not sure right now if I'm upset because the bottle is broken, or if I'm excited because I can finally get a good look at its contents."

Addie backed up slowly and then rushed behind the register, where she kept a small box. "We can put the pieces in this."

Lisa looked at me as if I had come unhinged.

Margaret reached in her back pocket, pulled out her cell

phone, and began to snap pictures. "Rae, what the hell happened? Is there something you want to get off your chest?"

"I dropped the bottle on purpose."

Her gaze locked on me. "Say again?"

"I was hoping it might help."

"Help what?"

"Break the curse?"

"Break the curse. Shit." Margaret shook her head as she tucked her phone back in her pocket and reached for the roll of wax likely holding the scroll. "Addie, can you get my white gloves from behind the register, as well as my kit?"

"Right."

Kit. Like a crime scene investigator, Margaret had her tools of the trade. Addie returned with what looked like a fishing tackle box and plastic gloves.

Tugging on gloves with a snap, Margaret surveyed the scene before her as if it were some kind of homicide. "Addie, tweezers. Best not to touch it with bare hands. The oils on my skin may damage the paper."

Addie fished out a pair of silver tweezers and handed them to Margaret.

Frowning, Margaret slowly peeled wax from the paper. "Get your camera, Addie. I'll hold it open while you snap a picture and then we can read the images on the phone. Less stress on the paper."

As much as I wanted to tear open the note, I let Margaret handle it. There was no margin for error.

Addie took pictures, and after ten or fifteen shots, Margaret allowed the paper to roll back up and then very carefully placed all the items into the box.

"What does it say?" I asked. Nervous energy raced through me like a defendant waiting on the jury's verdict. What I had done had been completely reckless, but I could not care less.

Margaret took the phone and studied the images. After a very long moment, she said softly, *"Vanquish all my pain."*

"Vanquish all my pain," I said, mostly to myself. "A very rational wish considering her losses."

Addie leaned over Margaret's shoulder and studied the image. "You should look at this, Rae."

Margaret held the phone to her chest. "Honestly, Rae, if I weren't so excited to see what was in that bottle, I'd smack you right now."

She handed me the camera and I studied the thin, shaky handwriting. "It was just like the first letters Patience wrote."

"Not quite as steady," Margaret said. "I'm guessing she was pretty stressed when she wrote the note, wondering if Faith would somehow sense it."

"Do you think all the women did it together?" Addie asked.

"It's believed these witch bottles were more potent if created at the full moon. And I'm guessing these three women planned to meet at the full moon together," Margaret said. "Faith was charged in Scotland for witchcraft and then again here in Alexandria where she was examined for signs of witchcraft. My guess is that they created their bottles before the examination."

"I agree," Addie said. "Faith was already living with the McDonalds by the December full moon."

"And if my ancestor's wish of no pain or grief became a curse, it stands to reason that if McDonalds don't feel pain, we also don't feel joy."

"Matchmaker with a heart of stone," Margaret said. "Sound familiar?"

I shook my head. "I'm not a cold woman. At least I didn't use to be."

"Losing your sister could have done it," Margaret said.

"That was horrible. Terrible, but . . ." I looked at the note, terrified Michael might somehow be doomed to my life. "I felt every bit of pain and anguish right up until I gave away my son."

Both Addie and Margaret stared at me in silence.

"My sister's death turned my world upside down. I made foolish choices. Got pregnant. My son, Michael, was born just before my seventeenth birthday." I would say or do anything to make sure Michael was okay. "When I handed him to his adoptive mother, my heart did turn to stone. First Jennifer, now Michael. Maybe the McDonalds can never be happy."

Addie laid a hand on my shoulder. "That's not true, Rae."

I shook my head. "Michael's in the hospital. He was supposed to be here tonight but there was a car accident. His mother called me and that's why I left in such a hurry."

"Is he okay?" Margaret asked.

"They'll know more in the morning. There was nothing else that could be done tonight."

"Rae," Margaret said. "You're a strong woman. I can't imagine a kid of yours that can't go the distance."

Lisa's eyes brimmed with tears. "He's got to be strong, Rae."

"We McDonalds have never had luck with our children. It seems every generation gets smaller and smaller. I'm the last female and Michael is the last male. So many of us have died far too young. My sister, before I was born, my brother."

"I didn't realize you had a brother," Margaret said.

"Neither did I until Amelia told me about him. He was just a baby when he died. I certainly understand my mother now more than ever." My glacier heart, warming now, tingled painfully. "I'm not sorry I broke the bottle."

Margaret shrugged. "Maybe it was meant to be."

"I'm glad you feel that way," Lisa said. She picked up her bottle, moved clear of mine, and dropped hers in one fluid motion. It too broke into three pieces along with Margaret's composure.

"Good God, woman, have you lost your mind, too?" Margaret reached for Addie's phone. "My heart is going to stop!" She began snapping pictures.

Lisa looked at me, the broken pieces lying scattered at her feet. Tears streamed down her cheeks. "I killed Jennifer," she said.

"What?" I asked.

"We were driving down the parkway, going way too fast." Her tone was heavy with sadness.

"That's not what the accident report said, Lisa. You didn't kill her."

"You don't understand. She wasn't driving too fast. I was."

"What? No. Your mother said Jennifer was driving."

"It was my fault. I lost control of the car and crashed into a tree. I dragged Jennifer out of the burning car. She wasn't moving. My head was gashed open, and I lost consciousness."

I stood still, trying to steady the weight of her secret. She glanced down at the open palms of her shaking hands. "When I came to, there were rescue crews around us. I heard them say she was dead. We never would have crashed if I hadn't been driving too fast and too drunk."

I stood still, fearing that if I moved, I would break and shatter into a million pieces. Jennifer's best friend in the world, the one person my mother seemed to admire and feel compassion, killed Jennifer and sent my life spiraling out of control. A thoughtless act had created so much destruction.

I could not think or breathe. I'd lowered my guard for the first time in years and let the full brunt of pain hit me. "I've got to go."

Lisa blocked my exit. "You can't leave without saying anything, Rae. Say something!"

I tipped back my chin. "What is there to say? You were

young, selfish, and your actions caused my sister's death. You would take it all back if you could, but you can't. No one can."

Tears welled in Lisa's eyes. "I've wished it back a thousand times before."

"Wishes don't do much good. If anything, they turn on us. Did you not learn anything today from the witch's bottles?"

"Rae, I would never have hurt Jennifer."

"But you did. You're responsible for this mess. Honestly, Lisa, you couldn't have done a better job of hurting me if you'd planned it. My big regret is that I trusted you and I felt sorry for you."

The pain sparked, slowly draining the color from her face. "Rae, please."

I was now aware that Margaret and Addie were staring but could not bear another second of this. Without another word, I turned and left the warehouse.

A Letter from Faith

MARCH 2, 1783

Dearest Children,

Mr. McDonald died today, and I fear I will soon follow him in death. However, I refuse to pass until Hanna has her child and Patrick returns home. Hanna's belly is so swollen and heavy, her time is very close. I fear Hanna will lose this child as she has her others. I will not die until I see my children safe. I forbid it.

Forever,
Faith

Chapter Twenty-Two

LISA, FRIDAY, OCTOBER 21, 2011

Seconds after the door closed behind Rae, Addie came up to me and took my hands in hers. "She's hurt and upset. She just needs a little time to absorb it all, and then she'll come back and talk to you."

I wiped away a tear. Secrets were meant to be kept buried for a reason. I knew this. And yet, I was compelled by the moment. "You don't know Rae or the McDonalds. Once they slip behind that wall of ice, they don't come back."

Margaret gaped at the shattered bottles. "That's the secret you've been carrying for all these years?"

"Yes."

The urge to drink rose in me like a demon wrapping around my mind and soul, chasing away the good sense that was still lingering. Just a couple of sips to take the edge off. Just one drink. I did not need an entire bottle.

I turned my head from side to side, wondering where Jennifer's voice was now. The voice that had stalked me for years was painfully quiet. Maybe she only lingered close to me while the secret was intact. Now that Rae knew, there was no reason for Jennifer to stick around.

"You were a kid," Addie said.

"A very foolish and spoiled kid. I never thought about the consequences."

"But a kid," Margaret repeated. "A clueless child."

"How many of them kill their best friend?"

"Lisa," Addie said. "It was a car accident. You were probably less intoxicated than Jennifer and got stuck with driving."

I stared toward the door. "So many times, I knew Rae wanted to tag along with us. So many times. But I did not want to share Jennifer. I wanted her to myself. She had a sister and I did not. I was jealous of Rae." In the center of the broken pieces of my witch bottle littering the floor lay the scroll covered in wax. Carefully, I picked it up and placed it in Margaret's hands. She peeled away the wax and slowly unrolled the parchment. Margaret studied it for a brief moment and said, "*Keep my past a secret.*"

"Did your mother know?" Addie asked.

"Yes. She made me swear never to tell. She said because it was Jennifer's car everyone would assume, she'd been driving." I shook my head. "We Smyth women were always good with secrets."

"Margaret," I said, my voice tinged with sadness. "I'm sorry I broke your bottle. But I thought I could break whatever spell is cast and life would settle onto stable ground. But I've only made it worse."

"You didn't screw anything up," Addie said. "Give Rae time. She'll come around."

I moved toward the door, pausing, but not looking back. "I'm sorry. And I know that's not enough."

The walk up Union Street and over to Prince Street took less than five minutes, but each step was labored. This would have been the time to find a meeting and reach out to my friends while I weathered this storm. But I did not feel as if I deserved any forgiveness or help. I had ruined too many lives to simply get a pass because so much time had separated me from murder.

I went straight to my car, not able to deal with Charlie right now. I drove directly to the grocery store with the huge wine selection. This time, I did not circle the aisles or pretend that I had come to buy other things. I went straight to the wine section and purchased five bottles. I could not even tell you if they were red or white. I did not even notice the price as the lady rang them up and I swiped my credit card. Nothing mattered other than getting home and forgetting.

I loaded the bottles in the front seat and leaned over to open one when I saw a police car pass through the lot. Getting arrested would stand in the way of me getting blindly drunk, so I held off while I drove the few blocks back to the house.

Inside, Charlie ran up to me, wagging his tail. God, the way he looked at me almost broke my heart. He was always so glad to see me and shower me with unconditional love. Even with all the changes in his life, he was never cross. I did not deserve him either.

"Hey, boy." I dropped my purse by the front door and kicked it closed with my foot. I let Charlie out the back door and when he bounded outside, I screwed off the top of the bottle and hesitated only a beat before I drank. The cool liquid poured down my throat, exorcising the despair from my body. Success and failure all wrapped up in one moment. Slowly, I slid to the floor and took another pull from the bottle. My head tipped back against the door as the tears rolled down my cheeks. It had been years since my last drink, but that did not count for much now.

"This is your chance to call me a dumbass, Jennifer. Tell me to put the bottle down and walk away."

Silence echoed in the house. Somewhere a clock ticked. Outside Charlie barked.

"What? Nothing? You've never been at a loss for words

ever over the last sixteen years. Why so quiet, now?" I drank from the bottle, burying this terrible day as fast I could gulp. My phone rang and I glanced at the display, half hoping it was Rae. Maybe Jennifer had come to Rae and they were rallying and coming to my rescue.

The realtor's name appeared on the display, but she did not leave a message. Seconds later she texted: *Deal on the house has fallen through. Back to square one.*

"Of course," as I took another pull on the bottle.

A Letter from Faith

APRIL 1, 1783

Dearest Children,

Hanna's birthing was not easy, but I stayed at her side the entire night. At sunrise she delivered a girl and told me she would name the babe Faith. I left her home and returned to my cottage which stood in the shadow of the big house where Mr. McDonald had lived. As I lay down, I heard the whispers of my mother and grandmother, beckoning me home. I am almost ready to leave this earthly realm.

Forever,

Faith

Chapter Twenty-Three

RAE, SATURDAY, OCTOBER 22, 2011

Worried about Michael and furious with Lisa, I barely slept that night. At one a.m., I called the hospital, but because I was not family, they refused to release any information. I explained I was his birth mother and that I had donated blood for him, but none of that mattered.

This long night would not allow me to sleep, eat, or sit still for more than minutes at a time. Would morning ever come?

By two a.m., I sat at the kitchen table with the box of papers that my mother had saved. I had given all the McDonald papers to Margaret except for those that belonged to my mother. She had been dead two years now, and though once or twice I had considered going through the stacks, I had avoided for fear I would stumble across her truest feelings, the ones that she had hidden so deeply for most of my life, as well as hers. Prying felt oddly invasive.

Carefully, I set the top aside and pulled out the binders of papers. No need to put things in chronological order because Mother had done that. She thought in straight, clear lines. Nothing was ever out of place. Notes were recorded in clear, precise handwriting. Receipts kept in order with notations. And pictures carefully marked, leaving no question of when and where they were taken or of whom.

We were so much alike, and yet toward the end of her life, we could barely speak to each other. Always polite. But we never talked about anything of substance.

Oddly, she had not saved as much money as her mother and the other McDonald women before her death. What mattered to her was condensed to a single eight-and-a-half-by-eleven inch box.

My brother's death certificate.

Jennifer's death certificate.

A petition for divorce from my father dated two months before his death. I remembered Dad traveled a lot during that time but did not believe he was so unhappy that he planned to leave my mother. She had never once let on that her marriage was falling apart.

My son's original birth certificate.

She had lumped Michael's birth certificate with the other tragedies in her life. Carefully, I set the other papers aside in their own pile. I traced Michael's name and then mine that was typed into the spot designated for *Mother*.

Rising from the table with Michael's birth certificate clasped in my hand, I went into my office, where the box holding the family Bible was kept. I set the book on my desk and switched on the lamp. Using my best ink pen, I found the space in the book just below my name and wrote *Michael David McDonald*, along with his birth date.

Sitting back in the chair, I studied his name in our Bible. A deep satisfaction warmed inside me.

Yes, Susan was his mother.

But he was *my* son. *My* flesh and blood. A McDonald. And no one could ever deny that.

Gently, I blew on the ink and only when I was certain it

was fully dried did, I close the Bible. As I lifted the book, I spotted the slight edge of a yellowed piece of paper that was peeking out from the back pages. I tugged, pulling it out.

It appeared to be an old envelope addressed to Mr. Samuel J. Smyth. Postmarked 1946, the letter had clearly been opened and resealed. Across the front, in bold letters, was *Return to Sender*. I removed the letter and carefully unfolded it.

December 2, 1948

Dear Mr. Smyth,

It has been a year since I returned to Alexandria. As you must know by now, I have married and plan to stay in the area. As you promised, I would like to see Amelia and work out a plan to transition her back into my life. Though I appreciate all that you and Marjorie have done for us both, this arrangement was temporary. I am able now and want my daughter back as soon as possible.

Yours truly,

Fiona McDonald Saunders

For a long moment, I read and reread the letter. Fiona had wanted Amelia back. And yet the Smyths and McDonalds chose never to tell her.

Written on the back of the letter was another note, scrawled in thick, bold handwriting. It read:

Amelia is a Smyth now. She knows only Marjorie as her mother and to remove the child from a loving home now would be cruel. You made your choice when you left Alexandria and now, we take this opportunity to remind you of the papers you signed that made this adoption legal.

Mr. Smyth

This was the letter Amelia needed. Had yearned for all

these years. I certainly did not owe Lisa anything, but Amelia deserved to know.

I arrived at the hospital seconds after visiting hours began. Pausing at the nurse's desk, I said without hesitation that I was Michael's family and that his mother was expecting me.

The nurse gave me a pass, and I went back to his room. I raised my hand to knock. I paused, wishing I had not come empty handed. But I had no idea what candy he liked or what he enjoyed reading.

I knocked and heard a man's footsteps move toward the door. I braced, suspecting Michael's father, Todd Holloway.

When he opened the door, he did not speak for a long moment as he stared at me. And then he leaned in and hugged me. "Thank you, Rae. Thank you for everything."

For a moment, I could not move, I was so taken aback by the physical contact. Slowly, I raised my hands to pat him on the back. "Is he better?"

Todd drew back and cleared his throat. "He is."

A rush of relief washed through every cell in my body. "Thank God."

"Susan told me you donated blood. Thank you."

"It's the least I could do. If he ever needs anything, please know I'm here."

He squeezed my hand. "I will."

"Can I see him?"

"Of course, you can see him. The doctors removed his spleen and repaired the internal damage that was causing so much bleeding. He also has a concussion which worried us and the doctors last night," he said, releasing a ragged breath. "But he's proud of his broken arm and the bruise on his face."

"I'll try not to make too much of it."

"Even if you did, I think he likes the attention. And tell your friend, Zeb, thanks. I appreciated him picking me up at the airport."

"Zeb picked you up himself?" I asked.

"He did. And he drove me to my house so I could get our other car. Solid guy."

"He is that."

He stepped aside and I moved into the room to see Susan sitting at Michael's bedside. He was indeed battered. His swollen, bruised right eye rocked me for a moment. I could not stop staring as I inventoried the damage. His right arm was in a full cast, locking it into an L.

Susan rose and smiled. "Rae. I'm glad you're here."

Even as I cringed at her weary face, my attention shifted to Michael.

"As you can see," Susan said, "he's looking a bit like he went a few rounds with a boxer." Her tone was light, but I heard the fear still echoing around the words.

I kept my tone even. "What does the other guy look like?"

Michael raised his fingertips to his eyes, a slight grin tipping the edges of swollen lips. "I wanted to post it so my friends could see, but Mom said no."

I took a step closer to him. "I think she's right, Champ."

Gingerly, he touched his shiner with a familiarity that suggested he had looked at it a lot. "I guess they'll just have to wait until I get back to school. My friends are going to be so shocked."

This nightmare for his parents and me was a grand adventure for him. "I'm sure you'll be quite the attraction."

Susan rose from her seat. "Rae, sit here. Visit with Michael."

I tensed. "I don't want to intrude."

"You aren't," Todd said.

I lowered myself into the chair, feeling the profound weight of her gesture. They were opening their circle of family and allowing me to join.

"How did it go with the witch bottles?" Michael asked.

"A funny thing about those. They have a big story behind them." I gave him the rundown of the women who had made the bottles and their wishes that instead became curses, according to Margaret.

"So, can I see the McDonald bottle sometime?" Michael asked.

"Well, it's in three pieces now."

"What happened?"

"I went to the warehouse last night straight from the hospital. I wasn't thinking too clearly and when Margaret suggested the curse could be broken with the bottle . . ."

Susan touched her lips. "Rae, did you break the bottle?"

"Yep. I dropped it right onto the floor. I thought Margaret was going to have a heart attack."

Susan's shocked expression gave way to amusement. "So, do you think the spell was broken?"

"I don't know if there ever was a spell. But Michael has turned a corner and that's good enough for me."

"Amen," Todd said.

"Do you really think the McDonalds were cursed?" Michael asked.

"He's a big reader," Susan explained. "Loved *The Hobbit* and *Harry Potter.*"

"Well," I said. "I don't think we're cursed anymore. But that doesn't mean there weren't a spell to be broken."

"What about the third bottle?" Michael asked.

"Lisa broke hers as well." As angry as I had been with her last night, I could not hold on to it right now. Like the bottle, the anger slipped away.

"What about her curse?" Michael asked.

"I don't know yet," I said.

"You should go see her today and ask her if she feels any different. You sure look different."

I did not hide my surprise. "How so?"

"More relaxed."

"Michael," Susan cautioned.

"It's okay," I said. "I can be a little stiff, and when I met you, I was pretty nervous."

His brow knotted into a frown that looked like mine. "That makes two of us."

"I think your mom was as well," I offered. I gave Michael life and I would always love him. That would never change. But Susan was his mother.

Susan gently brushed a strand of auburn hair from his pale blue eyes that mirrored mine. "I think it's okay to be a little nervous. It means we're all trying our best."

"What's that quote about courage, pal?" Todd asked. "Fear's fine, but you got to saddle up anyway."

The boy groaned. "Right, Dad."

The nurse came into the room carrying a small tray filled with cups holding pills. "Michael, it looks like you're having a party."

I turned, knowing he needed his rest. "He's quite the entertainer, but I've got to cut this short."

The nurse appeared pleased I had caught the hint. "You can come back tomorrow."

"How long will he be admitted?" I asked.

"A day or two more," Susan answered. "But please come back. Maybe you can give us an update on the third bottle."

"I'd like that," Michael said.

"Okay, I'll call your mom tomorrow and figure out a good time."

Michael grinned, wincing as his bruised lip stretched. "I really want to know."

I nodded to Susan and Todd. "Thanks."

"We appreciate everything you've done," Todd said.

I stepped into the hallway and took a few steps before the weight of the moment hit me hard. My body rushed with an array of sensations. Fear. Worry. Happiness. Joy. It was as if the floodgates had opened and long pent-up waters were flowing freely over me. I leaned against the wall, closing my eyes, not fighting or resisting, but simply allowing.

When I opened my eyes, tears fell down my cheeks. I brushed them away, amazed at the feel of the moisture on my fingertips. It had been years of feeling nothing.

A gentle hand touched mine and I saw the nurse who had been in Michael's room. "Are you all right?"

"Yes. I'm fine."

"He's a tough kid. His prognosis is good."

"I know. It's just such a relief."

"That was a good thing you did, giving blood. Your type is rare and hard to keep stocked."

"Glad to help."

She leaned in a fraction and lowered her voice. "He looks so much like you."

A lump formed in my throat. "He has great parents."

She winked. "All of them."

When I left the hospital, the air was dry and warm, the sun was so bright that I dug my sunglasses from my purse. Its rays warmed my face and chased away the chill that had lingered for what seemed like forever.

I drove to Prince Street, knowing I needed to see Lisa. We needed to talk about Jennifer. I needed to listen to her and remind myself that she was just a kid at the time of the car accident. No good would come from beating her up.

I found parking at the top of the hill on Prince Street. As I got out, I savored the view down the cobblestone street made from the rocks that, like the hearthstones, had been ballast in the sailing vessels of the 1750s. I could not help but wonder if some had come from the same place as the hearthstones on the McDonald property.

When I arrived at the house, I saw the *Sale Pending* sign

had been removed and the house was again on the market. I thought about Samuel and Debra. Had she finally confessed her real secret to him? Had it been more than he could handle?

I knocked on the door and heard the music inside. Charlie was barking. Parked on the street was Lisa's battered and muddy SUV. She was home. Why was she not answering?

No doubt she was angry and disappointed with me and willing to let me linger on the porch. I knocked again. Charlie barked louder, with impatience. When she did not answer, I turned to leave but was halfway down the steps when I felt what seemed like a tug on my sleeve. There was no one there, but the sensation echoed through my body like an electric shock.

I glanced back up at the red lacquered door and the pineapple brass door knocker. The music throbbed inside the house.

Retracing my steps, I went to the planter by the front door and tipped it back, searching for the key that Amelia always left there. It remained stuck to the bottom of the pot. I dusted off the dirt and opened the front door. Charlie bounded up toward me, barking away.

Rubbing the dog, I could see he was upset. "Lisa?" I called. "It's Rae. Can we talk?"

The music pulsed, but she did not answer. Lisa was annoyed and hurt. That was understandable. But she would have answered me if she were here.

Again, I had the sensation of hands on my back pushing me forward. Inside the hallway, I carefully closed the front door and with Charlie running ahead, I looked to my left and saw the empty wine bottle.

"Oh, Lisa. Tell me you didn't do this." The floorboards creaked under my feet as I moved down the hallway, glancing first into the parlor on my right and then the dining room on my left. Each was perfectly neat. Unless they were selling a home or expecting an honored guest, few kept their house so tidy. Most people kept the front rooms presentable, but these rooms had the feeling of having just been cleaned. Did she know the sale had fallen through?

Deeper into the house, I gripped the key, the tension in my gut building as if I expected to find something terrible locked in this house. I pictured Lisa drunk and lying on the floor. I pictured alcohol poisoning. Suicide.

The visions grew darker with each step, but I kept moving. Regardless of what I found, I needed to talk to her. Help her.

In the kitchen, the strong scent of coffee greeted me. I saw the coffeemaker on the white marble countertop dripping out the last of a full pot of coffee. Charlie ran up the back staircase and I followed him to Lisa's bedroom, where I found her lying on the suite's bathroom floor. The dog ran to her and sat beside her.

I dropped my purse and went to her, turning her on her back. She was breathing.

Eyes closed, she brushed me away, her words an unintelligible mess. Charlie nudged her.

"That's okay, boy," I said. "I've got this." I sat her up and opened her eyelids. Her eyes tried to focus but rolled back instead. "Lisa, can you hear me?"

Her head drooped to the side. I rose and went to the sink, taking a decorative hand towel and ran it under cold water. Wringing it out, I knelt in front of her and pressed the cold cloth to the back of her neck. She groaned and tried to push my hand away.

"No," I said with the force of my mother. "You need to wake up. If I can't get you up and moving soon, I'm calling 911, Lisa."

She shook her head. "Go."

I shifted the cloth to her forehead. "No." Rising, I remoistened the cloth and again pressed it to the back of her neck and her face. I repeated the process several times before her eyes opened and she looked at me. Her vision did not seem to focus, but she was trying to clear her head.

"Time to get you on your feet," I commanded.

Lisa shook her head.

I kicked off my heels and, with the dog watching closely, hooked my hands under her arms and braced my legs. I lifted her to her feet and propped her against a wall. She could barely support her own weight, but the fact that I had her on her feet was a good start.

"Go," she stammered.

"Shut up." I half carried, half dragged her to the small shower and turned on the cold water. She could not stand in the shower alone, so that meant I would have to get in with her. I deserved this as much as she did.

Drawing in a breath, I pulled her into the shower.

She screamed and arched, but I held on to her and forced her to endure the cold stream of water hitting her squarely in her face.

Charlie barked and pawed at the shower entrance.

"Stop!" she gurgled.

Ignoring her and the dog, I held her steady under the cold stream. "When you can stand."

"I can stand."

Loosening my grip, she immediately slipped, forcing me to catch her and haul her back up to the shower head. "That's not standing, Lisa."

"Go away."

"Not until you're sober enough to tell me why you got pissed drunk."

Eyes ringed with black mascara looked up at me. "I killed Jennifer."

The frigid water made my teeth chatter as the cold seeped through my clothes and into my bones. "You were a stupid kid. It could have just as easily been the other way around. It's time to climb down off your cross."

"It doesn't matter. She's dead. And I totally ruined your life."

A month ago I might have agreed. But not now. To change the past would wish away Michael, and I could never do that. "You didn't ruin my life. We both wallowed in our own self-pity and wasted our lives."

"Please turn off that water."

Her voice sounded a little more sober. "Can you stand?"

"Yes. No. But I'm freezing to death."

"We both deserve it." I turned on the warm water, allowing it to flow over us and chase away the chill. Neither of us spoke as we absorbed the heat.

"How much did you drink?"

"Doesn't matter."

"It does if you've poisoned yourself."

To prove she was improving, she pushed back her shoulders and leaned into the warm spray. "I'm not going to die. At least not today."

"Good."

I shut off the water and reached for a white fluffy towel hanging by the shower. Carefully, I dried her face and hair. "Open your eyes."

She looked at me, blue eyes ringed with redness.

"You took terrible."

"Do you," Lisa whispered.

"Can you get out of the shower?"

"Yes." I held her arm as she stumbled out and wavered for a moment. "I'm going to be sick."

Water dripping from my head, I helped her to the toilet and held her hair back. When she was finished, I handed her the damp towel and she pressed it to her lips.

"Doesn't get any prettier than this, Rae."

"Not exactly the kind of moment one puts in a scrapbook."

She sat down on the floor, propping her body against the tile as I reached for the other towel and dried off my own face and hair. Charlie came up and licked her face as she gently patted him on the head. Water dripped from my silk blouse, which was a total loss. My dark trousers, now waterlogged, drooped from my waist.

"Why did you come, Rae?"

"To tell you it's time for us both to move on. It's time we set the burden down."

"But you did nothing wrong, Rae."

"I've spent the last sixteen years in limbo, too afraid to live or breathe. Given my sister lost her life so young, it feels simply stupid to have wasted so many good years."

"What about the boy? How is he?"

"Michael is fine. He's even proud of his bruises and cast. Boys, I don't know why it's so exciting to them. He wanted to post a photo of his black eye online."

"He's a kid. Enough said." She closed her eyes. "I'm so glad he's okay."

I squatted so that we were eye level. "I am, too. He's a great kid, and I wouldn't wish him away for the world."

Bloodshot eyes stared back at me. "You wouldn't make a stupid kid. Maybe a little stiff, but definitely not stupid."

A smile flickered.

She moistened her lips as if she might get sick again. "Margaret must be freaking out."

"She was not impressed with our curator skills. But now she knows exactly what's in her bottles."

"Better to know than to wonder." She sniffed and shoved back a lock of wet hair. "Do you think we broke the curse?"

I sat down on the floor, cross-legged, and pushed back my hair. "I don't know if there ever were a curse."

Lisa twisted the damp hem of her shirt. "You know, I've been hearing her for years."

"Who?"

"Jennifer," Lisa said. "She's always there. Always talking to me. Does it sound crazy?"

"Perhaps it wasn't her at all. Perhaps it was you, talking to yourself. Your subconsciousness."

Lisa shook her head. "I thought so at first. But the more she talked to me, the more she sounded so real." She closed her eyes. "Your sister could push the right buttons."

Faint laughter rumbled in my chest. "That's an understatement."

"Bossy."

For a long moment, we sat in silence, each allowing our memories of Jennifer to settle in a more peaceful place in our hearts.

Gently, Lisa rubbed the dog's head. "She stopped talking to me the moment that bottle broke."

I stared at the patterned tile floor. "You told your secret, so there was no more reason to carry her or the guilt. Makes perfect sense."

"I sure could have used her last night. I tried to get her to talk to me, but she wouldn't. Completely ghosted me, no pun intended."

"Alone with your own thoughts."

"And look what it did. I have not had a drink in twelve years, and I blew it in an instant."

"You'll start again."

"It's not that simple," Lisa said. "I threw away twelve years."

"You did no such thing. You had twelve sober years that carried you here to us. That should mean a lot to you, and it doesn't mean you have to ruin the rest of your life."

With a bitter grunt, Lisa said, "It's never that easy."

I shook my head. "If it were, AA would be a vacation and we'd all want to join."

"The craving is always there."

"And it always will be. Accept it and start putting one foot in front of the other."

Lisa closed her eyes. "I can't face all those people at AA. And Colin. God, what will he think? We were supposed to go out tonight."

"If there's ever a group of people that understands where you are now, it's the AA people. And I have a feeling Colin isn't so easily scared off." I pushed to my feet. "I'll make you some coffee, get some food into you, and then we'll go to a meeting together. Think of me as your wingman."

"Right." She pressed her hand to her mouth. Her coloring remained pale and her hands trembled, but her gaze was clearer. "That's a good plan except for one thing."

"What's that?" I asked.

She rose and leaned over the toilet again.

"Sobriety looks pretty good right now, doesn't it, sister?"

A Letter from Faith

APRIL 15, 1783

Dearest Children,

The time is so near that the line between life and death is paper-thin, and I hear the spirits calling me. Patrick rode home today and kissed me on the cheek. He was injured but will survive.

I have no regrets in my life, save one. If I had the strength, I would find the witch bottle I made so many years ago and call back my curse. But it is too late for that, so I am tucking all the letters inside this box so that they will survive. I want the world to know the truth about me. I am mother to both the Shire and McDonald lines.

Forever,
Faith

Chapter Twenty-Four

RAE, SATURDAY, OCTOBER 22, 2011

The AA meeting was not easy for Lisa. I sat beside Charlie as she stood, puffy eyed, trying to slay a tremendous hangover. Her hands shook and she fought off tears.

"My name is Lisa and I'm an alcoholic." The group welcomed her as she paused and checked her watch. "It's been six hours since my last drink."

Several people leaned toward her, their eyes softening with an understanding only those in this group would have.

"I've been carrying a secret for years," she said. "It's weighed on my heart since day one. I thought I had it safely locked away and could keep it at bay. But yesterday, I released it."

"Can you tell us what happened?" the leader prompted.

She twisted a tissue in her hands, pulling at the edges. "I bought five bottles of wine at the grocery store and drank two of them. I can't even tell you what kind of wine it was. Red, maybe."

I could have confirmed they were red because I had watched the burgundy liquid swirl down the kitchen drain as I ran the tap. For good measure, I had rinsed out the bottles and, on the way, here, dropped them in a public trash can. There was no hint of it, not even the smell, left in the house. Lisa watched me do all this, but she'd been numb from guilt and remorse. That is why we were here now. To start again.

"How did it make you feel?" the leader asked.

"The first sip was amazing. Even better than I had remembered."

"How long did *amazing* last?"

"A minute, maybe two."

The leader sat back in his chair, his expression suggesting he already knew the answer before he asked. "What came after amazing?"

"Fear, shame, guilt. I quickly stopped tasting the wine."

"That's common," he said. "It's a knee-jerk reaction. The need overrides the pleasure of taste. How do you feel about yourself?"

Lisa twisted the tissue. "Weak. Stupid. Foolish."

"And now that you're here?"

"A little calmer." She reached in her purse and pulled out her key chain. She removed the twelve-year sobriety chip. "I can't keep this anymore. It's a reminder of my failure."

"It's a token of what you once accomplished and what you will again."

"I don't see it that way." She traced her finger over the copper edges. "I can't keep it."

I held out my hand. "Give it to me. When you hit your next twelve-year mark, I'll give it back to you."

She looked up at me with watery eyes. "No one knows where they'll be then."

"I know that I'll be giving this to you," I said in a steady voice. "I might not be the warmest person, but we both know I won't forget the date or the promise."

"Thanks, I think. But are you saying I won't remember?" Lisa asked.

"I'm confident you will."

"There are other chips," Lisa said.

"Give them all to me. I'll dole them out accordingly. If memory serves, you'll need to return here tomorrow for a twenty-four-hour token."

She shook her head. "I never collected one of those the last time. It didn't seem like such a big deal at the time."

The leader smiled. "Do you think it's a big deal now?"

She nodded. "It's huge."

The leader rose and crossed the room, opening his arms to Lisa. She slowly stepped into his embrace. The other seven people in the room approached and wrapped arms around her. She was starting all over again. But then again, weren't we all?

In my car, Lisa laid her head back against the seat. Charlie sat in the center of the backseat, still keeping a watchful eye on her. "I feel like I've been hit by a beer truck."

"Better to feel that than nothing."

"I haven't even asked you how you're doing?"

"I'm not entirely sure," I said. "There are moments when I feel like the steady, calm woman I was, and then I feel a rush of feelings. I want to laugh. I want to cry."

"Sounds human."

"I don't mind having the feelings, but I would like to control them a bit more."

Lisa laughed. "Don't we all."

"I see the house is back on the market."

"The couple buying it was engaged, but they broke up. The realtor wanted to hold them to the contract, but I told her to release them and their deposit. The house needs someone who wants to live in it."

"It should have no trouble selling."

"No, it shouldn't. But I'll wait until I get the bid, I need to take good care of Amelia as long as possible."

"I thought she was set financially."

"Depends on how long she lives," Lisa said. "She's put a lot of money back into the house."

I pulled into traffic, but instead of heading back toward Prince Street, I drove toward the Beltway.

"Where are we going?"

"To see Amelia."

She twisted in her seat and faced me. "Why?"

"I found a letter in the family Bible. It's from Fiona to Mr. Smyth."

"What does it say?"

"After she left Alexandria, she came back several years later with a new husband, new life, and wanted to see her daughter. She reminded the Smyths of their temporary arrangement and said she now wanted her daughter back."

"Really?"

"The letter was opened but then resealed and marked in bold handwriting, *Return to Sender*."

"The Smyths knew she wanted Amelia."

"They knew and reminded her she had signed a legal agreement that they interpreted as nonnegotiable. She was ordered to stay away."

"Shit."

"Amelia needs to be told that Fiona loved her and wanted her back."

"Agreed." She laid her head back against the seat rest. "I forgot just how bad a hangover feels."

"Too bad you can't bottle that feeling and get a taste of it before you drink another glass."

Eyes closed, she said, "Spoken like a nonalcoholic. When the power of the drink is so overwhelming, none of that matters. We're the consummate liars to the world and ourselves. 'Don't worry, the hangover won't be so bad because you'll have only one drink. Don't worry. Just a sip.'"

"A world without logic must be maddening."

"I have logic. I just need to hold on to it tightly and actually use it."

"Are there any more secrets you have to share?" I asked.

A wry grin crossed her lips. "Well, there was this one time when Jennifer and I short sheeted your bed."

"I knew that was you. I knew it."

She shrugged.

"If that's the worst, then you should manage."

"Let's hope."

When we arrived at the nursing home, we checked in and I asked to see Amelia. The duty nurse grimaced. "Amelia's status is degrading rapidly."

"Why didn't you call me?" Lisa asked.

She checked her computer screen. "According to these notes, we left several messages."

A sigh shuddered from Lisa as she fished her phone from her purse. The battery was dead. "I forgot to charge it last night."

"It doesn't matter," I said. "There was nothing you could have done. Can we see Amelia now?"

"Of course. She's resting peacefully."

"Thanks," Lisa said.

Amelia's room was bathed in shadows except for a single bedside lamp giving off a faint glow. Lisa sat in the chair beside the bed and laid her hands on Amelia's small, fragile hand. "Amelia, it's Lisa and Rae. We came to see you."

She did not respond, her breathing so slight I had to stare hard to see her chest move. The life was seeping from her body and soon would be gone. Charlie moved to the bed, sniffing her hair. Then his ears went back, and he sat on the floor beside her.

I took the seat opposite Lisa and pulled the letter from my purse. "Lisa, you need to read this to Amelia."

"Can she hear?"

"A couple of weeks ago I'd have said no, but I'm beginning to believe anything is possible. Plus, this is the answer she wanted so badly all these years."

Lisa unfolded the letter, the yellowed pages crinkling. Placing her hand back on Amelia's, she began to read.

"This needs to go in her baby book," I said when she had finished. "It's as much a part of her history as all her other memories."

Amelia drew in a deep breath and then slowly released it. We sat quietly in the room for well over an hour as Amelia's breathing slowed to a rasp. The color drained from her face and a complete stillness came over her. I called the nurse just after seven, and she came and checked her vitals.

"It won't be long now," she said.

Lisa and I each held one of Amelia's hands and minutes before eight o'clock, she stopped breathing altogether. The doctor pronounced her deceased, and after a few more minutes, the care center escorted us into another room where a counselor waited. There were papers to sign. Belongings to be gathered and boxed. In the end, Amelia had so few things with her. The quilt. The lamp on the bedside table.

There was little in this world to hold her, but she had tenaciously clung to life until Lisa had read the letter. Amelia finally had the answer she had sought since she was a little girl.

As we carried the box to my car, neither of us spoke. Even Charlie did not make a sound. From his slow gait and body posture, he knew Amelia was gone.

"Do you think she heard us?" Lisa asked.

I opened the trunk, loaded the items inside, and shut it. "I'm sure she did."

"I was so worried about money and what I'd do if she

outlived it. I had no idea how I was going to take care of her. And now she's gone. Once the house is sold, I'll have no more ties to Alexandria."

"That doesn't mean you have to leave. You can talk to Colin about keeping the house. Surely with market prices so high, there is equity in the house that you can draw upon without selling it."

"Maybe. But I don't know if I want to live there."

"Then live in the apartment Zeb is building on my land. It'll give you all the privacy you need."

"You don't have to do that."

"You're right, I don't. But I want to." A half smile curved the edges of my lips. "Maybe I'll put my matchmaking skills to the test and see if I can find you the perfect mate."

She laughed, her bloodshot eyes flickering with genuine humor. "Are you trying to chase me away?"

I slid behind the wheel and waited until she and Charlie were inside the car. "If I promise not to set you up, will you stay?"

"Maybe." Lisa picked an invisible thread from her jeans. "There's a lot I'd like to photograph here."

"This place is pretty happening," I said.

She laughed. "Rae, I think we're going to be just fine."

A Letter from Hanna

JULY 14, 1800

Dearest Daughter Faith,

On your wedding day, I am passing down a box of letters that your namesake entrusted with me. Protect it and see that no one reads it until the three witch bottles are no more.

Forever,

Hanna

Chapter Twenty-Five

RAE, TUESDAY, NOVEMBER 8, 2011

I was almost sorry when the construction on the garage and apartment was finished. I was getting used to seeing Zeb every day and visiting with Eric from time to time. Today when the red truck pulled up, I was sitting on the back porch drinking morning coffee and enjoying the blue skies. I rose and walked around the side path and greeted the two of them as they headed up to the front door.

"Good morning."

Zeb's grin was slow and steady and sent a shiver of warmth up my body that could have melted any ice. "Good morning."

Eric ran past his dad. "We brought you a glad-the-job-is-done present." He held up a box.

I accepted the gift and carefully opened it. It was a bottle of sparkling cider.

Margaret had given her public lecture on the witch bottles only when Michael's doctors and parents cleared him to travel. Pride filled me when I sat next to Michael as Margaret detailed the lives of the McDonalds, from Patience and Michael's trip from Scotland to the Virginia Colony and then all the way through to Michael and me. The boy seemed pleased by his long lineage that up until now he had known little about. I was glad not only that I had given him life but that we shared a rich ancestry. Perhaps one day it would allow us to be close friends.

"Are you going to tell her about the stones, Dad?" Eric asked.

Zeb sighed. "I was out in Loudoun the other day, and the builder who purchased your hearthstones had extras. I took all he had."

"You brought the hearthstones back here?"

"Only if you want them."

"I would. Do you have enough to build anything?"

"Maybe a fire pit. It will be first class."

"Sounds great." These hearthstones had a new purpose. Just like me. Lisa. Addie. Even Janet.

I leaned in and kissed Zeb as naturally as if I had known him all my life.

Zeb kissed me back. "Good."

Eric rolled his eyes. "I want to drink some of the fake wine."

Smiling, I straightened. "When Lisa arrives, we'll have a toast."

"When's she coming?" the boy asked.

"Soon. Real soon."

"Is Charlie coming?"

"Yes."

With Amelia's passing, Lisa was not under a lot of pressure to sell the Prince Street house. She had taken it off the market, knowing she would stay in town until at least the spring. It was nice having her around. We might not have gotten along as teenagers, but as adults, we have become close. She and Colin have been dating for a couple of months and she looks happier than I ever remember seeing her.

"I hear you're having a party?" Zeb asked.

"A little gathering. Rachel is catering the desserts."

Zeb's head cocked. "You aren't matchmaking, are you?"

"Mr. Talbot, I'm not a matchmaker, remember?"

He laughed. "Does Rachel know?"

"Not exactly."

He groaned. "Who is the poor man you have in your crosshairs?"

"One in particular, but if you want to find out, you'll have to come to the party."

His expression turned serious. "It's not me, right?"

Slowly, I shook my head. "No. I have someone else in mind for you."

A dark brow arched, and a sly grin crept across his face.

"I know this woman," I said, smiling. "She's local. Deep roots in the community."

He took my hand in his and traced the underside of my palm. "I hope she has red hair."

"It's not exactly red. I think of it as more brown with auburn highlights." I tipped my body closer to his, coaxing him to lean forward. He smelled of fresh air and sawdust—my new favorite combination.

"That sounds like trouble."

"Lots of trouble."

His smile warmed my heart. "Good."

Recipes

Rachel's Lemon Polenta Cookies

Rachel at the Union Street Bakery puts her heart and soul into her cooking, and she will tell you her recipe selections vary with her moods. She worked tirelessly to balance the flavors of this particular cookie. There were times when she used too much lemon and polenta, making the lemon polenta cookies slightly bitter. Other times, she was heavy handed with the sugar, creating a cookie that was too sweet. But these days, she feels as if she had found the perfect blend. She encourages everyone who makes her cookies to experiment. Feel free to mix in different flavors or try a unique topping. She wants you to find your favorite balance of flavors. Enjoy!

¾ cup softened butter
1 cup sugar
1 egg
1 tablespoon lemon zest
2 tablespoons lemon juice
1½ cups all-purpose flour
½ cup ground cornmeal
½ teaspoon salt

Preheat the oven to 350 degrees Fahrenheit. Cream/blend together the softened butter and sugar until it is well blended. Mix in the egg and lemon zest. In a separate bowl sift together the flour, cornmeal, and salt. Slowly add the dry ingredients to the butter/sugar mixture. Scoop the cookie dough by tablespoons onto a greased or lined baking sheet and bake for 12 to 15 minutes.

Never Too Much Chocolate Chip Cookies

1 cup softened butter
½ cup sugar
1¼ cups brown sugar
1 egg
1 egg yolk
1 teaspoon rum extract
2½ cups all-purpose flour
1 teaspoon baking soda
1 teaspoon salt
1 cup large chocolate chips
1 cup small chocolate chips

Cream/blend together the softened butter and the sugars. Add the egg, egg yolk, and rum extract. In another bowl, sift together the flour, baking soda, and salt. Mix the dry ingredients into the butter sugar mixture. Mix in the chips. Scoop the cookie dough by tablespoons onto a lined baking sheet and bake for 12 to 15 minutes.

Reader Discussion Questions

THE VIEW FROM PRINCE STREET
Reader Discussion Questions

1. The novel alternates between the eighteenth century and the present. Does this enhance the storytelling? How do the historical passages shed new light on the contemporary story?

2. Do you think the curse was real? Did Rae break it when she broke the witch bottle?

3. Do you think Faith regretted how she treated her half-sister Patience?

4. The car accident changed both Rae and Lisa. Do you think they can finally move on?

5. Do you think one's family history can affect future generations? How so?

6. Do you think Michael and Rae can build a strong relationship?

About the Author

Amazon Charts bestselling author, Mary Ellen Taylor's love of history and fiction is evident in her novels ***The Brighter The Light*** and ***When the Rain Ends***. For more, visit www.maryellentaylor.com

Also by Mary Ellen Taylor

The Union Street Bakery Series

Made in United States
North Haven, CT
07 August 2023

40066107R00207